NORTH
OF SUPPOSED TO BE
A Novel

NORTH
OF SUPPOSED TO BE
A Novel

Marcia Ferguson

FRANKLIN HANCOCK PRESS

North of Supposed to Be

Published by Franklin Hancock Press

Flying Pig Media

Book design by VMC Art & Design LLC
Cover Photo by Joy Brown

Published in the United States of America

ISBN: 978-0-9857810-0-2

For Pat and Bill – the dearest parents in the world

ACKNOWLEDGMENTS

Thank you to my family, friends, and readers who explored the early drafts of this book, offering suggestions and encouragement. Lillian Griffith Wargetz has shown unfailing interest and perspective. James D. Moore kindly offered ongoing encouragement and brilliant notes. Michael J. Macon has been a great sounding board, lending his ear to the steps and stages of the book's creation, and generously staying involved throughout the process. When I'd waver a bit about publishing, writer Jamie Ford shared insightful observations. One of my first supporters was Parker Ladd, and I thank him for his kind words and suggestions. Barbara Cloud has been a good friend and inspiration – the quintessential observer and sharer of life's simple pleasures. Sincere thanks go to George Musi for initially shaping the estate map, and John H. Shaver for the final version.

My research brought me to landscape architect Doug Reed; Mollie and Wells Moore who inspired the Lerner Garden of the Five Senses in Boothbay; Robert Cuccioli who kindly shared the funding dynamics of Broadway plays; Laura Hartman Maestro who generously offered estate map suggestions; Joy Brown whose photographs are spirit-soaring; and Frankie Still who lent his charming self as a nod to Snooks Von Krinkles. Much appreciated, Frankie.

I truly appreciate the publishing oversight of Kristin Lindstrom and Flying Pig Media. It's been a pleasure working with you.

My love of movies was fueled by Edgar and Twila Shaffer and their Roxy Theater in Slippery Rock. Those days were utter bliss. My view of the resonating pleasures of life mirrors my Great Aunt Mabel 'Meme' Davis, and her influence stretches across the years. Tommy Paton was larger than life and holds a special place in my heart.

Home can be a mercurial thing, but I've been blessed to enjoy the richness of home thanks to the dearest parents in the world – Pat and Bill. Our lives have been enriched by Ron, Deb, my niece Taylor and nephew Jordan, all of whom are much loved and appreciated. And family resonates from the past as well as the present, most of all my dear and loving Nana and Pappap – Bessie and Howard; my Grandma and Grandpa – Betty and Ross, with their Beaver 'big house' and 'little house'; aunts, uncles, and cousins; and my great aunts and uncles – particularly Eva and Bill, Ethel and Emil, Jessie and Edgar, and Twila and Edgar. I'm proud to come from 'good stock'.

NORTH
OF SUPPOSED TO BE

A Novel

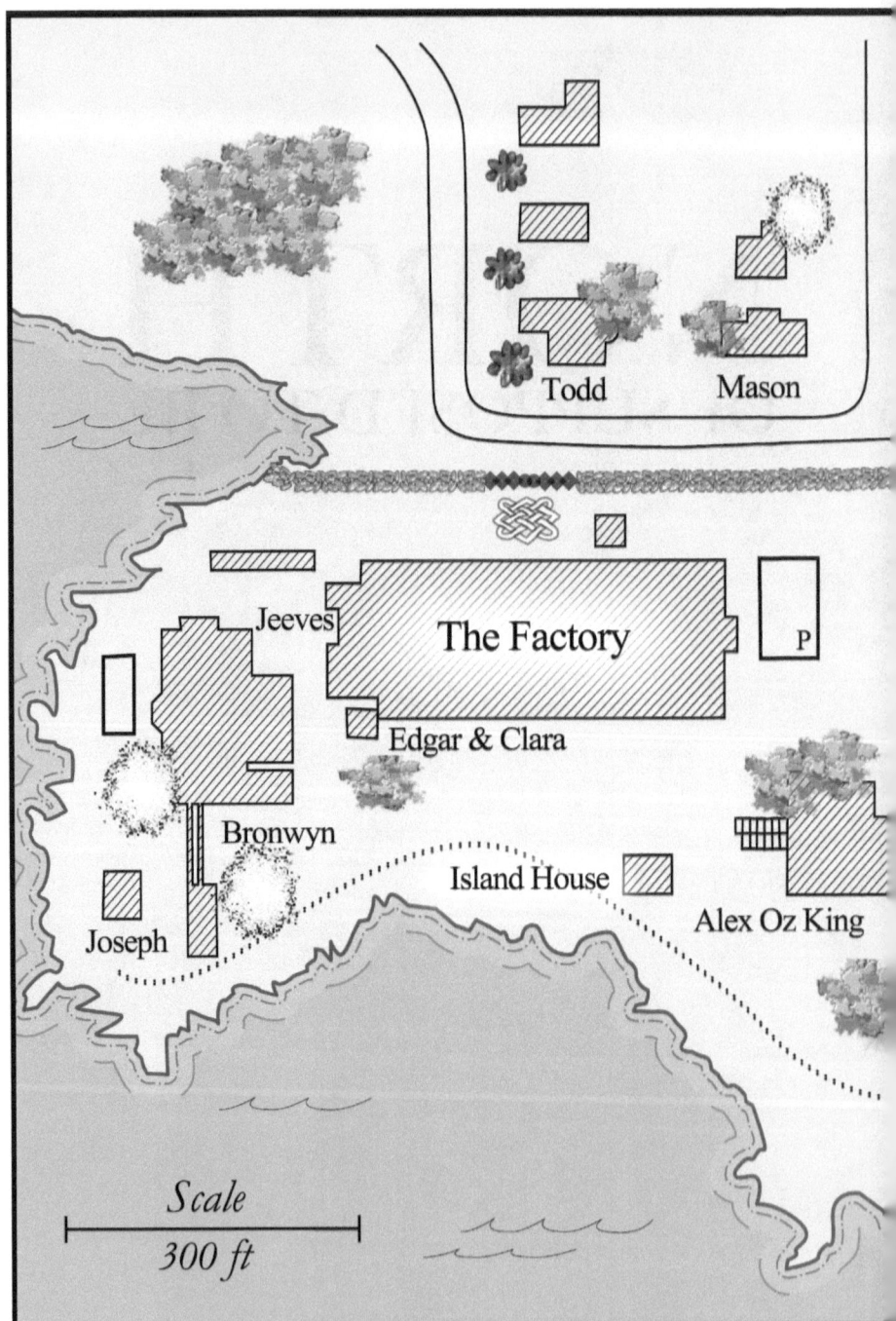

Todd

Mason

Jeeves

The Factory

P

Edgar & Clara

Bronwyn

Island House

Joseph

Alex Oz King

Scale
300 ft

Bronwyn's Maine Estate

Cotton

King Street

Davis

Palimore

Squirrel Hill

N

Atlantic Ocean

CHAPTER ONE

THE LOOKING GLASS
1997

Think of a puppy. A puppy with melting eyes and velvety ears, the shape of a cracker. A bouncy Boston terrier puppy, crazily chasing a ball.

Moments ticked by as the dog reverie failed to calm Bronwyn's racing heart.

A sunset over the ocean. No, maybe seagulls gliding on the wind.

Bronwyn breathed a choppy sigh. Her nerves were getting the best of her. Photographing celebrities was effortless, but the Prime Minister of Israel...that would be something else. Gazing intently at her reflection, Bronwyn's green eyes held a glint of panic; what she needed was vibrant confidence staring back. Waiting was torturous, and the hotel ladies room was like a chilly holding cell.

Two chattering girls came through the doorway.

"You can't, Mel. You can't just turn out the lights and go without locking up."

"Of course I can. Nobody's gonna know. It's just an hour. I've done it before. It's not like there's anything to steal."

"Really? You're sure? 'Cause I have so much to tell you about last night."

Bronwyn glanced up, catching sight of the bubbly girls as they left. She checked the time. A quick peek in the mirror bolstered her. To counteract the gloom of late winter Washington DC, she'd chosen a creamy pants suit and navy blouse with pleated cuffs drifting past her wrists. Turning slightly, she vowed to keep the suit spotless for the next fifteen minutes. No need for a sweep of blush; her cheeks were flushed pink with anxiety.

This was one of the many times she longed for her mother or father, or even her sister who would have been twenty one this year if she hadn't died seventeen years ago; if they all hadn't been dead for seventeen years. There was an overriding solitude to Bronwyn's days; always had been since she was eight, but she made an effort to move along as if she were part of a whole. As a photographer, she'd been called a visionary, but this morning her work seemed particularly insubstantial and an icy jolt of uneasiness merged with her butterflies.

Disgusted with dark thoughts fueling her nerves, Bronwyn squared her shoulders and decided to call Ollie Silkowski. He always knew what to say. She leaned into the mirror and whispered 'good luck' to her reflection.

She fed the pay phone, punched Ollie's number and waited. The girls were still talking in the hallway, in front of the 'about to be forsaken' travel agency.

"So, I'll see you at the food court in thirty minutes, okay? You're sure you can take a whole hour?"

"Yes," the friend groaned.

"Good, 'cause wait'll you hear everything that happened. I'm so psyched."

Ollie's phone rang and rang. Disappointed, Bronwyn waited to leave a message.

"Hi, Ollie. It's almost time to meet the prime minister. I'm nervous, but it's exciting. If he wants a sitting in the next couple of days, I'll be staying – if not, I'll be back in New York tomorrow night. I can't wait to photograph him." She paused a moment and said, "Well, actually I can't wait to meet him. I'd better go. I just remembered you're playing tennis with Tommy. Have fun. I'll call you tonight."

The giggling girls were gone and the richly carpeted hallway stood empty. A flash of childhood memory struck Bronwyn – her mother pinning flapping white sheets to a clothesline. The imagined sun forcing her mother into silhouette seemed to penetrate Bronwyn with calm, and the snapping sheets blew away her gloomy isolation.

Marching to the bank of elevators, she reminded herself she was successful enough to be photographing *Vanity Fair*'s cover story – she was a master who sliced light as if it emanated from her, assembling shadow and sending shades of gray, cavernous black, and jolts of white across the planes of an object until the thing's very soul was unearthed. When she chose to, Bronwyn could make color sing. By the time she reached the Presidential Suite, she wore a confident smile.

Once inside, she submitted to a pat down and wanding, turned over her navy leather clutch and portfolio, and sat in the foyer. Informed there would be a ten minute wait, she settled in, trying to unobtrusively sit on her left hand and then her right, discretely warming them.

As twenty minutes came and went, she approached a curved console table where photographs of a woman and several of two boys were displayed.

"Do you mind?" Bronwyn asked. When no one responded, she shrugged and said, "I'm a photographer, remember? May I look at the photos?"

She lifted the photos of the boys and searched for a resemblance to their father; surely these would be photographs of the prime minister's sons. She couldn't imagine the Presidential Suite would sport generic family photos.

"Are these the prime minister's sons?" she asked, but got no response.

Annoyed with their silence, she was finally ushered inside. Striding purposefully forward, she took the prime minister's extended arm and leaned upward to place her lips squarely upon his cheek in greeting. So much for the cold handshake.

Prime Minister Abraham smiled enigmatically.

"Miss McCall."

"Mr. Prime Minister." Bronwyn stopped herself from a slight curtsy, even as she wavered a bit on a slightly flexing left knee.

He gestured to a chair, and she placed her portfolio on the credenza.

"I've brought some photographs, Mr. Prime Minister. I'm staying at the Willard, so perhaps someone can drop them off when you're finished viewing them."

"I'm curious as to your vision. Christopher sent over a few magazines with your work. I think he aims to distract me from his article. He hasn't shared it with you?"

"Actually, I think you'll be pleased, sir. The scandalous part seems to be having you on the cover."

Prime Minister Abraham chuckled softly.

"Step around, Miss McCall, and tell me about these photos."

Bronwyn wondered what the writer had selected to represent her work. She thought it nervy that Christopher hadn't consulted her, but was bemused by his three choices.

"Well, this first one is of my friend, Graeme Woods."

"Yes, one of my favorite actors. I've dined with him in London."

"Oh? Well the photograph seems to work because he's recognizable in profile, despite the distance."

"You're being modest. It amazes." Bronwyn blushed.

"Did you enhance the colors of the rocks?"

"No. I don't manipulate film. I frame the moment and might wait for an eternity for the fading light, but the moment is pure. In this case, the Arizona desert and this particular rock formation had the perfect angles to echo solitude." She leaned over to tap the photograph. "You might think we used a wind machine, with Graeme's coat flying behind him, but with that panorama and the jutting rock, we couldn't have."

While the prime minister nodded, Bronwyn was struck with how oddly familiar he seemed.

"It proves Graeme's acting skill – he looks so contemplative, but we had loud leaf vacs pulling his clothes from behind.

"And this photograph of Roddy O'Neal is quirky, but people seem to like it."

"When did you decide he should be eating?"

"Roddy has always had a great relationship with food – he eats with gusto. So I convinced him to let me sit on a stepladder in this dining room – breakfast, lunch, and dinner. I sat through thirteen meals – like a *National Geographic* stakeout of an elusive animal. I always knew Roddy's face would be reflected in the very corner of the mirror – I'd been on the ladder long enough to figure that out. And I'm not surprised that a flaky croissant and Irish butter would have been the moment."

"But, Miss McCall, his face looks like a postal stamp on the page and the mirror sparkles – it's the beveled edge, isn't it? And somehow the mirror reflects nothing at all. Everything is colorless, except that little square stamp of his face. How did you manage it?"

"I call the dining room biscuit beige, because we plotted it to recede with silk covered panels. Again, don't forget how much time I spent on that ladder. He forgot I was there, but I never stopped watching him. I knew what I was waiting for."

"Extraordinary."

"And this last one is a classic portrait, as I plan for you."

"But I know this woman – she's difficult, a diva. In fact, I don't think I've ever seen her without anger and intensity. In this photograph, she's docile. Seems sweet-tempered and almost a girl's innocence."

Bronwyn leaned in and whispered, "She's listening to her music – we played her amateur CD's – over and over. And," Bronwyn rolled her eyes, "over."

Privy to the secret, the prime minister nodded with satisfaction.

"Mr. Prime Minister, these photographs have a tricky element – magazines want quirky expressions and unexpected composition, but your photographs will be straightforward."

She took in as much of his face as possible. He looked older than she'd anticipated, with frown lines, worry lines, smile lines, and smoking lines racing across his tanned face. His hair was more gray than dark, but his eyes were deep with a spark of youthful playfulness. Tall and smartly dressed, his broad shoulders didn't seem broad enough to carry the weight of his world.

"Excuse me, Mr. Prime Minister," interrupted one of the men. "We're running behind."

Bronwyn rose, as if jerked by an invisible string. "Your staff has my number at the hotel. Perhaps we can arrange a sitting within the week?"

"I expect we'll find time, Miss McCall. Enjoy your stay in Washington."

This time he leaned down and kissed her cheek goodbye. It was only a brief moment, but they eyed each other without pretense; more than a glance and less than a stare.

Relieved, Bronwyn rode the elevator to the lobby. She felt euphoric to have the meeting concluded without any embarrassment. Her mind racing, she vowed to create at least one photograph that would convey the power and aura she'd just witnessed.

The day before, she'd made a dry-run over to the hotel, wandering through the lobby, picking up magazines at the newsstand and strolling down the ramp past the magic shop leading to the connected shopping mall. Today she repeated her steps and felt like skipping. She glanced at the magic tricks, wondering if she should surprise Ollie with some enchanting sleight of hand. At the foot of the ramp, she took in the noisy food court and shoppers, catching sight of the two mischievous girls from the ladies room. Apparently anyone needing travel arrangements in the next hour would have to do the booking themselves.

Standing on the right side of the escalator, Bronwyn peered over at the seafood restaurant below, considering it a definite lunch possibility. She couldn't have guessed, but that was the last moment of life – as she'd known it.

Her gaze fell to the left side of the shopping level as the escalator continued its languorous descent, and she felt the flicker of concern before it took hold of her head. Two little boys were being whisked along by a pair of men in long overcoats.

It was the grim swiftness that wasn't right. One boy was jerked and then scooped up, while the smaller one was already in the arms of the other man. They headed to the up escalator, so Bronwyn stepped off and made a wide half circle, a few steps behind them.

With a shock, she realized they were the prime minister's sons from the photographs, and their eyes were large with fright. Her gut instinct kicked into gear.

A cashier riding the down escalator thought Bronwyn was signing to the deaf boy in front of her, but she had her finger to her lips, followed by a thumbs-up sign. It seemed strange the children were silent, but Bronwyn decided it was for the best. She'd felt rather feeble in the presence of the security men upstairs and these two had those expressionless faces, with violent intent beneath the surface.

Once they reached the top of the escalator, the men seemed conflicted between walking fast, and avoiding attention. Nevertheless, their long strides made it impossible for Bronwyn to seem nonchalant. She saw her advantage up ahead. The men were headed for the hotel lobby, but she knew the shortcut. If they passed the elevator to leave the hotel, she could catch up. Giving the older boy one more thumbs-up, she veered to the parallel hallway, past the ladies room and darkened travel agency to the out-only door she'd fruitlessly approached the day before. The men leaned into the revolving doors beyond her, while she propped open the out-only door with her clutch.

It was oddly serene outside, with no foot traffic around the hotel entrance. The kidnappers were a few yards from the curb as a black car pulled up. For a fleeting moment she imagined herself flinging her body upon the car's hood, but in a flash the urge was gone and she shouted "Mickey Mouse". Maybe it was because of a kick or a bite, but the boy was dumped to the ground. He grabbed the little one and raced back as Bronwyn yelled "Donald Duck". Bronwyn leaped forward and scooped them into her arms, shielding them from the gunfire she expected.

It came.

Her adrenaline made it surprisingly easy to kick her handbag, yank the door, and gain a few moments' time as she careened to the dark travel agency. Bronwyn reached on faith, jerked the office door open and awkwardly landed with the boys under a desk after kneeing the chair away.

Outside was chaos. On his way to Blair House, the prime minister's driver made two drastic right turns and jumped the curb as the kidnappers rushed across the pavers, arching toward the out-only door. They were brought down in a brief and bloody exchange of gunfire, while the trail of blood led inside.

Time seemed to slow and Bronwyn heard an odd rushing noise in her ears. The office was quiet, except for the slight hum of a small refrigerator. She whispered to the boys.

"What's your name?" Bronwyn asked weakly, clutching the smaller boy tightly against her while rhythmically patting his back with her right hand, just as her mother had patted her...one, two, three pats...one, two, three pats...one, two, three pats. Her mother was the best patter in the world, she thought wistfully, missing the boy's answer.

"Your name?" she asked again.

"Paul."

"Yours?"

"Samuel," the older boy said solemnly, his head above hers.

"You were brave," she murmured.

He stared at her.

"Have you been to Disney World?" She'd surprised herself with the Mickey Mouse yell.

Paul nodded.

"What did you like?"

"Everything," the little one answered, enthusiastically.

"Pirates of the Caribbean," Samuel told her, thoughtfully.

Bronwyn was losing her grip on consciousness. She held Paul even more tightly.

"Samuel. Lock the door if you can and listen for your Papa."

The boy backed away from under the desk.

"Samuel. Just open for your Papa. Okay? No one else," she rasped.

But there was no time to lock the door or listen for Papa; he was already there. The prime minister panicked when he saw the blood on Samuel's clothes. But when they pried Paul from Bronwyn's arms, he couldn't believe little Paul wasn't mortally wounded, so soaked in blood was the boy. He clutched both sons, kissing their faces and hugging them hard, but when they lifted the desk away from Bronwyn, the prime minister couldn't have been more stunned.

The sounds of rescue seemed for away. Bronwyn's wheezing echoed beneath the desk with a faint musicality, like a mournful bagpipe. The dark travel agency, the shadows beneath the desk, the blackness of consciousness leaking away, all conspired to dim the day. Bronwyn's last conscious thought was one of shocked finality. *This is how I die. I didn't know. This is how it happens.*

CHAPTER TWO

BRAM AND DAVID

During Bronwyn's agonizing recovery, she became aware of a man seated on a chair beside the bathroom door. Occasionally, he ducked into the bathroom; that's how she knew where it was. She still had a catheter.

Once, she saw him standing above her when she opened her eyes. She'd closed them trying to shield herself from the unrelenting pain, trying to remember vaguely good things in her life. He stared and asked if she was in pain. When she nodded, he asked 'from 1 to 10, how bad is the pain'. She weakly lifted one hand and three fingers of the other. 'Eight?' he asked. She closed her eyes again, but heard him berating someone in the hallway. Within minutes, they injected her with something that made her warm and cozy. It felt wonderful. After that, he came to her bed and would press a button if she indicated she was in pain. She began to depend on him. He always seemed to be there.

She had no real sense of time, but eventually she graduated to sitting in a chair and walking with tenuous steps across the linoleum floor to the garishly lit bathroom. The first time she made the trip without a nurse, the man took her elbow as she edged over with a walker. When she got to the door, she whispered for him to wait outside. He was visibly relieved and Bronwyn was pleased she'd noticed something outside of her pain and fear.

She hardly recognized her puffy face in the mirror. The short trip to the bathroom exhausted her, and when she opened the door, she asked the man if she could sit in his chair for a moment. Instead, he helped her to her bed; eight feet away, but seeming a mile. As he swept her legs up into the bed, he brought the thin blanket down upon her as if it were a cloud. She asked his name.

"Ernest Rose."

Exhausted, Bronwyn fell instantly to sleep, but she had a dream. Her friend Moss was in the doorway and that overwhelmed her with inert joy. She weakly lifted her hand in the dream, beckoning him to sit beside her. Then he was gone. She slept more peacefully, having had a dream visit from a friend.

"What is she doing?"

"The girl?"

"Yes. It's like she's signaling, waving."

"Probably a tremor. Let's get back. I've got calls to make and I'm hungry."

Prime Minister Abraham's old college friend glanced back into the darkened hospital room and then strode after the prime minister.

When they returned to Georgetown, the prime minister, chilled by the drizzling rain, donned a cardigan. He had dark circles beneath his eyes and a grayish pallor. Fixing glasses of whiskey for himself and his friend, he sat in a wing chair and closed his eyes.

"About the girl. What do you think, Bram? She was part of it?"

The prime minister shrugged. "Apparently not, but they've tossed her house. Taken everything. I almost hate to think she's an innocent. She'll have nothing to go back to. I don't know." Bram shook his head, sighing. "They've seen the meeting footage and the security cameras. She made a pay phone call before our appointment. It seems innocent. They feel she was at the right place at the right time. For me and the boys."

Bram frowned. "Her friend died the same day as the kidnapping. Seemed suspicious, but turns out he had heart problems, on record. So it seems a coincidence – playing tennis."

"They're saying she'll live?"

"Appears so. Didn't look good at the time. She flat-lined in surgery. The surgeons were amazed at the bullet paths." Bram leaned forward with his elbows on his knees, rubbing his eyes. "Maybe you could go by her house in a few days. See if there's anything salvageable. Knowing the teams, it's probably pointless."

"Give me her address and I'll go after dinner."

"It's in the Village. Look when you go back home."

"The Village. Greenwich Village?"

Bram nodded.

Moss's voice rose. "I thought you said she was a DC photographer."

"No, I said she was taking the photos for *Vanity Fair*. She's from New York. I have her portfolio over there," he gestured to a side table.

Moss's heart fluttered. "My God." As he unzipped it he saw her business card and flipped plastic pockets, coming to Susie and Allison's photo on the staircase. "You haven't looked, have you?"

"What's wrong, Moss?" Bram said as he reached for the photos Moss was thrusting at him.

"I know the girl! My God, I know the girl. Bronwyn. Bronwyn McCall. She's a friend of the family. I'm her attorney, for God's sake. I'm going back." And he raced to the hall tree, retrieving his raincoat.

As Moss rode through the Washington streets, willing the car to go faster, he thought back to when he'd first met Bronwyn. She was only eighteen then, but with such poise, she seemed older.

His wife had admired photographs in a Chelsea art gallery and with her birthday coming up, Moss took little Susie and Allison with him, to choose a gift. He didn't realize there was a gallery show that evening, or he wouldn't have taken a four year old and six year old. Bronwyn was there. If he asked Susie right now what Bronwyn was wearing, even though seven years had passed, Susie would know. The girls worshiped Bronwyn.

It was a wine and cheese party, with trays of hors d'oeuvres passing through the gallery rooms. Bronwyn emerged from the back with two plates of miniature sandwiches; orange marmalade and chopped almonds on crustless bread, cut into diamonds. The girls were entranced. Moss assumed Bronwyn worked in the gallery and asked her to keep an eye on the girls. When Moss came out of the rest room, he noticed a man on the pay phone, evidently calling a girlfriend. Moss never mentioned it to Bronwyn, but when he was introduced to the man, he figured Ellis

Fielding for a two-timer, which he proved to be. Bronwyn held Allison up to the huge photographs for a better look. Ellis Fielding crossed the room and possessively wrapped his arm around Bronwyn's waist to steer her away. Bronwyn shook her head, choosing to be with the little girls for awhile longer; Ellis made a face and moved on.

The most striking portraits were done by Bronwyn, and Moss was impressed. He didn't expect an artist of that caliber to be retrieving munchies for his munchkins. He introduced himself as Stanley Mastrofrancesco, attorney. He gave Bronwyn his card, said to call him Moss, and engaged her to do the first of several black and white photographs of his daughters.

Who would have thought that Bronwyn McCall would save the lives of his best friend's sons, seven years later? Why hadn't he looked at her in the hospital bed? Moss told himself the lighting was dim, her face swollen. But she'd lifted her hand, reached out to him, and he'd dismissively turned his back. It cut him deeply.

With his return to the hospital, Bronwyn was happy it hadn't been a dream and was relieved she wasn't quite so alone.

Ever since meeting Moss, she'd thought of him as the quintessential good guy. A touch of Cary Grant added to a Norman Rockwell dad. Bronwyn loved watching him laugh; he could make such dopey looking faces with his girls. Susie and Allison brought out the tender side of Moss.

His eyes were sunken and serious when he came to her bed in the hospital. He looked stricken and appeared as if gray had touched his hair overnight. She watched as he absentmindedly ran his hand through the thick thatch, burdened with sadness. She reached out to touch him and was reassured by the crisp starch of his shirt cuff.

Moss promised to return the next morning, leaving Bronwyn clutching at memories.

She'd recently shot a new portrait for Moss, a throwback to the thirties. His suit faded into the black background; his white shirt collar defined the dark tie; the fluff edge of a pocket square hinted at his heart; handsome hands crossed, seeming to float in darkness; ears, nose, forehead lurched from a landscaped face, all darkness and light.

Then there was the black and white photograph of Moss's grandfather. She'd taken advantage of an early misty morning in Bridgehampton to photograph the old man. The butt of a cigarette perched between his lined lips, and he sported grizzled stubble, a long crooked nose, a hint of tweed jacket and worn shirt, long ears; wild and unruly eyebrows obscured his narrow right eye and bright left eye. But most of all, his forehead was covered in a roadmap of wrinkles. Bronwyn took flattering photographs of the gentleman, but Moss loved that one, saying it was the man he knew and loved.

Another photograph of Moss was near the back of her portfolio. If she thought of Moss as a genial father, this was a view of him as solemn professional. Stanley Mastrofrancesco, and don't forget it, it seemed to say. After several tries, she shot it through a train window, perfectly timed, with Moss striding alone along the platform between trains, turning to stare at her with a gaze she'd requested – serious and unflinching. By looking at her, just that deadly serious, body striding forward, turning back to look at her, he added a furrowed brow above his chiseled face; a brow that seemed to ask her, 'is this what you wanted'? Others would read it differently – it was a complex range of emotion in a dark and light photograph, done in color, which was unusual for Bronwyn. The sharp face in the center of the photograph simply bored a hole through the viewer, with its intensity.

Her mind worked better thinking of the past, but she thought of her ideas for photographing the prime minister. Casual periwinkle blue and gray, she'd decided after meeting him. And a location shoot. As she pondered those ideas, she felt an internal shift. She realized she'd lost her nerve and although she hadn't thought taking photographs required nerve, she now knew it absolutely did – at least for her. She wasn't certain she could lift a camera and see anything at all. On the other hand, the hopeful spark still residing in her body whispered she might see more than she ever had before. With that thought, she closed her eyes and drifted off to sleep.

Moss visited the next morning and said he was leaving for New York. Before he left, Bronwyn asked him if the prime minister was still in Washington. When she learned he was staying another week, she asked Ernest Rose to see if the prime minister would come to see her.

What would seem an innocuous request raised red flags among the security forces. The counter terrorism unit had determined her innocence, but was she ready to admit some role in the kidnapping? For his part, Bram refused to wear a listening device. He had the room swept by Ernest Rose and met with Bronwyn, alone. No matter what she might have done, she had ultimately saved his sons. He was not about to punish her.

Bronwyn watched as Ernest Rose finished his sweep of the room, leaving her alone with the prime minister. She wished she felt stronger; even sitting in the chair was tiring. She asked the prime minister for a sip of water, and began.

"I saw you. When I was operated on. I saw you in the

operating theatre above me. You were wearing a dark green polo shirt, long-sleeved with a pink polo player."

She watched as he tried to remember what he was wearing. He recalled changing out of his bloody suit, and yes, they'd brought him a green jersey. Like the one she described.

He nodded, patronizingly.

"You said 'come back to me, come back to me, come back to me'."

That scored a hit. Bram jerked slightly back. He was certain he'd never said that aloud. True enough, he had thought it, he had fervently prayed it. Upon reflection, he wondered why the words in his mind hadn't been 'don't die'. Thinking 'Come back to me' was an odd thing, but he knew there was no accounting for what people said or did under stress. But no one would know he'd thought those words. He'd been silent. There was no way she could find that out. His shirt, but not what he'd been thinking. What game was she playing?

"When I died, when I was on the operating table and died, I went to the bright light, like people talk about." She scratched inside her ear, glad of some human touch, even if it was her own.

"Your brother was there, waiting for me."

Bram looked angry. "My brother. Who is my brother?"

"I don't know his name, but he said he was your brother."

Part of Bram wanted to leave, but part of him was fascinated by the girl's gall. To speak to him of his brother. The temerity of the girl. If she didn't look such a complete mess, tethered to wires and IV's, he would roar at her until she lay on the floor, weeping.

"Go on." Bram's head was tilted at an angle, signifying disbelief. "Did he have a message for me?"

She nodded her head. "He said he wants you to know he's always with you."

"How nice. And is that all he had to say? Only that? Always with me?"

She drew her thin robe around herself, feeling chilled. "He said he forgives you for making him lose the tip of his little toe. With the rock."

Bram's head jerked upright. His mind was racing back, landing on the perfectly recalled memory of throwing the rock, the blood, the vow to never tell. Then racing forward, trying to judge if he or David had ever, would ever, tell anyone that boyhood secret.

Bronwyn expected it would take some time for the prime minister to absorb the message. She was looking forward to spilling it out so she could sleep, blessedly sleep. It was a true burden, carrying and conveying messages from Heaven. Or, wherever his brother had been.

"I don't understand. You mean my brother told you something about a rock?"

Bronwyn could have nodded, but it seemed less effort to simply sigh.

"Anything else?"

"His dog was there."

"Well there you are, Miss McCall. My brother never had a dog. Ever."

"Maybe it was your dog. I just know he was beside him."

"And there you have it, again. I never had a dog and my children have never had a dog. It's as simple as that. You must have had a dream. Just a dream. You've been sedated for the better part of two weeks now. It's understandable."

Bronwyn hadn't thought of that. She studied her hands, hardly recognizing them with their purplish bruises and veins puffed by needles. Her lovely pale hands with the long fingers. They used to hold her wallet, she thought. They snapped photographs and slid up the long stem of a crystal wine glass. In the world. Out in the world. A world far beyond the walls of this hospital. She realized she didn't even know the name of the hospital or where it was. She felt very sad. She lifted her eyes and saw the prime minister sitting on her bed, watching her.

"What did the dog look like?" Bram surprised himself, asking. Well, the girl looked so disappointed, he thought.

"A border collie, I think. Long black and white fur, pointy black ears, white feet, white chest, white muzzle, but the rest of his face was black fur. His eyes glittered like black stars. He was very nice. I could feel his breath on my hand. That's why I looked down and saw him."

Something in the back of Bram's mind was clicking into place. A black and white dog with long fur. He vaguely remembered.

"He had a brass disk on his collar. I know that sounds weird, assuming he was in Heaven. I can't tell you if your brother was dressed or not dressed, but I saw the brass circle around Pal's neck."

"Pal."

"The disk said 'Pal' so I thought that was his name. His fur was very soft."

"Perhaps you'd like to get back into bed, if you think you've told me everything."

"Yes. That's all. Your brother said to tell you he's always with you."

Bram helped her into bed, realizing he seldom helped anyone these days. Even the boys had people to tuck them into bed. He laid his coat atop her blanket and the additional warmth sent her straight to sleep while he sat in her chair. He watched her sleep as tears coursed down his cheeks. When they were young, visiting Maine, he and his brother had biked all over town and had chased each other through the rocks nearly every day of their summer vacation. They ate their packed lunch and plotted their futures, gazing out at the bay. Yes, Bram had thrown a rock and nipped off the tip of David's toe, exposed in his sandal. They told their parents that David had tripped, and Bram couldn't imagine David ever telling anyone it was Bram's fault. However, you never knew what good intel could gather. But the dog. That was something else. They'd found the dog and played with it, trying to figure a way to keep him. Bram's mother would never permit it; they knew it would be a lost cause. But they loved the dog. It licked and kissed them, ran with them, laid its furry body atop them, brought sticks for them to throw. It had only been an afternoon, but when Bram reached through his memories, he knew both he and David had loved the dog. It broke their hearts when the owner walked through the woods, calling 'Pal'. The dog remained at their side while his name was called, but got fidgety and finally galloped to meet his owner. Proving the dog was his, the man showed them the dog's brass nametag.

Maybe it hadn't been Bronwyn who peeled back the tough layers of memory, revealing his heart. Maybe it was the brother he'd long missed, wanting Bram to know, world leader or not, that he was always with him. The thought occurred to the prime minister that perhaps his brother had led the girl, had used her to save the boys.

Bram rose and lifted his coat from Bronwyn's bed, whispering, "Truth lends itself to peaceful sleep."

The prime minister didn't return, and there were times when the man named Ernest Rose wasn't in her room. The shards of pain had lessened, but the endless hours hung over Bronwyn like an oppressive weight.

She supposed she could ask for a book or magazine, but she didn't have a peaceful mind for concentrating. She felt lousy. All she could do was clutch at memories, thinking of people she cared about, the people who were gone.

Ernest Rose had been kind enough to answer when she inquired as to the prime minister's boys. They were back home, unscathed. She doubted they were unscathed, but she was relieved they weren't injured.

She asked Ernest Rose to tell her friend Ollie she'd been in an accident, but was fine and would see him soon. Ernest Rose didn't say he'd convey the message, and there was something about the man's stoicism that made Bronwyn uncomfortable.

There was no question Ollie would be worried about her; they stayed in constant touch. But, if she kept improving she was certain she'd be in New York before long. Memories kept her company, just as they had always done. She tried to ignore the nurses and the smells, the endless blood draws and the Spartan room, and think back to the life she'd made.

After the nurse left, Bronwyn delicately shifted her position in the Naugahyde chair with its brass studs, knowing that once she managed to get in the chair, she'd be staying there awhile. She wished she had an afghan, like she had in the townhouse. Ollie's townhouse.

She reflected back to when they'd met, as teens in Pittsburgh.

She was at the creative arts high school. Ollie was 16 while she was 13, but she hadn't seen him at school. He was strutting down the runway of a Teen Board fashion show at the Joseph Horne Co. department store. She knew he was special. His hair was long, his body rangy, but it was his face. The features looked carved from marble, timeless perfection. His eyes were chocolate brown with lashes so long they seemed to burden his eyes. His high cheekbones were distinctively hollow, defining a bone structure supermodels would envy. But his nose was what made him special. It was uniquely exotic; beautifully curved in the most delicate way. It was Bronwyn's nature to observe people, and she'd never seen anyone who looked anything like Oliver Silkowski.

People who didn't know Ollie would think he was shy and quiet. It did seem as if being so uniquely handsome wore him down. He donned mufflers and knit caps and ragged clothes, seeking invisibility. When Bronwyn waited for him after the runway show, asking if he'd like to get a veggie plate at Stouffer's, his eyes crinkled and he showed her a shy smile. They were fast friends from then on.

Ollie was intrigued with Bronwyn's freedom. Sworn to secrecy, he kept up her façade, pretending as she did that her quasi-guardian, Judge Wheeler, maintained a residence in the William Penn Hotel. The judge paid well enough to keep up the pretense, leasing a two room connecting suite, leaving a few of his suits and his wife's dresses in the other room, in case anyone might suspect young Bronwyn lived alone.

It wasn't Bronwyn's preference, of course, but as it turned out it suited her perfectly.

When she was eight years old, her parents had flown to

France with her paternal grandparents and sister, Claire. Her mother's best friend, Gwen, kept Bronwyn, who was in school.

It had all gone terribly wrong. Bronwyn's family was killed in a plane crash. Bronwyn suspected something was wrong when Gwen took her to her father's Great Aunt Ida's house in Sewickley. Gwen was weeping and Bronwyn hated her for it. If she was leaving her with that old woman, she had no right to cry. Judge Wheeler was there. They said Bronwyn's family wasn't coming back, her house was being sold, and everything in it was gone.

With years of perspective, Bronwyn realized Ida might have felt guilty about selling everything at auction. What mattered to Bronwyn was losing all of the family photographs. Without them, she could hardly remember her family. She barely remembered her life. That was unforgivable.

Bronwyn imagined photos in the albums, closed her eyes and fell asleep. When she slept, her life was normal. Sometimes strange, but never as strange as the reality of the windowless hospital room. This time she dreamed about her father putting pieces of sod on their roof. At first Bronwyn thought he was making a grass roof and she loved the green of it, but he was just drying the sod out while men did yard work.

While she was sleeping, Ernest Rose was pulling up the kidnapping footage. He zeroed in on Bronwyn in the Presidential Suite's anteroom. He zoomed in and saw what the girl looked like without the facial puffiness from surgery. As Bronwyn glanced at the camera, unaware of its existence, she'd been well-dressed for the interview, with a charismatic smile. Ernest looked at the hospital bed. It was no wonder the prime minister's friend hadn't recognized her. Ernest could find nothing in the look of the girl to match the video, although she was a vaguely plain, ill version.

Bronwyn's mouth moved as she slept, and he watched to see if she would awaken. When she didn't, Rose returned to his laptop. Her friend, Oliver Silkowski, had been living in East Hampton with the actor, Tommy Gallagher. They'd been playing tennis together when Silkowski collapsed on the court. The men had been discreet. Their neighbors said Silkowski lived in the pool house.

Ernest Rose reviewed Silkowski's background. He was a student at the same Pittsburgh creative arts high school, and Bronwyn did the photographs for his modeling portfolio. The two had run errands for his grandmother, Daisy Coulter. When she died, her sister Nellie moved into Daisy's Homestead house on the outskirts of Pittsburgh, allowing Silkowski and Bronwyn to stay in her Greenwich Village townhouse. Tall and narrow, it had an Italianate façade and thirteen foot ceilings. No one would guess the recent disorder. Ernest Rose looked at Mastrofrancesco's photographs of the ravaged rooms. Rose wished instead that his teams had done the job. These people had made a ripe mess of things.

He leaned back in his chair. Brought into the situation by the prime minister's mother, he was to have Bronwyn's health and well-being in hand. He'd already failed miserably. He'd been overruled when the 'truth team' walked into her room, satchel of drugs in hand. True, they'd left satisfied; she had not been involved in the planning or execution of the kidnap plot, but it seemed unholy to inject her with thiopental sodium. Not after what she'd been through.

He scrolled down. The chap had modeled all over the

world while Bronwyn's career took off, showing in galleries in SoHo and Chelsea, with photographs in glossy magazines. Ernest Rose reviewed her early years before the New York move.

Bronwyn was waking up, but kept her eyes closed, using her memories to walk through the life she used to have.

Sewickley was a nice town. She fixed her own breakfast in Aunt Ida's old Victorian kitchen, usually cereal; that worked great because there was a staircase leading to the kitchen from her bedroom, like a secret passage. Sometimes she fixed peanut butter and jelly sandwiches when she knew Aunt Ida wouldn't be around. But usually she ate at Isaly's or jumped on the bus to Pittsburgh. She had numerous eating possibilities there. Her dad's friend worked as chef at the William Penn Hotel and he'd planned to join Bobby McCall, when he opened his first restaurant. Whenever she popped back to see him, she felt closer to her father.

Judge Wheeler gave her a nice allowance. When he realized she could handle money and enjoyed eating out, he didn't mind giving her restaurant money. He couldn't imagine eating with the old dowager.

Ernest Rose was pondering what sort of man Judge Wheeler had been. Stanley Mastrofrancesco had been helpful in rounding out intel on the girl. When Judge Wheeler retired to Palm Beach, he turned over the governance of Bronwyn's modest trust fund to Stanley Mastrofrancesco. Moss declined to explain how Bronwyn lived alone in a large hotel from the age of thirteen until she moved to New York at eighteen, but Ernest Rose knew the Judge had finagled it somehow. He had the uncomfortable feeling that Wheeler had reacted just as Rose himself would have done – pass the problem off and close your eyes.

The nurse came in, checked Bronwyn's vital signs and took her into the bathroom. She left Bronwyn there and before long, Ernest heard her call 'Leaves.'

He went to the door.

"Is something wrong?"

"Could you come in here a minute?"

He was relieved to see she was fully dressed and leaning on the sink.

"They want me to take a shower, but I'm supposed to sit on that chair."

"You need assistance?"

"I was hoping you could wash the chair for me. I don't know where it's been." For the first time, he saw a small smile from her.

"Certainly." He removed his jacket, rolled his sleeves and began to scrub with soap and paper towels, and then turned to her. "What did you say, when you called me?"

Bronwyn looked embarrassed and shrugged. "I don't know."

"It sounded like 'leaves'."

Rose knew he'd caught her at something. He put his hands on his hips; wadded paper towels in one hand, and antiseptic soap in the other.

"I may have called you Jeeves. I didn't mean to."

"Why would you do that?"

She was turning a light shade of pink which was a marked improvement over the deathly pale white she'd been every day. "I guess I've been pretending you were my Jeeves."

"Your Jeeves? I belong to you?"

"Well, like a manservant. It just seemed less scary to think you were my manservant instead of whatever you are."

"Whatever I am? Sorry, Bronwyn. I should have told you. For the past five years I've served as personal bodyguard for the prime minister's mother, and she's asked me to assume that role for you."

Bronwyn looked alarmed. "Someone's trying to kill me?"

"Certainly not. You saved her grandsons. She wants you properly cared for and that's my job."

He was about to return to his cleaning task when he asked, "Why would you want me to be your Jeeves?"

"You've only got to stand on Jeeves and fate can't touch you."

"Well, that sounds right, doesn't it? So, I'll be your Jeeves. Satisfied?"

It was late at night, and Bronwyn couldn't get comfortable. Sleep was eluding her once again; she was sad and alone. Ernest Rose had gone for the night. Twice she rolled a raggedy washcloth into a cylinder, imagining it as a teddy bear or something comforting to clutch as she fell asleep. The first time the nurse found it, she shrugged and tossed it in the hamper, but the second time she raised her eyebrows at Bronwyn and clucked. Sometimes Bronwyn cradled the back of one hand in the palm of her other, as if the palm could reassure her. But she could never outsmart the receiving hand. Somehow it always knew and couldn't truly be comforted. It was her dominant giving hand that focused her brain – how to hold, how to squeeze, how to pat, how to cradle. There was no surprise in her effort, but it still felt better to cradle one hand within the other than to let them lie separately.

Bronwyn feared she was losing her sense of self. All she could do was think of the life she'd been leading, wringing enough vibrancy from the memories to make them true. In the dark of night, it so easily slipped away.

Bronwyn's mother had no idea that Gwen would move. And Maggie McCall would have been devastated that Gwen moved without taking Bronwyn. They'd been best friends for years, and she'd chosen Gwen as 'God-forbid anything happens' guardian.

Gwen made one visit to see Bronwyn at Aunt Ida's, and when she saw what little clothing Maggie's daughter had, she raised the roof at Judge Wheeler's. Bronwyn went shopping with the Judge, but she never saw Gwen again.

If Maggie McCall had known what would happen, they'd never have gone to France. If she'd known they would never return, she certainly would have packed family photographs in Bronwyn's little suitcase. As it was, she did send something special along with Bronwyn's three weeks worth of school clothes. She sent along her own childhood Betsy McCall dolls – one brunette and one auburn, just like her daughters, Bronwyn and Claire.

As she unfolded the pages of her life, whiling away the hours, Bronwyn got choked up, thinking of her Betsy McCall dolls. Thank goodness they were safe, tucked under the floorboards of Ollie's townhouse.

The nurse came in, shining a small flashlight in her face. Bronwyn hated giving blood. It made her feel faint. She could feel the blood draining straight into the vial. She'd always been that way and if she didn't put her head between her knees or lie down, she would see stars.

Which path should her memories take her now? Back to the past, or a flight of fancy to Greenwich Village? She chose her past, saving New York as icing on the cake.

Sewickley and the Judge seemed like only yesterday.

She stayed in Aunt Ida's house in Sewickley for five years. Aunt Ida was gruff and Bronwyn did a good job avoiding her, but sometimes she'd offer to plant vegetables or pick up groceries at Select Market, just to have something to do. But age wasn't wearing well on the old lady and she was easily annoyed. So, Bronwyn became expert at being invisible.

She went to the movies as often as possible. Popcorn and movies always made her happy.

She saw enough movies that an idea took shape. She would ask Judge Wheeler if she could live with him. It seemed a splendid proposition. She could be just as invisible in his house and was confident he wouldn't mind seeing her.

She chose a day and prepared her speech. The delivery was flawless and she knew she'd reeled him in – until she stood in the hallway outside his living room pocket door, which had closed. Mrs. Wheeler was not agreeable. She wanted to travel. She wanted freedom. She didn't want to be tied down to the girl. Bronwyn knew this, because she could hear their raised voices.

Bronwyn trudged back to Aunt Ida's house beside the Judge. He reassured her, but most of all he made certain she went back. He needn't have worried. She wouldn't go anywhere if it wasn't an improvement.

That night she made a new plan, and the joy of it lifted her through the week until she took the bus to Pittsburgh. When she walked through the William Penn and visited her dad's friend in the kitchen, she felt more certain. She had lunch in Kaufmann's, bought herself a book, and returned to the hotel for tea in the lobby.

The next day Bronwyn called the Judge, to meet privately. Now that Bronwyn looked back, it was amazing the Judge was easily sold. She was just thirteen. What Bronwyn didn't realize was that the Judge had been grasping for a solution. He'd have taken the girl and was shocked at his wife's stance against it.

Judge Wheeler was a man who knew what money could buy, so he made unique arrangements with the hotel. He planned to see Bronwyn most weekends, taking her to the Symphony and museums. The front desk staff and housekeeping would look after her and Wheeler didn't mind paying well. It seemed the perfect solution. He told himself he was going to do a better job with Bronwyn than Gwen or the old woman had done.

Some of Bronwyn's happiest memories were the five years she lived in the hotel. She loved the bustle in the stately lobby, the activity of the streets, the unending excitement of the stores, and the city views beyond her windows. What a joy it was meandering through Pittsburgh, dining in restaurants, seeing plays, overhearing people's conversations in elevators, watching the seasons change in Mellon Square, finding Ollie as a friend, and discovering the camera.

Bronwyn's favorite course at the creative arts school had been photography. She convinced the Judge to buy equipment and set up a darkroom in the bathroom of 'his' adjoining room. Just remembering, allowed her to nearly smell the chemicals. She recalled how she opened the hotel windows, letting the chemical smell drift away. In her mind's eye, she could see the negative strips hanging; the basins for developer, stopper, fix, and the water bath. She visualized the red glow of the light, almost felt how slick the paper was when it came out of the fluid. She always marveled at how the camera lens bent light. It was an absolute miracle to her. Taking photographs was about seeing, but in her little pitch-black darkroom, the photographs were nothing except touch and instinct. She remembered that tiny bathroom as a new world for her.

Harry Plank had a portrait studio off the hotel lobby and she volunteered to be a photographer's assistant. Mr. Plank didn't realize how young Bronwyn was. With Ollie's help, she looked a few years older, but it was like living two lives – dressing for success on the job, and then running through the city as a free spirit. Mr. Plank groomed her, eventually allowing her to take photographs and create her own portfolio.

When she awakened the next day, Ernest Rose was in her room. He handed her a flannel nightgown and a fuzzy robe and was rewarded with a lovely smile.

"Thank you, Jeeves," Bronwyn said, gratefully.

He beamed at her.

"Jeeves, am I in a prison?"

"No, Miss. Why?"

Her mouth was a thin line. "This isn't a nice place."

Ernest Rose felt a stab of guilt. He wasn't being a very good Jeeves. "It's a military hospital Miss, not a prison. I'm afraid it lacks the modern touch."

"No one talks to me. The nurses do their work, but they don't talk to me."

"I don't believe you'll be here much longer, Miss. You must do as they say and get stronger."

"As soon as I get out of here," she said with a voice warming to a rapid clip of words, unlike her usual measured spooling of syllables, "I'm going to have lunch with my friend Ollie. You can come, too. We'll either have tea at the Plaza, which you'd like, wouldn't you? Or lunch at Saks. Maybe a milkshake at Serendipity."

He was unprepared for a glimpse of the life she'd lost. "Just gain your strength, Miss."

"I'm going to see those boys again. That's what I'll get strong for. Do you think I'll be allowed to see the boys? Samuel and Paul?"

"That's a distinct possibility, Miss. Their grandmother informs me the young gentlemen are anxious to see you."

Bronwyn was tired and closed her eyes, vowing to get strong enough to leave. It was a relief to hear it wasn't a prison, but it was still her prison.

She wondered if Ernest Rose would be surprised to know she'd been practically on her own since she was eight years old. The surprise would have been hers, however. Even without exchanging confidences, there wasn't much about her life that Ernest Rose hadn't discovered.

The food was terrible. People say that about hospital food, but the food was terrible and Bronwyn had no appetite. She convinced Jeeves to hide the food and throw it away so she wouldn't be scolded. Jeeves wasn't about to volunteer to eat the mess. He brought her a chocolate milkshake once and she devoured it, so the milkshakes were a go-to food when nothing tempted her. Today, they'd done just that, dumped the food tray, and Bronwyn was relishing a milkshake.

He pulled up a chair and brought out a small notebook. "I've a question, Miss."

Jeeves had begun calling her 'Miss' with his lovely English accent, and using more formal words in his new position of manservant. Bronwyn knew the 'Jeeves' game was a novel way for them to pass the time. She never doubted he was still whatever he was.

"Okay."

"When you were recovering, drifting in and out, they made note of something you said and I must ask what it means."

"I was talking? I don't remember."

"Not talking. Phonetically, it sounded like a rapid repetition. 'jewluhmeejewluhmee'. What does it mean?"

Bronwyn narrowed her eyes. "It's personal."

"I'm afraid, Miss, I must judge the significance. If it's personal, you know I'll not breathe a word. But you really must tell me."

The set of her jaw signified silence.

Bronwyn was angry he would bring something like that up, especially if she'd just gotten out of surgery. It was an invasion of privacy. She hadn't really looked at Rose until now. She wanted to judge this man's face and see why he'd become an interrogator. His dark hair was brushed back from a dominant widow's peak and tinged with gray at the temples. His eyes weren't friendly, they were beady. His nose was a junior version of Bob Hope's ski jump nose, and thinking of that made Bronwyn smile, giving Ernest Rose false hope. His most obvious feature was a prominent chin, like a tennis ball attached to his jaws, so pronounced that it created a deep crease between his chin and his lower lip. She wondered if he had to clean the crease with a Q-tip, it was so deep. She judged him to be in his late fifties. Admittedly, while her appraisal of his facial features seemed not to flatter him, he was a distinguished looking man.

"I must know, Miss."

He was so serious. Whoever 'they' were must think she'd revealed a secret code of some kind.

"I think it's time for a good faith gesture."

Ernest encouraged her negotiation.

"Certainly. Another milkshake?"

"What I want is to learn something personal about you. Then, I'll tell you what it means."

"Fine, Miss. You first."

"Nope. You first." She put out her hand, to shake his. As they shook, she said, "And if you lie to me, may God strike you dead."

It was odd, really. Something had shifted inside; it had actually registered with him, mattered to him. He would have aped acquiescence and lied like a dog, but the way she said it made him flip through his secrets to see if there was one he might offer up.

"To never be spoken of, again," he drew his face to hers, just inches away.

She nodded.

"My wife Deirdre died of cancer. Several years ago."

"More," she said. "Never to be spoken of, again. What's the rest of it?"

"I turned away from it. I turned my back on her."

Bronwyn stopped him. It was enough.

"Those were my mother's last words to me. The words you've written down. Right before she went down the tunnel, into the airplane. 'Do you love me'? When I want to feel close to her, when I need to feel close to her, I say those words over and over. Like a litany. Especially if I'm in pain."

He glanced at his notebook and then at Bronwyn. "More. What's the rest of it?" he asked, realizing she knew better than he did, there is always more of it.

"She should have said 'I love you'. Not ask me if I loved her. Those shouldn't have been her last words to me." He thought she might cry, but she didn't. Instead she said, "Never to be spoken of, again."

What she was thinking was that she had no idea if she'd answered her mother's question. She only remembered the question.

Ernest Rose was glad he'd brought her a milkshake; it had been kind, just like the robe and nightgown after she'd spent so long in threadbare hospital garb. He rather liked being her Jeeves. But the real gesture had been in giving Bronwyn his truth. Only the truth could create the fiber that bound them in that moment, laying down the first tracks for their journey together.

CHAPTER THREE

MAIN LINE

Anna Black was Sunny to her friends and the Main Line community, but her closest friends called her Menke – her maiden name.

When her son told her about the attempted kidnapping of her grandsons, she wanted to go to Washington, but Bram sent the boys back to Israel. He danced around the particulars about the photographer who saved them, but after Menke spoke to Samuel on the phone, she felt a deep debt of gratitude. That's when she sent Ernest Rose to the hospital as Bronwyn's protector.

Now that it was time for Bronwyn to leave the hospital, it seemed natural to bring her to Rose Lane. A physical therapist was scheduled for daily visits and Menke hired a home nurse. She wasn't certain what condition she'd find the girl in. Ernest Rose was no conversationalist. He only said that Bronwyn would be no trouble. Menke wondered if he'd been keeping her sedated.

With some trepidation, she watched the Infiniti pull around the driveway. She'd expected an ambulance, not an SUV. As Menke watched, she saw the attendant bring a wheelchair to the passenger side. The young woman tried to decline the wheelchair, but gave up. Ernest Rose walked behind and Menke watched anxiously as the girl was wheeled over.

Bronwyn attempted to step over the foot rests, but the reach was too much and she barked "Jeeves". With bemusement, Menke watched Ernest Rose hop to it and flip the two foot rests upward, offering his arm as the girl rose.

When Bronwyn looked up, she saw Anna Black and gave her a lovely smile, extending her hand.

Surprised at how cold the girl's hand was, Menke urged them through the door.

"I understand you're the prime minister's mother. I'm Bronwyn McCall."

"It's such a pleasure to welcome you, dear. I'm Anna Black, but my friends call me Menke." She gestured to the nearest easy chair, watched as Ernest Rose situated the girl with more gentleness than Menke could have imagined, and seated herself in an adjacent chair. She took a moment to have a good look at Bronwyn.

It was obvious she'd been through a great deal. Her skin was the palest she'd ever seen, but Menke noted a smattering of freckles. She had the look of someone sick, haunted around the eyes. For someone with such lovely dark hair, her eyebrows and eyelashes were strikingly pale, as if a mistake had been made in her creation.

For her part, Bronwyn was assessing the prime minister's elegantly dressed mother. Bronwyn imagined her carefully choosing what outfit to wear for the occasion of Bronwyn's sick-bed arrival. Mrs. Black was a striking woman and wore a deceptively simple open-neck white blouse of obvious quality, casually rolled at the cuffs. A black pencil skirt was topped by a grosgrain belt. She was tall, with short, honey blonde hair, swept back from her face in a deep wave.

"Do you mind me asking, where we are?"

"This is my home, Bronwyn."

"I'm sorry, Mrs. Black. I meant are we in Delaware? Pennsylvania?"

Ernest Rose's eyebrows shot up, but Menke answered, "Haverford, Pennsylvania, Bronwyn, near Philadelphia." At that, Bronwyn smiled. "And, please call me Menke. I noticed you smiled a bit when I mentioned we were near Philadelphia."

"It's just a Pittsburgh thing, Menke. Philadelphia is great with its Boathouse Row and restaurants, but I'm a Pittsburgh girl, and if you love Pittsburgh you always feel a rivalry with Philly."

"I see," she said, while clearly she did not.

"Your home is lovely. I noticed the wooden gates leading to gardens and the stone paths are beautiful. All the colors... brown and lavender and blues."

"I'm sure you must be tired, dear. Let's get you settled in your room and then we'll tour the house, later."

When the nurse insisted on the wheelchair, Bronwyn vowed to convince Menke to ditch the nurse as soon as possible, but she acquiesced and they glided through the living room. Bronwyn's head turned left and right. As they approached her room, Bronwyn asked about the ornately dressed monkey figurines she'd seen in the living room.

Menke explained, "They're Meissen. Porcelain. That collection is a Monkey Band. I'll put a few in your room if you'd like."

They crossed the threshold of her bedroom, with its

tones of beige and one straight back chair and a chaise. Bronwyn thought neither would suit Jeeves. The bed looked quite comfortable, but the focal point of the room was a long glass-topped vanity, skirted in white chiffon. A vase of white flowers sat atop, as well as delicate twin lamps, and the entire thing was framed in matching chiffon curtains parted to reveal a round golden mirror. When Bronwyn rose out of the dreaded wheelchair, her eyes fell to the lovely plush carpet, and it was then that she realized she'd gone from one extreme to the other. She would never miss the dingy scratched linoleum tiles of the hospital room and could hardly wait to be barefoot on the carpet. Something caught her eye; something with movement. She discovered a pale beige cat watching her from the corner of the room. Bronwyn smiled widely, realizing that she hadn't truly smiled in weeks.

"What day is today? What is the date?" Bronwyn was stunned to discover six weeks had elapsed since the day she looked in the mirror of the ladies room, certain her career was climbing ever higher.

"Bronwyn, have you any suggestions for the boys? They're not sleeping well and apparently they've lost their appetite." Menke was hoping to encourage Bronwyn's own appetite.

After a few moments, Bronwyn offered, "Maybe miniature food. You know, like tea sandwiches and little hors d'oeuvres. That way it's not overwhelming. And Ernest Rose hit on cocoa and milkshakes for me, and toast with peanut butter. If I can't face anything to eat, those usually work."

Menke nodded and thanked her. She decided to have Cook serve tea that afternoon, with tiny scones and finger sandwiches.

"Menke, if you have paper and a pen or pencil, I could draw the boys a picture and maybe you could mail it for me."

"What an excellent idea. Bram says the boys talk about you constantly. We'll fax them and they'll get them right away."

Bronwyn began drawing a detailed picture of the Meissen monkeys for Paul with their ruffles, masks, hats, instruments and extraordinary clothing, and then gingerly moved near Puff the cat, to capture her sleeping form for Samuel. She added a note to each and handed them off. Within the hour, both boys had faxed Bronwyn drawings of their own. It served to remind Menke that the three shared a bond.

Afternoon tea was a success. At one point, Bronwyn shared how she hoped to have boys just like Samuel and Paul. Menke was thankful she had the ability to appear impassive. She glanced at Ernest Rose but he turned away.

When Bronwyn settled in for a nap, Menke searched for Rose, finding him in the gardens. Just as she suspected, no one had told Bronwyn she couldn't have children as a result of the surgery. It was inconceivable to Menke, but the doctors hadn't spoken to Bronwyn; only the prime minister. Moss was coming the next day. Perhaps he could deliver the bad news her son hadn't bothered to share with Bronwyn.

When she learned that Moss was coming, Bronwyn realized he would know Menke. When he and Bram were in college together, he probably came for holidays.

Bronwyn dressed in a blouse, drawstring pants, and a cardigan borrowed from Menke. She planned to ask Moss to stop at Ollie's townhouse and send a few outfits to tide her over. She wanted to impress Moss with her progress. If she looked almost normal, he'd surely facilitate a quicker return to New York.

She expected he would come straight to see her, but she heard his voice near the kitchen. He was having a glass of bourbon to brace himself.

Moss had so much bad news to deliver. So much life-changing, life-robbing news. He'd mentally arranged and rearranged the order, but it would make no difference. He finally settled on 'Ollie is dead' as the first blow.

It seemed dreamlike to Moss. He waited for Bronwyn's reactions, but she didn't cry out. She didn't beat her chest. He braced himself for a delayed reaction, but none came. She simply asked if she could call Ollie's partner, Tommy Gallagher.

Moss had met Oliver Silkowski, when Bronwyn brought him to the Mastrofrancesco penthouse for dinner parties. He understood why she'd call Tommy Gallagher, but he suggested she keep the particulars of her absence a secret.

In a soft voice, she gave her condolences to Tommy Gallagher, asked how he was, inquired about Ollie's mother and told Tommy she'd been in an accident but was doing well, explaining away her absence. Then, she was perplexed.

"Yes. Well, friends did that for me. They didn't want to upset me about Ollie, so they just went ahead and moved things out." She turned her hand palm up, furrowed her brow and shook her head slightly, looking from Jeeves to Moss and back again.

"That's what I thought. Of course his aunt would sell the townhouse." It was obvious Bronwyn was learning about the empty townhouse and Moss was furious with himself for not telling her.

"No, I'm fine. I'm staying with friends. No Tommy, but thanks for the offer. Have you been in? Does everything look okay?"

Moss didn't know Gallagher's reply, but he had sent a cleaning company to restore order to the place. He doubted Silkowski's family would have any problem selling it.

When Bronwyn hung up, she looked alarmed.

"Where is everything? Where are my things?" she asked Moss.

"I'm sorry, Bronwyn. A counter-terrorism unit went in when they suspected your involvement. They took everything as evidence. I didn't know, or I would have stopped them. I swear to you."

Ernest Rose lifted an eyebrow. There'd be no stopping the men, but if Stanley Mastrofrancesco wanted to think so, let him.

"But where is everything? When will I get it back?"

Moss shook his head. "It's gone, I'm afraid. I've tried, but it's gone."

"I don't understand. My clothes? Cameras? Photographs?" Moss nodded at each one. "All of it? You're sure?"

He detailed his trip to Ollie's townhouse and assured her nothing was left. Bronwyn grasped his forearm and asked for a favor.

He agreed and called his wife.

For the next thirty minutes, the three kept vigil as Mrs. Mastrofrancesco took a cab to Greenwich Village and then pried up floorboards at Ollie's. To Bronwyn's relief Moss's wife found the two Betsy McCall dolls her mother left with her, years ago.

Moss's wife was aware of Bronwyn's mounting losses and was glad there was one small thing she could do for her. She'd used her house key to pry up the correct floorboard and found herself silently praying as she pulled back the thick velvet around the dolls. Even though Bronwyn told her there should be two dolls, she was taken aback when she saw they were Betsy McCalls.

She'd forgotten about those dolls, but remembered she'd owned one when she was a girl. A flash of memory brought back the way their clothes were packaged, with outfits illustrated on the box flap. She remembered gazing at them the same way she anticipated the Betsy McCall paper dolls in her mother's McCall's magazines. She promised to call Bronwyn as soon as the dolls were tucked in the Mastrofrancesco safe.

She held the two dolls tightly as she got into a cab. Pulling back the velvet wrapping from the tiny doll faces, she felt a kinship with Bronwyn's mother. As the cab edged its way uptown, she looked at the little dolls, garishly lit by the bursts of neon, and then darkened through the rainy intersections. The auburn haired Betsy was wearing a white flocked gown over a blue dress with a pale pink satin sash. The brunette Betsy was still jaunty in a riding habit, with brown felt jodhpurs, black vest, white top and pink chiffon scarf at the neck. She decided she'd never seen more exquisitely delicate and beautiful dolls than these vintage Betsy McCalls.

Once Bronwyn knew the dolls were rescued, she seemed to feel better. Moss was annoyed with his friend the prime minister, but it had to be done. He told her she could never bear children.

He didn't expect the wry smile she gave him. He knelt at her knees and took her hands.

"Why are you smiling, Bronwyn? What can I do?"

Her voice sounded hollow. "I'm smiling because I realize I've been here before, Moss. That last bit did it. I recognize the place I'm in. When I lost my family and my home and everything in it. Not many people lose everything. I've been riding along on the edge of despair and now I've notched down into it. I've been here. It's familiar."

She sounded matter-of-fact.

It wasn't until she went into the bathroom, ran the water in the bathtub and crumpled on the floor beside it, that her emotions overtook her. Ollie's death was sinking in. At first, no one knew where the noise was coming from, but as they approached the bathroom they heard a wail above the noise of rushing water. Ernest Rose listened at the door and when she finally stopped, he turned and faced the others.

"I'll make cocoa."

Moss rubbed his eyes with the heels of his hands and Menke left to turn down the bed. When Bronwyn emerged, her eyes were swollen from crying. Jeeves carried the cocoa while the others steered her into bed. Puff the cat gracefully leaped upon the bed and Bronwyn stroked her and smiled sweetly. "I'll be all right," she assured them, with as much voice as she could muster.

Having navigated the depth of life, she knew she'd be climbing up. The fall was unfamiliar, but she'd been at the bottom before.

Bronwyn and Bram's boys exchanged faxed notes each day, and she seemed to take more of an interest in the house and the gardens, beyond pleasantries. Her appetite was meager but she made an effort at tea, politely marveling at the various sandwiches and pastries. Cook basked in the compliments each time Bronwyn poked her head in the kitchen, and that appreciation sent her delving into cookbooks, searching for culinary ideas to please the girl.

If Jeeves hadn't slipped something into her cocoa most nights, Bronwyn's sleep would have been disrupted by anguish. He did it more for himself than Bronwyn; he hated seeing her swollen eyelids in the morning, so thin and ripe with grief they looked as if they might burst. Her eyes were normally so large, it was disconcerting for Jeeves to see how heavy-lidded her sorrow made them. He wondered if he might be forced to prop her eyes open with glue or a toothpick or a crane. The sedated cocoa was easier.

Both Jeeves and Menke were well aware Puff the cat avoided people, so it was intriguing to find her with Bronwyn. Even at night the cat slept on her bed. More often than not, Jeeves would find Bronwyn with her arms extended toward the sleeping cat. Bronwyn's right hand cradled one of Puff's feet while her left gently covered it…like a delicate 'cat paw sandwich'. Seeing this was torturous for Jeeves. It made him think his dear dying wife may have reached out for his loving touch, long ago and all for naught.

One morning Jeeves told Bronwyn she'd been sleepwalking, but she denied it.

"Why would you say that?"

"You were walking to the vanity, Miss. You opened the bottle of water, felt for the glass and poured yourself a drink. I was here, making certain you didn't stumble."

"I wasn't sleepwalking."

"Then, what were you doing?"

She didn't answer.

"It's nothing to be ashamed of, Miss. Nor frightened of…I'm always here for you."

She gave him an odd look and set her mouth.

"You must tell me."

Bronwyn realized he wouldn't be letting it go.

He sensed her indecision.

"Tell me. Never to be spoken of, again," testing to see if that would open her mouth.

"You know how it works, Jeeves. You give me something." Smiling, she added, "And may God strike you dead if you lie to me."

He was surprised that her answer must bear some gravitas. He thought what private secret he might share. Then he thought what lie he could create. Bronwyn couldn't see his mind spinning with options; he was cool with his calculations. When he looked at her, something made him disregard lies as an option. He wasn't sorry he'd mentioned his wife Deirdre before, but if the truth was necessary, he had only one option.

"I don't need to know, Miss," and turned to the window.

She sat on her bed, smiling. It pleased her enormously that he would choose not to lie. Several minutes passed, and when Jeeves turned around, she was waiting.

"I've closed my eyes at night since I was small, going to the bathroom, finding socks when my feet are cold, writing in the dark, pouring water. I've done it so I can take care of myself. I'm not saying I expect to be blind, but it makes me feel capable. You should try it. I think you'll find you can often see better with your eyes closed." She gathered her clothes and reminded him, "Never to be spoken of, again."

She could feel how far within herself she'd retreated, coping with the reality of losing Ollie. Finding him had been the best thing that ever happened to her. Even when he traveled to Europe, they were in constant touch. They had shared joyful discovery and laughter for twelve years. Memories of their southern road trips made her wistful. They always stopped at as many Cracker Barrels as they could find, like stones across a pond. And they'd become good friends with Mama Lou, the owner of a southern barbeque restaurant. Both Ollie and Bronwyn fell for Mama Lou's motherly ways – the way she hugged them and chuckled and called them 'baby' and mopped the perspiration from her dark face. Bronwyn couldn't believe Ollie would never see Mama Lou again. Never have her barbeque again. Ollie had become Bronwyn's family and she loved him dearly. She'd trusted that he would be with her for the rest of her life and it was a cruel and unbelievable shock to lose him.

When she seemed to accept Ollie's death, she found herself blindsided by the twisting, painful knowledge she'd never have children. The losses slapped at her until she felt like a robot, putting one clanging foot in front of the other, barely able to propel herself forward. Everything was an enormous, empty effort; empty of intention, empty of meaning.

But, as weeks went by, Bronwyn felt herself coming nearer the surface, coming closer to filling out her skin. She might have held back longer, silently suffering, but she needed to bolster Menke's spirits. Bronwyn didn't realize Menke's desolation was brought about by Bronwyn's predicament. She just saw the worry etching across Menke's forehead, and the deepening lines and shadows around her eyes. Bronwyn decided to gather strength and make more of an effort to endure.

Menke was pleased when Bronwyn agreed to venture out, and they began to have a few lunches at restaurants. She was more talkative, musing about the menu and chef, the décor and food.

One day, Jeeves convinced Bronwyn to use a wheelchair at Longwood Gardens, and Bronwyn's spirits were raised by over a thousand acres of beautiful flowers. It intrigued Bronwyn to learn how different the gardens appeared throughout the seasons, all part of the planning process. They interrupted their tour with lunch at the Terrace Restaurant and both Menke and Ernest Rose teased her when she ordered Chester County Mushroom Soup and then Kennett Square Mushroom Strudel. Jeeves was pleased with himself when he allowed Menke the punch line and she came through with it…what mushroom dish was she having for dessert?

Menke couldn't rest her mind, knowing how much Bronwyn had lost, simply because she saved Samuel and Paul, nearly dying in the process. Even the security staff assigned to protect Menke gave her sleepless hours. She trusted the men, but it was still unnerving, wondering how the kidnapping plot had been hatched. Giving Ernest Rose to Bronwyn was the least Bram could do, and Rose was more solicitous than Menke could have dreamed. He seemed fond of the girl. They'd even developed a give and take at restaurants, finding common ground in food. Menke watched as they exchanged looks with one another and she barely recognized the man who'd been protecting her the past five years. Originally intended as a temporary measure, it was Ernest Rose who suggested he be assigned to Bronwyn permanently.

If Bronwyn's safety seemed secure, the thought of children plagued Menke. Losing the opportunity to have children seemed the worst thing of all. Ernest had finally completed the kidnapping picture for Menke. It took courage, but Menke agreed to watch video of the hotel shooting. It happened in an instant, but when Ernest Rose played it in slow motion, she marveled how the boys fled the kidnappers, trusting the girl. Bronwyn must have shouted and it was sickening to see blood spread across her suit. She moved so fast, the boys' bodies were flung away from her while the bullets found their mark. If she'd clutched them, the boys would have been hit. By spinning away, they were saved. A split-second reaction had profound consequences. It was remarkable how Bronwyn's adrenaline must have propelled her through the door as it locked behind her. Menke now understood how Bronwyn and the boys had safely gotten inside. Samuel had told Menke about the desk. She could still hear his small voice on the phone telling how Bronwyn told him to listen at the door for 'Papa', while she held Paul beneath the desk.

Menke liked to pretend Bram's world didn't intersect with her own. Her second husband had provided her with a new name, new home, new friends and a new life. When he had a fatal heart attack, her life continued without missing a beat. Her anonymity was important to Bram, but the kidnapping and Bronwyn's predicament was a shocking reminder that her son's world was a dangerous place.

It was unimaginable cruelty to have destroyed Bronwyn's home, suspecting her involvement when she'd done nothing more than been their savior. Menke agonized over how to repay her.

The biggest surprise for Menke was Bronwyn's grace through it all. She was improving each day and her affection for the boys seemed to negate any desire for reparation. Moss had spoken to Bronwyn about litigation and Menke knew she'd nixed the idea. It was Ernest Rose who told Menke that Bronwyn would not entertain a civil suit, and he seemed to relish telling Menke he'd done everything he could, to convince her to make demands.

Rather than feel relieved, Menke felt more burdened. The early morning hours were the worst. She found Ernest Rose in the kitchen one night, around 3:15 AM. They sat together, sipping milk and munching cold turkey sandwiches, prepared by Ernest Rose. In all the years they'd spent in the house, they'd never shared a late night repast. As she watched him rummaging through Cook's cupboards, an idea struck Menke. She said nothing to Rose, but Menke called Bram as soon as she returned to her bedroom. The time difference suited her and it was good to pick up the phone, offer her idea, receive instant assent from her son and at long last, fall peacefully to sleep.

When Bronwyn survived King of Prussia Mall without too much exhaustion, Menke began to plan the surprise trip up north. She needn't have worried about Bram agreeing to her idea. He saw how his sons lit up whenever Bronwyn was mentioned or sent them a note. He knew how they kept her notes messily stapled together and slept with them under their pillows at night. There wasn't a day when he didn't think about Bronwyn McCall and wonder if he'd still have his sons if she hadn't been sent to photograph him for the magazine. Against everything he knew, he also felt less alone, pondering her 'Heavenly' message through the day and accepting it as he fell asleep each night.

Hearing a silent fanfare pounding in her ears, Menke finally broached the idea to Bronwyn, asking her what she thought of Maine. She was pleasantly surprised when Bronwyn said she'd always wanted to see it; her dad loved it as a boy and her parents had honeymooned there. With apparent calmness belying her inner excitement, Menke told Bronwyn she would like to show her a harbor town along the Maine coast. She and Bram had a house they wanted to give her, if she liked the town. Menke noticed Ernest Rose standing in the doorway, always a man with annoyingly impeccable timing. She expected the idea of Maine would be the last thing in the world to interest him, but he came to Bronwyn's side and waxed on enthusiastically about the idea.

It was settled. They'd all take a look.

CHAPTER FOUR

MAINE

*I*t was a tiring limo ride, but Bronwyn savored the Maine scenery. Signs indicated they were approaching the town. An airstrip was to the right and a small plane rose from pines. Although there were fast food restaurants and a miniature golf course, what caught her eye was a large expanse of majestic pines, thirty yards back from the highway. She mentally marked it to have a better look on the return trip.

Bronwyn caught sight of a few shops before Menke directed the driver to swing up the hill, past the bay. Large sightseeing boats were surrounded by colorful fishing boats, and docks dotted the water's edge. Birds were diving and Bronwyn put the window down, to hear their calls. She took a breath as the harbor faded from view and they wound through a residential area. They made a right onto Spruce Lane and Bronwyn caught sight of the harbor again. If she'd been looking ahead, she would have seen the Factory. After a left onto short Leopard Lane, the limo stopped. A seven-foot stone wall was on the right.

"Are you ready to stretch your legs, dear?" asked Menke.

Bronwyn stepped out of the car and waited a moment

for her achy and cramped body to recover. It was chilly and Bronwyn tucked her chin inside the high neck of her jacket. Menke spoke to the realtor while Jeeves surveyed the location, assessing its advantages and disadvantages.

"Here we go Bronwyn, if you're ready." Menke waited for Bronwyn and Ernest Rose to join them at the double iron gate, bisecting the stone wall. Bronwyn smiled appreciatively at the sight of the old Factory before her.

"It's huge. What did the Factory make?" Bronwyn asked.

"My great-great-grandfather built this Factory in 1832. It was called the Bayside Blanket and Toboggan Company. They provided blankets for the Civil War and there was a craftsman shop in the valley, where they made toboggans. A tunnel links the factory to the water for boat shipments. They say the tunnel was part of the Slave Railroad."

"Is the tunnel still there?"

"Possibly, but I think it would be unsafe. If it's not already closed, I'm sure it should be," Menke said, looking at Ernest Rose who nodded slightly.

"Where was the sign? Up there?" Menke nodded. "I bet it was wonderful to work here."

Menke gazed up at the windows.

"How long has it been empty?"

"My father closed it in 1962. Let's take a look. Max assures me the elevators have been inspected."

When they entered the garage, Menke pointed out an enormous turntable, large enough for seven cars, as well as a grease pit and lifts, dwarfed by the cavernous space. Bronwyn knew her dad would be impressed. The weekend before her family went to France, he'd taken Bronwyn to the Henry Ford Museum and Greenfield Village. They'd spent hours looking at huge trains, historic planes and automobiles. Yes,

Bobby McCall would be whistling under his breath. The Factory garage was the full length and breadth of the building.

Bronwyn's heart was racing. After looking in the freight elevator, they took the passenger elevator and Bronwyn noticed each level was two stories tall. Bronwyn left the elevator at each floor and walked the circumference, peering out the right side at neighboring homes of the opposite block; then swinging around to look out the windows overlooking the water. The water side had a sweeping lawn and tangled overgrowth leading to woods on the left, descending into a valley. The bustling harbor was in the distance.

"People must have loved working here. The view is gorgeous."

"I imagine it's a view they were used to, dear, and remember, they worked hard." Menke remarked. "But, my grandfather and my father had lawn fetes for the workers and games in the walled garden."

Menke was rewarded with Bronwyn's smile.

On the top floor, Jeeves found a folding chair for Bronwyn and handed her a pain pill. He deftly produced a bottle of water and saltines, like an odd magician. Menke and the realtor went back down and Jeeves stared out the bayside windows.

They rejoined Menke and her realtor, and walked to the family's homestead, about fifty yards from the Factory. A brick-walled garden beyond the house caught Bronwyn's eye, and when Menke showed her where the garden door should be, Bronwyn nodded her head. "A secret garden, like in the book." Menke began clearing vines away until Jeeves and the realtor took over. Jeeves yanked the door open, revealing an overgrown and neglected space.

"This garden will be beautiful before you know it,"

Bronwyn said with a clear voice, and then glanced apologetically at Menke. "I'm sorry. If you decide I can live here. I shouldn't have said anything."

"That's why we're here. Bram and I want you to live here. The Factory can be converted to condos or a hotel and with the money you receive from the sale, you can build whatever home you like. Just raze the old house and begin your life anew. Let's look at the loggia."

Bronwyn hesitated.

"I'd like to look inside the house."

Bronwyn carefully mounted the worn porch and Jeeves moved aside, allowing her to peek into the left room off the hallway, as well as the right. A curving staircase led to the second floor. Her breath quickened and she was delighted with the tall ceilings. Something stirred within and bubbled up. She recognized it as hope and it felt equally wonderful and terrible.

As they turned to go back, Bronwyn regarded the stone house, with loads of unrestrained ivy climbing the walls and a weathered picket fence along the sidewalk. She touched the rough picket's peeling paint and thought of Mark Twain's Tom Sawyer and his whitewashed fence, and her mind darted back inside the house, envisioning book-lined walls, a blazing fire on the hearth, and a cup of tea. Hope seemed more substantial now, than its usual gossamer-winged flight. Long giving inanimate objects a high regard, Bronwyn made a silent vow and joined the others.

Jeeves and Bronwyn waited while Menke and the realtor spoke. After several minutes, Bronwyn crossed the street, and looked up at the Factory. Jeeves decided she must be judging the privacy she could have with a hotel nearby.

Bronwyn turned and gave a little wave to the house

behind her. An older gentleman came outside. Bronwyn shook his hand as his wife joined them. They gestured toward the Factory, chatting away. Before long, a couple from the next house came over and the five were laughing and talking like old friends. Jeeves was intrigued, witnessing a Bronwyn he hadn't yet met, happy and engaged.

Menke returned and asked what Bronwyn was doing.

"Making friends, I expect."

When Bronwyn said her goodbyes, the neighbors retreated. She motioned for Jeeves to join her and Menke watched as they walked from the gate to the end of Leopard Lane. It was a distance of at least eighty yards and Rose seemed to be walking in three foot increments, pacing it off. How odd, Menke thought, with a furrowed brow.

Bronwyn was telling Jeeves if Menke was kind enough to give her the Factory and homestead property, she'd like to purchase the rest of the land to the end of the street. When she innocently looked at Jeeves, saying she thought she'd feel safe behind the wall if this 'pokey out part' of land was all hers, he was inspired to tell her he had savings, and perhaps they could do just that.

The realtor joined Bronwyn and Jeeves, and Menke was even more puzzled as he shrugged and gestured toward the car, shaking his head and holding his hand in front of Bronwyn.

"What you're seeing Miss McCall, is just the bracelet on the wrist of the hand. You see, the land you've stepped off, is the wrist. The stone wall is like the bracelet. But what you can't see is how massive the property is beyond these woods. It curves out and if you saw it from the water, you'd know it's huge. Just think of it that way. Maybe you could afford the wrist, but you could never afford the whole hand."

"Still, I'd still like to know who owns the rest of the land. You'll let me know?" Bronwyn urged, returning to the car.

Bronwyn's mind was crammed with ideas. On their way out of town, they headed up the peninsula. When they approached the stand of pines she'd mentally marked, Bronwyn asked the driver to pull over.

"I'm not quite ready to leave, if that's okay. I want to look here, just for a minute."

Menke was dumbfounded. Bronwyn turned her back on the highway, lifting her head to see the tops of the pines. She made a little circle, seeming to memorize the area.

Bronwyn returned to the car. "Thank you so much for bringing me to Maine. It was wonderful, Menke. My father visited Bar Harbor and Boothbay when he was young. Camden, too. I see why Maine was so special to him."

Menke had been annoyed, but Bronwyn's sincerity tempered her. "Tell me Bronwyn, why did you ask to stop here? I mean, right here and not farther down the road?"

"I noticed it when we were getting close to town. I marked it in my head, past the car wash and before the miniature golf. The pines are so dense and green. When we were leaving town, I wanted another chance to see Maine up close, in case I fall asleep on the ride home."

Menke touched her hand. "Would you like to see the shops? After all, this will be your home someday."

Bronwyn sat forward. "You should take time to think about it. You should think about it and talk to Bram and Samuel and Paul. I didn't realize your father lived there. You must all have memories."

"We've discussed it, Bronwyn. It's decided. Now, let's see the town, shall we?"

The driver dropped Jeeves and Bronwyn in front of the drugstore and continued on with Menke. With an hour for lunch, Bronwyn had a burst of energy.

The drugstore was wonderful. Unlike most drugstores, it still had a lunch counter. She and Jeeves ordered grilled cheese sandwiches and chocolate frappes, once the counter girl explained the difference between frappes and milkshakes. They walked through the store, Bronwyn assessing their magazine selection and cosmetics; Jeeves reviewing the array of cigars. When they left, Bronwyn grabbed Jeeves' elbow and said, "Wait."

He turned. Even Bronwyn didn't seem to know what she'd caught on the wind, but then she said, "There," and Jeeves saw she meant the park across the street, half a block down.

"Wait for me."

Jeeves frowned. It was all well and good if he chose to sit in the car while she made nice with the neighbors, but ordering him to stay behind now, was cheeky.

While Bronwyn crossed the street and sat on a bench, Jeeves did the same on his side of the street. She was sitting beside an old gentleman and began petting his red dachshund.

"What's her name?"

"Snooks Von Krinkles. Isn't she a character? She sure does like you, and she doesn't like everyone."

"I'm Bronwyn McCall," she said, extending her hand.

"I'm Gus Townsend, Bronwyn."

"Snooks Von Krinkles looks like she has black eyeliner around her eyes. She's quite beautiful," Bronwyn admired her. "I'll be moving here, someday. It seems like a really nice town."

"Aye. Oh, look at Snookie. I think she wants to be held."

Bronwyn worried the squirmy Snooks Von Krinkles might jam a foreleg into her heeling wounds, but she scooped her up and held her lightly against her chest. It was apparent Snooks was a big Bronwyn fan, giving her so many kisses that Jeeves could hear Bronwyn giggling across the street and couldn't help himself. Jeeves grinned happily at the sight.

When Snooks snuggled on her lap, glad for warmth, Bronwyn tucked her jacket around her and asked, "Do you know anything about the Bayside Blanket and Toboggan Company?"

"Indeed I do, Bronwyn. Had a great Uncle work there, years ago. A lot of folks have ties to that old factory. I remember Uncle Ralph telling how they'd play ball on their lunch breaks and have picnics some Sundays and I remember he said at Christmas they all got turkeys. People were proud to work there."

"Have you ever been inside?"

"Haven't been. Know where it is, though. Are you thinking of going over?"

"Actually, I just left there. It seems like it's holding up well, after all these years being empty."

"Doesn't surprise me. Yankee workmanship."

"Snooks is sleeping. Look at her little eyes squeezed shut. How old is she?"

"Just got her a year ago. Missed my wife so much after she passed, I had to get a weenie dog for company. Best crazy thing I ever did."

"You're lucky. She's great. My dad had dachshunds when he was growing up."

"Does he have any, now?"

"No, my family all died when I was eight years old."

Gus clucked. "I'm sorry to hear that, young lady. Truly. How are you getting on? I noticed that gent across the street with you. Is he your uncle or grandpap?"

Bronwyn smiled. "Actually, he's my bodyguard. His name is Ernest Rose, but I call him Jeeves, like my manservant."

Gus nodded, touching his cap toward Jeeves. "Well, Bronwyn, I hope he keeps you good and safe."

Bronwyn glanced at Gus's watch. "I'd better go. We're heading back. Would you mind if I wrote sometimes, so I could find out what's going on in town?"

"Good idea, Bronwyn. Little Snookie will want to know what you're up to. I'll write my address and phone number; call me any time."

"Thanks, Gus. Here, I'll write an address for you, too. Here you go. It's my attorney, Moss. I travel a lot, so this way mail can reach me."

"When do you think you'll be moving, Bronwyn? Sooner the better, I say. This town could use a nice young girl like you. Have you had any lobster, yet?"

"Wow, Gus. You're right. I just had a grilled cheese and now we're leaving without lobster. Next time. I don't know when I'll be moving. Probably not for a few years. But it'll be great when I do. You and Snooks Von Krinkles will be my best friends."

She handed Snooks to Gus, who set her on the ground. They rose and Gus gave her a light hug.

"I promise I'll write soon, Gus. Nice to meet you."

"Likewise, honey girl."

Bronwyn slept longer after her trip than any time since her surgery. Jeeves and Menke took turns checking on her. When she arose, Menke was relieved. She directed Cook to start breakfast and asked Bronwyn to join her on the screened-in porch.

"Bronwyn, I've spoken to Bram this morning, and it's all settled. We're giving you the entire Maine property. I understand you inquired about the land beyond the Factory. That's ours as well, and we want you to have it. Perhaps you'll decide to build something on the far side instead, and you'd have room for gardens and a guest house."

Bronwyn was stunned. "All of it? To the end of the street? Jeeves and I were going to buy as much of it as we could afford."

Menke was amused at the thought of Ernest Rose paying for anything.

"Bram and I have fond memories of Maine, but that's all. Memories. Neither of us has any desire to live in Maine. We have other properties here and there, so think nothing more about it. The Factory's history was important to you, and that means a great deal to both Bram and me."

"It's too generous. Really." Bronwyn looked uncomfortable.

Menke changed the subject. "Did you like the town, dear? It really is quaint. What did you like?"

"I liked it all. I want to go on a sightseeing boat next time. The sign said they go out to see seals, puffins, and whales. And, I want to have lobster. The town was great and I liked meeting the neighbors across the street. Did you know both of their houses belonged to Factory foremen? So, the Factory means a lot to them. They'd appreciate it if the building wasn't standing empty anymore."

"Well, my realtor is ready to put feelers out to the hotel chains."

"I don't think I want a hotel there."

"Oh. Perhaps you don't understand, dear. Selling the Factory is what will make you a wealthy young woman. You should be well set, after that."

"Maybe, but I want to make sure you and the prime minister have no regrets, and then I just want to wait awhile."

"I see. Well, I have another surprise for you. I told Bram how you stopped out of town."

Bronwyn was puzzled.

"I wondered why you chose that place. We own two pieces of property in town. Where you asked to stop, is the other. As soon as I told Bram, he said you should have it." Menke smiled serenely.

Bronwyn gingerly rose and walked to the window, gazing at the garden. Puff left the sunlit patch of carpet, stretched and sashayed across the porch to join her. Bronwyn's shoulders lifted in a sigh, and she realized her wounded lung was seldom inflated to its capacity.

Bronwyn took Menke's hand. "I didn't think I should tell you this if your son hasn't told you. I'm guessing he didn't."

Menke looked concerned.

"When I was on the operating table, I died. There was a bright light, like people say, and a man was there. He was Bram's brother. When I told Bram, he said his brother was David."

Menke gasped and withdrew her hand.

Bronwyn took her hand again and looked at Menke earnestly. "I told Bram his brother had a message for him. He can tell you what David said to me." She saw comprehension dawning on Menke. If David had been to Maine, maybe Bram was gifting the memory of David, more than Bronwyn.

"I wanted to tell you because you've been so kind to me.

Not just about Maine, I mean your kindness and generosity while I recover. I can't imagine getting better, without you." She looked directly into Menke's eyes. "His eyes looked into my eyes, and I'm sorry it was me seeing him and not you."

Menke looked into Bronwyn's eyes, tears filling her own. "You said he had a message for Bram. Did he have a message for me?"

"I'm sorry. I'd have told you right away if he did." Bronwyn could see her disappointment. "I'm sorry, he didn't."

"Nothing? He said nothing?" Menke's voice was constricted.

Bronwyn turned from Menke, deep in thought. She watched Puff the cat, and a faded memory took shape. "There was something."

"What? Tell me dear, what?"

"I remember he turned me around, and as I was moving forward his hand gestured off to the right, to a building. Maybe a house." Bronwyn's brow was furrowed. Ernest Rose came into the room, so Menke sent him on a pointless errand.

"What did the house look like, dear?"

"I could draw it for you." Menke found a white notepad and Bronwyn began to draw. "I just saw the corner of it, like the rest of the building was faded or shrouded. There were tall pillars, two stories high and it was white-washed adobe or something. There were three steps up to the open narrow porch wrapped around the side of the house, and there was one cat in this chair, here, and another cat on this second step, right at the corner. That's all I remember. Do you recognize it?"

Menke shook her head. "I don't remember ever seeing it, dear. Is that all? Nothing more?"

"There were vines and…" Bronwyn got up and took a

pain pill from the vial inside her pocket. "There's something else. When I was moving forward, David said something to me. I just heard the voice and he must have been behind me. It kind of whooshed into my ear."

Bronwyn sat back down with Menke. "He said it's the 'forever' house. I thought he meant it was Heaven. It must have been."

Certain her beloved David had sent a message after all, of course he would send her a message, his mother, his loving mother; she stared at Bronwyn's drawing. She'd never seen it. She'd never lived there. It was unfamiliar. Menke came up empty.

"Can I get you something, dear? You needed pain medication? Some cocoa perhaps?"

Bronwyn said cocoa would be nice, and sat back into the plump cushions, closing her eyes against the dull pain.

Ten minutes later, Menke came rushing out of the kitchen, without cocoa. "I know, Bronwyn. I know. It was the vines that made me remember." Menke sped to the couch and took Bronwyn's hands. "It's our trip to Greece. This is exactly the place we stayed. I remember the cats always lazing about. David was only nine or ten. We had such a lovely time there. We needed it desperately, before the divorce. Bram and his father were loading the car. I remember." Her voice was rising, agitated. "I told David that I could live there forever, we'd had such a nice time and the weather was just superb, sunny and fresh. It was dazzling. David told me it was our 'forever house'. No one would know that, Bronwyn. No one would be able to draw this house. And the angle was exactly the angle of the house, from where the car was parked!"

Bronwyn nodded; happy her after-life encounter with

Bram's brother had given some peace to this woman who was so utterly kind to her.

"You see, when we returned, it marked the end of our marriage. The trip to Greece was only a respite. Everything that followed was so acrimonious; I'd almost forgotten we'd ever gone to Greece. We fought furiously over the boys. I left, divorced, came to Philadelphia and married a year later, moving here to Haverford. I only had the boys on vacations. Even that was a struggle." Menke glanced around the room. "It was difficult being without the boys."

Menke nodded slightly, the memories unveiling themselves.

Cook brought the cocoa to Bronwyn and she sipped at it while the pain medication took hold. Menke turned and stared deeply into Bronwyn's eyes. Anyone looking at the pair would have been beyond curious.

Tears fell from Menke's eyes and Bronwyn's own eyes were glistening.

"Oh my dear, you're upset?" Bronwyn shook her head. "What's wrong?"

Bronwyn didn't answer, gathering her emotions.

"Please tell me, dear. Tell me. You'll feel better," Menke urged, no longer crying.

Bronwyn placed a raspberry silk pillow on her lap, using it as a buffer as she leaned over, slightly rocking. She stroked Puff the cat, who was sleeping at her feet. Bronwyn spoke to the floor. "I don't understand why my family wasn't there, waiting for me. Where was my father? Where was my mother? Why was Bram's brother there and not my own family?"

Menke had no answer, but moved closely beside her and gently patted her hand.

CHAPTER FIVE

GRAEME AND SIR WINSTON
1997-1998

*T*here was buoyancy to Menke's days; not just finding peace about David, but also convinced she might undo some of the damage done to Bronwyn. For her part, Bronwyn began to sense possibility in her future. Jeeves' own musings conveniently ignored the reality of Maine's colder days, in favor of the imagined bliss of boating on seamless water.

Menke gathered dozens of home design magazines, and was pleased to see how Bronwyn diligently marked pages and made notes.

She'd overheard Moss offering to replace Bronwyn's camera equipment and Bronwyn answered she was finished being a photographer. Moss tried to laugh it off, saying of course she had to take more portraits of his girls, but Bronwyn shook her head.

Now Menke had an additional worry. If Bronwyn was unable to work, it was imperative to sell the Factory and get her on good financial footing. Reluctantly, Menke asked Ernest Rose to speak to Bronwyn, and point out the advantages of the Maine estate as a secure, smart solution.

When Ernest Rose returned with Bronwyn's plans, Menke was surprised. Bronwyn would wait before building a house. Meanwhile, she was planning a London trip to see her actor friend, Graeme Woods. From there, she and Ernest Rose would visit Sir Winston Watkins in Bath. Bronwyn had often stayed with them, and she was confident it would be just the ticket for a few months. Then, she'd take Ernest Rose to Pittsburgh to show him the sights, before flying to Palm Springs the first of the year, to visit Sir Winston at his winter home.

As Menke watched Ernest Rose, he seemed a bit giddy in relating their itinerary. Whether he'd been harboring a longing for the rich and famous, or just wanted to impress Menke with Bronwyn's well-laid plans, she couldn't tell. Bronwyn had been an easy and thoughtful guest, so it wasn't difficult to imagine her staying with friends. However, Menke doubted Ernest Rose's guest-worthiness.

One thing was certain; Bronwyn and Ernest Rose were finding a way to live together. She didn't treat him as if he held authority over her, and that pleased Menke. Bronwyn evidently found him amusing at times, and he seemed to bask in her pleasure. They bantered back and forth comparing notes on New York restaurants. Jeeves talked about Pastis and Bronwyn simply said 'Braised Beef with Glazed Carrots' and then he responded with 'Smoked Trout with Warm Potatoes and Horseradish' and Bronwyn wrinkled her small nose and guffawed. She suggested 'Croque Monsieur and Croque Madame' and he replied wistfully, 'yes, yes.' Then he pronounced 'Carrots Vichy and Gratin Dauphinois' and Bronwyn clapped her hands. With a wink and a raised eyebrow he offered 'JG' – she inquired, 'Melon'? – and met his grin with 'bacon cheeseburger and cottage fries'.

Apparently Bronwyn had never been to a place called Brass Monkey, so she listened with interest as Jeeves described Beef and Guinness Pie, Beans on Toast, Fish n' Chips in Brass Monkey Beer Batter, and Bangers and Mash. Bronwyn nodded and Menke marveled at Ernest Rose's descriptive abilities. He had them both salivating, even though Menke knew she'd never order Bangers and Mash, under any circumstances.

He said 'A Salt and Battery' and Bronwyn dissolved in laughter. Menke asked if it was a restaurant and Bronwyn told her about the battered beets, chip butty, and mushy peas. Ernest Rose added the details of a Shandy – English lemonade with a splash of Bass Ale.

It was the Payard Bistro that interested Jeeves. He mentioned the Wild Mushroom and Chestnut Soup and Bronwyn was familiar with it. She offered the Dark Bittersweet Chocolate Soufflé with pistachio ice cream. It gave Jeeves an opening, once Menke left the room.

"I understand your position, not wanting to visit France. But actually, Miss, I believe you might find what they call 'closure'. We could go after England."

"No, thanks."

"Or, I can locate your mother's friend for you. Gwen. And Judge Wheeler." He scanned her face for a reaction.

Bronwyn shook her head and left the room, but came right back.

"You've already found them. All of them. You know exactly where my family died, where Gwen is, the Judge. All of them."

Jeeves was taken aback. "Were you struck by lightning at some juncture?"

Bronwyn's lips drew back in a smile. "No. I was just gut shot."

Jeeves grimaced. "Really, Miss. We must find a more delicate term. It's distasteful to say…well, you're aware of your terminology."

"It was more distasteful to live through."

He agreed, but watched her impassively.

Bronwyn offered, "Bullet pierced?"

Jeeves shook his head.

"Bullet kissed?"

Again, he indicated not.

"Hole punched? Air-conditioned? Shard studded?"

Each suggestion caused him to make a pained face.

Finally she said, "I have it. Dotted Swiss. I was dotted Swiss!" and that made Jeeves laugh.

One morning, he said she'd mentioned Ellis Fielding in her sleep and asked who he was.

Bronwyn doubted him. She didn't believe she'd been talking in her sleep. She was certain Jeeves had done his homework and knew about Ellis. After all, he'd mentioned Gwen and the Judge, out of the blue. Surely Moss would have related her sad story about Ellis. Jeeves was manipulating her. She was disappointed, but appreciated the lesson.

It was tempting to allow Jeeves a look into the kaleidoscope of lost dreams, known as Ellis Fielding – they'd planned a future; he proposed only after Ollie saw him with another girl; then cancelled their wedding shortly after, married his young assistant and kept Bronwyn's honeymoon reservations, except with a different bride. She stopped eating, stopped sleeping, stopped loving, and stopped being a fool. He had made her happy and then, devastatingly sad.

Instead, she gazed at Jeeves evenly, and simply answered, "He was a man I once knew."

Jeeves tested her. He wanted to know.

"Miss. I'm not certain you realize how easily I can make things happen for you. I accept your answer, but permit me to ask once again. May I take you to Gwen, your Judge Wheeler, Mr. Fielding…your family?"

"No."

He got to the point. "Do you find it difficult to forgive, Miss?"

She smiled, and Jeeves was surprised to see the smile reach her eyes. She covered the distance between them and answered in a calm and measured voice, not unpleasantly but with a slight chill, "I don't forgive."

Bronwyn ordered a flower arrangement for Gus Townsend and Snooks Von Krinkles. Filling the order in Maine was a florist named Jen Cotton and she'd gone to school with Gus's son Luke. When Gus wrote, he filled Bronwyn in about the hard times Jen was having. Gus was a wealth of information.

Graeme Woods also wrote, saying how anxious he was to see her again, how sorry he was about Ollie Silkowski, and how much he missed Bronwyn. She had warned Graeme she'd be bringing a bodyguard at Moss's suggestion.

Envisioning months spent with Jeeves, Bronwyn told him he was free to come and go, once she was settled. Jeeves seemed pleased and she could see his wheels turning, making leisurely plans of his own while on Prime Minister Abraham's payroll. It was the only way Bronwyn could imagine being with Jeeves. She didn't want to suffocate the way Menke seemed to, with her constant guards.

Those men in suits were better at fading into the background than Jeeves, who appeared on the periphery often enough to be jarring. It was mid morning when Bronwyn asked him to sit beside her.

"If you care about me, Jeeves, you'll drive down to Decatur, Georgia."

She read his curiosity.

"There's a restaurant I want you to see, and then you can tell me what you think. I've been there once and I'd love to go back, but I should save myself for England. I think you'd really like it."

"And the name, Miss?"

He didn't seem as interested as she'd hoped. "Watershed. Creamy shrimp grits. Fried catfish with hushpuppies. Gingered beets."

He was incrementally perking up.

"New potato salad with sour cream and bacon. Pimento cheese sandwiches."

She offered the coup de grace. "Hummingbird cake."

"Oh my. Intriguing." He was imagining a Hummingbird cake. "Shall I leave today?"

"The sooner the better. Then get back and tell me all about it."

Menke was shocked that Ernest Rose did as he was told. Perhaps Bronwyn would be able to handle him after all. When he'd gone, she watched Bronwyn expectantly.

"Yes? Did you want something, Menke?"

"No, dear. I thought you wanted something." Bronwyn looked perplexed. "I thought that's why you sent Ernest Rose away. I assumed you needed to talk."

Bronwyn laughed. "No, I just thought we needed a break."

Menke's face was transformed by a lovely smile. She drew her legs beneath her, closed her eyes and leaned back into the silk cushions.

After a few moments, Bronwyn got an idea and leaned forward. "Menke, I think I'll fix supper and invite Cook. Wouldn't that be fun? The three of us?"

It was a wild idea, in Menke's book. Menke didn't even know Cook's name. Now, to have her dining at the same table seemed almost shocking, but she nodded.

It didn't take Bronwyn long to investigate the kitchen pantry with Cook. She came back, whispered in Menke's ear, "It's Avis. Her name is Avis," and dashed back to the kitchen.

Bodyguards moved wing chairs into the kitchen, and Avis and Menke became her audience. They laughed together as Bronwyn dramatically showed each step of her preparation, with flourish and celebrity chef aplomb. She started home fries in a skillet and while they cooked, she created a frittata with bacon, cheddar, asparagus and peas. She promised a special dessert and Cook wondered what it might be, unaware Bronwyn had sent bodyguards to the store.

The three women enjoyed the simple food; Cook had never made breakfast for dinner at Menke's house. When they finished, Bronwyn returned to the kitchen and invited Avis and Menke back to their kitchen chairs. It was apparent what dessert would be, with ten cut-glass banana split dishes lined up.

Bronwyn made a great show of demonstrating her hot fudge recipe, taking a large Pyrex measuring cup and adding $\frac{1}{4}$ cup of light corn syrup, $\frac{1}{2}$ cup of half and half, and 6 oz of semi-sweet morsels. She microwaved on high for two minutes, stirred, another minute on high, stirred, and a final minute on high, added a little vanilla, stirred again, and let it cool. When she was done, she made a second batch.

While the hot fudge cooled, Bronwyn sautéed banana

slices with brown sugar and butter, then thinly sliced strawberries, and browned sliced almonds in a pan. She scooped toasted almond fudge ice cream and added butter pecan. Then, she dressed the splits with the bananas, strawberries, and almonds. The final touch was hot fudge poured into ten individual silver pots.

The seven suited guards joined the women, and they congregated around the kitchen island, drizzling fudge from their own little pots, plopping extra almonds in their mouths, squirting whipped cream clouds on the ice cream and laughing.

When Jeeves returned, he was surprised to hear Avis called by name, and felt keenly left out of the banana split party. He wondered why it took his absence for Bronwyn to have fun, but he realized the more jovial atmosphere was a good way to leave. And Bronwyn was so interested in every detail of his Decatur experience, Jeeves decided he hadn't been 'had' after all.

Bronwyn took Jeeves along on a shopping excursion and asked if he'd like to buy Menke some wine.

"Pardon, Miss, for what reason?"

He had a vacuous look and Bronwyn got annoyed. Jeeves was playing dumb and she didn't care for it.

"Because we've been her guests and it's proper to leave thank you gifts."

"Gifts."

"Yes. I know you're well-versed in wines. You've told me so. I was thinking wine would be a suitable gift."

"You're giving a gift?"

"I know what I'm doing. I'm just trying to help you."

She felt her face getting hot and Jeeves looked out the window. She wondered if it was possible he didn't feel a kinship with Menke.

"Okay, we need to tell the driver. Do you want to get the wine at the end of our trip, or get it over with now?"

If he didn't answer, she was ready to go alone to see Graeme. She didn't need Jeeves; she didn't need anyone.

Jeeves sensed a watershed moment and then was amused. She'd sent him to Watershed in Decatur, and it tickled his funny bone.

"Whenever you like, Miss."

Returning home, Bronwyn was happy with her purchases, and she'd found a wicker basket and fancy shredded paper for Jeeves' wine.

"Here's a little gift tag. I can fill it out for you, if you like."

Again, Jeeves gave her a vacant look and she wondered if he'd been raised by wolves. It occurred to her that she had never heard Jeeves say 'thank you'.

"You know, Jeeves, I've been lucky to visit with friends for long periods of time. I'm not proud of it, but not having family it just seemed to work out that way. I've always been grateful to be invited and it's important to thank people. That's what we're doing."

"We're doing."

"Yes. And, we'll do the same thing at Graeme Woods' and at Sir Winston Watkins' house."

She realized he wasn't used to hearing he 'had' to do anything. He wasn't getting the 'Jeeves' part of 'Jeeves' at all.

"If it makes you feel better, I spent a lot more on Avis than I did on Menke."

Jeeves found that keenly amusing, hiding his grin as he looked out the window.

Bronwyn placed a few gifts throughout Menke's bedroom and bathroom...a Longwood Gardens photo book, a video of the movie *Find Me*, a small drawing she'd made of Menke wearing a Geoffrey Beene gown, the hot fudge microwave recipe, and a box of Godiva chocolate.

When it was time to leave, there were tears and hugs.

As Bronwyn waved through the car window, Menke felt profound loss. Fortunately, she found a long, heartfelt letter from Bronwyn sitting atop her pillow, but it was Cook who bellowed great gasps of sentiment when she read Bronwyn's long letter of thanks. Later, when Cook opened the pantry door, she found a red Kitchen Aid mixer, a periwinkle cardigan, and a long gold chain and pendant, engraved with 'Avis'.

Even the suited men of Menke's watchful team received thank you notes. Not knowing their names, Bronwyn wrote 'Man at the gate', 'Man who looked at flowers in the garden with me', 'Man who bought the banana split dishes for me', 'Man who faxed for me', 'Man who picked me up when I stumbled', 'Man who sat in the office' and 'Man who drove the car' on the envelopes.

Cook was still rereading her letter when Bronwyn was buckling her seatbelt on the jet. It was the first time she'd flown with physical manifestations of wounds and scars and fear. The man beside her was her very own Jeeves, but it was imagining Graeme Woods with his toothy smile, disheveled blonde hair, and welcoming arms that gave her sufficient peace to fly across the ocean.

As they flew, Bronwyn told Jeeves about her actor friends. First they'd be visiting Graeme Woods and his wife Angela in their Mayfair flat, and probably their Chipping Norton home in the Cotswolds. Jeeves had seen a few of Graeme's films and Bronwyn wondered if *Find Me* was one of them. She didn't tell Jeeves, but she'd made that movie with Graeme, two years before. It was her only movie, and no one seeing it would know it was her, but it had solidified her friendship with Graeme.

She expected Sebastian Hughes would drop by, 'Sea Bass' to some of his friends, and 'Hughie' to her. How to describe Hughie, she mused, while Jeeves watched her grasping for elusive adjectives. Peter Pan, perhaps. Jeeves wasn't certain he'd seen his films, which made her gasp.

"Don't tell him that, Jeeves. You'll destroy him." She was glad they were on a private jet. It would seem a betrayal if other passengers heard Jeeves' ignorance of Hughie's hand-wringing career.

Hughie was all sophisticated elegance on the red carpet; insecurity vying with bombast, off it. Actresses watched for a new romantic comedy coming down the pike, hoping they could grab box office success with lucky charm Sebastian Hughes. But he'd had critical success and an Oscar nomination two years ago, playing a cad. It had given him joy that he rode like a wave, but he was always perplexed about follow-up roles.

"He's quite nice looking, Jeeves. His nose is narrow and sharp; he's average height, thin, a few freckles like mine, although he hates them, and beautifully dressed. You'll like that about Hughie. He's one of those men who look like a million bucks even if he's in jeans and a sweater. He's much more handsome than he realizes – he's definitely too hard on himself."

"You're fond of him, then?"

"Very. He can be aggravating, though. After he wraps a movie, he always cuts his hair. Then, the producers are up a creek if they want any reshoots. He doesn't mind looping dialogue afterward, but that's it. He thinks he's sending a message by cutting his hair. He's done. It's kind of juvenile, but that's Hughie."

"Is he spoken for?"

"He's been living with a model for awhile. Charlotte Tritton. They make a gorgeous couple, but she's a little hard on him. He needs a lot of hand-holding."

Bronwyn described the triumvirate she called The Boys: Graeme Woods, Roddy O'Neal and Sir Winston Watkins.

"Why do you refer to them as The Boys, Miss?"

"They like having a nickname and they're so often together. And, they're close friends. I think you'll find them amusing. I know it seems like we'll be visiting Sir Winston for a long time, but you can come and go. If it seems too long, we can always leave. We're not locked in. I used to go with Oliver Silkowski."

Jeeves was relieved she could say Silkowski's name without tearing up. She started to speak, hesitated, then said, "Sir Winston's wife Elizabeth is often in one of their other homes. We may not see her, but she's lovely.

"We'll also probably see Conor Frost." She didn't say that with the enthusiasm she'd shown for the others. "He tends to come by."

Jeeves had seen Conor Frost's films. English classics, if he recalled. He was serious and good looking. Jeeves was surprised that Bronwyn was anything but thrilled at the prospect of seeing Conor Frost. After all, Jeeves was looking forward to it. Wouldn't his Mam and Pap be thrilled to see the stars, he thought. They seldom missed a Saturday night at the flicks when he was growing up.

Just as Bronwyn predicted, Sebastian Hughes dropped by Graeme Woods' flat the second evening. He was lazing around the fire, growing lengthier by each stretch of his long arms and legs, like a cat. His eyes were closed and Jeeves thought he was sleeping in the midst of his visit.

There was a rap at the door and Conor Frost was ushered in. Frost was taller than he seemed on the screen, probably 6'4" or so, with clothes hanging off wide shoulders, but a slender frame. He carried a solemn elegance and seemed just the sort of stately young gentleman that Jeeves would choose for Bronwyn.

However, she and Frost seemed to have little time for each other. Jeeves wondered what created such animosity, especially on Bronwyn's part. When Frost arrived, he looked as if he wanted to embrace her, and then thought better of it. He said how sorry he was about Oliver Silkowski; she nodded and curtly thanked him. Then he inquired as to her health, indicating he'd heard she had an accident. When Bronwyn didn't respond, Jeeves stepped in.

"Indeed. She had several internal injuries. Collapsed left lung. It was dire. Touch and go, as they say, but she's mending. I'm with Bronwyn as bodyguard, by the way. Ernest Rose. She prefers to call me 'Jeeves'."

Bronwyn gave Jeeves an odd look, wondering why he had suddenly turned into Chatty Cathy. Conor looked stricken and his hand clutched at his jacket. Bronwyn gazed into the fire and had nothing to say. She wished Jeeves had just kept quiet.

Even Graeme was surprised by the extent of her injuries. When they went in to dinner, Graeme and Conor both tried to help Bronwyn into her chair and she remembered yet another reason why she liked Hughie. He was oblivious. Bronwyn hadn't given Hughie a definitive answer when he'd asked her to read four scripts he'd brought along. Now, Bronwyn promised to read them right away. Seeing his instant delight was rewarding. Hughie was easy to move, this way and that. Like a doll. She smiled affectionately at him.

As they rose from the table after dinner, Jeeves detained Graeme Woods and asked if there was some serious disagreement between Bronwyn and Conor Frost, professing surprise in Bronwyn's demeanor as she usually seemed sweet.

"I'm not certain you'll always find her sweet, especially with Conor, Mr. Rose. But I assure you she's a dear, wonderful girl. For some reason, she and Conor have been jealous of each other. Roddy, Winston, and I have known them both for several years, but apparently each believed they were our 'favorite', unaware of the other. So, when they visit at the same time, it's quite good fun seeing them go for the upper hand. I'm ashamed to say just how very much we've enjoyed it. Beyond amusing." Graeme stood with his arms lightly folded, chuckling. "Once, we told them we were going pheasant hunting at three in the morning. We knew they'd show up in the drawing room.

There they were, probably had never gone to sleep, afraid to miss the chance to tote our guns or some nonsense. I drew the short straw and crept downstairs to see their frosty wait. Utter silence. I said we'd changed our minds about going, and they trundled off to bed, glaring at each other. Perhaps it's shameful how we've set them up, watching their tempers get the best of them, but it's oddly delicious." Graeme gave Jeeves his toothy grin and tee hee'd into the living room where they found Bronwyn sitting by the fire.

The heat from the flames licked her with warmth, so even though Conor Frost had taken up the seat Hughie vacated, Bronwyn stayed. She caught Conor looking at her, out of the corner of her eye.

"Is something wrong?" Bronwyn barked.

Angela Woods shook her head, as if to say, 'here we go again'.

"No, Bronwyn. I hope you're feeling well. You look thin."

She rolled her eyes and then felt a little ashamed. He seemed sincere.

"You're staring, Conor. I'm fine. You don't need to be looking at me." She said it with petulance and felt even more ashamed. Why was she acting a little fool in front of Jeeves? He'd think she always behaved this way and he wouldn't know it was only around insufferable Conor Frost. "Are you sure something isn't wrong, Conor? What are you looking at?"

"Your hair, I suppose."

"What's wrong with it?" she snapped.

"I was just watching how the fire highlights the ginger in your hair. Like the sun does, when you're outside."

She looked dumb-struck. "Ginger. In the sun."

"Yes, the way it finds the red strands, amongst the dark

ones." Conor felt foolish and turned to the fire, wondering how to gracefully leave now that he'd checked on her.

"The sun makes my hair look red?" Her voice was thin and reedy.

"It does."

Bronwyn gingerly rose from her chair and walked over to Conor. He couldn't imagine she'd hit him, but they disliked each other, so he braced himself. She took his hand in hers and brought it to her lips, kissing the knuckles.

"That is the nicest thing anyone's ever said to me, Conor."

Frost's eyes weren't the only ones becoming enormous.

Bronwyn sat back in her chair, smiling to herself, smiling sweetly to Conor and turning back to the fire. Conor decided he'd remain awhile longer and was rewarded by more sweet smiles from Bronwyn while he tried to remember what she'd been drinking. He was certain she'd only had water, due to her medication, but perhaps it was her medication creating some delusion.

Conor Frost would never know what the turning point had been, and Jeeves was no help answering Graeme's inquiries – he simply didn't know Bronwyn well enough. But Bronwyn knew why in a moment's time, she had embraced Conor Frost as a dear, special friend. When he looked at her, he saw red hair. In a rare convergence of the redheaded minority of the world, her maternal and paternal grandparents had been redheads; her mother and father, both 'only' children, had had red hair; her sister Claire had been blessed with auburn hair. Only Bronwyn was brunette. If Conor Frost saw red hair, however unlikely, she could never ask for anything more.

Occasionally, Jeeves hinted to Graeme at Bronwyn's homeless plight. Assuming it was Oliver Silkowski's death removing her from Greenwich Village, Graeme was sympathetic enough; Jeeves didn't need to paint a more forlorn picture. Yet, Jeeves said her flat had been robbed of everything. Graeme called Stanley Mastrofrancesco to confirm the tale. There was something about Ernest Rose that seemed detached and calculating. It was time to see why Ernest Rose was suddenly part of Bronwyn's life.

Moss stuck by the robbery story and assured him of his credentials. Moss said Bronwyn shouldn't be alone, and having a bodyguard seemed a good solution. When Graeme hung up, he still puzzled over Ernest Rose's role. Perhaps when Rose saw how the staff functioned at Sir Winston's, he'd learn to keep more distance.

After Graeme had spoken to Moss, Jeeves observed how Graeme treated Bronwyn even more gently. Jeeves made a show of accompanying Bronwyn to the best London restaurants, intimating her recovery mandated good food and bustling conviviality, even though Bronwyn seemed to find it tiring. By Jeeves' calculations, they could wander from friend to friend for a year or so. Bronwyn was obviously a sweet and easy visitor; if Jeeves kept from rocking the boat, and morphed into her deft invisibility, they'd be set for awhile. It was her good fortune to be surrounded by men of means, happy to care for her. Only Sebastian Hughes lingered near a restaurant bill, incapable of taking it. Jeeves was fascinated to watch him, wondering how he managed to be impervious to payment while at the same time, remaining charming and beloved.

When Bronwyn announced it was time to move on to Chipping Norton for a few weeks, Conor Frost showed up to take her to lunch. It was surprisingly easy to spend time with Conor. They seemed to have plenty to talk about, and yet enjoyed quiet moments. She surprised herself when she told him a little about the Maine property, and her hesitance in deciding what to do with it. She said she was disappointed in herself, not doing whatever had to be done, to find herself a home. Conor suggested they both had silent passions, and just because she wasn't certain what to do about Maine, it didn't mean she didn't have great passion to live there. It would happen before long, he said with quiet assuredness.

Conor was aware she'd lost several of her things in Ollie's townhouse, and wondered how much was gone. 'All of it?' he asked and she nodded. She was shipping things to her attorney, she said, for safekeeping. Moss had emptied a large office in his Madison Avenue law firm, installing shelving and wardrobe racks until she had a place of her own. She was embarrassed, but admitted to Conor that an empty office in a New York office tower was the only home she had.

Conor asked what she missed most of all, and when she said books, they went book shopping. He asked for Moss's New York address and promised to ship the books.

She'd said 'books' and not 'jewelry', but the truth was Bronwyn was very sorry she'd lost her jewelry. She never had many pieces, but Graeme had given her diamond studs after filming *Find Me*, Ollie had bought her some gold pieces, Ellis Fielding had given her a double strand of pearls, and she'd bought a few turquoise pieces. Even if they were miraculously returned to her, she'd feel they'd been in dirty, filthy hands and they wouldn't be the same. There was no justification for any of her jewelry to go missing; it would never shed light on the kidnapping, even if she'd been involved. She could be angry, but her sense of loss only triggered sadness.

When it was time to say goodbye to Conor, Bronwyn became emotional. He was due to start training for his next film, renewing his riding skills and working with the armorer. It unsettled Conor, seeing her on the verge of tears, and he reassured her he'd come to Sir Winston's in Bath, at his first break.

That night, she cried burning tears, muffling her sobs beneath the covers. She had a terrible feeling of panic, fearing she might never see Conor again. The last weekend she'd spent with Ollie in East Hampton, she'd been blissfully confident they'd have forever together. Whether it was saying goodbye on a street corner, at the townhouse, in the Hamptons, at a restaurant, it seemed she could remember turning and walking away from Ollie over and over. She could lose Conor just that swiftly, turn around and find him gone. Finally, since their relationship had turned on the head of a pin, she trusted they were destined to have more time together.

Disappointed to leave London, Jeeves tried to dissuade Bronwyn, but she'd decided Jeeves was enjoying the high life a little too much. She noticed how his eyes glittered as he traveled in Graeme Woods' London circle. Cigars, oysters, fine wine. It was time to live the cottage life for a bit and Bronwyn was happily anticipating Graeme's Cotswolds home.

Chipping Norton was not what Jeeves expected. The gardens were lovely and he could see how Bronwyn would enjoy the surroundings. Graeme's house was more modern than Jeeves expected, and for that he was grateful. White and beige furnishings were cheerful. It wasn't the depressing needlepoint and stone floor, dried herbs from the ceiling, damp cottage he'd been dreading. Their bedrooms were small but tidy, and Jeeves was relieved to see a live-in cook. It just simply didn't compare to the London flat in Mayfair. He had even hinted to Graeme that the grass and trees of the Cotswolds might be hard on Bronwyn's lung capacity. He remembered Graeme nodding sympathetically, but he didn't realize Graeme knew Bronwyn, and when she was ready to move on, she'd go.

Graeme settled them in, and then left with his wife for a location shoot. Jeeves had imagined returning to London, but he wasn't comfortable leaving Bronwyn in the cook's protective custody. Would there be a defensive battle of cast iron skillets? He tried to make the most of it. She promised they'd soon be moving to Bath, where Sir Winston Watkins had a huge staff, capable of caring for her in Jeeves' absence.

With time to herself, Bronwyn found herself missing Ollie Silkowski. They'd enjoyed spending time in Graeme's houses and the quiet solitude brought Ollie close to her heart. That grief led to longing for her family and the sounds of nature did nothing but amplify her emotions.

Graeme had kindly gathered books from Jaffe & Neale Bookshop & Cafe, and she devoured them. Jeeves wore his beleaguered face as Bronwyn read and regained her strength.

Conor Frost came one afternoon, bringing more books, and food hampers from Harrods and Fortnum & Mason. Jeeves circled the hampers with childish delight, attempting restraint. They waited to see how long it would take him to launch into the cellophane. Finally, with Bronwyn's urging, Jeeves tore into them, lifting Greek chestnut honey, shortbread, caviar, Scottish salmon, truffles...calling out each item. Rather than spinning the hampers, he walked around them, presenting breakfast marmalade, pâté, Kalamata olives, savory nuts; each item as if Conor would be just as surprised.

"Should I bring him his own, next time?" Conor whispered.

She laughed, knowing the exotic tidbits suited Jeeves and Conor more than her, and vowed to remember how to cheer Jeeves in the future...the old Food Hall hamper trick.

Sir Winston Watkins' grand mansion in Bath was the dark, dank and drafty home Jeeves had anticipated in the Cotswolds. He thought it made sense why Bronwyn had chosen to stay in Mayfair and Chipping Norton before coming to Bath. It could only have depressed her to sit in damp rooms with tapestries and gloom.

On the bright side, they were welcome as long as they wished. The staff was as large as Bronwyn promised. It was obvious that Sir Winston took the 'Sir' part very seriously.

It shouldn't have surprised Jeeves to find Bronwyn with the staff more often than with Sir Winston. After all, she'd been friendly to Menke's security team and staff. But it was apparent a longstanding closeness and mutual fondness existed in Bath. Sometimes Jeeves would find her polishing silver, folding bed linens, slicing carrots. Bronwyn obviously enjoyed the chores and she chatted openly with the staff. He understood why she desired a long visit to the gloomy digs; she was happy here.

Jeeves finally met the actor Roddy O'Neal and his round wife, Eimear. O'Neal was just what Jeeves had imagined...a bit crusty with a silver beard, an Irish brogue and complete confidence. His days as a heartthrob may have been behind him, but he had a charismatic energy. Roddy was glad to find a drinking buddy in Jeeves, warming up nicely while the others were cold around the edges. They had lengthy discussions of wine and scotch, punctuated with numerous samplings.

Jeeves was pleased when Conor Frost made a trip up to the land-of-gloom. Sebastian Hughes arrived that weekend with the vision named Charlotte Tritton, before his new film was set to begin.

After a day, Charlotte returned to London, bored with Bath. That left Bronwyn with Conor and Hughie, as Conor explained his role in the newest Jane Austen film.

"Hughie, I really can't abide these dance roles. I should have turned it down, straightaway."

"Nonsense, Frost. I've seen you dance. You're a grand dancer. Have you seen him, Bronwyn?"

"Sure. In films. But I know what he means. I'm not a dancer."

Sebastian Hughes loaded the CD of Conor's practice music and pressed 'play'. "Oh, let's have a look, shall we? Conor, give it a go with our Bronwyn."

Conor rose and extended his hand with a sweeping bow. She shook her head. "Honestly, Conor, nothing could make me dance. I truly can't dance."

He shrugged it off, moved a few chairs and began a majestic dance with complicated moves, all with an imaginary partner. The music transformed the room and Bronwyn sensed another world. Conor was lithe on his feet, despite his modest protests. He hardly noticed when Hughie slipped into his embrace.

"Whoa, old man. Are you gone in the head?" Conor was turning scarlet.

"Give a fella a chance, Conor. I'm no dosser. The day may come when Jane Austen calls for me. It's only Bronwyn watching. Come now, take a chance."

It took her urging before they made a few awkward steps together, and then fell into a lovely rhythm. As Bronwyn watched, she smiled affectionately. She remembered quite clearly Sebastian Hughes starring in a highly regarded costume drama. As competitive as actors could be, she suspected Conor knew Hughie could waltz.

"Is there a prohibition movie you should both prepare for? Foxtrot? Quickstep?" she asked, giggling. It was a memorable afternoon, watching her two friends inexplicably dancing together.

When they parted, breathless and grinning, Conor nodded to Hughie. "It's quite alarming actually, how well you fill the bill in the lady's role."

Sebastian Hughes beamed as if it were the highest of compliments.

Before the week was over, Bronwyn watched as Conor and Hughie galloped on horseback across the countryside. Bronwyn wished she could ride again, but doubted she would. Something about her injuries; it was as if her organs were tucked in, waiting for attack. She loved the horses, though, and spent part of each day brushing them and offering carrots and apples. Often Jeeves had to haul her out of the stables near dinner time, as if she were a reluctant child.

The night before Conor and Hughie left, they chatted about movie roles and Sir Winston suggested they watch *Find Me*, yet again. They complimented Graeme's performance as if he'd been there, and Jeeves wondered why Sir Winston and Bronwyn glanced at each other throughout the film.

During their time in Bath, Jeeves made several trips in and out of the place. Bronwyn had no idea where he'd gone, unaware if it was business or pleasure. She breathed more easily with the freedom of life without Jeeves, but she was genuinely happy to see him when he returned.

While Jeeves was off on a trip, she began sketching. It occurred to her that she might take the land in Maine, the part with the pine trees by the highway, and build a home there. She played with the sketch, imagining a nine hole golf course. Her trust fund wasn't large, but it might be enough; she'd ask Moss to make some inquiries. A small cottage for her and another cottage for Jeeves would be nice.

The Factory excited her and she felt honored to have it fall into her hands. She wanted to transform it into a museum of some kind, acknowledging the workers and the history of the Bayside Blanket and Toboggan Company with historical artifacts and photographs.

When Jeeves returned, he wasn't pleased with Bronwyn's 'cottage in the pines' idea. His reaction made her wonder if she was underestimating the bayside property. She liked the neighbors on Leopard Lane; the land seemed private and the view was lovely. She revised her ideas, thinking she could build cottages at the Homestead and still create the nine hole golf course out of town.

The next time Jeeves returned from a trip, he seemed more interested when he learned Bronwyn was back to building homes beside the Factory. She showed him a rough layout of golf holes. She'd done her homework, listing Tiff Eagle for the greens, Paspalum/Bermuda 419 for the fairways, Paspalum for the tees and collars, Zoysia/ Bermuda 419 for the rough. She wanted bunkers and some dense vegetation, but no water hazards. Excellent playability was important to her, with gentle slopes. Her desire to keep most of the pines meant the fairways would be tree-lined. She wanted children and new golfers to enjoy the play, so she was leaning toward a mix of easy and challenging holes. He couldn't help himself; Jeeves liked seeing what she'd done, and he offered suggestions for the green shapes. Bronwyn was surprised how Jeeves confronted the bunkers...he seemed a master at protecting the greens.

One evening, he observed Bronwyn on the phone, rolling her eyes and making faces. Sebastian Hughes was calling from location, somewhere in the Czech Republic.

"Hughie, I know it's cold, but it's cold for everyone," she said, encouragingly. "Hang in there. You'll be back to Pinewood for the interiors in a couple of weeks."

Jeeves saw her exasperation.

"Hughie. You don't want me to call you 'Drawing Room Hughie', do you? If you shoot outside, you're going to be part of the elements. It's that simple. If you always shoot indoors, people won't see how the sun heightens your natural glow," Jeeves admired her attempt. "I know there's no sun, Hughie, I'm just saying get through this and then don't think about limiting yourself. I like seeing you out of doors. You're really too handsome to be contained in one space. I really don't think that's the answer. I'll have Conor call you. I'm sure he understands what you're going through.

"Oh, I didn't know he called you. I know he's in Poland. It's cold there, too. Well for what it's worth, I hate being cold, Hughie. Give me an electric blanket and a cup of tea by the fire any day. You just spoil yourself when you get back to the hotel, okay? I love you too, Hughie. Call me."

She hung up, and then called his agent. Jeeves was curious to see Bronwyn's aggressive side. "Reggie. It's Bronwyn McCall. Sebastian says you're pushing the animated film. Do you want to end his career?"

Bronwyn began to pace. "I'm telling you, and you know I'm right – if you put Sebastian in a studio, he's gonna show up in pajamas, do 'Beauty and the Beast, the Sequel' and then move on to 'Bugs Bunny at the Speedway' and 'The Chipmunks See New York'. He'll never film a real movie, again. Is that what you want? Think about it, Reggie. Think who you're dealing with."

She made a face. "If you listen to his insecurities, you're going to cripple him. He always does this. If you're tired of it, maybe he needs a new agent."

Bronwyn continued to clip ideas from design magazines. When she had enough files to fill a box, she shipped it to Moss for safekeeping. Bronwyn assured Jeeves his home would be 'wonderful' and he expected her plans would wow him.

With trips in and out, the time at Bath went surprisingly fast for Jeeves. For her part, Bronwyn was ready to show him Pittsburgh at Christmas, before flying to Palm Springs in January. As they packed, she assured Jeeves that Sir Winston's Palm Spring's mansion was similar in décor, but sunny and bright outside. Jeeves couldn't fathom how the grounds would make up for the gloomy interiors.

The grand Pittsburgh tour was just what Bronwyn hoped it would be. On the way in from the airport, she insisted that

Jeeves sit up front, beside the limo driver. She was rewarded when he had the perfect first-timer reaction to the startling revelation of Pittsburgh at night, blasting all his senses as they emerged from the Fort Pitt Tunnel. Even the limo driver chuckled at Jeeves' response and it set a nice tone for their visit.

Bronwyn felt closer to Jeeves, as they explored the city. He enjoyed the department store holiday windows, watching the children point with awe. It was contagious enthusiasm. When Bronwyn pointed out the old wooden escalator at the top floor of Kaufmann's, he marveled at her memory and attention to detail.

The staff at the William Penn Hotel embraced her as a long-lost daughter, and Jeeves didn't mind the behind-the-scenes view of the kitchen and laundry areas. Almost everyone had known Bronwyn when she lived there.

They spent the end of December traveling throughout the Pittsburgh area, eating at restaurants along main streets and nestled along the countryside. Jeeves enjoyed the rolling hills, bridges wherever he looked, and rivers converging at the Point. He knew the relevant addresses in Sewickley and noticed Bronwyn avoided those streets.

Jeeves didn't mention his own childhood or hometown, so she was happy to bring her own dim history into his consciousness. For his part, Jeeves seemed to pounce upon each place, glad to discover and experience all that Bronwyn showed him. He'd had his MI6 time in big cities, sweltering jungles, desolate motel rooms, buggy huts, and splintered shacks. He'd been cold, unhappy, bored, isolated, drenched in sweat. What he suppressed was his early life, his young marriage, his dear Deirdre. Whatever Bronwyn handed him helped to press those early days down so flat they seemed to disappear. He only had so much room in his head, and these new memories were potent. Life at Bronwyn's side was sufficiently vibrant; he could almost excuse the very tiny remnant of his heart.

One day they drove to Beaver, and had an early lunch at Bert's Wooden Indian, her dad's favorite restaurant. They ate ham Bar B Q's and slender French fries in napkin-lined wooden baskets, and sipped milkshakes while Bronwyn told Jeeves about the juke boxes that used to be at each booth. They looked at Bert's photos on the wall, some as far back as 1948, and Bronwyn vowed to locate old photographs of the Bayside Blanket and Toboggan Factory.

After Bert's, they drove through the picturesque Beaver cemetery and walked down Third Street with Bronwyn pointing out the architecture, streetlamps and brick sidewalks. They looked at houses, sat in the park, bought Cherry Cheese Pockets at Kretchmar's, and having killed enough time to settle their stomachs, drove to the Brighton Hot Dog Shoppe. She pointed Jeeves to a booth and placed their order at the counter; a hot dog and French fries for Bronwyn and two chili dogs, chili cheese fries, and a shake for Jeeves. As they left town, Bronwyn described Jerry's Curb Service not far from Bert's, and giggled that their driver would have to know the 'rules' if they ever ate there...back your car in and turn your parking lights on for service. They made plans to eat at the Back Door Tavern next time. Jeeves would be flabbergasted by The Giant Fish Sandwich and all the imported beers and microbrews, not to mention the sports memorabilia. There was the tiniest up tilt to his lips as she described it.

The Grand Concourse on Christmas Eve took Jeeves' breath away, and they had a pull-out-all-the-stops meal in a breathtaking atmosphere. The old train station bustled with wait staff, echoing the cacophony of china and conversation. The elegance of a by-gone era arched magnificently above them. They stood along the train tracks, watching boats go by and breathing in the frosty allure of the city blazingly lit, across the river. Jeeves didn't know if her love for Pittsburgh was contagious, or if he always would have appreciated the city, but he knew that night, stomach full of bouillabaisse and Stilton hash browns, he felt a contentment he hadn't known for years.

After Christmas, they were taking a private jet to Palm Springs, but Bronwyn wanted to check her NYC 'closet'. That's what she called the office space Moss had reserved for her, down the hall from his own suite of offices. She was curious if her boxes had arrived, and she was relieved when Moss unlocked the door to reveal drawers filled with her new Pringle sweaters; garment racks; wooden cabinets with her files neatly organized, and bookcases of her new books. She had a young woman to thank – Grace Cloud. Grace was handling their bills and expenses, but also Bronwyn's 'closet'.

Grace was obviously a clotheshorse. Wearing a sleeveless tweed shift despite the snow outside, and black leather boots with astronomically high heels, she had large dark brown eyes, dark fringy eyelashes and beautifully groomed eyebrows. As Grace explained her filing system for Bronwyn's interior design files, Bronwyn was fascinated by the look of Grace's eyebrows. They seemed to float away from her face, as if they weren't attached at all. It was extraordinary. She had an engaging smile, a hearty laugh, and exceedingly glossy long dark hair. Although her slightly hooked nose wasn't her best feature, everything about her was attractive. Bronwyn thought her name was fitting; she carried herself with grace.

Moss suggested the two young women have dinner together, before Bronwyn flew to Palm Springs.

Bronwyn wanted to dress to impress. She hit the stores that afternoon and found a white silk blouse with ruffled cuffs and a black georgette silk skirt. When they met for dinner at Bronwyn's hotel, Grace was wearing black corduroys, a black turtleneck, and black toggle jacket with a huge silver necklace and hair drawn back in a ponytail. They had a good laugh, as each had dressed more like the other. It was a good sign of friendship. They chatted about fashion throughout dinner and made plans to shop the next day, delaying the trip to Palm Springs.

With Grace's help, Bronwyn chose some resort-wear for California. Grace promised to wardrobe the heavy clothes Bronwyn had brought from England, and helped her pack for California. As they worked in the 'closet', Grace handed Bronwyn a note and pointed to several green and white boxes on a corner shelf, some large and some very small.

Whenever you do have a house, dear Bronwyn, I hope these will add to your Christmas. Until then, know that houses reside in your Closet, until your Closet becomes your house.

With great fondness, Conor

While Bronwyn read the note, Grace unpacked one of the boxes. Bronwyn turned to see a Department 56 lighted house. It was mesmerizing. Grace was so happy to see her enthusiasm that she got a light strip and set up three more houses, placing trees and small porcelain figures in front of them. Just then, Moss entered. The lighted houses seemed rather pathetic, displayed on an office shelf, but it pleased him to know Bronwyn's friend was adding to her days, giving her some measure of hope for the future.

They said goodbye, and Bronwyn was happy she'd made a 'closet' visit, seeing an old friend in Moss, making a new one in Grace, and being reminded of a dear friend she'd almost discarded before she'd ever really met – Conor Frost.

To Jeeves' way of thinking, it was as if the entire Bath estate had been transplanted to Palm Springs. It was gloomy and had to be the only ancient home in the desert. Whatever happened to the New World, he thought. At least there were stables of Arabians to distract Bronwyn.

The sunny weather suited Jeeves. If he turned his back on the three story mansion with its steeply pitched mansard roof and closed his eyes, he could almost pretend it was the Riviera.

The weeks slid by, with Jeeves making trips to San Francisco and Las Vegas. On this day, however, he dropped Bronwyn off at the kitchen with a light bag of groceries, and then lingered at the stables, after parking the car. A veterinarian was examining the hooves of one of the horses, and Jeeves watched him work.

Having promised Sir Winston she'd make bread pudding, Bronwyn began to lay out ingredients across the kitchen island. The household staff had the day off, so her plan was to make a nice vegetable soup with cheese croutons and the bread pudding for dessert. Sir Winston was in the walk-in pantry, when someone lunged into the room.

"Where is he? Where's the bastard?" the man shouted, waving a gun.

The pantry door gently closed.

Bronwyn had seen this man before; he was the producer, Oakley Forse.

"Who? Who are you looking for?"

Oakley Forse had a naturally wild look, but this day he looked utterly insane. His curly hair was unruly and uncombed; his face shadowed and unshaven; his eyes gleaming with rage.

She leaned forward against the large island, as if everything was normal.

"Sir Winston's not here. Did you want me to give him a message?"

"Where the hell is he?" Oakley Forse walked toward her and waved the gun. He seemed steadier, committed.

"He's out. I'm making dinner."

His head jerked awkwardly. Forse looked around the kitchen, listening carefully to a house holding its breath with emptiness. There was no sound at all.

Bronwyn wondered where Jeeves would be. How soon would he appear? She knew there were cameras throughout the house. That was one reason Jeeves didn't mind leaving her, but she knew now the cameras would only record events; they weren't going to save her.

"Put the gun down, Mr. Forse. Tell me why you're upset."

He didn't put it down, but he seemed more than willing to share his grievance.

"Winston took my boy, he did. My little princess. My little Polynesian princess."

She thought he meant his son, then his daughter. It was confusing. Bronwyn recalled Sir Winston had been involved with an exotic would-be actor. It reminded her of Sir Winston's vulnerability. Roddy and Graeme had warned her Sir Winston's bisexuality was bound to be found out, and his career wouldn't weather the storm. If he'd 'stolen' his new love from Oakley Forse, it meant she was in the eye of the storm. Sir Winston had ducked for cover and Bronwyn wondered if his pantry locked. She was on her own.

"He isn't here. You don't want to do something bad right now." She watched Oakley Forse, carefully. "I know you don't want to make a move you can't undo. We can just forget…"

He shot her. She saw the flash at the same time she felt the bullet rip into her shoulder. It was a searing pain, a pain she didn't remember from the DC shooting. It surprised her. She held his gaze. The thought occurred to Bronwyn that she could finally see someone hurting her. It was empowering and calmed her. Time seemed to lengthen and she was aware of her breathing. Bad things happened to her, people disappeared forever, and she was stripped of everything, all of it, but always behind her back, when she wasn't looking. This was different. It was just a gun, and Bronwyn could see it.

Unwilling to break his gaze, she grabbed a tea towel and wadded it up. She pushed it into her wound, thinking it was high up on her shoulder; surely not a bad wound. She wanted to think Sir Winston would come out; she wanted to think Jeeves had heard the shot and was coming. Neither happened.

Bronwyn didn't know if Oakley Forse was drunk or high or insane, but she knew he'd meant to shoot and it satisfied him.

"Who are you?" he asked, as if he was only mildly curious and hadn't just shot her.

She didn't answer. He came closer and lifted his gun to her forehead. It was only six inches away. He waited for her to flinch, to beg, to pray, to bury her head. She held his gaze. Her eyes didn't dare him; they didn't beseech him; they simply looked at him. He cocked the gun and before he fired his eyes gleamed more brightly – until a cloud took the spark away, when he fired and nothing happened. Their eyes were locked on each other. Finally, Oakley Forse's hand dropped to his side. He backed away, and broke the gaze.

Bronwyn spoke quietly. "There are cameras, everywhere. Everywhere." He looked doubtful. "You know Winston. You know he'd have cameras. You'd better go."

Oakley Forse looked up, then around, nodded and backed out of the kitchen.

"Are you going to call the police?" Sir Winston heard him say, but he couldn't hear Bronwyn's reply.

She tried to measure the situation as she felt lightheaded. If Winston had been at the sink, he'd be dead. She was at the edge of a scandal. Winston was nothing, absolutely nothing, without his image and career. She wouldn't repay his kindness by being part of his downfall. "Are you going to get your checkbook?" she answered Oakley Forse.

Moments later, she slid down to the floor, and called weakly to Sir Winston, "He's gone."

Sir Winston was a mess, shaking and crying and vowing never to love again. He was far removed from the award-winning actor everyone respected and revered.

Stars flashed as she was on the verge of fainting. "Winston. Get Jeeves. Get the vet. Don't call the police. Call Moss. Say it. Say it!"

Winston answered, "Jeeves, the vet. No police. Call Moss."

CHAPTER SIX

OAKLEY'S MOTHER

*B*ronwyn recovered in Carmel, three thousand miles away from Menke. After all, Jeeves was being paid to protect Bronwyn. It was bad enough to deal with Stanley Mastrofrancesco; he didn't want to face the prime minister's mother.

The money was Jeeves' saving grace, even though he'd had nothing to do with it. It had been Bronwyn, of course. Bronwyn who warned Oakley Forse about the cameras, Bronwyn who insisted Watkins get the vet, Bronwyn who said to call Moss and not the police.

Jeeves viewed the security tapes from three different angles – why on earth did Sir Winston have three cameras in his kitchen; what delights did he cook up there? Jeeves caught the maniacal glint in Oakley's eye, when he held the gun to Bronwyn's head. There was nary a flinch on her part and it was obvious Forse had expected a bullet to round out his fun. It was most disturbing.

Lip readers indicated Bronwyn asked Forse if he was going to get his checkbook. Jeeves allowed himself the pleasure of watching that part again – his favorite part. 'Are you going to get your checkbook?' As much as Bronwyn wanted to build her dream home in Maine, Jeeves wouldn't have expected that; not moments after she stared into a .357 Magnum.

The bullet to Bronwyn's shoulder hadn't pried the money from Oakley Forse and his fleet of attorneys. It was the clear desire on Oakley's part to put a bullet in her head. Moss refused to allow Bronwyn to be questioned, so the attorneys asked it of Jeeves. Why didn't she flinch? Who would look into the gun and not beg for mercy, not put their hands up to deflect the bullet, not close their eyes?

Jeeves had no answer, but it bothered him. Was she so sad about her life, that she was ready to die? Did a sixth sense tell her there'd be no bullet in the chamber and she was cool enough to gamble? Did she think she was saving Sir Winston Watkins as he sat cowering in the pantry? Was she in shock? Jeeves was at a loss.

At least Oakley Forse was on Jeeves' radar, with a tamper-proof locator device around his ankle, all part of the negotiated settlement.

Jeeves contacted an old MI6 friend to join them in Carmel. Van Tsang came down from San Francisco and Bronwyn enjoyed his company. He looked younger than forty six, was trim but powerful, with a gray-tinged black crew cut and dimpled smile. Jeeves was tight and proper, whereas Van Tsang was calm and Zen-like. It was a pleasant change for a few weeks.

"There's no need to be concerned about Oakley Forse, Miss."

"I wasn't worried, Jeeves. Moss said the transfer of funds has been made. It's beyond generous. If Oakley Forse wanted to renege on the amount, I wouldn't have a problem with it."

Jeeves looked at Bronwyn as if she were insane.

Bronwyn was confused by his look and wondered what Jeeves meant about being 'concerned'.

"Do you mean you think he'd hurt me?"

"I was merely informing you that matters are in hand." Jeeves busied himself packing for their flight to London. "You've no reason to worry."

Bronwyn confronted Jeeves. "What have you done?"

Jeeves had no intention of responding, but such was the problem of living together. He'd have to come up with something, and reaching for something other than the truth took too much effort.

"We've relocated his mum, but don't be concerned. She's in a nursing home, a keener one than where we found her."

Bronwyn's right eyebrow lifted higher than the left. "You've kidnapped her?"

Jeeves turned to fold his shirts. Bronwyn touched his arm and then gave it a pinch.

"You've kidnapped her? You're crazy! Think how confused she must be." Bronwyn's freckles swam in a field of flushed pink and her mouth puckered with distaste.

"You've no idea how important you are to the prime minister, Miss. I've taken you into my confidence and now you know there's no cause for concern."

"Where is she?"

"I'm afraid I can't say, Miss."

Bronwyn settled in a club chair and smiled. "I'll figure it out when I see the road signs, Jeeves."

Instead of their lovely trip to London, Jeeves and Bronwyn spent the next month in rural Ohio. It made Jeeves wish he'd moved Forse's mum to Palm Beach. The inn was cramped in so many ways that he felt like Goldilocks without finding the 'just right'. The bed was too high, the mattress too hard, the hallways too narrow, the steps too creaky, the lighting too dim, the rugs too shabby. They would have moved if it hadn't been for the food, which was sublime. He ate tartine of smoked salmon, cheese plate with wine-soaked raisins, and crisp calamari. At dinner he enjoyed fingerling potato salad, roasted beet salad with pomegranates and who would think he could find a lovely coq au vin so far from civilization? The food made each day palatable for Jeeves, literally and figuratively.

When Bronwyn met Mrs. Hrubochak, Oakley's mother, Jeeves reminded Bronwyn that the prime minister was paying nursing home costs and they should be on their way, but Bronwyn shot him a furious look. As far as Bronwyn was concerned, Mrs. Hrubochak deserved kind-hearted visitors (Jeeves disqualified himself), lovely pillows and quilts, melt-in-your-mouth chocolates, and regular hand patting.

Shortly after Bronwyn's arrival, Moss flew in. Accompanying Moss was an attractive native-born South African, Zuleika Zannini, and a Swiss banker.

Zuleika and Bronwyn took an instant liking to each other. In her early forties, Zuleika was uniquely beautiful with an aquiline nose, wide-spaced dark eyes, a long face, and a rather voluptuous figure. Her husband, Jean Luc, was a New York City restaurateur with five restaurants, which intrigued Bronwyn. Zuleika would handle Bronwyn's newfound wealth, and the Swiss banker reviewed her new account. With that settled, the Mastrofrancesco group departed.

Bronwyn became increasingly worried about Mrs. Hrubochak's health. The woman seldom spoke and was often confused. Her doctors warned Bronwyn how rapidly she was failing from congestive heart failure, so Bronwyn made her days as pleasant as possible, renting videos and recapping her son's most popular films. Each weekday afternoon, Bronwyn watched *The Young and the Restless* with Oakley's mother, and kept a running commentary on Victor Newman and Jack Abbott. Interestingly, Jeeves never missed an episode.

One evening, Jeeves mentioned that Oakley Forse had changed his name several years ago. Jeeves was obviously aching to fill her in. Bronwyn wanted to leave him hanging, but felt compelled to know. Apparently Oakley had killed his twin brother when they were fourteen.

She realized if Jeeves was willing to 'relocate' Mrs. Hrubochak, he'd enjoy blackmailing Oakley Forse. Jeeves needed to find a hobby.

As Bronwyn's attorney, Moss had carefully studied Sir Winston's security films before negotiating the one hundred million dollar settlement, and he was aware Jeeves had uncovered Forse's past. It seemed prudent to put additional clauses in place. Oakley Forse referred to the clauses as Pre-Vi and Post-Vi agreements, alluding to his Pre-Nups and Post-Nups. If Oakley Forse violated the 'within 100 yards' restriction, Bronwyn would receive four million dollars... a 'Pre-Violence' agreement. If there was any additional violence, she would receive an additional two hundred million dollars on top of the four million...the 'Post-Violence' agreement. Moss couldn't conceive of Oakley Forse's lack of interest in the money, but worse, it had been Oakley who proposed the enormous sums. If Oakley Forse didn't care about the money, what would keep Bronwyn safe?

Therefore, Moss was stunned several weeks later when Bronwyn asked Oakley to come to Ohio to see his mother, and Bronwyn planned to be there, waiving the 'within 100 yards' restriction during the visit.

A fuming Jeeves watched Bronwyn and Oakley in the hospital cafeteria. Bronwyn was leaving his mother in Oakley Forse's hands, now that Mrs. Hrubochak was near the end of her life. She and Jeeves had loudly disagreed on the matter, with voices rising through the Inn's thin walls. Now, three of Oakley's attorneys were observing, just two tables away from Moss and Jeeves.

Bronwyn and Oakley Forse sat across from each other. Jeeves thought he'd jump out of his skin and stared at them with unblinking eyes. He didn't know if Bronwyn was out of control because of her financial windfall, or if she always would have been willful. Perhaps he should have shared more of Forse's dossier with her. Well, perhaps not, but that was the point, wasn't it?

Moss was there to oversee the situation on Bronwyn's behalf. Watching Jeeves gave Moss an insight into the unsettling world of MI6. He hoped Jeeves was unarmed, although he had every reason to believe Jeeves had stashed a variety of weapons up his sleeve, down his sock, under his salad bowl. Moss envisioned extreme violence, not from Bronwyn's table, but from his own.

"I'm sorry Oakley, that we moved your Mother."

"The nurses tell me she was doing well. Until recently." Oakley gazed past Bronwyn, unseeing. "Anyway, I wasn't much of a visitor since I put her in the other place. Too busy, but that's no excuse, is it? Important man, big producer."

He sounded wistful. "Isn't it odd? She's more lucid, now that it's almost over. She called you my girl."

Bronwyn frowned. "Hardly lucid."

Oakley cocked his head to the side, smiling.

She was unafraid, but uncertain how much to trust his apparent friendliness. He noticed how composed Bronwyn was, with a quiet sadness that was almost elegant in its simplicity. Each of them reached the same conclusion, that the other was sincerely saddened by the oncoming death of Oakley's mother.

Forse caught his breath, realizing how near he was to losing his last living relative. Bronwyn thought of her own mother, how she would never have the chance to be with her at the end, but not envying Oakley's opportunity.

Bronwyn lowered her eyes and noticed his hand shaking until Oakley caught her looking and put both hands in his lap. He did have the most extraordinary light gray eyes. They'd been wild, insane-looking when he'd shot her, but they still had a weird quality. She figured anyone working for him probably cowered whenever he entered the building. He seemed unbalanced, on the verge of something extreme, but today he was a stricken son.

"We have my father to thank, Bronwyn."

"Sorry?"

"If it hadn't been for my mother, cleaning house for my father, you and I wouldn't be enjoying all of his money."

"I thought the settlement was your money. From your films."

"That's different money, Bronwyn. Most of mine is off-shore. I decided to share my father's wealth with you. You wouldn't want to know how my father got his ugly money, or his father before him. I rarely touch it."

"How did your mother come to marry your father? He fell in love with her?"

Oakley Forse looked carefully into Bronwyn's eyes, appraising her. "My father never married my mother, although he did take good care of her, once we were born. I had a twin brother, you know." He watched for her reaction. "He died tragically, and it's hard to explain what losing a twin is like. You lose the biggest part of yourself. It's always missing."

Bronwyn nodded.

"My father never thought he'd have children, so when we came along he shipped us off to Chicago. I guess he thought it would be safer for us, and my mother changed our names. Before my father died, he set up the Swiss accounts for me. It's an obscene amount of money, Bronwyn. I've had two ex-wives, and they never had a clue. It makes us almost like brother and sister, you know? You and me. If it weren't for 'our' mother, loving my father, you wouldn't have this lovely money."

"That's a reach, Oakley. You know we're not related – or even, friends. She's your mother. We never should have taken her. It wasn't right."

"I know you didn't take her, Bronwyn." He offered a wry grin. "Thank you Mother, for getting the money for Bronwyn and her bad brother Oakley."

Oakley Forse looked down and shook his head. When he glanced up, his eyes were glistening.

"Cream roses."

"Sorry?"

"Cream roses. She loved cream roses. My father always remembered her birthday, and she was happy for days when he had cream roses delivered from half-way round the world."

Bronwyn imagined a doorbell ringing and a long floral

box delivery to a young Mrs. Hrubochak, hopeful and glad. Bronwyn had a lump in her throat, now that the time had come for cream roses, once again.

"I'm sorry, Oakley. She's very special." Bronwyn said, rising. "Will you be okay?"

Oakley suspected Bronwyn would stay as long as she was needed. He had minions aplenty, anxious to do whatever he wanted, to stay in his good graces and get ahead. Even his attorneys were attentive only in billing hour doses. He sensed how far removed he was from normalcy, standing across from this kind-hearted young woman who he'd nearly murdered with a bullet to her head. Those same green eyes looked at him with unblinking, unwavering steadiness, just as they had in that kitchen. He wasn't a bit sorry he'd fired the gun; in fact he was glad he could take her down his sodden path of riches, lined with filthy, vile money. It had been a lonely burden.

Oakley nodded and the two stood.

"The truce between us has expired, Oakley. I won't see you again. Take care," and as a bristling Jeeves watched with revulsion, Bronwyn shook Forse's hand goodbye.

CHAPTER SEVEN

SNOOKS VON KRINKLES

A visit to Maine was important to Bronwyn, before heading to Sir Winston's in Bath. Jeeves was on board. He looked forward to walking the Maine estate, investigating the town, and having plenty of lobster. But what Bronwyn most wanted, was to see Gus Townsend and Snooks Von Krinkles.

Jeeves realized how anxious Bronwyn was to see Gus, so he invited him to dinner at the harbor motel. After a meal of baked stuffed lobster, Bronwyn asked if she could stop by and see Snooks. Instead, Gus invited her to spend the week and was rewarded with Bronwyn's delight. Jeeves declined his invitation, planning to prowl the estate to his heart's content.

Arriving at Gus's cozy house, Bronwyn found Snooks Von Krinkles at the door, bouncing on her toes. The little red dachshund was certainly compact and sturdy with a loud and piercing bark, but she was also quite beautiful. Her oval eyes were deep and soulful and the room's lamps bounced light off her satiny red hair. Bronwyn decided her nose was aristocratic in its length. Snooks' cheekbones curved daintily beneath her eyes and her long ears were soft with an intriguing fold creating a tiny pocket at the underside. As Bronwyn admired Snooks, she found a beautiful swirl of hair across the dachshund's chest, centered right beneath her shoulders.

Bronwyn petted Snooks as Gus listened quietly to her abbreviated tale of Mrs. Hrubochak's death. Gus empathized, reminisced about his wife, and retrieved photo albums, recapping the Townsends' happy life together. Bronwyn was slow to turn the pages, visually wringing the photos, absorbing each captured moment of life. Snooks slept peacefully beside Bronwyn. Sometimes her long ear twitched, when Bronwyn let the photo album dip near the dog, but Bronwyn knew she was deeply asleep because her broad chest was rising and falling.

Gus noticed Bronwyn covering Snooks with the corner of her sweater, so he brought a blanket over and tucked it around the dog. She sighed deeply, dug her stubby feet against Bronwyn and slept more peacefully. Bronwyn felt at home.

"This little dog. I've had other dogs, but I never knew one who understood so much of what I tell her, and then absolutely doesn't care. She disobeys me even if I tell her to do something I know she wants to do. She is so stubborn and smart, but mind you, so brave. Maybe her daddy was a little warrior. Her papers say his name was Kimmel Von Dragmore. That sounds fierce enough."

"I think she's just perfect, Gus. Was she tiny when you got her?"

"Yep. Had to tape off the bottom of the sofa, or she'd crawl under and get lost. You wouldn't know she was so teeny to see her now. And those little puppy teeth were like needles.

If I laid my sweater down, she'd burrow into the sleeve and sleep there. Right down one arm, like a sausage. I've no idea how she could breathe! She was a beauty, just like now. Such a mind of her own. She can pull you down the street. Look at me, fit man that I am. And look at her. Thirteen pounds of dachshund will-power trumps the strongest man. If it's raining and I want her to move, forget it. She's a dog with purpose."

"Do you know how many movie stars had dachshunds, Gus? You're in good company. Clark Gable, Errol Flynn, Marlon Brando, John Wayne, Paulette Goddard..."

"I'm surprised you've heard of Paulette Goddard."

"Of course. And Carole Lombard, John Gilbert, Noel Coward. And Geoffrey Beene, the fashion designer. He had pairs of them. Three times, I think. The writer PG Wodehouse had Bertie. William Randolph Hearst had two. And Picasso had one named Lump."

"What a name."

"And Andy Warhol. He was from Pittsburgh, you know. Like me. His wiener dogs were Amos and Archie. He had cashmere sweaters made for them, in Paris."

"Who would think you'd know so much about doxies? I bet Snooks would like to have a cashmere sweater. Then again, she might chew it up. She has some cat friends and they seem to like it when she sneaks up on them. All but one, anyway. That one doesn't appreciate her tactics. Even with the fence, she starts burrowing underneath if she sees a rabbit. I've caught her making a right mess, like Stalag 17."

"Does she have a great nose? I remember my dad saying his dogs were like bloodhounds. And they loved digging, too."

"She digs in bed. You should see her arranging the pillows and getting deep under the blankets. She's definitely a burrower. And a prankster! Well, you'll find out, the more you're with her. She's reserved with people, Bronwyn. But not you. She's chosen you and she'll give you just as much affection as you give her."

"Look at her." Bronwyn gently adjusted the blanket around her little head. "She looks like a thoroughbred horse. Strong and beautiful. Look at the color of her fur. So red. Little racehorse. And look at these little paws." She lifted one. "They're just so perfect. See how the fur swirls around her wrists?"

It was nearing midnight, and Gus figured the way to convince Bronwyn to call it a night was to have her sleep with Snooks.

The next day, Bronwyn was out in the front yard with Snooks on her leash, and admired a weathered driftwood sculpture.

"I put red berries around it at Christmas. Like a driftwood tree," Gus explained.

"Is that a lobster crate, under it?"

Just then, a large young man came outside from the little house next door.

"Mornin' there, Tiny. Meet my friend Bronwyn."

"Hello, Tiny." Gus appreciated that Bronwyn made no comment regarding Tiny's height and girth. "Snooks is excited to see you," which was evident from the dog pulling at her leash.

Bronwyn picked her up and walked over to Tiny, who lifted one leg and gracefully cleared the fence. Bronwyn shook his monstrously large hand.

Gus was nicely dressed with a white polo collar poking above his navy sweater. He wore tan corduroys and was puffing on a pipe. His face was lined, not from weariness, but from decades spent on lobster boats, courtesy of the sun's harsh rays and whipping weather. Bronwyn was just as casual with khakis and a mocha sweatshirt. Snooks Von Krinkles donned her red leather collar, but it was Tiny who could be seen from space. His pants were raspberry cotton. A turquoise crew neck sweatshirt was pulled over a yellow and black plaid shirt. Bronwyn had no idea what size his feet were, but they were wearing undeniably rubber shoes, in a taxi yellow shade.

They sat on Gus's porch, with Tiny holding Snooks until she squirmed and insisted on being put down. Bronwyn noticed Tiny's disappointment, so she engaged him in conversation about living beside Snooks Von Krinkles.

"She barks so loud, Bronwyn, but she has a bark just for me. Doesn't she, Gus? It's like a wail, Gus says. A wail. Bark, Snooks. Wail for me, Snooks."

Bronwyn laughed and promised Tiny she'd recognize the wail, whenever Snooks wanted to call him. That seemed to satisfy Tiny. She looked around the painted white porch and Bronwyn once again, felt quite at home. A crisply ironed white cloth draped over an old wooden table. Gus brought a tray of iced tea and Bronwyn poured.

"Gus, have you shown Bronwyn the lobster things? What are they called?"

"Buoys, Tiny."

"Can I show her? Can I?" And Tiny walked Bronwyn over to Gus's lobster boat shed, where colorful wooden lobster buoys decorated the fence and hung from the walls.

"Have you ever been lobster fishing, Tiny?"

"Gus won't let me." Bronwyn had found a sore subject. "My mom and dad never would, either. Wanta see my house? Do you wanta see my house?"

It was amazing to Bronwyn that Tiny could live in such a small house, but he seemed content and proud of his home. Suddenly distracted, he told Bronwyn there was a television show he had to see, and Bronwyn said her good-byes as Tiny settled in to watch *The Price is Right*.

That afternoon, Gus's son came to visit – Mayor Luke Townsend. Bronwyn spent two hours with him, discussing town improvement ideas. She wanted Luke's promise that when she built her estate, renovated the Factory, built the golf course and made town improvements, he'd facilitate permits and variances. Luke Townsend pushed Bronwyn to implement her plans; it was just the growth impetus he needed to create his legacy. Bronwyn sniffed his ambition, so she demanded his sincere commitment. Bronwyn warned him that if she was restricted by the town, forced to jump through hoops, she'd move elsewhere. When they shook hands, both Luke Townsend and Bronwyn McCall firmly squeezed the other's hand and didn't let go, holding the other hard and fast, to keep their word.

At week's end, Bronwyn deeply regretted leaving Gus and Snooks, and now, Tiny. She was liberal with her kisses and hugs, but when she walked out the front door and turned to wave, emotion choked in her throat. The sight of Gus holding Snooks, and Tiny blowing into his huge handkerchief, was half the picture. The other half was Gus's weathered house and fence, framing colorful boats sprinkled across the sun-beaded harbor. Maine had cast its enchanting spell, it seemed like home, and now she was leaving.

CHAPTER EIGHT

THE PALL

*M*enke urged Bronwyn to visit, before flying to England. Wilmington's *Nicholas and Alexandra: The Last Imperial Family of Tsarist Russia Exhibit* was about to close and Menke remembered Bronwyn reading *The Last Tsar.* She was right; Bronwyn very much wanted to see the exhibition.

It had been a year and a half since they'd seen Menke, and Jeeves wasn't keen to return. But as much as Jeeves dreaded the visit, Bronwyn embraced it.

The exhibit was emotional for Bronwyn. She toured with audio earpieces, walking slowly with Menke; but afterward Bronwyn left her and Jeeves in the lobby and returned for another look.

Beautifully lit satin ballgowns and jeweled Fabergé eggs were breathtakingly intricate. The Tsarina Alexandra's grand piano anchored one room and Bronwyn imagined Alexandra's hands on the ivories. Focusing, Bronwyn could very nearly catch just an echo of melody. But the photographs, telegrams, locks of baby hair, letters, and photos were what lured Bronwyn back.

The photographs mesmerized her. The royal family had

been ethereal in their beauty. Whether they wore delicate finery, lawn dresses with pearls or fur-draped wool, their faces were timeless. The photographs of the Ipatiev House made her feel uneasy; its starkness was unnerving. She moved to the photographs of elegant picnics, well-dressed tennis matches, and Alexei with his valiant companion, Nagorny. The photograph of Joy, Alexei's spaniel in Ekaterinburg, brought tears to Bronwyn's eyes. The room was dark, with pinpoint lights focused on displays; perhaps no one was aware of her emotion, or perhaps others were containing their own rampant sadness. What most saddened Bronwyn were their last words, before the unspeakable happened. She regarded Alexei's last letter, written before the boy's death; then cast her eyes on Alexandra's diary entries before looking at the inevitable last words, written just two hours before her death. They floated above empty space, if only...

Bronwyn was quiet on the drive home and Menke found herself second-guessing the wisdom of seeing the exhibit. She hadn't realized the kidnapping of Samuel and Paul might bring it too close to home for Bronwyn.

Indeed, that was part of it, but she was overwhelmed by the gloomy desolation of a family obliterated from the earth, and the rain-filled skies did nothing to alleviate her somber mood. Bronwyn peered out the car window, pretending the speeding scenery snagged her attention.

Menke cast her a miserable glance, but Bronwyn turned to thank her, saying the exhibit had been a moving experience, a once-in-a-lifetime opportunity, and she was grateful that Menke had suggested the visit.

The Main Line visit didn't last long, just long enough for Avis to whip up every delicious thing she could create.

Jeeves was amazed at what Avis could lay upon the table and began to wish for a longer visit.

He found himself musing about Oakley Forse. The interaction between Forse and Bronwyn at the hospital had been bizarre. As much as it rankled Jeeves, he knew he'd witnessed a bond between them. He didn't believe Oakley would ever hurt Bronwyn again. That contemplation set his wheels to turning, and gave Jeeves an even bigger appetite.

In Bath, Jeeves offered to delay his planned London visit, surprising Bronwyn. Maybe he was concerned that she hadn't shaken off the horror of the 1918 Romanov murders, or the death of Mrs. Hrubochak.

"Jeeves. The only way this will work, is if you have a life and I have a life. I enjoy having you around, but I've been alone all my life and if you were with me all the time, I'd smother."

Jeeves' eyes narrowed.

"I'm saying you should go to London. Or wherever you'd like. For as long as you choose. I'll enjoy myself in Bath and sometimes you'll be with me as the years go by, and sometimes you won't."

"You don't mind my leaving, Miss?"

Bronwyn laughed and made a slight bow. "I am prepared for your absence, Jeeves."

Having just spent time with Bronwyn, Menke called her grandsons. They were wild with questions about her, so Menke made a plan with her son. The boys would go to England to surprise Bronwyn.

When the long black limo swung around Sir Winston's circular driveway, Bronwyn was clueless. She was standing near the corral, wondering who'd been invited, when the door opened and Samuel and Paul came tearing across the grass. Bronwyn dropped to her knees and threw her arms out to embrace them both. No longer the tiny boys she remembered, they almost bowled her over.

Samuel and Paul were nine and six now, and followed Bronwyn around as if she were a Pied Piper. She swung into the kitchen and the boys trailed after. She strolled to the horse barns and the boys nipped about her like puppies. They even joined her at bedtime, piling into her enormous bed along with Sir Winston's chocolate Labradors, Buster Brown and Coco. When word got out what a sight it was, the servants peeked in.

Bronwyn and the boys slept more peacefully than they had since the kidnapping attempt. Aided by the large, warm bodies of the dogs nestled around them, they were also simply glad to be together again.

One morning, Bronwyn awakened before the boys, recalling the dream she'd just had. She was at the White House and had knelt in a corridor, welcoming the younger versions of the two boys. Then, for some reason, the President of the United States insulted her at dinner and the prime minister left his table. The president lifted his arm to slap Bronwyn for going to the kitchen without permission, and it seemed Bram was going to slug him and the next moment Bram had his arm around Bronwyn's waist, dancing to beautiful music. Bronwyn recognized the music as *Concetta*, and settled into the pleasant reverie of dancing. Bronwyn's gown was layers of navy and copper chiffon with a fitted bodice and Bram's arm was so tight around her waist, pressing her against him, that her feet were a foot off the ground. The gown's skirt billowed as they twirled. Now Bronwyn remembered Menke in the dream, standing beside Geoffrey Beene. Bronwyn never had to dance a step in the dream; Bram just swirled her to the music, across the dance floor. Bronwyn remembered the people murmuring as they watched Bronwyn and Prime Minister Abraham and the beautiful pair they made. When the music was over, Bram set her back to the floor; she lifted his hand and kissed the inside of his wrist. When she did that, Bram disappeared. It was one of those magical dreams, so real and so pleasant, that Bronwyn replayed it over and over.

She smiled at the boys with their rumpled pajamas and arms flung over dogs. What a full bed it was. She remembered how sleeping with Snooks Von Krinkles had allowed Bronwyn ten inches of space at the edge of the bed. Snooks would maneuver until she claimed as much bed as possible. At least Buster and Coco plopped and snored, nothing more. Bronwyn eased herself out of the bed, quietly coaxed both dogs out, and covered the boys.

Sir Winston's horses were an attraction, but Samuel seemed most intrigued when the vet visited. Paul fed and brushed the horses, and gave them unending carrots, apples, and sugar cubes. Bronwyn asked Paul's bodyguard if he might be allowed to ride a gentle horse and when they got the prime minister's permission, she let the bodyguard tell the thrilled boy. Astride the horse, Paul almost gagged from his trilling giggles, and his smile threatened to reach his ears.

Eimear and Roddy O'Neal came down, and Graeme and Angela Woods arrived the following day. They wanted to see Bronwyn and her happy band of boys and the show was worth it. No one had seen Bronwyn in such a happy state.

Even the boys' bodyguards were a bit sad when the visit drew to a close. They had looked in on the 'bed of lads and dogs' and were well aware how happy and carefree their two stunted charges had become with Bronwyn.

When they returned home, Samuel and Paul burbled tales of Bronwyn, the luscious food, the bed of dogs, the stable of horses, and the vet. When the boys asked if they could see Bronwyn soon, it was an easy thing for Bram to promise, 'yes'.

Eventually the laughter and stories trailed off and the boys reverted to their guarded, quiet selves, but each backward day made the prime minister anxious to arrange their next visit with Bronwyn.

CHAPTER NINE

THE BOSTON TERRIER
1999

*I*t had to be a Boston terrier. There were so many breeds to choose from, but Bronwyn knew Roddy O'Neal had a soft spot for Bostons. The O'Neals were buying a Malibu home close to Graeme's, hoping the warmer weather would be good for Roddy's health. The medical nudge was something Roddy had resisted until now, and Bronwyn was certain a puppy would be just the thing to make Roddy feel at home.

Eimear O'Neal was agreeable, so getting the puppy would be the pièce de résistance as they planned Roddy's birthday party. The two women cooked up the surprise at Sir Winston's and Bronwyn promised Eimear she'd get to Los Angeles and make the arrangements.

The restaurant Bronwyn chose was ideal, featuring an elegant back room and French doors leading to a Mediterranean style patio. Bronwyn dashed back and forth from Graeme Woods' place in Malibu. Jeeves accompanied her on her party excursions, but planned to be in Las Vegas during the party. He pleaded disinterest in the insular movie crowd, detesting the Hollywood lies…scripts were brilliant, every director fantastic, each writer a genius.

Jeeves didn't mind sorting through puppies though, and agreed with Bronwyn when she selected a tiny little gentleman, all black and white and dignified. They got the proper gear together, stashing the life-with-a-dog purchases at Graeme's place until the big reveal the next day. Jeeves said his goodbyes and Bronwyn happily played with the puppy.

The day of the party, Bronwyn brought the puppy along to meet the restaurant owner and he suggested if Bronwyn wanted to change into party clothes later, she could use his bathroom for privacy. She held the puppy up to the office security cameras, letting him have some 'face time', while the owner laughed. He regretted missing the party that evening; he'd like to see Roddy's face when he saw his puppy.

Before the party began, Bronwyn fondly patted the puppy and managed to sneak him outside for a short walk. She attempted to tie a big red satin bow around his neck, but he was squirmy. Luckily, Graeme stopped in to help and the puppy relaxed in his large, warm hands.

Graeme darted across the hall and his toothy grin was ear to ear as he motioned for Bronwyn to sneak in the back door. Roddy was seated at the head of the table and Bronwyn placed the puppy on the floor. A quiet descended upon the room, with murmurs and gestures. With no coaxing at all, the Boston terrier walked straight down the length of the room and over to Roddy's chair.

It was a preview of Roddy's old age…he was spluttering with a childlike rapture, gushing over the little puppy and crying emotional tears.

"Aye, look at the fella. Look at him everyone. Knew

me right away, he did. Came to Papa." Roddy held him high in the air, as if the pup were a prize, and then clutched him to his breast, stroking him with extreme love.

Eimear whispered to Roddy, telling who was responsible, and when he caught Bronwyn's eye he smiled with private knowledge. Of course Bronwyn had listened. Of course Bronwyn knew his heart's desire.

Bronwyn nibbled and listened to the conversation around her. Roddy was talking to his puppy, promptly named 'Jiggy'. He seemed to have no problem drinking and eating, talking and petting, all at the same time.

Graeme and Angela Woods were telling Bronwyn about their lunch at the Ivy.

"You have to try the warm anadama bread, Bronwyn, it's the bomb." She grinned at him. "And Angela's quite a fan of the Ivy gimlet, now. Aren't you darling? The mint leaves looked like a shrub. Imagine what we saw? This little tart gets out of her limo, poses for a papo shot in front of the patio, and then jumps back in the limo and speeds off. Didn't even have a proper meal. Just for the publicity. Cheeky bit o' fluff," Graeme guffawed.

While Bronwyn was laughing, someone familiar was greeting Roddy.

The hairs on the back of her neck stood up, as Oakley Forse walked down her side of the table, leaning in to whisper.

"Hello, Bronwyn."

It was an expensive move at the private party, bound to cost him the 'pre-vi' four million dollars.

Bronwyn glanced at Graeme and smiled weakly in the candlelight. It was evident Sir Winston hadn't told anyone about the Palm Springs shooting, not even Graeme. Oakley reached over the flowers and shook Graeme's hand, talking the usual guff. Then he leaned over Bronwyn and whispered, "I know about Graeme Woods."

She was stunned. There was no way he could know Graeme's secret. But if she wasn't blasé, Oakley Forse would know he'd made a lucky guess.

Oakley had moved to the end of the long table. She looked down at her plate, hoping he had gone, but he was in the back doorway. He beckoned her and Bronwyn reluctantly excused herself.

She thought Jeeves would flatten her if he'd been there, but Oakley had said the one thing she hoped she'd never hear. 'I know about Graeme Woods'. It seemed all her friends had secrets.

It was amazing how many things Bronwyn noticed as they crossed the hall. Earlier in the day, she hadn't registered the mini blinds covering the office and door windows. She hadn't noticed how far the office was from the kitchen area. But when Oakley Forse closed the door, Bronwyn realized she'd paid attention to the cameras. She knew exactly where they were positioned. Four of them. Four corners. Four angles. Four views. She guessed the 'Graeme' bit had been a ruse; Oakley Forse was intently observing.

Had she entered the room, all alone, because she didn't care? She honestly didn't know the answer. She would have run the other way if this was happening right after the Palm Springs shooting, but she'd made a connection with Oakley Forse when his mother was dying. Bronwyn trusted him just that much, to be standing in the office across from him. Her mind was peppered with self-doubt and uncertainty; she wondered what was going on in Oakley Forse's mind.

"Why haven't you built your house, Bronwyn?"

She noticed he barely moved his lips; he'd learned a lesson with the Palm Springs cameras.

"Why, Bronwyn?" He spoke with his head down, near the door. "I know the answer." Her heart skipped as he methodically removed his shoes and socks. She was stupid, stupid, stupid to be there.

With adrenalin lifting her fighting spirit, shock was sucking that spirit right out of her. She stared at him, waiting for his next move.

Oakley held his socks, slipped his bare feet into his patent loafers and then reached into his pocket. As Bronwyn watched, he dropped some coins into one sock, saying through unmoving lips, "Because there's never enough money, Bronwyn. No matter what a person has, it's never enough."

His smile was sad, and he rolled the sock in a ball and slipped it inside the other, knotting it.

"I've been here Bronwyn. Same as you. Boarding school for me. Hold onto the desk. It won't hurt much. Think of the house."

With her face smothered in a raw steak, Bronwyn realized how far she'd sunk.

She'd placed the call to Moss; a call she was ashamed to make. Following his instructions, she waited in the back of the kitchen for the arrival of Moss's security men and attorneys. She'd tell them about the four cameras of course. She'd remind them to secure all the footage and get her two hundred million dollars. No, two hundred and four million dollars. She'd earned it. Earned it with no defense, no fight, no reason to resist. He'd only smacked her face with a sock. Fifty times. A hundred times? That's all. No real harm done. Certainly nothing to be proud of, either.

She heard someone schmoozing in the kitchen – a voice she recognized from the movies. The actor, Keiran Kish. Bronwyn was tucked behind a pillar, near the chef's table.

"What do we have, here?"

Kish bent down and took the meat from her face. "Ouch. That's probably gonna puff up. Hey. I know you."

Kish seemed more intent on remembering where he'd seen her.

"I just saw Roddy. You caddied for him in that celebrity Pro-am in Wentworth. We were in the group behind you. Remember?"

Bronwyn gave him a half-smile, half-grimace.

"You're waiting for rescue, then?"

It occurred to Bronwyn that the steak must be doing its job. At least Keiran Kish didn't seem perturbed by the look of her.

"I take it Roddy doesn't know? Want me to tell him you're with me? Make your excuses?"

Bronwyn wondered why he didn't ask about the details of her porterhouse facial, but was relieved when he promised to be discreet and not worry Roddy.

While he was gone, she mused about a world where beatings were commonplace, money exchanged hands, and X-rays were available through back entrances of plastic surgeons' plush offices. She heard the Moss attorneys and security men coming through the kitchen. While she told security about the cameras, the attorneys regarded her puffy face.

Keiran Kish returned.

"Why not come with me? Whoever smacked you won't find you. I have a place in Holmby Hills and you can recuperate." He looked at the attorneys, at Bronwyn, and back again.

She knew both attorneys. They were with Moss after the Palm Springs shooting. One answered, "That could work. Better than a hotel. Ernest Rose caught a flight and should be here, shortly. Do you mind having an extra guest or two, Mr. Kish? I'll bring Bronwyn after her X-ray."

Seeing Jeeves, was the last thing Bronwyn wanted to do. The very last thing. She was ashamed. Ashamed she'd gotten into the situation, ashamed she'd offered no defense, ashamed she'd let Jeeves down.

Surprisingly, Jeeves didn't seem upset when he got to Kish's house. Instead, he patted the top of her head and returned with a cup of cocoa. Bronwyn was so relieved Jeeves didn't seem angry, that she actually fell asleep after sipping the cocoa.

The next morning she was slightly stiff and sore. She whispered to Jeeves that the beating hadn't amounted to much, but she was surprised when she looked in the mirror. Jeeves nodded and looked satisfied, murmuring about delicate skin.

He convinced her to sit outside by the pool. Jeeves was certain her spirits would lift if she felt the sun. A few pain killers, glossy magazines, and a pair of large sunglasses were all she'd need to get through the afternoon.

Jeeves watched as Keiran Kish dragged himself out of the house that afternoon, looking rumpled.

"Good morning, Mr. Kish," Jeeves said sarcastically.

A huge Great Dane, white with black spots the size of small plates, loped down the lawn and Bronwyn sat up, excited to see him.

"What's his name?" She asked Keiran, putting her arms around the dog's neck. The enormous animal lay down beside her, yet his head was still higher than the chaise.

"Herman. My girls named him."

Bronwyn tried to smile for the first time, but her mouth was resisting on the left side.

"Your daughters?"

"Monterey and Chelsea. Named them after where they were conceived. Brilliant, right?"

Neither Jeeves nor Bronwyn thought that was particularly 'brilliant'.

"Do they live here?"

"No, but you'll see them soon. They're always stopping over to see Herman."

Bronwyn tried to shake her shoulders a little, as if she were chuckling, since the smile wasn't working.

"Let's have a look at you."

When Keiran pulled her sunglasses off, Jeeves thought the look on Keiran Kish's face was priceless. Unprepared for the sight of Bronwyn, swollen and colored almost unrecognizably, Kish grimaced. He hadn't seen the aftermath of real violence before. He said to stay as long as they liked, promised to keep mum about the mysterious beating, and left for a location shoot later that afternoon.

Jeeves knew there was no location shoot for Kish. He'd weenied out of town at the mere look of Bronwyn. His destination was a secluded floating fishing lodge on British Columbia's coast. Keiran Kish had run away, stricken by discomfort.

Jeeves tried to persuade Bronwyn to recover in Carmel. After all, it was such a charming town, but she refused. So, under the guise of house-sitting, plant watering and dog walking, Jeeves and Bronwyn settled into Keiran Kish's house.

There was a problem with the Oakley Forse settlement. When the Forse attorneys viewed the camera footage, they questioned Bronwyn's lack of defense during the beating. They pointed out she'd entered the room willingly, even unlocking it, and let Moss know it wasn't a simple settlement, after all.

Moss was certain there would be no debate, once they saw Bronwyn. He had an ace in the hole with Bronwyn's fair skin. She was so pale that the bruising was a kaleidoscope of spreading swollen color and they had to meet soon, before she began to fade. It was a clinically detached tactic, but there was a fortune at stake. Bronwyn's face needed to be paraded now, while it was still a mess.

The meeting was on the eleventh floor of a Los Angeles high-rise. Jeeves stayed outside the closed door; the attorneys feared he'd be too volatile for the room.

This time, Bronwyn had to make an appearance. It was a go-for-the-gold meeting, with two hundred four million dollars on the line. Bronwyn wasn't happy about being there. She didn't want to see Oakley Forse, and the attorneys for both sides assumed she was fearful. She wore large, dark sunglasses and Moss promised she wouldn't have to speak. She doubted that. There was too much money at stake to sit on a throne of silence.

She kept her head down as Forse and his team entered the conference room. She was seated toward the far end of the table, with Moss attorneys flanking her and Moss across the table. An empty chair separated each team, with Oakley Forse seated on Bronwyn's side of the table, four seats away. The usual squad of attorneys surrounded Oakley.

They ran the security footage three times.

There were questions, but Bronwyn let her mind drift away. Oakley Forse had said to think of the house, and that's what she tried to do. She could hear Oakley tapping his pen. She wondered why someone didn't make him stop. Moss kept interrupting the proceedings, saying she didn't need to answer, but finally the silence on both sides seemed to indicate they were waiting for her. She focused.

"Sorry?"

"What made you leave the party? Why did you go to the office with Mr. Forse, a man you profess to be frightened of?"

"I don't profess to be frightened of Oakley Forse. He deliberately shot me. Then he put a gun to my head and tried to murder me."

Eyebrows rose on both sides of the table. She sounded stronger than they'd expected.

"Noted, Ms. McCall, but that's an issue that has been resolved. We're talking about this recent action. Why did you go to the office with Mr. Forse?"

"He mentioned a friend of mine. I thought something might be wrong."

"What did he say was wrong?"

"He didn't."

"Then, why did you assume 'something was wrong'?"

"By his tone and implication."

"I see. Who was the friend?"

"He didn't say."

"I'm sorry. He didn't say?"

"No."

"What exactly did he say?"

"I'm not the one who did something wrong. I don't know why I'm answering questions."

"For clarification, Ms. McCall. We're all trying to understand what transpired. Now, what did Mr. Forse say to you? Exactly."

"I'd planned the party with Eimear O'Neal and he wasn't on the guest list. As soon as I saw Oakley Forse, I was concerned. When he mentioned a friend of mine might be in trouble, I thought it must be legitimate, or why would he come into the room when he saw I was there?"

"You say you don't know the name of the friend?"

Bronwyn shook her head.

"Sorry, Ms. McCall. For the record. You don't know the friend's name?"

"No."

"Perhaps we can ask Mr. Forse for the friend's name. Mr. Mastrofrancesco?" Moss shrugged.

Oakley Forse spoke for the first time. "I told Ms. McCall a friend of hers was in trouble."

"And what friend was that?"

"I didn't say."

"I see."

"Ms. McCall. We've reviewed the security footage and it appears you made no effort to defend yourself. In fact, we see no indication that you spoke, throughout the incident. Why not cry out for help? Ask him to stop? Were you complicit?"

"Complicit?" she asked with astonishment. She heard the tap, tap, tapping of the pen and then it stopped. She looked over.

Oakley rose from his chair. She knew the rangy movements of his long arms and legs. She kept her head down, looking at her hands, not wanting to make eye contact while he poured himself a glass of water at a corner table.

He made his return trip the other way around the table. She shivered.

"I don't believe she's even injured. I think this is all a ruse to extort money from me. Take the sunglasses off and you'll see it's all a good makeup job."

When Oakley Forse rounded the end of the table, Bronwyn took her sunglasses off, revealing bruises of olive green, eggplant, and deep purple.

In an instant, Oakley spat upon her face, rubbing her cheek so forcefully with his white handkerchief that Bronwyn fell off the chair, fainting from the shock of the pain. Jeeves heard the disturbance and flung open the door just in time to see Moss flying over the table, leaping on Oakley Forse, while coffee cups flew across overturned chairs and onto the floor.

Jeeves quickly restrained Moss and the only casualty besides a briefly unconscious Bronwyn, was the effort to derail the two hundred four million dollar payment. Even Oakley Forse's attorneys were appalled at his behavior.

Accusations were shouted from all sides, and results from an HIV test were demanded from his attorneys, as well as Bronwyn's. No one knew if Oakley Forse's saliva might have compromised them, and no one was willing to risk it.

Bronwyn wasn't worried, though. She recognized a theatrical scene shift when she saw it. She was surprised so many industry attorneys had missed the dramatic change in dynamics. The issue of complicity was dead in the water.

It was when they returned to Holmby Hills, weary but victorious, that Bronwyn handed Jeeves a note, stating 'I'm not talking for awhile.' She continued to pass notes, although Jeeves heard her talking to Herman the Great Dane. That reassured him. If Bronwyn needed silence, he'd let her have it. He supposed adding two hundred four million dollars to her largely untapped hundred million would take the wind out of anyone's sails.

Sleeping didn't come easily to Bronwyn. Thoughts of the beating and then the meeting kept replaying in her head. At the conference table, she'd been thinking about Maine and her house, while the attorneys argued. But now a different thought stabbed at her. She and Oakley Forse weren't pen pals. Other than meeting at the hospital as his mother lay dying, they'd never spoken nor written. Why did he ask about her home?

Before the meeting, Bronwyn would lie awake and imagine how she could have, how she should have, avoided the beating. She focused on the weighted sock, landing again and again, so many times that the sting became a song, as if it would never stop. It was only after the meeting that she began to replay it all; from Oakley leaning in at the birthday table, to the office, to his socks. She remembered. When he took his socks off, Oakley was wearing his monitoring bracelet, just as he was supposed to do. He rose, his pant legs dropped to his patent loafers, but she had seen it. The bracelet.

She pondered why she had to keep one step ahead of Jeeves. She knew in her heart that Jeeves would never hurt her; really hurt her. And if she breathed even a word of her doubt to Moss or the prime minister, she was certain removing Jeeves from her life would mean removing Jeeves from his.

Bronwyn was a silent workhorse going through her design files, sent from New York. She made numerous sketches and site diagrams, handing Jeeves notes requesting graph paper and new sketch pads, as the need arose.

Moss arranged for a cook, but Bronwyn's appetite was

minimal. Sometimes Jeeves made a run to Pink's, amusing Bronwyn with his Guadalajara Dog with relish, onions, tomatoes, and sour cream. She still opted for a plain hot dog, no matter how enthusiastic the normally sullen Jeeves could become. The next time he tried wafting a Bacon Burrito Dog under her nose, and when he had a Pastrami Reuben Dog with sauerkraut, she feigned running from the room. When he presented her with the Harry Potter Dog, with Polish sausage, grilled onions, grilled mushrooms, bacon, and nacho cheese, she wrote with all sincerity, 'I don't get it. What's Harry Potter, about that?' She still enjoyed sitting with him, though. Jeeves was so utterly human when he was enjoying food.

One afternoon, Bronwyn handed Jeeves a note, and as Jeeves reached for it, she held on, making him read it from her hand. It said *'Do I need to worry about Oakley Forse hurting me again?'* Her eyes challenged him, but he wouldn't look at her. Jeeves simply said, 'No, Miss' before returning to the pool.

Bronwyn called Moss; she needed reassurance about all that money. It seemed too much like a dream. Moss sent Zuleika Zannini, Grace Cloud, and a Swiss banker, hoping to put Bronwyn's doubts to rest. He seriously considered finding a shrink, specializing in 'acquiring obscene wealth', but Jeeves said Bronwyn was finally making plans for Maine.

Zuleika explained her expertise in global asset management, tax law, and foundations. The Swiss banker calmly detailed her astounding financials, and Grace was well-prepared to handle day-to-day expenditures and construction expenses whenever Bronwyn was ready.

Kish's girls, Chelsea and Monterey, stopped often,

enjoying Bronwyn's company and filling her in on the young Hollywood world of seven and eight year olds. They were exceptionally pretty girls, composed for their age, and chatterboxes. Chelsea was softer and more vulnerable; Monterey more worldly.

Keiran Kish called and enjoyed Bronwyn's updates about Monterey and Chelsea. He agreed the girls could see New York with Bronwyn, and they made plans for a NY weekend in late summer, revving the girls up about 'Frr-rozen' Hot Chocolate at Serendipity and toy shopping at FAO Schwartz.

Eventually, Bronwyn ended her silence with Jeeves, with the pronouncement, "I think we're ready to build in Maine."

She was concerned what Menke would think about the money she'd be spending. Jeeves suggested she simply say it was an inheritance. The prime minister was well aware of the source of her fabulous wealth; Moss had told him the truth.

Satisfied, Bronwyn told Jeeves she was going through with the nine hole golf course out of town, adding a clubhouse and several homes around the course.

"You're not suggesting we live at the golf course, Miss?"

"No, Jeeves. But you'll enjoy the course and clubhouse. Gus Townsend recommended the school district's business manager, Margo Storey, and I've hired her to oversee my local foundation."

Jeeves noticed how matter-of-factly Bronwyn was discussing her plans. It was obvious she'd made great strides in embracing her wealth. More than he'd imagined.

"Her daughter Laura has an MBA and she's done a retail study; a wish list for businesses. You know how much we enjoy towns, right?" Her inquiry didn't seem to require a response, but he nodded enthusiastically.

"I have plans for the estate homes, Jeeves. And big plans for the Factory. My problem is the construction site manager. I know who I want, but it's going to take some convincing."

"Why is that, Miss?"

Bronwyn filled Jeeves in. Alex Ozwald King was the man she wanted for the job. His credentials were precisely varied enough and he had expertise to spare, but he'd left the construction field. He'd lost a man in a high-rise accident, and hadn't recovered. Apparently he was spending his days on the beach, unable to work, unwilling to work, uninterested in work.

"So, first we're going to Pittsburgh and then we'll stop in New York to see Zuleika and Jean Luc. Eat a few nice meals and then head out to the Hamptons. It's time to meet Alex Ozwald King."

Pittsburgh was 'on the way' to New York, so Bronwyn couldn't resist a stopover in Sewickley. She wanted to observe the town and take in the lovely old homes before she committed to her projects.

Jeeves and Bronwyn walked to The Sewickley Café's patio, where outdoor heaters were blasting away, and Bronwyn noticed the chandeliers hanging from the tent.

Jeeves ordered a lobster club sandwich, saying it was a nod to their Maine future. While they ate, it was impossible not to overhear the conversation from the two other diners braving the cold.

"Oh, Nan. You know I love your brother. More than anything. But he won't let me help."

"He's depressed, Laura. He's never lost a patient before. Not like that. And it's not just the malpractice suit, it's his reputation. He thinks everyone expects Peter Larchmont to be perfect. He expected to be perfect. He just can't handle it right now."

Bronwyn thought she might know their Peter Larchmont. When she was young, she'd gone to Quaker Valley games and Peter Larchmont had been the star quarterback.

"He's turned away from me, Nan. It's not just the separation. I'm afraid he's not going to practice medicine anymore."

Bronwyn heard a gasp and the scraping of a chair. "I am so sorry, Laura. I'm late. I've got to get back to the hospital. Call me tonight. Please? Call me tonight."

Bronwyn looked at Jeeves. She wasn't certain what silent message they were conveying to each other. He could have been nodding affirmation to anything...should they have dinner at Ruth's Chris Steakhouse before leaving... should they stay an extra day...should they have dessert inside, where it was warmer. But in fact, his nod was followed by, "Go ahead, Miss. Have a word with her," and they were in sync.

Before the day was done, she'd hired Peter Larchmont as her private physician. He agreed to move to Maine, with the promise of a huge Sewickley-style home on Bronwyn's new golf course. Jeeves suspected the doctor would be highly paid and well rewarded for very little work. Normally he'd resent Dr. Larchmont's good fortune, but Jeeves thought it a wise move, a preventive measure. Perhaps if they had a doctor of their own, their days of shootings, dramatic rescues, and makeshift vet surgery would be over.

❧

In New York, they enjoyed dining wherever Jean Luc Zannini guided them, and Bronwyn felt more comfortable about the money. As a test, she'd asked Zuleika to donate substantial sums to an animal rescue group and an animal sanctuary. Bronwyn half expected the checks would bounce, but Zuleika walked her through the lightning path of money infusion, placing a call to both groups so Bronwyn could hear the rewarding tinkle of happy receivers. Bronwyn began to believe.

Two days before their Hamptons visit, Jean Luc arrived late to their lunch.

"I am so sorry. It's an issue I'm dealing with. The place on Broome Street."

They placed their orders and Jean Luc fumed. "My chef is such a fine gentleman. So proper, competent. Not the visionary that Laurent is, but a dream. Now, he's become a total disaster."

Jean Luc shook his head and Zuleika's lips were drawn to a fine line.

"Are you saying you're going to fire him?" Bronwyn asked.

"It's not my wish, but there's no other option. I have been far too kind."

Zuleika filled them in. "You see, Edgar rides the subway from Brooklyn. He was mugged two months ago, and I understand his fear. I do, truly. But, he misses work. He's frightened. I've seen it in his eyes and it's getting worse."

"Old fool," Jean Luc muttered, under his breath. Then, aware Bronwyn was frowning, he added defensively, "It's really best that he just stay home."

Jeeves noticed Bronwyn picking at her food.

"He's a good chef?"

"Oh, yes. It will be a loss. But, I am too soft. The time has come."

In a requiem of sorts, Zuleika and Jean Luc expounded on the culinary delights created by Edgar Davis, with each remembering yet another high point.

After their lunch, Bronwyn huddled with Zuleika back in the Mastrofrancesco offices. It was Zuleika's first glimpse at Bronwyn's ability to plot to perfection.

The next morning, Bronwyn's driver took her, not to Brooklyn to see Edgar Davis, but to a restaurant on the Upper East Side. She'd left Jeeves back at the hotel.

Laurent Davis was the sous chef at Jean Luc Zannini's newest restaurant and in line for promotion to chef. Zuleika had been surprised when Bronwyn announced her plan to pluck him for herself, but Zuleika recognized it as a power move, to test Zuleika's loyalty and punish Jean Luc.

Laurent Davis was completely gray at twenty seven, and his stoic demeanor made him seem older. He was wearing chalk-striped chef pants and a blindingly white double breasted chef jacket. Bronwyn sat across from him in his empty restaurant. He listened with dubious interest.

"Why come to me? Why not just ask my grandfather?"

"Because I want all of you."

"All of us? Who do you mean, Miss McCall?"

"Bronwyn. Please. Bronwyn. I want your grandfather and grandmother, your dad and your mother. And, you."

"Well, I'm afraid you're not getting me, Bronwyn," he said with an incredulous laugh. "No offense, but it's just your home. Just you. You don't have a family, it's way off in the future, and you don't need a sous chef. But, I think it's great you're considering Granddad as your chef. I don't know if he'd be interested, but he's a great chef."

Bronwyn didn't respond. Laurent glanced around the darkened restaurant, wondering if he'd offended her.

"Here's the thing, Laurent. I want you. I've come into an obscene amount of money, so anything we plan, anything we ever plan, there's enough money. So, let's not even think about how you and your family will live, and if you'll have enough money in your lives. You will. It's that simple. Let's not talk about that.

"I've bought a three story bank building, and it will be converted to an arts center with galleries, classrooms, music rooms, and a state-of-the-art kitchen. That kitchen will be a culinary classroom and a catering center. I'd like you to teach there, or at least help staff it. I think organic food, youth gardening, food-based fundraising can be promoted there. I believe good food travels the shortest possible distance between farm and table and it promotes a healthy local economy. Don't you?"

Laurent nodded, with his head cocked slightly to one side.

"Your family will live on my estate. Your grandparents will be over by the Factory, closer to me. It used to be the Bayside Blanket and Toboggan Company, and it's a beauty. I have a rough drawing of the houses I've planned for you and your parents. See, they're on the other side of the estate, on a small private street. This is your place and this is your parents'. Here's the gate and the new security gatehouse in front of the Factory. All behind a stone wall."

"But, you haven't spoken to my parents, or my grandparents?"

"No. I came to you first."

"Because you thought I'd help you talk them into it."

"Laurent, I wouldn't want to talk anyone into anything. I'm twenty seven years old, the same as you. I've never had a home. I mean, I haven't had a home since I was eight years old. I might as well tell you I was an orphan at eight. I don't want your sympathy. I want you to understand that I have yearned for a home of my own since I was eight years old. Now I have millions of dollars and I can make that happen. You didn't realize it, but the moment I walked through that door, your world shifted. Like the plates of the earth, there was a shift. And, instead of a bad thing, it's a good thing.

"I know your grandfather is afraid. I know that fear. I really do. I want to offer him my arm, and drag him to safety. And, your mom."

Laurent sat silently and Bronwyn sipped her water. They exchanged tentative smiles and Laurent found he liked Bronwyn McCall. He couldn't buy into her scheme, but he liked her.

With a lighthearted tone, she began again. "Did I tell you my father planned to open a restaurant? My parents went to France with my grandparents and they spent weeks, scouting restaurants and cafes. Restaurants meant a lot to my dad, well, to my parents really, and they mean a lot to me. My house will be the last one built, but it will have a private club attached, and three connecting kitchens – one for my house, a baking kitchen and a commercial kitchen for the club. I have friends who know good food, so you wondered if all the cooking would be done for me. Not always. Sometimes there'll be guests. And, I want the retirement home in town to have upgraded food facilities and you could be an adviser for that."

"You have big plans."

"I figure it will take three years for everything to be in place."

"So, you're not asking any of us to decide, for a few years?"

Bronwyn smiled. Laurent had said 'any of us', so perhaps he was closer to boarding than he realized.

"It's now. The decision is now. The salary begins now. I need suggestions for kitchen design, and things will be hectic because there's so much building to be done at the estate and in town. But I'll build your house and your parents' house right away. And your grandparents can stay with your folks till their home is built onto the Factory."

"Why do you want my parents?"

"From what I understand, your dad is a maintenance worker at a school. I need a maintenance man. And, Zuleika says he's a really nice guy. That's important to me."

"But, you haven't met him."

Bronwyn shrugged.

"So, what if you meet him and you don't like him? You'll withdraw the offer?"

"That's not me. If we shake hands, it's a done deal. For life."

Laurent looked skeptical. "Does Jean Luc Zannini know you're here?"

"No."

"I don't think he'd like it. In fact, there'll be hell to pay. And, he'll find out. You just said you talked to Zuleika about this whole thing."

Unperturbed, Bronwyn looked blankly at him.

"Well, Bronwyn, you've given me a lot to think about, but I like it here. I like living in Brooklyn and I like my job. I'm happy."

A smile snuck across Bronwyn's face and she bent her head back, gazing at the walls and up to the ceiling.

"I'm glad for you."

Laurent's words seemed to echo a little; his pronounce-ment of happiness surprised even himself. He was angry with Jean Luc Zannini; the boss owed his grandfather more respect, more compassion. Laurent wasn't even certain he could stay with Jean Luc's group, disgusted with their in-fighting. The hints they might promote him to chef meant that Chef Robert would lose his job, and they just had a baby.

"Why did you come to me first, Bronwyn? It's my grandfather you really want."

"You're the key."

"I don't understand."

"If I don't have you, I don't have your mom. If I don't have your mother, I don't have your dad. Without them, I don't have your grandparents. You all love each other. You're family. I understand that, better than you think."

Laurent became fidgety in his chair and Bronwyn welcomed the response. She had wondered what it would be like, populating her estate. Apparently some fidgeting would be expected before they said 'yes'.

Bronwyn's voice took on a different tone. Laurent noticed she was slightly melodious, as if she was irresistibly shaping each word into something special. It wasn't a matter of enunciation. It was more like she'd relaxed and embraced her thoughts so dreamily that they blossomed into what words should be. "Look here, Laurent. See this house of yours? It's linked by two wings, to your parent's house. They're integral walkways, and they create a courtyard of greenery between your homes with a retracting solar panel. Sunshine and fresh air on nice days without leaving the house, without setting foot on the porches." Laurent realized Bronwyn knew his mother was agoraphobic. "There's nothing I won't do, to make your home perfect for you. I hope you'll feel independent and content in your own home, but this will only work if I link you to your family with walkways."

Laurent was impressed. How long had she been planning this, he wondered. There was no way he'd ever believe it had only been one night.

"What will it take, Laurent? I understand you have a good life here, but we'll have an organic garden, maybe a henhouse. Uncork your Maine imagination. Cranberries and blueberries, crab and lobster and local producers. I know you'll find the best and with your input, we can support dairies and farms. Maybe you'll want your own restaurant. That's possible. And, maybe you'll want to write a cookbook. That's possible. What do you want?"

"A boat?"

Zuleika had to admit that she'd underestimated Bronwyn. She caught all the Davis family in her net, and Zuleika was moving significant money into all of their accounts. They were now officially part of Bronwyn's estate. She was right about Bronwyn and her husband, Jean Luc. He was stunned Bronwyn would take the old man off his hands, while costing him the visionary talent of Laurent. Bronwyn's calculation paid off with Laurent; he must have encouraged her to poach Katrin Karlsson as her pastry chef. Zuleika listened half-heartedly as Jean Luc went on and on, wringing his hands and ranting with histrionics. It was an impressive coup, despite the overplayed agony of her Jean Luc.

CHAPTER TEN

ALEX OZWALD KING

Finding three carrots with tops seemed an odd necessity, but Bronwyn insisted she needed them before meeting with Alex Ozwald King.

King wasn't aware they'd be meeting. Bronwyn had called, and he'd declined. Then Jeeves followed him to a diner where he conveyed Bronwyn's respectful request to meet. It didn't surprise Jeeves when Alex Ozwald King would have none of it. Jeeves knew the look of men who'd given up. He doubted anything would bring the man back to the surface; not after the front page and 'News at Six' reporting of a fatal high-rise accident. Lawsuits were directed at the building conglomerate, but King was a gentleman at heart and was destroyed by the mess. It had been over two years. Time enough. The man was rot.

Jeeves knew where Alex Ozwald King would be. He was a man with a schedule. A cup of coffee at 6:45 AM, followed by a nice sit at the beach. His slight British accent was largely unvoiced in the midst of his silent days. Maybe a walk along the water before a visit to the public loo. A take-away bite to eat and back to the beach for scribbling in a notebook or pondering. Visit the local tavern for wings and a pint. Mosey back to his messy room when darkness fell. Nothing of interest there except the smell of surrender.

It was admirable how focused Bronwyn could be. She sat in the car and asked Jeeves if he'd mind watching her satchel. He expected her to haul out a huge stack of folders, flipping through plans that might intrigue the man. Instead, she lightly tapped Jeeves' knee, clasped her three carrots with green tops, opened the car door, and marched through the sand.

Jeeves braced himself. If the man was a bolter, Jeeves planned to nab him, but Alex Ozwald King seemed a gazelle. Tall and lanky, King looked the natural athlete, even when he'd taken his bar stool. Bronwyn asked Jeeves for a description so she'd approach the right man, but the beach would be nearly deserted at 7 AM. He described King's curly black hair and café au lait skin, courtesy of his Jamaican grandmother. He warned her that King would undoubtedly cut her off with disinterest. Jeeves glanced at his watch and made a self-bet as to how long she could ride the bull. Jeeves decided she wouldn't last three minutes.

At first, Jeeves had his hand on the car door. One never knew with desperate men; King might lash out at Bronwyn. But as the ten minute mark passed, Jeeves settled in to watch.

Alex Ozwald King remained seated in his folding chair. Bronwyn made a half circle in the sand, moving to his left and right as she talked. At one point, Bronwyn seemed to collapse on the sand, but Jeeves decided it was for effect. She was kneeling before King, imploring him. Jeeves knew the importance she placed on landing him to head her construction. There was no point in trying to dissuade her.

She made a semi-circle trough in front of the webbed chair and Jeeves thought how simple it would be to merely interview a dozen top men who would beg for the job. She was setting herself up for failure. Nothing was going to bring Alex Ozwald King back from the brink.

Glancing at his watch, Jeeves saw twenty five minutes had elapsed.

From her pocket, Bronwyn extracted a pointer, pulling it into an impressive length. She turned her back on King, and to his credit, he leaned forward in his chair. Bronwyn drew shapes in a ten foot wide area. She stepped behind them and turned.

Jeeves tried to read her lips, and then judge her body language. She was speaking and then allowing time for absorption. She walked from side to side, with the sand drawings between them. She'd stab her pointer into the sand, and once Jeeves saw her laugh. How astounding. Quick as could be, Bronwyn dashed around the sand, scraping it into a rough smoothness with her bare feet.

Bronwyn seemed more relaxed, making fresh diagrams in the sand, but now she faced King. Jeeves decided she wasn't getting anywhere, really getting anywhere, until such time as King got off his webbed throne. That would tell the tale.

She drew a large oval and carefully leaned over it, drawing other shapes within it. King sat back while Bronwyn retracted her pointer, put it in her pants pocket, and stood before him, hands on hips. It seemed she was waiting, but Jeeves could see King's head moving slightly; probably speaking. Bronwyn had never set the carrots down, clutching them in her left hand. Now she dangled one in her right hand and handed it to King. They seemed to be having a give and take, and Bronwyn gave him the second carrot. She turned and faced the ocean. It was as obvious to Jeeves, as it was to her, that Alex Ozwald King was connected to Bronwyn at that moment, as if they were both grasping the final carrot.

Bronwyn seemed relaxed looking out to sea, as if King wasn't even there. Jeeves watched her shoulders rise and knew she'd taken a deep breath. He reminded himself he must urge her to do that more often. She was a shallow breath dweller and it simply wasn't healthy. When she turned around, she had a peaceful countenance. Bronwyn handed the final carrot to Alex Ozwald King and this time, Jeeves saw exactly what she said. *Freedom.*

Bronwyn knew it would niggle at Jeeves, not knowing why she had carrots, and more importantly, how she'd convinced Alex Oz King to take total control of her entire construction project. She waited for Jeeves to ask, suspecting he was too proud to do so. Perhaps he'd ask Alex Oz King, she thought. Then she decided, probably not.

In fact, she'd drawn King a rough diagram of the Factory and estate homes. Then, she evened the sand to show him the land she was reserving for him and his two million dollar home. In the valley. That was the first carrot. He seemed interested. Engaged. He suggested his salary be a million dollars and she insisted on two. That was the second carrot. Bronwyn assured King he would never have to work again, after devoting three years to her projects. He'd have his home, he'd have money, and Jeeves was correct; he'd have *freedom.*

Alex Ozwald King might tell his friends and family

that he'd been lured by carrots, but he was ready to join Bronwyn on her quest when she'd hit her knees. He saw the same emptiness and despair he knew so well, but when she spoke of her hopes and dreams, he was drawn in. She could have saved her carrots. But he was no fool. Three carrots it was.

Chapter Eleven

The Estate

"I'm sensing a theme, Miss."

Bronwyn laughed and stepped onto the deck. Her motel room was clean and neat, but the location was the peachy part, with the town across the water and the lobster pound to her right. The dock below was studded with fancy powerboats, fishing vessels, and yachts anchored nearby. She and Jeeves enjoyed walking around the docks and finger piers, pretending which boats were theirs. Somehow the reality that she could purchase any boat didn't register with Bronwyn. And although it never escaped Jeeves, he played the 'this would be mine' game with her.

She watched the staff through the dining room windows, setting up for dinner. The food was the best part of the motel, and Bronwyn could hardly wait for creamy lobster bisque and chunks of lobster sauté. She kept her eye on the tablecloth progress, and explained, "I'm giving people a new start. We're grateful, aren't we? For our new lives?"

Jeeves didn't reply.

"I want people who'll appreciate the estate, so they'll stay."

"What if we prefer they go, Miss? Perhaps they'll be bone idle."

"I'm trusting that the right people are falling into my lap."

"Really, Miss. I have grave doubts about Matthew Brodie's wife. I'm afraid she has a larger personality than you've anticipated."

Bronwyn considered his opinion. Jeeves noisily flapped open the New York Times and she pretended to look at a magazine.

The day before, despite the chilly April weather, she'd finally gone on a seal spotting cruise. They bought tickets and waited for boarding time. Bronwyn sat beside a bespectacled young man with a handsome Scottish terrier named Coolidge. As Bronwyn patted the Scottie, admiring his stately beard, she noticed his master looked forlorn. Apparently they'd been turned away from the cruise, even though he'd been allowed to board with the dog the previous year.

Jeeves enjoyed watching as Bronwyn bought all the unsold tickets and tipped the ticket master fifty dollars. Matthew Brodie couldn't thank her enough. As the boat pulled away from the dock, Bronwyn sat atop with Coolidge warmly sandwiched between her and Matthew. She admired the dog's solid body, remarking on his keen expression. Jeeves handed them blankets and went below.

It turned out that Matthew had more disappointments in life than just having Coolidge rejected from the boat. He'd been director of a university computer department until three months ago; the university outsourced it, and he was having trouble adjusting. Bronwyn thought he might be in his late twenties, but Matthew was a surprisingly boyish looking forty three, with twenty years at the university. She tucked her blanket around Coolidge, and dashed down below to ask Jeeves about their computer and security requirements. Jeeves suggested they would be wise to conduct interviews, but Bronwyn would have none of it. If Matthew Brodie managed a university department, she was confident he could handle whatever needs Jeeves might have. She suggested he interview Matthew while she had a cup of coffee.

Matthew waxed on about his gone-up-in-smoke career, until Jeeves steered him into fact and achievement. Jeeves found Matthew to be knowledgeable, but more importantly, keen to learn new technologies. It was obvious he missed the daily opportunities to adapt to changing technologies and use his inventiveness. Matthew promised his resume showed skill levels in networking, software, operations, helpdesk, and communications; happily, it was apparent Matthew was capable not only with computers, but also Wi-Fi, RF engineering, and bespoke systems. Jeeves asked Matthew what he'd think of a tech training period in London and Hampshire.

Bronwyn rejoined them on the top deck and Matthew was gaga with excitement. But, as much as Matthew loved Maine, his wife was intent on relocating to Florida. When he mentioned Linda Brodie, Bronwyn sensed fear in Matthew's voice and realized Linda wore the pants in the family. Bronwyn made plans to meet Linda that evening, but first sussed out her background. Matthew said she'd rather entertain, make crafts, or clean house with a vengeance, than teach her sixth and seventh graders family consumer science.

It hadn't taken much, really. Matthew made a commitment, contingent upon Linda's approval.

If Matthew Brodie looked like a kid, his wife looked like his mother, although they were only three years apart. No wonder she was bossy, Bronwyn thought. The four met for dessert at the motel restaurant, and Bronwyn found Linda to be engaging, but intense. Shorter and larger than Matthew, she had glossy hair, worn in a bob. Bronwyn noticed her bangs shrinking as the evening wore on. Linda's flushed face may have been from the wine, but a sheen of perspiration encouraged a bouncy curl in her bangs, revealing brighter and brighter eyes. Linda had a cackling laugh, slapped the table too much, and nudged Matthew too forcefully.

Bronwyn invited her upstairs, leaving Matthew with Jeeves.

"I love your dog. Coolidge."

"Isn't he great? He doesn't look mischievous, but he is."

"You're right. He looks like a stately Southern colonel."

Linda laughed and Bronwyn was glad the cackle seemed to be gone.

"Matthew says you enjoy crafts and cleaning house?"

Linda looked surprised, then answered, "I suppose I do."

"What crafts have you done?"

Linda relished describing her Christmas edibles, like truffles in organza gift bags, spicy cashews and pistachios in cornucopias, and glasses of cranberry ginger orange conserve in jelly jars with lacy white stencils.

"They sound beautiful."

"Well, I think they were. At least people seemed to like them. And my gingerbread houses had cranberry wreaths on the doors, with dark green icing walls, white shutters, and the roofs were done in shredded wheat, like thatched cottages. Then I sprinkled white powdered sugar on top, like snow, and added coconut on the base, for snow flakes."

Bronwyn thought they sounded enchanting. "What else have you done?"

"I made a pumpkin train along our porch steps, with holes cut for windows and punches to let the light shine through. I decorate our apartment for all the holidays."

"Tell me about your cleaning. You enjoy doing your own? You've thought about it as a business?"

"I've always imagined it could be a fall-back job someday, but I'm not sure I'm up for people's dirty homes."

"You know I'm considering Matthew as a computer expert on my estate. It's just a mile or so from here, and construction is starting. We're building several homes and converting an old Factory. Maybe you'd want to be the Household Manager for the estate."

Linda's eyes gleamed.

"It's a management job. Ideally, I'd like you to clean my house and Ernest Rose's. We'll have a day staff. Maybe twelve workers.

"You and Matthew would live in the Factory. One third of the second floor will be for my pastry chef." Linda's eyes widened when Bronwyn mentioned 'pastry chef'. "The rest of the floor is yours, with water views. I'm doing the interiors in a lodge style."

Linda wrinkled her nose.

"I'm definitely interested, Bronwyn. But, I really don't think western sounds like me."

"Actually, that's firm. I have some pictures."

Linda waited while Bronwyn sifted through files. She showed Linda a clipping of an enormous stone fireplace two stories high with a long wooden mantle, surrounded by leather furniture, trestle tables, pegged floors, exposed ceiling beams, a horn chandelier, and a grand wooden staircase leading to an upper level with balconies.

"Upstairs you'll have offices, a media room, his and hers dressing rooms like these…"

Linda touched Bronwyn's forearm and murmured, "His and hers bedrooms."

Bronwyn nodded, without missing a beat.

"Your kitchen and dining room will be lodge style, but you'll have every appliance you'd want. Gourmet. Coolidge will have a little room of his own upstairs, and grass planted on the balcony so you won't have to take him downstairs. And look at this little nook for him in the kitchen. His own private retreat."

Linda was about to speak when Bronwyn suggested, "This is what might interest you." She had a separate stack of clippings and showed Linda a colorful cottage exterior of sage green with pale lavender and aqua trim, and a picket fence and gate, beneath a rose covered arbor. "You'd have a retreat, like this. An Island House, just for you; although you and Matthew would stay there while your Factory home is built."

Bronwyn dropped another picture on the pile. It showed a white beadboard kitchen with white cabinets and glass fronts; pastel mixing bowls and an old fashioned milk shake mixer on shelves. A long counter separated the kitchen from the dining area with a bolster clipped to the beadboard counter, over an equally long bench at the dining table. Additional slip-covered chairs sat around the cheery space. Linda was tempted to greedily snatch the whole pile of photos from Bronwyn's hands.

A loft bedroom was simply misty, with white sheers drifting from a metal four-poster dressed in white linens, with a weathered armoire.

"This could be your work area." The photo revealed little white lights strung around the ceiling. A painted table sported a pink panel inset, with a shell-shaped tea service. An intriguing white iron light fixture dropped from a chain.

The last two pictures showed a white living room with red gingham accents, pine wreaths on the windows tied with red ribbons, red rolls of wrapping paper in brick red metal baskets, and tea-stained snowmen everywhere; then flag buntings of Old Glory, draped across a porch and railings. Bronwyn hadn't forgotten Linda's holiday ardor.

"We can add an art studio with tons of windows for natural light."

Linda sifted through the pictures.

"What do you think, Linda?"

She giggled, nonplussed. "How could you know how perfect this is? You've just met us, today. It's amazing. And, you're right. Matthew would love the Western stuff. And a place of my own. I can't believe it. I can do my crafts there, and paint."

Bronwyn smiled at her. "It's settled then? You're interested."

Linda enfolded Bronwyn in her cushy embrace.

"No kidding," she said gleefully.

The following morning, Bronwyn awakened from a good night's sleep, whereas both Linda and Matthew had been tossing and turning and giggling with astonishment over their good fortune. However, as the dawn grew bright, the Brodies grew concerned. It defied logic that Bronwyn Dai McCall was serious.

Their phone rang and Bronwyn invited Linda to see the estate, while Jeeves arranged a conference call for Matthew and some people in London.

Linda expected to see inside the Factory, but Bronwyn chose to walk the grounds. They ventured along a hillside that meandered gently to a valley. Bronwyn walked to the edge of the rocks and asked Linda to turn around. The Factory was an imposing structure. Bronwyn explained how balconies would run the entire length. Linda realized how high the ceilings must be, as the windows were so tall.

"Take a look at the second level of windows. That'll be your home. We'll build the balcony out, ten feet or so. Over there, to the right, we'll have two levels of balconies. The lower one with a grilling area and Coolidge's little outdoor retreat on top of it.

"The Factory's third floor is for guests, so it'll require maintenance cleaning," Bronwyn gestured to the factory.

"A living area runs the length of the third floor, with five bedrooms to the left, street side; then three suites on the waterside."

"You expect the third floor will get a lot of use, Bronwyn?"

"Maybe not. I don't know. But, it'll be great fun whenever people are there, don't you think?"

"I'd be up there all the time."

"I saved the best for last. I'm putting in an authentic soda fountain."

"Pinch me."

"I feel like that, too. How do you feel about hanging out?"

Linda hesitated. "You mean killing time?"

Bronwyn laughed. "No, I mean clothes. Do you ever hang on a line, rather than use a dryer?"

Linda's smile was wide. "You bet."

"Turn around. This is where your Island House will be, close to the water. What do you think?"

They spent several minutes pacing off the rooms Bronwyn envisioned, as well as the picket fence.

After a quick peek at the Secret Garden, with plenty of space for clothes lines, the women crossed the front of the estate.

"There'll be a knot garden here, in the turnaround; a three level security gatehouse here. The security man is so sweet. Van Tsang. He thinks he'll be living in the gatehouse and he will. For awhile. But, I'm surprising him with a beautiful home, over there."

Bronwyn walked to the head of King Street, with her back to the stone wall.

"First is Jen and Ken Cotton's house. They have a little boy, Augie; he's five. She's a florist and Ken is in training to be the estate groundskeeper."

"Like Matthew will be training."

"Exactly. And behind their house, we'll have a greenhouse, flower gardens, and an herb garden. Maybe a henhouse."

Linda was surprised to see how much land there was beyond the Cotton's house.

"Across the street from the Cottons will be Van Tsang's modern glass house with an indoor koi pond."

"Wow."

"Beside the Cottons are adjoining homes for my sous chef, Laurent, and his parents, Tom and Valli Davis. The wings will frame a little courtyard between the houses. Tom's our maintenance supervisor."

Turning her back on the Davis property, she gestured across the street. "Then, three guest cottages across the street, beside Van's. They'll be similar, white with porches. Hopefully, charming.

"My construction site manager will be building in the valley. You asked the order of building. Your Island House will be one of the first homes built."

"And then, the Factory?"

"Yep. Let's see. I told you my pastry chef will be on the second floor with you. Katrin Karlsson. She'll be training in Paris for several months, although she's *really* brilliant. Her brother and sister-in-law will have a bakery in town.

"Then, the Factory's top floor will highlight the history of the Factory and the rest will be my Business Manager's home and office, Grace Cloud. Everyone answers to her. Oh, and a swimming pool on the roof."

Mentioning the pool reminded Bronwyn of Edgar and Clara Davis. After all, Bronwyn had nixed Jeeves' idea of a pool as too indulgent, until she learned Laurent's grandmother Clara could make good use of one, for her heart condition.

"Two additions will go onto the Factory. Ernest Rose's home will face my house, two stories high with a glass enclosed staircase rising from it. My chef is Edgar Davis, Laurent's grandfather, and he and his wife Clara's home will run across the back of the factory, with the new balconies rising above."

"So, the Factory will be done and then, your house. How long will it all take?"

"These houses on King Street will be first. I'm hoping they'll be done by the end of the year."

"Really? You haven't broken ground."

"Well, I don't know how extensive Alex Oz King's home will be, but I don't think any of the others will be a problem. Your Island House won't take long. The Factory should be renovated the second year and my house, the third year."

Linda was thinking if she had Bronwyn's money, she'd be doing her own house first, not last.

"Parts of the Factory will be operational for the work crews – bathrooms, showers, laundry facilities in the basement, a large kitchen on the third floor. When it's ready, Edgar will be serving meals there. So we'll need your cleaning staff up and running."

Bronwyn realized she'd forgotten the basement of the Factory. Although Factory families would have storage space, there would also be racquetball courts, an exercise room, boxing ring and locker rooms. They laughed about forgetting all that.

The four said their goodbyes. The Brodies would be on the payroll within the week, and Linda would only have two more months of teaching before summer would signal the start of a new life.

As the morning dawned, Bronwyn had a good feeling. With her staffing wrapped up, architectural plans drawn, and construction schedules roughed in, she felt things were coming together. Out of town, clearing for the golf course was underway, as was the foundation for the clubhouse. She planned homes around the course's perimeter, and named the place, *Bergamot Nine*.

Anticipating a quiet day, Jeeves decided to try the local barber shop. He doubted the Walt Harris Barber Shop could hold a candle to his favorite clippers in London and New York. Bronwyn waited on a bench outside, soaking up the town's atmosphere.

A small boy sat on one side of the bench and Bronwyn noticed damp eyes when he lifted his face.

He looked at his hands, squeezing and unsqueezing them as he sighed.

"How old are you?"

"Six."

"What's your name?"

"Charlie," he said, with no expression.

"Charlie, I'm Bronwyn. Bronwyn McCall. Where's your mom? Or, your dad?"

"Mom's working inside. She cuts hair." Bronwyn noticed the hair salon beside the barber shop.

"So, she watches you while she works?" Bronwyn asked, hopefully.

"Guess so." He seemed deep in thought. There was something very endearing about Charlie. It could have been the way his ears were attached to his head; perhaps the translucent quality of the skin pulled across his face, with light blue veins near the surface of his temples. He reminded her of Samuel and Paul, but he wore the pain she'd known as a child, with the weight of the world on his tiny shoulders. Everything he was, everything he loved, everything he'd lost seemed to be barely contained within his tiny taut frame. Bronwyn recognized abject loneliness when it was sitting right beside her.

"My Dad's not here. He works at a fancy place. Acatootha."

Bronwyn was interested. "Acatootha? That's the name?"

"Yeah. It's an Indian."

"What does your dad do, Charlie?"

"He fixes things. Like mowers and stuff. And he bosses people around. He can fix anything."

Bronwyn heard quiet sniffling. He *was* sniffling. She rummaged through her satchel and handed Charlie a Kleenex.

He snuffled into it and Bronwyn noticed how sharp his shoulder blades were as they heaved a bit. A few freckles dashed across his nose. When he looked at her, pale lashes framed huge brown eyes, and his nearly white hair was ruffled.

"Where's Acatootha, Charlie?"

He began to cry. Bronwyn looked to see if his mother was watching; when no one came she moved over and patted his thin back.

Bronwyn called Gus Townsend and asked if he'd call the barber and vouch for her, so she could take Charlie to lunch.

Gus did one better. In ten minutes' time, Gus appeared. He popped his head into the beauty salon, then the barber shop, and told Jeeves where they'd be.

Charlie mumbled his sad tale – a common tale, but sad nonetheless.

After they walked him back to the beauty salon, Gus supplied the details. The year before, the boy's mother filed for divorce, took Charlie, and left with a boyfriend. Now they lived in a crummy apartment just out of town. More often than not, Charlie could be seen wandering around town. He'd already made the acquaintance of Snooks Von Krinkles, several times.

It was wise of Bronwyn to find someone to vouch for her because it had been Gus's friend Jess Jackson, owner of the Men's Shop, who read his mother the riot act about Charlie's wanderings

Bronwyn wondered what kind of a father Charlie had. After all, Vicki Palimore had left Teddy Palimore for a lowlife. Surprisingly, Gus only had good things to say about Teddy. He came down most weekends, sitting in the park with Charlie, standing at the docks, and munching sandwiches at the drugstore, as they'd just done.

Wondering where the resort was, and if the name was really Acatootha, Bronwyn discovered it was an effort for Teddy Palimore to come down to the bay. The Acatootha Resort was over four hours away, upstate. She asked Gus what he thought the outcome would be, but Gus held out little hope. He'd seen women's willfulness before, and although he didn't consider Vicki to be any prize, and the rumor mill indicated the boyfriend wasn't interested in making an honest woman out of her, Gus doubted she'd go back to Teddy.

Two days later, Bronwyn was in New York, to review renderings with one of her architects. The land beside Laurent's and his parents' home was about to have a Spanish style home with four wings safely enclosing a beautifully tiled courtyard. Just the kind of place to keep Charlie Palimore safely out in the open air.

It surprised Bronwyn that she'd overlooked the location, beautifully situated on a curve above the water.

Bronwyn ordered a high-power telescope for Charlie to use in an astronomy tower she planned for the top of his bedroom. Bronwyn called Splash Flanagan at the Lobster Pound and asked if she could install a signal tower on his roof. Splash was enthusiastic about the idea; Charlie would be responsible for remotely indicating the weather forecast by firing up different colored lights. Bronwyn remembered her mother's stories about emerging from Pittsburgh's Fort Pitt Tunnel, and being entranced by the Gulf Building's skyscraper top, aglow with weather lights. Bronwyn thought it was a good thing to give Charlie some responsibility.

The Acatootha Resort wasn't happy to lose Teddy Palimore, but he was delighted to hire on with Bronwyn and was willing to spend the next four months sleeping in his truck until his house was finished. He'd do anything to spend time with Charlie. As the newly appointed Estate

Manager, Teddy was anxious to meet Tom Davis, his new maintenance man, and Ken Cotton, his groundskeeper.

Bronwyn rented another Mountain Air Trailer for her Factory 'circle of wagons'. Now Teddy would have more comfort than his pickup truck, with his trailer sidling up to Alex Oz King's. A third trailer was Chef Edgar's, beside Grace Cloud's larger one.

She told Jeeves about Teddy Palimore's homeless truck idea, thinking Jeeves would be impressed with his dedication. After all, it was an old truck, undoubtedly drafty and uncomfortable. When Jeeves mentioned he could find Teddy a fully functioning cherry red 1951 antique Ford pickup, Bronwyn was surprised. She had no idea Jeeves was into antique vehicles. She urged him to get it as a surprise for Teddy, and asked if the new hangar at the airport would be a good place to stash it. She assumed there was plenty of space for a couple of cars along with shipments of materials, salvaged décor, and furniture they'd be receiving.

"I've another idea, Miss," he mentioned. "The hangar should suffice, but I've an idea to reward our Matthew Brodie."

"Actually Jeeves, I want everyone on the estate to have a new car. Within reason of course, except for you," she smiled, expecting a response. He gave her nothing but a slight nod. "The sky's the limit, for you."

"Excellent idea, Miss," Jeeves responded, suppressing his thrill at having unlimited auto autonomy. "You purchase the vehicles, and they're responsible for upkeep and insurance. Just a thought."

"So, you have a car in mind for Matthew?"

"Actually, I was thinking of a gift auto, in addition to his new vehicle. Just as Teddy Palimore will have his classic Ford."

Once she gave Jeeves the go-ahead to do some recreational car shopping, Bronwyn met with the Portland interior design team, doing the Palimore house.

"I want this railing made from Louisville Slugger bats. See? And look at this chair. It's a baseball glove chair made of glove leather and a foam and feather cushion. See the stitching? This is Charlie's room. The loft is designed like a ship's prow, with a ladder leading to a study area upstairs. Gorgeous flooring, just like this. See how it has black caulking along the boards, so it looks like a deck?"

"Yes. We should be able to work with this, Bronwyn. An authentic life preserver on the wall, reclaimed boat light fixtures."

Bronwyn nodded.

"Okay, for his dad's room, I want Teddy to have a loft, as well. Woolrich style. The bedroom will be large enough for a seating area. Burgundies, navy, warm medium-toned wood. I've no ideas for the bathroom..."

The design team clucked in good-humored amazement.

"Okay, I guess I'm thinking an India black granite with seafoam green. Clean. Masculine. Maybe glass block in the shower." Bronwyn smiled, "So surprise me next time. The building materials should inspire you. The house is a Spanish style with stone columns, stucco, and clay-tile roofing. The front door will be handmade and distressed, so it looks aged. They're putting together a barn from weathered board-and-batten siding. There's already a Seckel pear tree, very stately. If you can find a handmade tree swing, rustic, that would be great. Charlie's a little boy, remember."

"So, the house is a male retreat."

"There isn't anything here that I wouldn't like. Oh, Teddy's putting in an American flag gate for the fence. It's a replica from a folk art museum. I'd like to see your lighting thoughts."

"Teddy Palimore must have impressed you, Bronwyn. This is a late addition to the mix. What's he like?"

"He's a good dad. Guess that's the big thing. He also knows his stuff. Oh, I forgot to tell you. The basement under the garage wing is a basketball gymnasium. It'll have a floating floor system of pads two-thirds of an inch thick, under two layers of plywood and strip maple. Special wall panels."

The design staff made copies of her clippings and jotted additional notes.

"And downstairs, a bunk room like this with trundle beds tucked below. Nautical bedding and ladders, navy and white, with red for the walls. That way, six kids can sleep over. This bar area is actually a boat, cut in half, with overhanging oars. The stools need higher metal rungs for kids to put their feet. We'll need a Foosball table and the media room should have recliner chairs like these."

"Sauna?"

"Not in this house. You asked me what Teddy Palimore is like. He's the kind of guy who just came on board this week, but was willing to live in his truck till the house is done. He's the kind of guy who went to the Humane Society yesterday and adopted a beagle. Muffin. So, you're not just putting this house together for Teddy Palimore, you've gotta get it done for Muffin."

"And, Charlie."

"Yes. Charlie's the best. Are we done?"

CHAPTER TWELVE

THE ROOF
2000

*J*eeves couldn't fathom why Bronwyn would set foot in Sir Winston's Palm Springs home, ever again. But when Bronwyn heard that Oré Diaz Dominguez was visiting Sir Winston, before they started filming their Three Musketeers film, she was intrigued.

It took some convincing, so Bronwyn tried the direct route, saying she was determined to meet Oré Diaz Dominguez. With Jeeves scowling and sighing, they settled into Palm Springs.

Bronwyn manned the windows, hoping to see Oré by the pool. She reminded herself he was more a 'movie star' than an 'actor'. The Boys alone had a combination of ten Academy Award nominations, and each had his own little gold man. Even Conor and Hughie had nominations.

It was Oré's socialite wife Bronwyn met first, all tan and leggy, ultra thin, with dark hair and kohl-rimmed eyes. When Jeeves caught sight of her, Bronwyn suspected he wasn't quite so distressed over the visit. It was always difficult to detect a pulse with Jeeves, but his mood improved.

Oré's daughter, Dominique, was a beautiful child; three years old with white gold ringlets, a dainty demeanor, and a squeaky voice echoing off the tall ceilings.

Jeeves was astounded that Bronwyn turned shy and avoided meeting the actor. They took their meals in her room, and when Jeeves suggested they leave, she looked offended.

"Of course I don't want to leave."

"I'm sorry Miss; I'm not grasping the situation."

"I don't want to talk to him, but I want to look at him. You know," she tried to coax him into understanding.

"Perhaps I could procure some surveillance footage," he suggested, "and we can both look to our hearts' content."

She shot Jeeves a dirty look and walked to the window for the fiftieth time, hoping to see Oré.

Jeeves was unhappy at Sir Winston's. It reminded him of Oakley Forse, and Bronwyn's stated mission was a bust. She hadn't even laid eyes on Dominguez.

Bronwyn was annoyed with the clothes she'd brought and detested the hot weather. She was cranky and out of sorts, until the maid said Mr. Dominguez was off the property. Bronwyn ventured out, finding little Dominique playing in the sitting room. The happy look on the little girl's face gave Bronwyn a lift, and she told Dominique to get her picture books. It was the perfect place for fairy tales and storybooks, with a full suit of armor in the corner and musty, well-worn tapestries of unicorns and flowers. They whiled away the afternoon until Sir Winston returned with Oré.

Bronwyn decided to eat in the kitchen and apologized to Jeeves for being backward. If Bronwyn could bear to visit the damnable kitchen, Jeeves decided he could join her.

"I noticed when I was playing with Dominique, her nanny didn't come around."

Jeeves shrugged, but the maid nodded knowingly.

"Quite right, Miss. Never notice her a bit. Spends time with the Missus, she does."

"I wonder why? The girl is her job, isn't she?"

The conversation switched to the skimpy clothing of Oré's wife, the strain on her bikini top, and her willfulness with the staff. Jeeves decided there was more interesting conversation in the kitchen, than the dining room.

The next day, Jeeves left to fetch takeaway from Pomme Frite. When he pulled out of the driveway, Oré and Sir Winston were dashing off in the Porsche. He checked on the guard at the gate; the last thing Jeeves wanted was another incident, especially on the staff's day off.

While Sir Winston, Oré, and his wife had ultra elegant dinner reservations, Jeeves wasn't about to feel the poor relative. Hence, the quick jaunt for sand dabs amandine at Pomme Frite, or perhaps Flemish prime beef stew. The profiteroles were a must, so Jeeves had no dilemma over dessert.

Bronwyn was happily anticipating Jeeves' return. She hoped Jeeves wouldn't forget the frites. That was rather the point, after all. She took a magazine and went to the third floor sitting room, wondering if she'd see little Dominique again. The little girl's doll was on the floor. She peeked into the hallway, but no Dominique. As was her custom these days, Bronwyn glanced out the window.

Constant cooing drew her attention, and when she leaned out the window, Bronwyn gasped at the sight. Crawling along the gutter of the steep roof was Dominique, following a mourning dove.

Bronwyn's thoughts were flying; Jeeves was gone and no one was around. She remembered it was the staff's day off, and, of course, the Dominguez nanny was nowhere to be seen.

Deathly afraid of heights, Bronwyn looked at Dominique and called as quietly as she could, "Dominique. I see the bird. Don't turn around sweetie. Just stop, okay? That's right. You stay there and I'll come over and we'll just let the birdie go, okay?"

Startled, the bird flew away.

Bronwyn didn't realize she was going out onto the roof until she heard herself say so. Her heart was pounding out of her chest and she felt sick. Hoping her fear would subside, she hauled herself over the window sill, silently cursing Sir Winston for not having a one story ranch home.

Dominique was dangling her legs over the edge, looking toward Bronwyn. She told Dominique to stay, and debated whether to stand and walk or keep one knee in the gutter, dragging her left knee shimmy, shimmy across the tiles. She decided the crawl method was more likely to work.

That only lasted for two knee crawls. The slant of the roof and the rounded tiles made it difficult. Dominique was blissfully unaware, confident Bronwyn would scoop her up and they'd be reading stories, lickety-split. Her ringlets were blowing in the wind and Bronwyn worried if the wind would blow them off the roof, but decided little girls with silken thread for hair often had wisps blowing about.

Dominique was ten feet away, but to Bronwyn, it seemed a hundred yards. She glanced to the horizon, and saw no imminent rescue. Girding herself, Bronwyn slowly rose. She simply could not make her brain connect its 'move' instruction to her leg's ability to respond. She was in an instant pour of sweat. Fiercely biting her lip, the taste of blood unblocked the connection. Bronwyn slowly moved with her left leg leading and her right leg shyly catching up. Little by little.

Bronwyn was so focused that she didn't see the little girl standing up. When she was within five feet, Bronwyn heard Dominique sobbing.

Moving faster, Bronwyn touched Dominque's arm just at the moment she slipped off the roof. With more reaction speed, strength, and balance than she could rightly have possessed, Bronwyn reached down, jerked, and tossed Dominique in the air with one swift motion. A searing pain tore through Bronwyn's shoulder as she pressed the little girl against her.

The pain in her shoulder became secondary to the task at hand; how to turn around. Bronwyn wondered if she could sit back against the steep roof. She felt paralyzed. Dominique was sobbing, "I want my Mommy," and Bronwyn reassured her.

Still facing the wrong way, she had no idea how to get her feet turned the other way. She avoided looking down, imagining what people would think if she fell with the girl. Even rescuing Samuel and Paul, she'd been under suspicion. If she fell today, would people think it a murder-suicide? Would no one understand she saw the girl and came out to rescue her? She took a deep breath, but her weak left lung didn't fully inflate and her injured shoulder pierced her for the effort.

"Put your arms around my neck, and you can put your legs around me if you like. How 'bout that?"

What seemed an excellent idea to stabilize the girl was a horrid idea for Bronwyn's journey back across the roof. Now, she couldn't see her feet.

Bronwyn found resolve. She hadn't reached the girl against all odds, only to spend an eternity on the roof, or worse yet, fall off. She prayed she could make it, moved her feet into a shaky balletic first position, and turned her body to home, trusting the feel of the gutter before each step.

When Bronwyn reached the open window, her legs turned to jelly. The most difficult part became finding the courage to step down onto the chair. Her legs were failing her. It wasn't easy, but once inside, she hopped awkwardly to the floor, carefully clutching Dominique. Focusing her fury, rather than succumbing to fear's aftershock, she sat rocking the girl against her.

Bronwyn had no idea how much time elapsed. The house was eerily silent, although Bronwyn heard rushing in her ears. At long last, Jeeves walked down the hall with his bags of fragrant food.

Bronwyn handed him Dominique and dashed off on a nanny hunt.

She found the nanny in bed with Oré's wife, scantily clad and snorting lines of cocaine with a silver straw and mirror. Bronwyn would have knocked them both off the bed with a single mighty blow, but she could see in their eyes it wouldn't have registered. Instead, she wound Oré's wife's hair around her fist and yanked her upright, growling the story at her. She pulled it for emphasis and shook it for the sheer joy of seeing her head bob around. She sneered at the nanny and warned Oré's wife that there had better be a new nanny or she was telling Oré all about it. *All* about it.

Bronwyn returned to the sitting room to find Dominique happily drinking milk and eating cookies. Jeeves waited while Bronwyn went into the powder room. After retching, she admitted she needed a doctor.

It took several hours at the hospital before they got back. Sir Winston was relieved Bronwyn wasn't badly hurt, and suggested it was pointless to upset Oré, since Sir Winston's staff had already made arrangements for an English nanny. Oré was unaware of the roof ordeal, but Sir Winston shrugged that Bronwyn could tell him, if she thought she must.

It was cunning of Sir Winston. How would Bronwyn tell Oré Diaz Dominguez that she risked life and limb scampering across a thirty foot high gutter to save his daughter, when she'd been too shy to lay eyes on him for the past week?

Jeeves regretfully remembered the food. He settled her into bed, promising to return with eggs and toast. As he fried bacon, Jeeves ruminated about the cursed place, and if it wasn't, at least he was cursed in the place. He knew no one could have anticipated the little girl would be adventurous; she seemed such a bookworm.

Once Bronwyn's dislocated arm had been set, the shoulder tear addressed and the pain medication administered, Bronwyn had filled Jeeves in on the details. She gasped about her fear, giggled at her own bravery, and Jeeves praised her courage.

It wasn't until she was tucked into bed that Jeeves watched the security tapes. Bronwyn hadn't mentioned Dominique nearly falling off the roof. No wonder she'd torn the shoulder and dislocated it. How extraordinary that she could wait in silence for his return, and then stomp down the hall to give the nanny hell before getting to a doctor. How was he to guard and protect Bronwyn when she exploded in his absence and was the model of serenity when they were together?

Bronwyn couldn't sleep. She kept replaying every millimeter of her march across the roof. She was glad to be safely in her bed though, with plump pillows and soft blankets tugged up to her chin, and her sleeping pill should kick in soon.

There was a quiet knock at the door and Bronwyn waited

for Jeeves to come in. Another knock, this time louder, brought Bronwyn out of bed. It was Oré Diaz Dominguez with Dominique.

"I am so sorry, Bronwyn. We haven't met. I am Oré Diaz Dominguez." In the darkness of her room, she turned slightly and eased the sling off her shoulder.

"My daughter tells me she cannot sleep until she sees you." His teeth gleamed in the dim hallway light and Bronwyn felt actual pain with her intake of breath. His eyes were large and sparkling in person and his dark hair framed his face seductively. His nose was the perfect punctuation point to sit in the midst of a sublime face. He had a courteous demeanor, almost formal.

"Actually, she tells me she must sleep with you." He leaned over and whispered in Bronwyn's ear. "Perhaps she could lie with you just until she falls asleep, you know? Then, back to her bed. Would you mind, awfully?"

Bronwyn smiled at his daughter.

"Of course. Come on Dominique. Let's get into bed."

It was evident little Dominique hadn't forgotten about their ordeal. She clung to Bronwyn with fists of steel. Oré turned on a small lamp and Bronwyn knew if her hair was ever a mess, if her pajamas were ever disheveled, it was this night. Poetic justice, she decided. She'd avoided him when she didn't look half-bad, and now here he was.

It got worse. He pulled up a chair and placed his feet on the bottom of her bed. If there was one thing Bronwyn abhorred, it was someone watching her sleep. But sleep she did, and Oré was entranced.

He had no idea what to expect, when he finally saw the elusive Bronwyn Dai McCall. He understood her avoidance of him; he had that effect on people. But he enjoyed this chance to gaze upon her, without conversation or limitation. Her face was milky white, revealed beneath the dark waves of her hair. Her exquisitely formed lips moved slightly as she slept, and her nose was sprinkled with freckles.

Sir Winston had warned him how rapidly Bronwyn could color, and not to embarrass her. It seemed he was anxious for them to meet. The old man had waxed on so long about her large eyes and their astonishing shade of green, that Oré wondered if Sir Winston was at least a little in love with her himself. Oré hadn't seen those green eyes in the dark room, but the pale lashes and eyebrows were a contradiction from her dark hair. He reflected on Bronwyn's dodging through the house, just around a corner or through a door, always missing him, and decided she was worth the wait.

His emotions began to get the better of him. He adored his little girl, and to see Bronwyn and Dominique holding onto each other with such fierceness, perhaps desperation, brought him near tears. Why was her mother so distant? He should be looking down upon mother and child and it saddened him.

An hour passed with Oré circling the bed, gazing down upon them, returning to the chair, and watching them until he fell asleep with his feet propped on the bed.

Despite the sleeping pill, Bronwyn's pain awakened her. She wanted to get downstairs to whatever pain relief Jeeves could mix up, but didn't want to waken Dominique. Oré was silhouetted by the dim light behind him. He appeared to be sleeping, since his head was lolled off to the side.

She finally made her move, tickling Dominique's cheek until she stirred and turned over. Cautiously, Bronwyn edged out and covered Dominique with the blanket.

As she neared Oré's chair, he stirred and took her hand. He whispered, "You're awake?"

She could smell him and it was evocative and pleasing. She felt warmth emanating from where he sat, which was remarkable in the drafty room.

Bronwyn whispered, "I'm going to the kitchen, but I'll be back."

That was forward, she thought. He already said he'd take Dominique back to her room.

"I'll warm the bed for you, shall I?" and he kissed her cheek lightly as he rose, and embraced her. She felt the plush softness of his knit top against her cheek, the solidity of his body against her. He breathed in the smell of her hair and became aware of the narrowness of her back as he pressed against her. It was just a moment, but the embrace sizzled.

He hugged and kissed women all the time, sometimes more than that, but this moment of restraint at almost four in the morning, coupled with his daughter inches away and the long unfettered analysis of Bronwyn, struck him.

As he climbed into bed, she headed down the oriental carpets of the hallway.

"Jeeves," she called quietly at his door and he responded immediately. He hadn't slept, dwelling on her dangerous roof escapade. She whispered her state of pain; he scolded her for removing the sling, and prepared an injection. They sat together, waiting for the pain medication to take effect, and Jeeves offered to make cocoa.

"I've seen him, Jeeves. Oré's in my room, with Dominique."

Now Jeeves suspected why the sling was off.

"He's incredibly handsome. Really. Just like I thought he'd be. I wish my friend Ollie could see him. Even though

Ollie was unbelievably handsome, you know, he was a model? He appreciated what people looked like, just like I do. I know the variations two eyes, a nose and a mouth can take."

As he poured the cocoa, Jeeves marveled at how quickly the pain medication took effect. Bronwyn usually spoke sparingly; certainly in the dead of night, good for a grunt 'yes' and a grunt 'no'.

"So, he was just dark, with the light behind him, but even then he had such presence. That's why I didn't want us to meet him, Jeeves, or I mean for me to meet him. You could have met him. You could always have met him. I didn't keep you from meeting him, did I?"

"When you finish your cocoa, Miss, you may sleep in my room, if you'd like."

She smiled sweetly, shaking her head. "No, I'll go back upstairs."

Even though she surprised him by saying they'd leave in the morning, Jeeves didn't believe her. Now that she'd seen Oré Diaz Dominguez, and he suspected more importantly, now that Dominguez had seen her, they were in for a long stay at Sir Winston's.

He walked Bronwyn to her room, and was perturbed as she slipped through the door, closing it quickly. He knew there'd be no sleep for him. He'd be returning to the kitchen for more than just cocoa.

Bronwyn was true to her word. After a few hours of wistful Oré observation, she greeted the rising sun with an awkward struggle into cargo pants and a hoodie. Shy again. And on the road.

A few pleasant days in Carmel began to feel like a habit. First, they descend on Sir Winston's Palm Springs home. They wait for an inevitable disaster; find medical attention, and then motor up to Carmel to recuperate in a fairy tale world of sunshine, art, color, flowers, and tea at The Tuck Box.

Because they enjoyed Carmel so much, Bronwyn was reluctant to ask Jeeves if he had second thoughts about Maine. Shoveling snow probably didn't occur to Carmelites, and Jeeves turned his face upward to get a full-on smack of sun when he walked down the streets. But if she'd asked, Jeeves would have said he longed for the anonymity and safety of Maine; it reminded him of home. He held no particular fondness for the curse of California.

But Jeeves did enjoy Carmel. It was as if Bronwyn's sentimentality washed over him, for just as she imagined her father in the various restaurants they frequented, Jeeves knew how much his own dear mother would be taken with the quaint charm of Carmel. When they ordered blintzes and Swedish pancakes at Katy's Place, he thought of Mam. When he ordered boneless short ribs at the Carmel Chop House, he thought of Pap and even when he slurped his root beer float, he could hear Mam scolding him. They made it a point to stop at the Patisserie Boissiere often, not just for pastries, but for the delicious hot almond milk. Life with Bronwyn was more pleasing than Jeeves could have guessed. He may have dreamed of the sunny Riviera, but the reality of sipping hot almond milk across from amusing Bronwyn was more rewarding.

While they had crepes at The Cottage restaurant, Bronwyn updated Jeeves with her plans. First they'd stop in Pittsburgh for a few days, before checking on progress in Maine. After that, Sir Winston had asked her to join him for a few days in Bath. They agreed; Jeeves would accompany Bronwyn to England, and then he'd continue on with his own travels. He didn't mind Bronwyn visiting dreary Bath without him and Bronwyn filled their reunions with obscure details and amusing tales.

In Pittsburgh, Jeeves was delighted that Bronwyn still had wonderful places to show him. She dealt them like a deck of winning cards.

They stayed at the William Penn Hotel, but made a trek back to Beaver for dinner at the rustically elegant Wooden Angel. She watched to see if Jeeves recognized Bert's as they swung through the parking lot, and was pleased when he did. She steered him into the Wooden Angel, explaining how one brother had the Wooden Angel while the other ran Bert's Wooden Indian.

Jeeves enjoyed his rack of lamb immensely, but the dinner's highlight was Alex Sebastian inviting Jeeves to see his wine cellar of over 10,000 American wines.

On the drive back to Pittsburgh, it was the most animated Bronwyn had seen Jeeves. He was going to be one happy camper when she surprised him with his own private wine cellar.

Samuel and Paul were scheduled for a Maine visit the following week and Bronwyn couldn't wait. They liked to race from one construction site to the next, with their heads bobbing beneath their yellow hardhats. Samuel, Paul, and Maine – an unbeatable combination.

CHAPTER THIRTEEN

ORÉ'S DINNER

*G*lad to be in Bath, Bronwyn was even happier to see Sir Winston's wife. Sir Winston had also invited Conor Frost and his girlfriend Nova, Angela and Graeme Woods, Eimear and Roddy O'Neal, as well as Sebastian Hughes' girlfriend Charlotte Tritton. Hughie was waylaid in London and was relying on Charlotte to give him the news. Bronwyn was astonished when the guests were buzzing about the pending arrival of Oré Diaz Dominguez

It was easy to sink into Graeme's comfortable world in Mayfair and Chipping Norton, but Bronwyn no longer dismissed Sir Winston's rather garish Bath home. Now that she was in the midst of major construction, she was more observant, wandering and appraising her surroundings.

Back in Maine, construction was ahead of schedule. The Factory was underway and estate houses were finished, except her own. Pedestrian gates and reclaimed streetlamps were being installed, with landscaping by Reed-Hilderbrand.

When work did begin on her house, Bronwyn hoped to recreate the cozy warmth of Graeme's homes in her snuggery, library, and warming room. There wouldn't be much of the Sir Winston dazzle, but aspects of the Factory might reflect some of his exuberance. Items were being procured and shipped from all over Europe, and the third floor of the Factory was receiving salvaged pub and hotel décor as well as shop fittings from various European closings. This week, they were expecting antique glazed display cabinets and colonnade railings.

Oré wasn't expected for two more days, so Bronwyn strolled the halls of Sir Winston's country home, taking in the bold furnishings. The hallway fronting her bedroom had deep blue and gold latticework on the walls, and Empire period sconces. The curving staircase was covered with chocolate brown carpet sprinkled with pale mint flowers. Bronwyn admired the open look of the railing, punctuated by gold flowers. There was nothing vertical about the railing as the metal looped in romantic swirls. The staircase walls were adorned with pale pink wallpaper, laden with yellow-flowered trees, egrets, and romantic bird pairings.

Whenever Bronwyn entered Sir Winston's drawing room, she was reminded how different their tastes were. The walls were wildly striped with turquoise and azure blue, and there were raspberry velvet couches and chairs. So many rooms had a vivid over ripeness.

Sir Winston's living room was more sedate. Several settees and club chairs sported dark green flowered fabric, with matching drapes covering eight arched windows. The ceiling was awesome with magnificently grained wood. Thirty candles rose out of crystal flowers from a stunning light fixture of black enamel and gold. When lit, the glow was unforgettable.

Bronwyn's bedroom was lovely; its bed canopied by

Brunschwig & Fils in a dove gray check, with cream colored bed linens. The toile chairs were charming, and its bathroom had a soaking tub that fit her back perfectly.

Despite Oré's marriage, The Boys encouraged her. She never doubted their affection for her, especially Graeme's, so she didn't dwell on his marital status.

Conor Frost was another matter; deeply disturbed by the scenario. Graeme clucked at him, but Sir Winston told him to leave if he couldn't abide Bronwyn's happiness, which made Conor all the more determined to stay.

The day before Oré's arrival, Sir Winston was transforming his library into an all-red theme. Not only did he have red candles and red ilex placed throughout the room, he'd had his chairs and sofas recovered in vibrant red. It had a warm ambiance, but Bronwyn admired the baroque dining hall. Its bronze ceiling had heavy medieval light fixtures with fleurs de lis curving around them. The table seated fourteen and was dressed in layers of forest green. Chairs on either side of the table were armless except for the chairs at either end. Black iron sconces hung on cream colored walls, and she expected Sir Winston would have candles everywhere. He was a master of effect.

The next day, Oré arrived in late afternoon. The Boys met with him in the red library, losing no time in assessing his interest in Bronwyn. Satisfied, they relaxed with pre-pre-dinner drinks, sending word to Charlotte that 'all systems were go'.

As Bronwyn dressed, she wondered what the others would be wearing. The set-up seemed contrived, rather like a 'Clue' dinner – maybe Miss Scarlet would carry a candlestick to meet Colonel Mustard in the library. In fact, Nova was wearing pale blue tight-legged silk slacks with a long sleeved Indian embroidered red silk tunic, while Charlotte trotted out a deep purple dress, long-sleeved and high-necked.

Nova nodded approvingly at Bronwyn's white charmeuse blouse and long black skirt, slit on one side to reveal high black leather boots. She was impressed with Bronwyn's smoky eyes. Charlotte reached over and unbuttoned one of Bronwyn's buttons.

Oré, in his navy Brioni dinner jacket, flashed the dazzling smile that had beguiled audiences all over the world. He was pouring on the charm, with his handsome features in animation. His wavy hair was longish and brushed back, tucked behind his ears. It seemed a hidden key light flashed off his chocolate brown eyes, but it was the way he stared at Bronwyn, combining his flirtation with a pout that caused her to stare in wonderment. That face. That extraordinary face. When he wasn't watching her seductively, he was throwing his head back with pure abandon, enchanted with life. His laughter provoked good humor throughout the room and everyone congratulated themselves for the small part they were playing as Oré worked the room. Bronwyn was undeniably drawn to the life-force he offered.

Pre-dinner cocktails were served in the Red Room, with most trying an Ian Fleming style martini…Gordon's Gin, 42 Below Vodka, Lillet Blanc, shaken not stirred. Bronwyn wasn't surprised the men would spend a moment in James Bond's shoes. As actors, it was always just a script away from reality.

Sir Winston ushered them into the dining hall and as they took their seats, Bronwyn whispered to Charlotte that she'd forgotten her pain medication injection. Charlotte offered to take care of it; did she want it now? Oré was sitting and Bronwyn said she'd wait. Charlotte whispered to the butler, and took her seat beside Dominguez.

A trio of appetizers opened the meal...a tiny cheese soufflé, a ceviche of lobster and artichoke, and a tiny scallop sauté with cauliflower. Storytelling rolled into high gear as the main courses were presented. Bronwyn didn't eat much. She was too excited and hadn't realized how painful her shoulder was. Bronwyn found herself watching Oré as much as he observed her; neither aware of the knowing smiles directed their way from all their tablemates, save Conor Frost. Before dessert was served, Bronwyn caught Charlotte's eye and she accompanied Bronwyn down the short hallway into the kitchen.

Oré had a clear view, via the angled hallway mirror. The reflection took his breath away as Bronwyn unbuttoned her blouse, dropping one sleeve to reveal a bustier. He slyly returned his gaze to the mirror and his heart sank with disgust. Charlotte Tritton was filling a syringe. His hopes and dreams for Bronwyn McCall were dashed with the revelation of the needle. He'd had his fill of weak women, yearning for drug highs. She was no different and without shame, shooting up in the kitchen in full view of the staff. Bile rose in his throat and he looked away.

After a few minutes, Bronwyn and Charlotte returned. Sir Winston quietly asked Bronwyn if she was 'all better' and she did seem relaxed and happy. Damn her habit, Oré thought.

Bronwyn gave him a shy smile from behind the flickering candles, left her seat and beckoned the wait staff to remove his dishes and silver. With the guests transfixed, she sat on the table in front of him and lifted her feet onto either side of his chair. The split made her skirt fall between her legs and one over-the-knee boot was revealed, before she dropped into his lap. She slowly kissed his forehead, eyelids and crease of his neck before pressing her lips to his, kissing lightly. He responded, in kind. She could taste a hint of tobacco and Amontillado sherry. Everyone at the table was mesmerized, slightly embarrassed, decidedly excited, except for Conor Frost who was glaring from behind horn-rim spectacles.

Wordlessly, Bronwyn stood and returned to her seat. She motioned for his place setting to be returned and asked, "What's for dessert?"

"I'm not quite certain how to reply, my dear Bronwyn, but most of us are having sherry trifle," Sir Winston said, delightedly.

In the flickering candlelight, Bronwyn missed the change in Oré's demeanor. Her kiss had made an impact, and for that instant he'd forgotten her moment with the needle. But his gaze was no longer open and welcoming. The same kiss that meant 'hello' to her, meant 'goodbye' to him.

As they finished their dessert, Roddy O'Neal announced he and Eimear were taking Bronwyn's room as Oré was now in Sir Winston's. This was news to Bronwyn and everyone's good humor seemed to skim over her lack of sleeping quarters. Graeme and Angela snatched rights to Roddy's room and the musical chairs continued. Bronwyn wasn't comfortable with the inference she'd be sleeping with Oré, but if she wasn't willing to take the next step, why had she kissed him so blatantly? She hoped for the best. If Oré wasn't interested, Sir Winston's enormous bed would suffice, if sleeping was the thing.

Oré excused himself after dinner and went up to Sir

Winston's room. Bronwyn sidled up to Conor Frost as everyone else urged her upstairs. Bronwyn was embarrassed and decided it was better to go, than be teased mercilessly in the Red Room.

The butler accompanied her, asking if there was anything she needed before retiring. He'd drawn a bath for Mr. Dominguez and offered her one of Sir Winston's dressing gowns. Bronwyn opted for one of Sir Winston's white dress shirts, instead. She opened the door and beheld the perspiring actor in his bath.

With a tentative smile, she approached the bath with more boldness than she thought she possessed, flinging her right leg over. Straddling the side of the tub, the tail of her shirt was beginning to soak. Anticipating a romantic moment, she was aware of the bright lights of the bathroom and glanced at Oré.

He had a look of distaste, chilling her. If she hoped the look would be fleeting, replaced in a flash by a welcoming smile or even a resigned expression, she was mistaken.

"Pardon me. Sorry," was all she could manage as she lifted her leg out of the water. She walked to the door, hoping something might make him ask her to stay. He did not. Once she closed the bathroom door, she was a flurry of activity, removing the shirt, donning her skirt and blouse, and ringing for Arthur.

Good old Arthur. The butler arrived within moments.

"Arthur, do you think you could drive me to London? And please, don't say anything to anyone."

"Certainly, Miss. May I tend to anything for you before we depart?"

"Are the O'Neals in my room?"

"I'm afraid so, Miss."

"Well, right inside the door, my handbag is on the floor

of the closet and I need my moccasins. Do you think you could get them?"

Within five minutes, Arthur was back. He'd even managed to retrieve her jeans. He stepped out as she put them on and slipped into the moccasins. Arthur held out one of Sir Winston's waxed cotton jacket.

The next morning, Conor Frost was pounding at Hughie's door. Bronwyn pretended not to hear, but when Hughie was obviously somewhere deep in dreamland, she went down the hall and peeked through the spy hole. This wasn't the way she wanted to dwell in her state of morose solitude, but she had no choice. She let Conor in.

"Arthur told me all about it."

"I doubt that."

Conor looked uncomfortable and she shrugged.

"I'm sorry things didn't work out."

Bronwyn shuddered each time she thought of standing in Sir Winston's bathroom, wishing she could turn the clock back. If she could, she'd have simply eaten her dinner like the lady she'd always thought she was, nodding goodnight without any funny business and returning to her bedroom without the musical chairs.

"Thanks," she said, lightly embracing him. "I'm going to try to get some sleep." Bronwyn disappeared into Hughie's sitting room. She spent ten minutes on the couch, wide awake and drumming her fingers on her two front teeth. She looked in the mirror and flinched. She tried to plump out the crease on her cheek; an imprint from Hughie's wildly brocaded couch. She was still in the charmeuse blouse, and although it had withstood the night, she found she despised it.

"You didn't happen to bring any of my things?" Bronwyn called out, opening the door a few inches. No response.

Padding down the hall, she found Conor fussing in the kitchen.

"Did you bring any clothes for me?"

Conor turned, flummoxed.

"Afraid not, Bronwyn. I can dash back. What do you need?"

"That's okay. Hughie can lend me something. I'll make tea and then you can hold my hand and cluck over me. How's that?"

Bronwyn rolled the afghan into a ball and they settled onto the couch, sipping tea. Neither of them wondered where Hughie might be. He may have owned the place, but he was uncomfortable in trying times. He'd be indisposed for awhile.

Bronwyn attempted to tell Conor what happened. Searching for the right words, she felt a clutching sensation in her throat, and her eyes began to well up. Conor glanced at her, with a pained expression.

"It's hard to explain, Conor. Oré didn't do anything wrong. Not really. It's just that he looked at me with distaste. I'll never forget the look on his face." She turned away. "It's my own fault for being that vulnerable. I should have just laughed and left. How could I have been so wrong about him?"

Conor's brows were knitted and he looked sorrowful.

Bronwyn shuddered again.

Conor held her hand, occasionally patting it.

After several minutes, Conor moaned, "Well. This is something."

"What, Conor?"

"I'm afraid there'll be distaste on *your* face. I can't bear to look at you. Everything seems to have changed, just so quickly."

Bronwyn shook the afghan out, clutched it to her neck,

and tucked her feet under. "I'm thinking, Conor, that you and I have been drawn to people very different from how we are. Nova and Oré have passion and abandon. We're quiet and thoughtful and careful. Aren't we? I don't dance or sing or have fettuccini hanging off my eyelashes. I don't do anything with gusto, actually. Maybe we need that in our lives. Not to be like them, but we're drawn to their warmth and energy. They seem more alive. Do you see what I mean?"

Conor nodded, thoughtfully. "I suppose I do."

Bronwyn feared she'd hurt Conor's feelings. She certainly didn't want to hurt him – not the way she'd just been hurt.

"Is something wrong, Conor?"

He paced the room, occasionally opening his mouth to speak and seeming to think better of it. Bronwyn found it odd. She couldn't imagine him being tongue-tied in any situation.

Finally, her wait was over. "It's this, then, Bronwyn. Nova's with child. I mean to say, she's pregnant. There. That's it."

Bronwyn's eyebrows shot up. Conor's face was unreadable, but his body was jumpy.

She patted the couch. "Sit here, Conor, beside me. That's wonderful news, don't you think? To be a father? Now, I'm not saying you have feelings for me, but I should tell you I can't have children. So, that makes having a family with Nova a wonderful thing. Right? Like it was meant to be." He looked at her with wide eyes. "I'm happy for you. I expect us always to be close."

Conor sighed, deeply. "Bronwyn. This could be our chance. We could consider being together." She didn't answer him. "Are you saying you'd turn me away when you don't have a chance of being with Dominguez?"

"I meant what I said, Conor. I adore you. You mean too

much to me to lose you foolishly at some point. With or without Oré, I see why Nova appeals to you and why Oré appeals to me. It's fate, Conor. This baby is fate. It's probably a shock, but just digest the reality and start getting excited. I am *so* delighted for you." And when Conor looked at her, she did appear to be delighted.

He nodded, slowly. "We'll always be close, you're saying. This doesn't mean I'll lose you? In my life? You're certain?"

He looked wistful.

"Yes Conor, friends forever. A friend means everything to me. You mean everything to me. Now, I think you should wake Hughie up and get shopping. I need a bra, a nightgown and a sweater…I guess you say a jumper. If you come back here with what I need, which is most of all a bra, then we'll have lunch somewhere and maybe find Nova an engagement ring."

"I say, Frost, what do you think of this? All lacy and fussy." Hughie held up a red lace push-up bra.

Conor wished he was anywhere else but the lingerie department. It took people awhile to recognize them. If Hughie had kept his pie-hole shut, they probably could have been in and out by now. Conor heard girls whispering, "There's Sebastian Hughes…oh look."

Conor watched him. Hughie was aware of the attention and didn't even try to do the job and get out. The plonker was strutting and preening, looking at the girls as much as he checked out the merchandise. How did Charlotte stand being out with him? On the other hand, Conor thought, Charlotte probably got the attention, not Hughie.

"Miss, what we're looking for is a simple brassiere." As soon as Conor approached the clerk, he wished he'd gone to the more mature saleslady.

"Does Sir wish a convertible? Something padded? A Racer-back?"

"Conor, old girl, I think she should have something black, don't you? Lift her spirits and all?" Hughie held it up, imagining it on the lady in front of him. "Lift her up, I mean to say? See how it covers the naughty bits?"

He wanted to crown Hughie for calling him 'old girl' in front of the giggling shoppers. Hughie seemed to forget their bra mission, plucking thongs and g-strings off the display racks.

Conor took a deep breath, pulled out Bronwyn's note and strode as manfully as he could to the more matronly clerk. "Madam, I'd like something simple, white, probably cotton, in," he checked the note, "a 34C, American size I suppose."

While Hughie was scooping up gear for Charlotte Tritton, Conor decided he'd lend Bronwyn his trench coat to sleep in. He simply didn't have the energy to endure the nightgown section.

When they returned to Hughie's flat, Bronwyn was relieved to have the bra. She'd regretted not taking one before she left Sir Winston's, but she'd asked enough of poor Arthur. The bra brightened her spirits immensely, and she borrowed one of Hughie's shirts for Conor's ring excursion.

They stopped at Fortnum & Mason, where Bronwyn found a nightgown and robe in far less time than Hughie's selection of garters and lace-up teddies had taken. Their chances of finding food at Hughie's would be dicey, so they decided to have a big lunch at The Fountain Restaurant, and afterward, headed to the Parlour Restaurant for ice cream. Bronwyn so enjoyed Conor's company, she briefly considered claiming him for her very own. He ordered the Knickerbocker Glory sundae, but Bronwyn chose the Patio Nut Delight with pistachio, praline and coffee ice creams, caramel sauce, roasted almonds and whipped cream.

As they sat twirling their long spoons, Bronwyn updated Conor about her home, vowing she'd soon be serving Knickerbocker Glories in her Factory soda fountain. When they'd eaten all the ice cream they could handle, they gathered themselves and went to Armour Winston Ltd. It was ring time.

Bronwyn didn't mind trying rings on. It seemed complicated to explain that Bronwyn wasn't the bride-to-be. She watched Conor's reactions to the rings, but he was, in turn, watching her. Finally, they agreed on a spectacular 4 ct emerald cut ring, with baguette diamonds on the shoulders. Bronwyn pointed out the long rectangular lines of the stone looked purposeful and sturdy, and Nova would be rocked by four carats. Bronwyn waited near the door as Conor finished the sale.

An oblivious Jeeves would arrive soon, and they'd be returning to the States. Arthur delivered Bronwyn's luggage and news of Oré. He'd heard The Boys berating Mr. Dominguez, but Arthur gathered they'd come to an understanding. Bronwyn took that to mean Roddy O'Neal had been restrained from killing him.

That night, as Bronwyn was tucking her blanket beneath her chin, Conor knocked softly at the door.

"I've something for you, Bronwyn." He held a long slender box. "So you'd always know we have that special friendship of ours."

He had a doubtful look on his face, but when he handed her the box, he brightened.

Bronwyn opened it, touched at his gesture, and was astounded by the beauty of a pink gold watch with a diamond case. It had a black silk strap and said Cartier. He'd somehow managed to add to his Armour Winston shopping.

She hugged him tightly, held him hard, and dwelled in the land of second guessing as soon as Conor left her room.

CHAPTER FOURTEEN

CONSTRUCTION

*B*ronwyn flew back to the states to spend a few days with Jeeves in Colonial Williamsburg. From there, they drove across Virginia and visited with Bronwyn's old friend, Mama Lou. Mama and her family fussed over beaming Jeeves as if he were royalty, filling him with ribs, brisket, pulled pork, mac & cheese, and cornbread. In a satiated fog, they headed to Maine, where they anticipated lobster at Splash Flanagan's restaurant and prepared to check on construction progress.

Her first stop was Gun Townsend's, delivering a blue vine Williamsburg bedspread. Then Gus walked with Bronwyn over to Tiny's, where she gave him a set of Colonial Tavern dinnerware, explaining what the King's Arms, Chowning's Tavern and Christiana Campbell's were like. Tiny listened with rapture, his mouth hanging open as if he could taste the food. Bronwyn decided she'd ask Edgar to drop by Gus's one evening and put his *Colonial Williamsburg Tavern Cookbook* to use. Perhaps he would delight Tiny and Gus with peanut soup, Brunswick stew, and pecan pie. She'd arrange it for when she and Jeeves left town, or else Jeeves would be racing Tiny to the dregs of the stew.

Luke stopped in during Bronwyn's visit, and pressed for a list of town improvements for which he could take credit. Bronwyn wondered how gentle Gus could have such an aggressive politician for a son. When Luke left, Gus proudly shared that Luke was planning a run for governor.

It would still be several months until the Factory renovations were completed. Matthew and Linda Brodie were staying in the Island House, while Edgar and Clara stayed with their son Tom and his wife, Valli. Grace Cloud was in one of the cottages beside Van Tsang's house, and Katrin Karlsson was staying with her brother and sister-in-law above the new Euro Bakery, in town.

Jeeves was barely hiding his petulance that his flat was unfinished, but he'd promised to wait before seeing it. Earlier, Bronwyn had asked Jeeves if his name was really Ernest Rose. With unexpected candor, he'd shared how his mother had a penchant for all things Oscar Wilde, and his dear wife had loved roses. So Bronwyn had done his kitchen as his wife may have liked, with cheerful red rose wallpaper. He'd also be finding a complete set of Oscar Wilde books in his library, including *The Importance of Being Earnest*.

Jeeve's only request to Bronwyn had been space in the basement, which he planned to use as a secret Operations Room.

A glassed Orangerie was being positioned off Edgar's kitchen and linked by walkway to Jeeves' flat – intended as a crystalline sanctuary, especially in the winter when it would be triumphantly aglow.

Bronwyn divided the estate's interior work among

several interior designers. A London hotel design firm was handling the elegant fourth floor of the Factory, as well as Jeeves' flat and Bronwyn's home. She'd recently met with the London team at Hughie's, and saw the travel team when she returned to Maine, giving them the same marching orders as the other five design firms she was using...*no shortcuts, no substitutions, no surprises, everything perfect.* It was her mantra and she said it often enough that she heard it from the designers in greeting, as beauty emerged from the construction chaos.

A Pittsburgh group did the Larchmonts' Sewickley-style mansion at the Bergamot Nine golf course. The home looked as if it had sprung out of the Maine woods: stately, elegant, and permanent. And even though Bronwyn's sales pitch to Doc had been a connecting guest house for Laura, his wife happily confided they'd reconciled.

A Boston firm did the Bergamot Clubhouse, and was coordinating the Factory third floor; much of it architectural reclamations, including the soda fountain installation.

Moving Valli Davis, Laurent's agoraphobic mother, was accomplished thanks to Doc Larchmont who accompanied a sedated Valli on the trip north. A Brooklyn interior designer had taken photographs of Valli's Brooklyn home and worked with much of her furniture. Although her new home was larger, it was harmonious and a relatively painless transition from Brooklyn to Maine.

Bronwyn had surprised Valli with an indoor vertical garden flowing off the kitchen and soaring upward past Tom and Valli's bedroom balcony. Interior windows brought the essence of the conservatory's waterfall and tropical atmosphere into the bedroom, or closed it off for viewing. Bronwyn was relieved to know that Valli often ventured over to Laurent's. The enclosed walkways had been an inspired idea, linking their homes together, and a classic stable and corral sat behind the Davis house, with five miniature horses taking up residence.

A Portland firm was finishing the Swedish-style Factory apartment of pastry chef Katrin Karlsson, while other designers were nearing completion on Linda and Matthew Brodie's lodge-style home in the Factory, across from Katrin's. The Factory's pièce de résistance was the domed rooftop pool design – a Mediterranean vision of turquoise, white, and aqua tile.

It had taken years of dreaming, but all those balls in the air were plopping one by one into Bronwyn's upturned hands.

Bronwyn spent a day with Douglas Reed and his gregarious dachshund, Pookie, walking through the multiple garden and landscape areas of the estate. She'd chosen the Reed-Hilderbrand firm because she'd met Doug Reed with Menke at Longwood Gardens. He was a consultant there, and she'd seen his Children's Therapeutic Garden in Wellesley, Massachusetts.

He'd created paths that wound through the property, joining a circuit bike path. The terraced fields surrounding Squirrel Hill, her animal cemetery, were beautifully cradled by low stone walls with narrow ten inch gravel paths gently curving through the grass. Near Jen Cotton's house, cutting gardens fell into herb gardens and her greenhouse and potting sheds were surrounded by wildflower gardens.

They crossed King Street and looked over the wooded ravine, leading to the plateau of Alex Oz King's home and gardens. As they walked, Doug Reed explained how everything would change with the four seasons. His enthusiasm for the winter vision was contagious. Bronwyn couldn't wait to see the estate in its frosty glory, punctuated by the reclaimed streetlamps.

Behind the Factory, Doug had created grape arbors, stone walls, and serpentine gravel paths to form private areas for Edgar and Clara. A large vegetable garden was tucked beneath the final wall, open to sunshine and cultivation. Bronwyn appreciated Doug's unique vision. He'd honored the natural beauty of the place, while recognizing the needs and whimsies of the people. Her own shaded lawn was an excellent example. Bronwyn wanted a simple expanse of lawn, but he encouraged shade with trees sheltering the loggia and its covered walkway and enfilade to the side. Her bluestone patio would feature a remarkable idea of Doug's... he was cutting a narrow ten inch channel of water into the bluestone, allowing the watercourse to flow across the lawn and spill onto the craggy rocks, forty yards beyond. He'd succeeded in creating a rural compound amidst cultivated areas, exactly what she wanted for the Factory and its surrounding land.

When Jeeves wasn't making veiled comments about his home's low priority, he was prodding Bronwyn about her home. He implored her to answer why she had so much money, yet they were vagabonds on their own land; which only amused her.

She hoped her Leopard Lane neighbors were weathering the construction and noise. Bronwyn had promised the Todds and Masons $25,000 for each year of construction inconvenience. She'd given them checks last December, explaining they could use them for a vacation, home improvements or even a new car so they'd have some enjoyment amidst the chaos. Handing over their second $25,000 checks, Bronwyn said the plan was to finish construction by late 2001, when they'd receive their last gift checks.

After five days of construction meetings, Bronwyn was looking forward to spending a day downtown. The renovated Roxy Movie Theatre had just opened, as well as the Arts Center in the old bank building. The first floor of the Arts Center housed a gallery and reception area; the basement featured kitchen and culinary classroom facilities; the second floor had rooms for photography, quilting, and art; the top floor was soundproofed for music classes.

When the Euro Bakery was in its early planning stages, Bronwyn hoped the town bakery wouldn't panic. She was determined to support both bakeries and chose a location several blocks away for the Euro. She'd met with the town bakery owners, promising to provide new equipment whenever they needed it. The meeting sailed into giddiness when she placed standing orders for doughnuts and sandwiches for her construction workers and added standing orders for the local teacher lounges every Wednesday and Friday. But the town bakery's popularity soared when the Pine Manor residents enjoyed rotating baked goods each day – brownies, iced cookies, cupcakes, doughnuts, tarts, bagels, and rugelach, courtesy of Bronwyn. The local bakery marveled that their biggest ally was the young woman who'd just built a new bakery in town.

Katrin's brother and sister-in-law ran the Euro Bakery and lived upstairs. Its pale blue exterior had white gingerbread trim and a porch with iron tables for outdoor dining. Bronwyn didn't want traditional baked goods sold at the Euro. Instead, brioche, panettone, stollen, pashka, macarons, Breton cakes, Paris-brest, cannelés bordelais, pain au chocolat, and croissant aux amandes were displayed on doily lined trays. Anna was excited to feature her almond sponge cakes, cashew terrines, caramelized apricot crème brulée, autumn cakes with white chocolate and raisin mango nectar, caramelized apple tarte tatin, and lemon brown sugar meringue tarts. Bronwyn stopped in to make sure everything was going well, updated Katrin about her Factory apartment, and felt her own heart sing with the thought of one day living near both bakeries.

Margo Storey, her Foundation Director, lived one block from the Euro, so they met at Margo's house. Margo was surprised Bronwyn had missed the grand openings of the Roxy and the Arts Center, but Bronwyn didn't want the attention. Offering fruit tarts in buttery pastry shells, Margo moaned about the pure bliss of living by the Euro Bakery.

After their meeting, Bronwyn stopped at Bergamot to see Jim Phipps and Babe Barclay. The men already had success stories with her Scholarship Partnership program. Twenty two high school students were working with local senior citizens to do yard work, shovel snow, pick up groceries and do chores, earning money for college tuition, dependent on successful service to their senior partners. Jim and Babe showed off their new homes at Bergamot; Jim on the seventh hole and Babe on the eighth.

As Bronwyn left Bergamot, she felt thankful for her Maine lucky streak. Seeing how invested Jim and Babe were with the scholarship kids, she appreciated having good people around her. She'd observed since she was eight years old, soaking up the best parts of Pittsburgh, Sewickley, and Beaver. But she realized the Maine successes weren't hers alone, nor was the beauty springing forth from the estate. She was just the conductor.

The next morning, Margo's daughter, Laura Storey,

filled her in on the Business Assistance Group, and Bronwyn thought Laura was an absolute 'wow' – full of ideas, inspiration and energy.

When Bronwyn visited The Book Nook, she asked Jane Jackson what she thought of the Assistance program. Jane was as enthused as her husband Jess was, over at the Men's Shop. Bronwyn stopped in several other stores, getting feedback and listening to ideas. Bronwyn promised that whatever merchants needed to update their façades, upgrade operation systems, and increase profits, she would provide with short turnarounds, via Laura. Bronwyn was glad she'd put Laura in the renovated apartment above the Roxy Movie Theatre. Laura would have a great view of every town activity, parade, and holiday event. It didn't hurt that she was a local, just like her mom.

Back at the estate, Alex Ozwald King invited Bronwyn to tour his home. He had a renewed energy, eager to justify a home he'd barely imagined. He had worked brilliantly the past twenty two months, handling the chaos as he sniffed the finish line. Bronwyn had been naïve to think the enormity of the construction projects could run smoothly, but Alex didn't mind her being blissfully unaware. She believed in him and her prolonged absences gave him time to resolve the inevitable problems.

When Alex showed her around his valley, Bronwyn had to admit it was outstanding. A winding road led to a circular driveway and a large garden in front of his imposing two story house. Flanking the home were a pair of long buildings; one, a five car garage with a workroom above and the other, a workroom below and a guest house above. A stream fell into the bay behind the house, with a beautifully finished second floor balcony connecting to a bridge over the creek. It anchored rising steps to the steeper hillside behind.

Bronwyn followed Alex's dogs up the steps, to Linda's Island House. She gestured back down the hill. "Let's call it 'Oz Valley'. We can say, where's Alex? Oh, he's in Oz Valley."

After meeting with Linda about the cleaning crews, Bronwyn and Jeeves said their goodbyes. The next time they returned, Jeeves would be seeing his completed flat for the first time. Bronwyn could hardly wait; he would be flabbergasted.

CHAPTER FIFTEEN

BRONWYN'S HOUSE
2001

*B*e careful what you wish for, Bronwyn thought, as she sat on her bed. Spending her first night in the home she'd yearned for, was unnerving. She wondered if Jeeves was somewhere in the bowels of the house, rattling metal and tapping on pipes. How was it possible that she could spend so much money, and yet there were noises, when the other estate homes were serenely quiet every night? Why was there any noise at all? Should her first admonition have been, make my house silent?

The house was too big, she feared. Bronwyn expected to feel safe by keeping her snuggery and library small and having only two bedrooms upstairs. The Silk Club, lobby, and Carnegie Suite were closed off, so why did she feel overwhelmed? And, nervous? And, afraid?

Earlier that evening, Jeeves seemed surprised when Bronwyn told him she'd settle in, alone. He shouldn't have been surprised, she reflected. He had his home; she had hers. She had no intention of giving Jeeves the satisfaction of knowing she was unnerved. She sensed the earth tilting;

the other side of the estate was populated by happy families while her side held a solitary home with an isolated occupant. If her side was weighted by supposed bags of gold, it was proof that money wasn't everything. Her heavy heart was only tilting it more.

For five years she'd been planning this life. She'd pictured items in drawers, how many steps would take her to the second floor, what shelves would hold cookbooks and which ones would hold mysteries. How had the echoing enormity of the house eluded her?

The same house that had brought her great joy each day, even this very day, had turned into a ravenous maw of soul-sucking anxiety. This is why people have a glass of wine before they turn in, she thought. But then, she wouldn't be able to save herself if she was in a stupor-induced dreamland.

She sighed.

What did she expect to happen? An invasion of the Huns? Her list of fears kept growing. She'd made the ceilings too high. What had seemed a stately and elegant environment was in shadows at night. Her bedroom balcony exposed her vulnerability. Yet, the reasonable side of Bronwyn knew how protected the estate was, and the house was alarmed three ways.

She fetched a bottle of water and some Saltines; then considered calling Conor Frost. He wouldn't laugh at her. Perhaps he'd have his own tale of homesickness.

But, this couldn't be homesickness. If it was, what on earth could she be homesick for? She and Jeeves had been nomads for five years, staying with The Boys and constantly traveling. She hadn't been lonely in Greenwich Village when Ollie moved into Tommy Gallagher's place in East Hampton. Thinking back to the William Penn Hotel, there were people behind each door, down every hall, on all the floors. Those five years at the hotel, from thirteen to eighteen, she hadn't felt alone in her room. Now, she did. With millions of dollars, this is what she had to show for it...knees drawn up to her chin, shivering with uncertainty, waiting for dawn.

Eventually, Bronwyn spent her first night outdoors, on the narrow balcony just off her office, wrapped in blankets to ward off the chilly night air. Rather than count sheep, she mentally ran the roofs of the estate, imagining the settled breathing of everyone but her.

She didn't return to the balcony the second night. She began in her own bed, but then wandered up to the top floor and snuggled into a bunk bed.

The third night, Bronwyn drew on her inner courage and was boldly alone. She found a notepad and listed sleepover invitees, beginning with Gus Townsend, Snooks Von Krinkles, and Tiny. They'd be her first guests, the sooner the better. She jotted down 'Menke', circling her name and underlining it three times. She added Charlie and Augie, and then Graeme with an exclamation point. She underlined Samuel and Paul. Then, added Mama Lou & Family, and Susie & Allison.

Jeeves observed her on his laptop as she wrote, and then was mildly disappointed when Bronwyn settled in. He waited two hours to see if she'd bolt, but when she didn't stir, he closed the screen and retired to his own plush bed.

Of all the possible reasons for anxiety, Bronwyn hadn't settled on September 11 as one of them. As most Americans, sleeping was difficult. She'd just moved into her house two weeks after that horrific and ominous day. Security at the estate had been fully implemented, and the gates were secured at all times. ID cards were issued and additional security precautions were imposed. Although guests were still invited to the estate and meetings held on the Factory fourth floor, life wasn't so easy and casual anymore.

As the days went by, however, the house began to feel more comfortable, and Bronwyn wrote to Menke with a rejuvenated spirit.

Oct. 10, 2001

Dear Menke,

I'm sitting in my 'snuggery' and rain is pounding on the window. It's been two weeks since I moved in. The leaves are turning and I have a nice view of them from here.

Jeeves has been teasing me to 'brace myself' for the Maine winter. He calls Maine the Kingdom of Cold. I've told him how I'm a shoveling expert...we've had plenty of snow in Pittsburgh.

It will be wonderful to show you my house. Please call when you feel up to the trip. Until then, I'll share a preview of my finally finished home. You'll see it's been a mental work-in-progress, for a long time – since the first day you showed me the Factory and homestead.

First, I should tell you about the knot garden, which is almost done. It's planted in front of the Factory turnaround, because so much "sewing" was done in the Factory.

The original homestead still has ivy climbing the walls, as well as the little white picket fence around the sidewalk, and the window boxes are still there, with pink petunias.

The snuggery is small, like a little living room. The chairs, ottoman and couch are old-fashioned, done in chintz. They're white fabric with faded red flowers and mossy green leaves and then roll arms with candy striped pink and white insets. I think it's very English. This is the room where I usually read. There's a nice powder room with a frosted door and a rough wooden cabinet with a silver bowl for a sink. The snuggery is to the right, where your great-great-grandfather's parlor was.

I should mention the little front porch. When I met with the first architect, he didn't want to put a screen door in. When he handed me the first draft of his plans, I mentioned the screen door and he was actually offended. He said it was a grand house and I must not be aware that a house like this would never have a screen door. He suggested I drive through some nicer neighborhoods (nervy) and I'd see that the homes had massive front doors, with nary a screen door. I should have reminded him that I was the one who planned every inch of the space, but I said my parents and grandparents had screen doors and I would, too. I remember how he looked snooty and said "surely this isn't a deal-breaker" and I said "No, it's a deal broken." That part was funny. Alex Oz King found me a London architect and he had no problem with the screen door (although Alex probably gave him a clue).

When you enter the house, the library is on the left. I remember how glad I was to see the high ceilings on our first trip to Maine. The windows have raw silk panels overlaying damask, and tassel fringe. Back-to-back leather couches have a sofa table between them and pendant lights overhead. One couch faces the fireplace with a wing chair, leather chair and ottoman (kind of crowded.) That fireplace must be at least three feet deep. The framed photograph of your grandfather is over the mantel. Jen Cotton (the florist) says she has great plans for the mantel at Christmastime, with huge boughs of greenery. We made a concession to modern times with a flat screen TV on the wall beside the doorway (I say "we" but I mean Jeeves). I do see his point. It's great for watching sports. As bright and cheery as the snuggery is, the library is dark and masculine.

The best part of the library is a display of Dickens houses. Have you ever seen them, in Christmas stores? A new bay window curves onto the front porch, and the display fills the window and extends into the room – about 7' wide and from the table top, maybe 4' tall. It's breathtaking. Do you remember the brass sheaths that covered revolving doors in department stores overnight? Maybe at Strawbridge and Clothier? I remember them in Pittsburgh, at Horne's and Kaufmann's. The little houses have one of those, to keep dust out. Sound effects play with the push of a button and solar lighting from the porch keeps it glowing in the evenings.

The kitchen has been enlarged. I also added a wing that I call the Silk Club. I named it the Silk Club after my best friend who died. You remember, Oliver Silkowski. I know how much he'd love the place because we enjoyed restaurants so much. It's part Belle Époque and steakhouse. Really gorgeous chandeliers, dark wood, sparkling mirrors and some frosted glass. When Jeeves saw it for the first time, his jaw dropped, so you know it's pretty nifty! Between my kitchen and the Silk Club is a baker's kitchen and then a commercial kitchen for the Silk Club. It even has a sunken counter for ice.

The Silk Club also has a bar. I had it dismantled and shipped, piece by piece from Dublin – a burled red mahogany bar with brass stools. It's been waiting in the warehouse, for two years. A long mirror behind the bar has twisted columns separating it with acorns and oak leaves carved in the wood. I brought over six booths from an Irish pub in Galway and we put old subway tile on the floor, just like the original, and old mirrors at the tops of the booths. Very private. It took a lot of work to crack and peel the black paint, to make it look like it did in Galway (we had photographs). It looks old and I honestly think your Factory ancestors would love it. The architect and designers said I rescued the bar and booths. Those old, beautiful things deserved being rescued, that's for sure. Jeeves couldn't believe we went to so much trouble to make the bar authentic (although he loves it) and he told me I "cling to memories like boulders" but the truth is, those old things make me feel lighter than air.

From the outside, the Silk Club is turn-of-the-century, with a glassed veranda and moss green iron work. The rest of the exterior is stone, like the house.

Behind the baker's kitchen is a new little room I call the warming room. It's done in tartan plaids, mostly dark green and navy, but a little red plaid, too. The green wing chair has a patina, from slightly worn corduroy. The warming room is a cozy little TV room, and Jeeves usually joins me there for supper. I have a small campaign desk there, with an antique inkwell, a silver creamer to hold odds and ends, and your father's little framed photo.

Across from the kitchen is still the dining room, although we extended it. The chandeliers are neoclassical in gilt bronze with alabaster shades, from France, around 1910. I had no idea I liked lighting fixtures so much. The iron chandeliers in the Silk Club bathrooms have alabaster tulips draping down from them.

I think you'll enjoy the little tea room we added off the dining room. It reminds me of England. Behind the dining room is a china room with a ladder. Graeme Woods gave me a lobster tureen. It's unbelievable and get this – it's from Meissen! Like your monkeys! And, he didn't even know! It's gorgeous, with a lobster draped across the top of the lid.

There's a laundry room behind the china room. Linda Brodie is my housekeeper. She hangs clothes out in the Secret Garden, when the weather's nice. After the Secret Garden was cleared out, my gardener planted what he calls "old school" things – English Ivy along the walls, lilacs, holly and azaleas. Along the walkway to the loggia are crape myrtle, rhododendron, bleeding hearts, sweet peas, hydrangea, peonies, smoke trees, japonica and more azaleas. The Secret Garden has plenty of room for Samuel and Paul to play soccer. I remember you told me your grandfather had picnics in there.

I know this letter is getting long, but it's fun writing it. At the back of the house is a new wing, like a hotel lobby. It has a 25 foot ceiling and a massive fireplace. Even an old, ornate brass cash register at the marble registration desk.

Off the lobby is a suite for your visits. I call it the Carnegie Suite. It has a living room and bedroom, with a dining area and small kitchen. We tried to make it like an elegant 1900's seaside cottage. The colors are calm – gray, taupe, white. Two small rooms for your bodyguards are above, and a balcony. This back wing of the house can be closed off, and runs parallel to the Silk Club. A hallway leads

*from that wing, to a side entrance. The architect
calls the hallway a copper ghost wall – very
reflective.*

*Upstairs, over the snuggery is a walk-in
closet. Over the library is the spare bedroom
and bathroom.*

*My bedroom has an elegant dressing room
– Jeeves says it looks like a British links locker
room. It looks alot like HIS dressing room.
My bedroom ceiling is covered with narrow
strips of mahogany that have been layered with
shellac. It's shiny and reflective and looks very
New England to me. A balcony overlooks the
lobby. When you visit, I can wave to you from
my bedroom balcony!*

*The attic staircase has been redone and
the attic has a bunk area – Samuel and Paul
should enjoy it in December – and a small
movie theatre. Storage is now in the basement,
and we're using the tunnel your great-great-
grandfather put in, to link the Factory to my
house. Ready for snowy weather.*

Are you excited to visit? I hope so.

*You asked me on the phone what my
favorite thing is, and I think it's the heated
towel racks. They're in the other homes and I
wasn't certain I'd bother, but I'm so glad I did.
They're wonderful. In fact, I've ordered several
for the Animal Rescue League. Cozy nights
ahead for the dogs and cats! I'm glad I got the
idea from your house. Thanks!*

Yesterday, when I draped a throw over that

patina corduroy chair, it reminded me of Paul when he visited in Bath a few years ago. He climbed into a leather chair and had his little argyle pajamas on. Do you remember those pajamas? You know how his big toes kind of splay out. Well, his little bare feet were hanging over the edge and he looked so dear, sleeping. I had his bodyguard take him up to bed. He was trying to stay awake so he wouldn't miss any action at Sir Winston's. I can picture him now.

Yes! Do bring some of your rose cuttings when you visit. I'd like to have your rose bushes climbing the wall here.

Clara Davis (my chef's wife) has a lovely nosegay garden right outside her sewing room and she's asked me to invite you for lunch. You'll like her, Menke.

I think you'll be surprised at the town with new brick sidewalks and flower boxes. Several stores have replacement windows and most have new signs and awnings. Big planters of flowers are along two of the streets. The bookstore is still chugging along. I love that place. And, so is the drugstore. All the old favorites are doing well. I renovated and reopened the movie theatre – the town needed one.

Please accept my heartfelt *thanks for giving me a new life. Your generosity is something I think about every day. Not many people in this world can say they've handed someone a new life. It's because you did that for me, that I've tried to do that for some of the people here.*

*I'm glad Samuel and Paul have given you
their perspective as the estate has rounded
into shape. I know they've enjoyed seeing the
progress. They'll be surprised to see my house,
finally done.*

*With heartfelt love and affection,
Bronwyn*

Winter grabbed hold of Maine with a vengeance, and Bronwyn was relieved the prime minister was allowing Samuel and Paul to visit in December, as they'd done before.

Jeeves and Bronwyn interrupted the boys' visit with a Broadway show, and then flew Moss's girls back with them to Maine.

Samuel and Paul had known Susie and Allison all their lives. Alex Oz King took the four of them to Sugarloaf to ski, something Susie especially loved. She'd chosen to attend Bennington College, partly because of their winter sports. Susie gave Oz a run for his money on the slopes, while Allison was the sixteen year old overseer to the boys, to the amusement of the boys' bodyguards.

Returning to the estate, they settled into their Factory suites. Bronwyn had allowed all four of them to choose their room décor. Susie and Allison had stayed in the Factory before and Samuel and Paul dashed about the estate during construction, but seeing Bronwyn's house was a novelty for all of them.

One night, they went to Bronwyn's and stayed in the third floor bunk beds after enjoying a movie marathon. It was satisfying to have them all under her roof, but she was lonely when they returned home. Bronwyn realized she couldn't think of them as 'children' much longer, but her thoughts turned to her original 'estate child'…Charlie.

Teddy Palimore's estranged wife concerned Bronwyn. She knew Charlie missed his mother, but Vicki was still living in a dumpy apartment and having money problems because of her gambling boyfriend. Bronwyn worried she'd be shaking Teddy down for more money and she didn't want Charlie caught in the middle.

She convinced the hair salon owner to send Vicki to observe at a top New York Salon so her business would improve. But that meant Vicki would be gone until Christmas, and Charlie considered it an ill-timed field trip.

To lift Charlie's spirits, Bronwyn and Jeeves embarked on a Kittery outlet shopping excursion with the boy. Charlie earned money washing cars in the Factory garage, but Bronwyn was still surprised at the fistful of cash he pulled from his pocket.

She successfully guided Charlie through Dana Buchman and Anne Klein, supplementing Charlie's money with her own guilt-driven cash. If Vicki was coming back a new and improved stylist, she might as well look the part. Bronwyn picked up a few things at Claire Murray before they settled into seats at Warren's Lobster House.

Charlie dove into his plate of chicken nuggets, slurping chocolate milk and craning his neck left, then right, looking around. Bronwyn caught Jeeves watching him and they smiled. Evidently Charlie didn't get out much. Bronwyn echoed Jeeves' order, trying the lobster thermidor and a 'pile of lobster claws'. All three agreed they'd have to return.

Jeeves usually left for parts unknown over Christmas. Bronwyn didn't know where he went, nor did she inquire. Grace Cloud offered to fill Bronwyn in, but Bronwyn didn't want to know. She liked thinking of him with family over Christmas, and preferred not knowing if he wasn't.

Other than the lovely holiday dinner she'd promised her neighbors, the Todds and the Masons, Bronwyn let Christmas slide by without her.

New Years Eve, the television was on in her warming room, but Bronwyn wasn't watching. She was reading a newspaper story about Mayor Luke Townsend touted as the early frontrunner in gubernatorial polls. The election was ten months away and Luke was anxious for Bronwyn's town projects to be completed. The town green was reconfigured and four parklets were added to the east and west sides of town. The indoor and outdoor basketball and tennis courts were a big success, and other than improvements to the animal shelter and Pine Manor, most projects were caught up.

Laurent was bringing over some New Years Eve nibbles. Bronwyn kept her eye on the clock and reached for her Christmas card holder.

She opened Conor Frost's card and looked at the photo of little Luca. Smiling to herself, she recalled Conor's regal London wedding. Bronwyn and Jeeves had stayed at the Dorchester, applauded the bride and groom and dined well that week, trying to keep their spirits up. Jeeves seemed disappointed that Conor was marrying, and Bronwyn matched his melancholy at the time. But Bronwyn was upbeat by the time little Luca was born that summer.

It always tickled Bronwyn when people on the estate sent her Christmas cards. She held Katrin and her new husband's card and reflected on meeting Mark Palimore for the first time.

Bronwyn had stayed at Jeeves' flat, while her house

was completed. One afternoon, she went to a Roxy matinee, and standing beside her at the refreshment stand was a guy in his thirties, hinting to Bronwyn that he knew the Roxy owner. She nodded with disinterest, but when she took her seat and began chomping her popcorn, he sat one seat away, continuing to brag about his supposed close relationship with Bronwyn McCall, friend of his brother's...Teddy Palimore. When the movie was over, she dashed down the alley and waited ten minutes before heading to her car. Back home, she asked Edgar to make a picnic for everyone, and she deliberately arrived last, anticipating the look on Mark Palimore's face. It was priceless. She didn't mention the movie, nor tease him and he'd been grateful.

As a fourth grade teacher in Kansas, Mark Palimore was spending the summer with Teddy and Charlie. At the end of August, he managed to get a job substitute teaching in town and asked Katrin to marry him, moving from Teddy's house to Katrin's flat without missing a beat. Some people were shocked at the quick courtship, but Bronwyn admired Mark's desire to stay. They made a nice and affectionate couple, beaming with a happiness that seemed to gall Linda whenever she saw them.

Laurent Davis had also embarked on an expanded life.

In the spring, he had asked to meet with Bronwyn, to see if he could sell the antique 1930 Chris Craft deal sweetener she'd bought for him. Laurent wanted to ask a widow with two young girls, to marry him. He intended to show good-faith to his Kristine by financing the girls' future college educations, starting with the sale of his boat. Bronwyn reminded him college funds were in place for all the estate children and that would include Kristine's girls, Josselyn and Nicole. Laurent began to protest, but Bronwyn encouraged him to sell the boat and use the money for anything he'd like.

His Kristine was a lovely girl with a beautiful spirit. Her fine blond bob was highlighted and her huge eyes were only narrowed by her lilting laugh. She seemed to have a perpetual smile and her sweet disposition topped how pretty she was. Bronwyn was thrilled that quiet Laurent had been the one to capture her heart. Even more thrilled when she learned Laurent wasn't moving away. They even planned a home wedding, so his mother could attend.

Bronwyn heard Laurent mounting the steps from the tunnel to the kitchen. She dashed over and helped bring up trays of hors d'oeuvres.

"You didn't need to bring a whole party," Bronwyn said with a smile that belied her protest. "What did you bring?"

Kristine popped into the kitchen with a basket filled with the makings for raspberry Bellini's. Bronwyn took their coats as Laurent called, "Bronwyn, where shall I set up? The warming room or the snuggery?"

"It's your atmospheric moment, Laurent. Wherever you like. I could turn the heater on in the Silk Club bar, if you'd like."

"That's the spirit, Bronwyn," Kristine laughed. "Sweetie, what kitchen do you want to use?"

They lifted foil covered trays from a large box and Bronwyn craned her neck to catch a glimpse inside. Although pocket doors had closed off the Silk Club for the winter, the pub had low ceilings and a fireplace. It wouldn't take long to warm up.

"Be seated, lovely ladies and I'll start the fire and serve the Bellini's."

The two women caught up on their Christmas, with

Kristine sharing how much her girls enjoyed giving gifts at Pine Manor. It was something Bronwyn encouraged the estate children to do, and it was nice hearing how it went for the girls.

This was the first year Bronwyn and Grace Cloud had a Secret Santa shop for the Pine Manor residents. They encouraged town shops to donate items, which they were surprisingly eager to do. Then, Clara donated piccalilli and jars of jam and Linda knitted beautiful scarves. Tins of fudge were available courtesy of Valli, Katrin filled cookie tins, and Bronwyn donated dozens of L.L. Bean items. The residents drew names and the ladies went in first for private shopping in the Pine Manor dining hall, and then the men. It reminded Bronwyn of the Joseph Horne Co. in Pittsburgh, except no one was dressed as elves. Maybe next year.

Laurent sat across from Kristine and Bronwyn in a booth, offering trays of cocktail meatballs, sesame chicken strips, mini potato pancakes, fried green beans, and lobster spring rolls; then refilling the nibbles again before putting out Clara's tiramisu squares and Kristine's chocolate truffles.

It was genuinely fun for Bronwyn, and, at one point, Laurent caught her eye as she was biting off the end of a spring roll.

"I'm happy here, thank you," and he said it in an off-hand way, just as he'd done that morning in New York City.

"I'm glad for you," Bronwyn answered, leaning her head back to look at the ceiling and then leaning over Katrin for a blank perusal of the bar area.

Kristine was bewildered, but smiled as both Bronwyn and Laurent laughed heartily at each other.

"Really, Bronwyn. Thank you."

"I am glad for you," she answered and leaned across

the plates to kiss his cheek. Then, she gently elbowed Kristine. "I'm glad for both of you."

They offered to stay longer, but Bronwyn insisted they get back to Tom and Valli's where the girls planned to stay awake till midnight. Bronwyn bet they'd never make it past 10:00, and Kristine predicted she was right. She thanked them again, and they headed down to the tunnel.

Midnight wasn't significant to Bronwyn, so she went to bed at 10:30, musing over the past year.

Laurent and Kristine's marriage and Mark and Katrin's made Bronwyn rethink her pride in foresight and planning. Although Laurent's home was large for him, it only had two bedrooms. Katrin's apartment featured three bedrooms, but her apartment was much smaller than Linda and Matthew's on the other side of the Factory. Bronwyn hadn't anticipated the need to make them larger, and it reminded her how one can only plan so much. Both couples seemed delighted with their homes, but Bronwyn entered the New Year thinking she'd made a mistake by not foreseeing the happiness of others.

Over Christmas, Conor warned Graeme that Bronwyn was lonely. In the midst of filming, Conor had no time for a visit, so The Boys decided it was time to resurrect Oré Diaz Dominguez.

The plan was to urge Jeeves and Bronwyn to visit Pittsburgh in late January, with The Boys swinging by to pick her up in a luxury VIP motorbus. They'd make the trip to Lancaster for some outlet shopping, and Jeeves would pick her up five days later, in the jet.

Bronwyn had shopped with Graeme before, and knew

he had a retail bent, but she approached the Lancaster visit with a bemused attitude. Somehow she couldn't picture Roddy O'Neal, Sir Winston Watkins and Graeme Woods, with wives in tow, dashing incognito in and out of Lenox, Bass, and Christmas Tree Hill.

The motorbus was impressive, all black leather with white and red appointments. It had a kitchen, shower, beds, and a tour host in addition to the driver. None of The Boys had been to Lancaster and they were eagerly anticipating the shopping, picturesque landscape, quaint Amish farms, and Pennsylvania Dutch food.

When they approached Lancaster, Sir Winston had urged Bronwyn to brush her hair, which she thought an odd suggestion considering he was wearing a checked newsboy cap, track suit and galoshes. As she scanned her outlet map, the bus pulled over in front of a stately brick Bed and Breakfast with candles at the windows. She thought the idea was for them to sleep on the bus for the duration, but as Roddy steered her down the steps, Oré Diaz Dominguez was striding down the front walk to meet her.

The next morning, they all met at Miller's Smorgasbord, having reserved the back section. If The Boys expected some reaction from Bronwyn about her Oré reunion, they were disappointed. She seemed neither happy nor sad. She plotted shopping strategy, sitting comfortably beside Oré. No one seemed to recognize the famous group, which Bronwyn thought was disappointing them. She offered to be the runner for breakfast buffet refills, cheering them by warning there might be autograph seekers. She wouldn't say they were a motley crew, but The Boys had an odd approach to outlet shopping, disguised as couch potatoes with bucket hats.

The Lancaster trip was a grand success, so much so that Jeeves had to make room for all of Bronwyn's purchases on the plane, and Oré Diaz Dominguez, too. It was time for Oré to see the home she'd described all week long.

Fortunately, the plane ride was relatively short, as Oré, Bronwyn, and Jeeves buried their noses in books and scripts to avoid the possibility of speaking. Sometimes Oré caught Bronwyn's eye and she had to smile. She'd called Edgar to plan some special menus, and Edgar said the ladies of the estate were all atwitter at the prospect of Dominguez visiting. She told Oré, and she realized he expected nothing less.

Oré seemed genuinely interested in her house. Being with him was nice; but, she hadn't forgotten the look on his face at Sir Winston's. Even if she never saw it again, she always seemed to see it.

He raved about her house and she found herself liking him all the more. But almost from the first, he encouraged her to add an enormous bathroom to her master bedroom. The bathroom off the staircase was used by her bedroom and the spare, and she thought that was sufficient. After all, there were several other bathrooms in the house. She felt quite flooded with plumbing. She didn't know if he was correcting a glaring omission, asserting himself into her life, or psychologically dealing with their Bath bathroom fiasco. He stood beside her dressing room, and showed her how obvious the placement was. He claimed it was as if she deliberately didn't add a master bath, and she could see Oré's point. There was definitely room for a large bathroom above the baker's kitchen. She agreed to bring the architect back. Just when she thought construction was finished, it was about to begin again.

Then he pointed out space for a cottage, just beside the loggia. The setting was exquisite with a view of the Lobster Pound and the harbor, unlike anywhere else on the estate. How had she missed it? She reminded Oré the Carnegie Suite was for guests, but when he said he wanted to take her to San Sebastian, she guessed he meant the cottage for when his parents visited.

Things were moving fast, but Bronwyn surprised herself by not being angry or defensive about his building suggestions. His ideas made sense, seemed to grow out of love and affection, and she began to feel a partnership with him, beyond the physical.

Edgar did a yeoman's job with Oré's food. He managed to work golden calamari, gazpacho, gratin of salted Atlantic cod, shellfish paella, and pistachio topped flan into the menus. And Edgar was thrilled to find a compatriot in the oyster department and indulged himself with Oré, offering Nootka, Lasquiti, Kumamoto, Blue Point and Cove oysters on the half shell, served on ice at the raw bar of The Silk Club. It was a men's event and even Jeeves was blissfully satisfied.

On Valentine's Day, Edgar expected to create an intimate dinner, but Bronwyn opted for surf and turf with Jeeves, Van Tsang, Gus Townsend, and Tiny joining Oré. Nevertheless, Edgar surprised Bronwyn that morning with a romantic breakfast for two on her bedroom balcony. Oré gave her a bronze necklace of squared watermelon tourmaline, whiskey quartz, and amethyst which she proudly wore to dinner that night.

The next day, they walked across the estate to King Street, drifting over to the miniature horses. Bronwyn told

Oré the women were enjoying his visit. She seemed on the verge of saying something else and when he asked, she said, "They think we're lovers."

"We are lovers."

"But, I know they think about it and wonder." He stepped in front of her, looked into her eyes and gave her a long knee-buckling kiss, observed by Jen, Kristine, Katrin and Valli, all ducking down at the window in Kristine's office. They'd gathered as Oré and Bronwyn progressed down the street and across the yard. First the women collected in the living room, then peered out the kitchen window, and finally fell over each other getting to the office window in time for... the kiss. It took a swooning moment to collect themselves before Kristine prodded Valli to get through the connecting walkway to her house and ask them in for coffee.

Bronwyn was beginning to trust his feelings for her. They'd each made a good-faith commitment. Bronwyn was building the cottage beside the loggia and the bathroom of Oré's design. For his part, he made travel plans for Bronwyn in April. They were meeting his parents.

CHAPTER SIXTEEN

ESPAÑA
2002

*V*an Tsang accompanied Bronwyn to Spain, handing her off to Prime Minister Abraham's bodyguard. Bram was concerned about Bronwyn's safety, particularly with the Basque separatist movement, and insisted his own man travel with her.

Jeeves stayed in Maine, feigning disinterest in Bronwyn's romance. While Bronwyn had packed for the trip, Jeeves was glad she hadn't purchased diaphanous nightgowns. When she'd said her goodbyes, she was wearing a lined twill coat, suede sneakers, turtleneck and corduroys. That's my sensible girl, Jeeves thought.

If Jeeves had asked, Bronwyn might have shared her determination that Oré wouldn't enter her bedroom while at his parents' home. She didn't want Bram to know she was sleeping with him. Oré was known as the 'world's greatest lover' – a modern day Valentino. She knew Jeeves wasn't thrilled; she suspected Bram would be even less so.

Oré's Spanish home was large and bright with yellow washed walls and brick floors, and strikingly patterned carpets. The bathrooms had some of the features planned for her home, with marble everywhere and separate vanities, creamy with intricate fittings.

Although Bronwyn's father had dreamed of seeing France and its restaurants, he would have enjoyed the Spanish gastronomic societies and Basque food. Oré proudly called it unending gluttony, telling her the French popped over to enjoy Basque food, more original and less expensive than in France. Bobby McCall would have loved the traditionally all-male eating clubs. If he'd lived, if her life had traveled the same path, perhaps she'd be handing her dad over to Oré and his family for a true submersion in the dining culture. She hoped her family had made it over the border to Spain at some point. At least she hoped they'd been to nearby Biarritz in France, when it was so close.

The beauty of San Sebastian delighted Bronwyn. It was achingly elegant with sand the color of pearls and a lovely shaped bay. The promenade seemed suspended from a past time, and Bronwyn gazed at the architecture. The Old Quarter was beautifully lighted at night. After dark, lights ringed the harbor like a sparkling necklace encircling a deep amethyst throat, and mountains reached into lavender clouds.

Bronwyn hadn't expected Spain to suit her. She couldn't imagine wine-soaked lunches that would last hours, and joining his family for a nap at the day's midpoint allowed her to experience the happy active hours of Spain at night. It truly was another world.

She had no idea Oré had been a young member of the city's Orfeón Donostiarra, one of the top amateur choirs of the world. When she heard his voice, she implored him to consider Broadway. It was lovely finding so many surprises in Spain.

Each day seemed abuzz with potential. In quiet moments, Bronwyn reflected how she normally spent her days skittering like a stone, barely landing on life; but with Oré, she was submerged and amazed at the world and its wondrous depths. He yanked her deeply into life and she was surprised by the bright reverberations she felt.

One day, he walked up the gravel driveway, leading a goat by a rope. Bronwyn was sitting on the porch with his mother, grandmother, and great-grandmother and didn't think there was a more stunningly handsome man in the world. Oré's hair was long and parted in the middle, all dark power framing his face. He wore a black pinstripe three piece suit and stark white shirt. She noticed how his white teeth flashed in an angelic smile and tried to make a mental imprint that would last as long as a photograph. This was one of the times she regretted abandoning photography. The goat was gracefully handed over to his great-grandmother, renowned for her goat's milk fudge, and he lavishly shared his kisses with all the ladies, including Bronwyn.

Oré's parents were handsome people, looking younger than she'd expected. His mother could have been on an opera stage with her buxom figure, lush features, and black hair cascading in waves, pulled away from her face. Her lips were full, her face heart-shaped, and her eyes were huge beneath striking black eyebrows.

His grandparents were as affectionate together as his parents were; gray haired but still youthful and laughing. Every time Bronwyn saw his grandmother, she was laughing. On the other hand, his great-grandmother was a hard-working, wrinkled, no-nonsense granny, always wearing a full apron and usually with a knife in her hand. Unlike

Oré's parents and grandparents, she spoke no English, but she and Bronwyn communicated well enough with hand gestures, smiles, and mobile eyebrows.

Bronwyn half expected to find Oré's wedding photo on display, but if there had been one, it was hidden. Once, his mother warned Bronwyn to beware of his wife; she'd do anything to keep him. She said it kindly, but Bronwyn hadn't missed the curl of her lip as she spoke of her.

There came a point when Bronwyn no longer wanted to hear about Basque food. She hadn't missed her dad this much in years. Everything in Spain was too brilliant, too poignant, too emotional, and too alive. Even though Paris was twenty two years and five hundred miles away, Bronwyn felt her dad's presence and wished he'd been on this journey, instead of her.

One afternoon, Oré announced he had a surprise for Bronwyn. He produced a tiny car and put his great-grandmother and Bronwyn in the backseat while Bram's bodyguard joined him in the front. He called his great-grandmother 'Bisabuela' so Bronwyn patted her hand and said "Bisabuela" with a smile. As they traveled along the road, Bronwyn closed her eyes. Oré enjoyed himself in front, singing along with one of his favorite CD's. The bodyguard sat impassively, which made Oré crank up his volume, even more. When Bronwyn opened her eyes, she saw signs for Hendaye-Irun and Biarritz. They were approaching the border crossing to France. He was taking her into France.

"Oré. I need to use a bathroom, Oré, I mean it!"

He pulled into a restaurant parking lot and Bronwyn flew out the door. In the rest room, Oré's great-grand-mother found Bronwyn sitting on the floor and when she bent to join her, Bronwyn wobbled up and declared, "No, no, Bisabuela."

His great-grandmother waited while Bronwyn put a wet paper towel on the back of her neck, looking thoroughly miserable.

Pointing to Bronwyn's stomach, she asked, "Bebé"?

Managing a smile, Bronwyn shook her head, emphatically. "No, no bebé."

She tilted her head back, examining the ceiling. His grandmother was inches away, worry etching her face.

"Parlez-vous Francais, Bisabuela?"

That evoked a smile. "Mais oui!"

Bronwyn wasn't so enthusiastic. "Ma Francais…un peu. Je entreai France, jamais. Jamais." Oré's great-grandmother looked shocked and Bronwyn suspected she might be thinking Bronwyn was a fugitive.

She used her hands. Clutching her heart, Bronwyn explained, "Mon père, ma mère, ma soeur, ma grand-mère, mon grand-père, tout mort." She made a sleeping sign. "Toute le monde mort. En France. Explosion. Je entreai France, jamais." Bronwyn drew her finger across her neck. "Toute famille. Toute alles." With a whisper to his great-grandmother's ear, "Je déteste France."

The old woman enveloped Bronwyn, holding her until the bodyguard opened the door. Oré made apologies to the ladies and entered the rest room.

"I can't go to France, Oré, I just can't."

He looked at his great-grandmother and she pronounced, "Retourner chez moi."

Everyone treated Bronwyn gently upon their return. His mother didn't mention it and Bronwyn had no idea what translation the great-grandmother could have made of her terrible French. Even Oré didn't ask questions, but she had the feeling his bisabuela had made Bronwyn a sympathetic character in their eyes.

For his part, Oré was perplexed. He cursed his knowledge of the English language. He was certain Jeeves had told him she'd love to go to France.

"I missed you, Jeeves, I really did."

"That's kind of you, Miss."

"It just didn't seem right being there with all that food, when I knew how much you'd love it. You've got to go there sometime."

"Perhaps we can go together, Miss."

"Well, I don't think we could sneak in without seeing Oré's family."

"Was it not a good visit, Miss?"

"No, it went fine. It's just easier traveling with you. We're good travelers, aren't we? It's always simple together."

Jeeves nodded while his eyes danced with pleasure.

"I must show you the new bathroom, Miss. They've made remarkable progress. Are you home to stay?"

"Well, Oré's filming for two months, but he's planned a June trip for us, to Bora Bora. I didn't even know Bora Bora was a real place, I'm ashamed to say. He says the rooms are on stilts above water and you can see tropical fish underneath, with glass panels in the floor. It sounds a little unnerving."

"Actually, I've been, Miss. It's what I always imagined Bali Ha'i would be. Of course I was there years ago, before the popular crowd discovered it. Bora Bora offers great serenity."

"Well, we should go someday. I always want to share things with you, when you aren't there. What did you like most, Jeeves?"

"I believe the crystalline water. One scubas into 85 foot depths. It's quite exhilarating."

Bronwyn looked thoughtful. "You know, it's not my kind of place. Mosquito nets and sun. I'd get sunburned."

"I'm sure Mr. Diaz Dominguez will find you a thatched umbrella. You'll have a grand time."

"Then, too, he wants me to go to Barcelona for Christmas. He says the boulevards are filled with flowers and it'll be balmy. He says the Las Ramblas is the most beautiful street in the world. Have you been there?"

She was impressed when Jeeves nodded.

"Oré says it's lined with banana trees and palms, and the cafes are trimmed with garlands and bows. And they have cages of chirping canaries on the streets and wonderful pastries and chocolate shops and he wants to take me to a restaurant named after its seven doors."

"Restaurant 7 Portes. Yes, Miss. Quite extraordinary. I particularly enjoyed the succulent fish soup and platters of seafood. Actually, it rather reminds me of your Silk Club. You'll see when the two of you visit."

Jeeves had mastered stoicism a lifetime ago, but Bronwyn knew he was having a hard time imagining her travels without him.

"Maybe you'd like to spend Christmas in Barcelona, Jeeves. It would be fun."

"Rather the third wheel, I'm afraid."

"Nonsense. You always have a place with me." But they both knew she'd been relieved he hadn't made the trip to San Sebastian.

Plans for Bora Bora were going strong, until Linda discovered she had breast cancer. Linda was devastated and Bronwyn ached to ease her fear. Doc Larchmont accompanied Linda and Matthew to Manhattan for her surgery, while Bronwyn made an appointment to see Vicki Palimore, Charlie's wayward mother.

Vicki was killing time, perusing the industry publications she'd been getting since her styling internship, when Bronwyn walked in.

"Hello, Vicki. I'm Bronwyn McCall," she said evenly.

"I know who you are." They faced each other. The receptionist was on her way out.

"I'm your appointment, Vicki. I'm here for a haircut."

Vicki was stunned. "You're kidding."

"Nope."

Annoyed, Vicki shampooed her and got to work. When she was finished, Vicki's lower lip quivered.

"If you use this wax, you can give it texture."

"Don't worry," Bronwyn said quietly. "It's just what I wanted."

"Why did you come to me?"

Bronwyn shifted her gaze to see Vicki's reflection. "Because I knew you'd do it."

The truth sat heavily between them.

"You have good bone structure. It doesn't look bad."

"My cheekbones have been missing in action for a long time, Vicki. I'm always chipmunk-cheeky."

Vicki grimaced and her eyes were hard.

"Even though we haven't met, I know I haven't treated

you well. I was afraid you'd hurt Charlie, so I kept you away from the estate. I deserved to have you be the one to cut my hair."

"Everyone says how nice you are, but I don't think you're nice. More like nasty."

Bronwyn didn't seem affected one way or another by Vicki's low opinion of her.

"People will think I did this on purpose."

"You know it looks good. Just drastic, but it's a good cut." Bronwyn stood, dropping a fifty at her station. "My hair grows fast. It'll be okay."

And then she was gone.

Bronwyn slipped into her house, unnoticed by anyone except Van Tsang who opened his mouth, but nothing came out. Bronwyn sat in her bedroom and phoned Oré, canceling the trip to Bora Bora and telling him about Linda and her schedule of radiation and chemotherapy. Then she went to bed, but not without running her hand through her inch long cap of hair.

Worrying about Linda filled Bronwyn's idle time. She took to dog-walking, but it was amazing how her thoughts could race out of control, even walking and talking to the estate dogs.

Bronwyn scooted across the front of the estate, leash in hand, deciding Jack Spot Cotton might like to walk through Oz Valley with her. Normally she took Coolidge for Wednesday walks, but Matthew had him at the groomers. So, Jack Spot Cotton was about to get a surprise.

Bronwyn heard voices on Jen's patio when she rounded the bend, and was surprised to see Vicki sitting with Jen, sipping lemonade. Vicki's eyes widened and Jen stumbled for words.

"Hi, Bronwyn. Vicki just stopped by a minute to see Charlie. She was walking by. Out front. You know, see Charlie if he was around. I mean, if he was here. With Augie. Or, walked by."

It was so pathetic, that Bronwyn had to smile at both of them. She asked if Jack Spot was around and clipped the leash on the excited wirehaired fox terrier. They left before Jen could offer Bronwyn some lemonade. Jen was cursing her luck; Bronwyn didn't come by on Wednesdays. It wasn't the first time Vicki had visited Jen, getting a chance to see Charlie on the estate. But Jen wanted Bronwyn to know Vicki had never been down the street to Charlie's or even as far as Tom and Valli's. Jen felt like she'd been caught red-handed.

When Vicki saw how upset Jen was, she tried to leave, but Jen was too kind to let her. Instead, they sat uncomfortably together until Charlie and Augie returned from their neighborhood bike ride.

Bronwyn wondered where Teddy Palimore was. She listened for his voice on the wind, or some loud physical labor. She found him in his courtyard.

Tom Davis was tending to the miniature horses, well aware that Teddy's ex had been sneaking on the estate to see Charlie. It was only a matter of time until Bronwyn caught on. When he saw her walking purposefully to Teddy's, Tom felt sorry for the guy.

"Hi, Teddy. How's it going?"

"Hey, Bronwyn. Good. What's up? You're walking Jack today?"

"Yep." She looked around the courtyard, and then glanced up at the sky. Teddy wondered what she was gearing up to say.

"You know Teddy, this is your house. I probably gave

you the impression that Vicki wasn't welcome here on the estate. I may have said it or made sure you knew it. I don't even remember. But, I'm sorry. This is your house. Charlie should see his mother as often as he'd like. Over here. So, what I'm saying is, if you'd like her to visit or whatever, it's fine with me. Do your thing."

She expected to see surprise on his face, but instead he looked instantly happy. Bronwyn hated herself even more when she saw that. Charlie had lost time, and no one knew what a crime that was more than she did. And it was her fault.

Still, Bronwyn was surprised when Vicki moved in with Teddy and Charlie, five days later. Her boyfriend had left town and Bronwyn suspected Jeeves sewed up that loose end, but maybe the guy was ready to move on. Maybe.

There was an immediate benefit to Vicki moving in. Everyone noticed Teddy was more relaxed; perhaps a remarriage was on the horizon. That outlandish possibility gave everyone a distraction from worrying about Linda's health.

Oré called Jeeves in early August, asking to meet him in New York. Jeeves was baffled. Unless he needed birthday ideas for Bronwyn, it was a mystery.

As it turned out, a tearful Dominguez told Jeeves his wife was pregnant. Somehow she'd found out about the Bora Bora trip, and when Bronwyn cancelled, there was no reason not to take his wife and daughter. Oré was sobbing, a sight Jeeves found distasteful, coming from a man with no physical inducement.

"I'm certain our Bronwyn will understand."

"She'll never forgive me. Never. Never."

"On the contrary man, I believe she will. You know, forgiveness is her very nature."

"The baby may well not be mine, Sir. I have my doubts." Oré was looking at Jeeves with a wisp of hope in his eyes.

"Well, there you have it. But, I don't imagine it will matter to Bronwyn. All will be fine."

Jeeves gave him large doses of hope and convinced him Bronwyn's birthday would be the perfect time to tell her. She'd be happy and full of bonhomie and all that. When they parted, Jeeves was quite happy and brimming with bonhomie. At least someone's gotten happy news, he thought.

The morning after her birthday dinner, Bronwyn left Oré a farewell note on her pillow, urging him to stay the week. Several estate families had plans to entertain him, and she knew Valli was particularly enthused because Oré always spent time with her.

It was dawn when Bronwyn walked over to Van Tsang's, saying she was driving to Bar Harbor for the week. He insisted on accompanying her and called Jeeves with their plans. The day was surprisingly chilly and dreary to suit her mood.

She reflected on the night before. She wasn't angry Oré's wife was having a baby. It actually settled things between them. Even though he said the baby might not be his, he couldn't deny it might be. He declared it was in man's nature to have relations with his wife, and he said it in such a stately way that Bronwyn couldn't get angry or defensive. He'd just pointed out the factual nature of his marital status and the romantic atmosphere of Bora Bora; a trip she'd cancelled.

Oré began sobbing and Bronwyn took care to comfort and bolster him. She pointed out how much his daughter needed him, that this new baby would need him to be a wonderful father, and that fate had merely intervened. Bronwyn was calm, but adamant about fate yanking him back on the path of his marriage. While she cooed, she remembered what his mother had said. Oré's wife would do anything to keep him.

Bar Harbor was a good distraction for Bronwyn. She enjoyed the place and whenever she visited, she felt closer to her parents. Her dad had visited in his youth, and he'd taken Maggie to Bar Harbor on their honeymoon. She remembered hearing her mum telling about the gift shops, Sherman's Books and Stationery, Cadillac Mountain, and whale watching. Bronwyn was glad to find the Edenbrook Motel had vacancies; she liked to stay there because her parents did, so many years ago.

Jeeves was in constant touch with Van, and relieved that Bronwyn was doing well, as if she was simply on a getaway. They had a quiet breakfast at Testa's and then boarded a whale watching excursion boat.

Van was more surprised than Bronwyn when they heard Oré's voice and turned to find him on the upper deck. Van and Jeeves gave the couple privacy, no one daring to approach the two unsmiling men with arms folded and feet apart. Bronwyn glanced at Van and Jeeves. They might be in for a surprise if they don't grasp the railing, she thought.

Bronwyn put her arm through Oré's and pulled her blanket over him. He looked like the dregs of the earth in a washed-out hooded sweatshirt, dirty sneakers and ragged jeans. It was obvious he'd been crying, with eyes ringed in red. She wondered if it was possible Jeeves had taken a toothpick and Elmer's glue to stick bits of yellow in the corners of his eyes and little specks of food in the stubble of his beard.

Surely the outfit had been Jeeves' idea. She could imagine him rubbing dirt on the sneakers. He could convince Oré to go unwashed, opting for sympathy, knowing she might have second thoughts if she saw the normally gorgeous Dominguez. But, looking at him, she realized no amount of grooming could rehab him this morning. He was a sad sight.

The boat was powering through the cold and windy water, sending most people below decks for warmth. Jeeves stood guard, well protected by his down jacket, while Van popped below to get four cups of coffee. Bronwyn took hers, but she saw Ore had the shakes – from the weather, his nerves, or both. Bronwyn decided Jeeves brought him in that condition, because Oré harbored false hope and Jeeves wanted Bronwyn to reject him with finality. She wished she could stun Jeeves, but he was right. She just didn't want to do it as Oré froze to death on the gray sea, in his gray sweatshirt, with gray pallor, gray stubble, and was that gray gills? He looked wretched.

She took him down below; there was no worry about anyone recognizing the world's greatest lover today. She bought him two hoodies in successive sizes, molding him into a rotund Michelin man with large/xl/xxl. He was so chilled, that he put all three hoods up, fastening them snuggly like a three year old playing in the snow. They staked out a remote table, and when others went atop, she stayed, soothing him with reassuring words.

"I'm sorry, Oré. I shouldn't have left without talking to you. I wasn't trying to trick you. I really thought it would be easier for you, to just enjoy the estate. Everyone's excited for your visit." He was on the verge of tears. "I want you to buck up, kiddo. You're going to be a father and I'm happy for you. It's okay. I'm not angry. Now, let's just see some whales, shall we? And we can have some popovers and tea at Jordan Pond. Then you can go back and have lobster with Charlie and Teddy. And then see Valli and the horses. You know they're all expecting you."

"Cariño. Are you certain there's no future?" Bronwyn gave him a loving look and firmly shook her head.

CHAPTER SEVENTEEN

IRONY

*U*sually a fan of irony, Bronwyn didn't appreciate it this day.

Laurent had golfed with Doc Larchmont and one of Bronwyn's pilots, Pete Giordano, the day before. He returned to the estate with a plan – he and Bronwyn would take a sightseeing excursion in a Piper Seminole, flying above Maine's autumn leaves. Then, they'd drive up the coast for their farm stand jaunt, as planned.

The day had begun with blissful perfection. Laurent offered homemade doughnuts and chicory coffee. It was chilly and tendrils of mist curled along the runway. Giordano began the take-off as Bronwyn and Laurent strapped in and exchanged grins. The plane flew low enough to see white church steeples punctuating the landscape, and colorful boats dotting the water; a glorious infusion of color tucking into their souls. The flight path along Maine's sunny coast offered magnificent views of reds and golds accenting the blues of the water – a visual rhapsody.

They called out tree colors, pointing and grabbing each other's arm. Bronwyn called out burnt umber, canary, rust, sienna, crimson and gold. Laurent matched each call with one of his own: tangerine, mango, pumpkin, plum, lemon, sweet corn. Then, when she sensed a theme and challenged him, Laurent dug deep and came up with banana, tomato soup, and mac & cheese. Finally, Bronwyn yelled "Fern", Giordano shook his head and called back, "Nope, pine."

When they climbed out of the plane, the pilot accepted Bronwyn's thanks for a nifty flight path, and shared his plans for another afternoon of golf. Pete told Bronwyn how content he and Bob Mikush were with their golf course homes.

"Not a bad place to 'land'," Bronwyn laughed. "At a golf course like Bergamot where it's more Heaven than earth."

Both pilots used to live in New Jersey, near the airport that housed Bronwyn's private jet. But after 9/11, the prime minister preferred the jet be stowed in Maine, so the runway was lengthened, additional snow plows brought in, and security cameras and fingerprint recognition controls installed. After the pilots saw the golf course homes she offered, they were sold on the move.

Pete told Bronwyn the Bergamot Nine was their 'happy place' with pot bunkers and Guinness on tap. They enjoyed eating at the Country Club and when Laurent asked about his favorite meals, Pete said he was partial to the Pinehurst chili with pepper jack cheese and Bermuda onion; Mikush liked the Polish sausage dog, and both were hooked on the root beer floats. Laurent and Pete discussed the treachery of the sixth hole, and then Pete related how much his mother enjoyed visiting Maine.

"She was amazed at the roses everywhere. Not just around the course and the club, but around my house. When I showed her the rose arbor, she said it was smothered with roses, and she's right. It is smothered. Good thing I love my

Mom because she can't wait to come back. We went up to the Cabot Mill antiques. And she got herself walking shoes at Colburn Shoes over in Belfast. You know how I found that Glasgow railway clock? She wanted me to get her one, so I just packed mine up for her. She's anxious to meet you next time, Bronwyn, if you wouldn't mind."

"Just let me know when she visits. We'll have tea and your mom can see Jen Cotton's gardens. Laurent couldn't survive without his buttery mache, could you? Flowers and veggies; she'd have a lot to see."

"Laurent said you're going to a produce stand today. They have things you can't grow?"

She laughed. "We like to spread the love. It's not just having fresh produce; sometimes it's seeing the people."

They said their goodbyes and Laurent drove Bronwyn north to Ridge Farm where they bought fruits and vegetables, maple syrup, apple cider, and cornstalks. When they loaded the car, old Mr. Ridge moseyed over with a wide grin on his round face. Bronwyn always found him to be a charming old fellow. He was perfect for a photograph, and she tried to imprint the look of him in her mind. No matter the weather, no matter the heat, Mr. Ridge wore a tattered dress shirt, buttoned to the neck. The excess of his belt became a longer flapping tongue, each time Bronwyn saw him; his waist was dwindling. Pleated pants didn't hide the fact that he was shrinking, but his shoes remained large anchors. He walked with a rocky motion that his cane tried to steady, but his toothless smile was what warmed Bronwyn. In fact, his bald head, prominent ears, spongy little nose, and ear to ear grin made his round head seem almost like a pumpkin you'd pluck from his fields. They say men and women tend to look alike, as the married years go by; in this case, Mr. Ridge was starting to look like his beloved produce. The old man giggled when Bronwyn hugged him goodbye.

It was almost 12:30 and when Laurent suggested a sundae at Taylor's Shake Shack, she was agreeable. It seemed the day was only getting better.

They returned home and decided to walk around town.

Parking at the top of the hill, they popped their heads into Euro Bakery to say hello, but were talked into café latté on the little porch.

Walking down the hilly street toward the harbor, Bronwyn gestured and looked around. Laurent noticed her intensity and did the same. People were friendly to Bronwyn, but some were almost reverential. Bronwyn was nonchalant, but Laurent felt his chest puffing up. It was a shared glory, bestowing good things to the town. He knew he had no part in it, but just being with her felt rewarding.

Passing the diner, there was a rap at the window and Bronwyn looked in and waved. She asked Laurent if he could stand another cup of coffee. They sat in the back, with a bunch of retirees and Laurent observed how comfortable she was with the old guys, laughing as they teased, and part of the gang.

Mabel was behind the counter, and directed their waitress to bring blueberry pie for the tables, 'on the house'. Bronwyn waved to Mabel and thanked Heidi, who had a big blueberry stain on her apron.

When Heidi got a break in the action, she said how much she was enjoying college, thanks to the Scholarship Program. She was home for the summer, and was still visiting her senior citizen partner. The men trailed off their conversations to listen, and then one thumped the table in front of Laurent, telling him what a grand person Bronwyn was. Bronwyn good-naturedly cut him off and said they had to get moving. At the door, she blew them a kiss, which got a cackling reaction from the men.

They walked to the hardware and Bronwyn popped in to see the owners, and then continued their trek around town. When they reached the Arts Center, she gestured to one of the benches.

"Did you know we're starting etiquette classes in November?"

"Really?"

"They're doing children's etiquette for party manners… introductions, phone courtesy, dining etiquette. It should build confidence."

"What ages?"

"They're going to start with nine to eleven year olds. I took etiquette classes for a few years, in Pittsburgh. It helped me to be more comfortable around adults. I may not put a coat on properly, or stand in hesitation, or enter a car correctly, but I definitely know how to, and that makes me more confident."

"I admire your confidence. I'm going to talk to Kristine. The girls should go. I think they'd enjoy it."

"I think they would. They always have fun together. They're doing one for high school kids, but I don't know if that'll be popular. I hope so. It's shocking to me how many kids don't know what it's like to order in a restaurant, to leave a tip, even to relax and enjoy food. They're doing a business etiquette course, too."

They continued strolling. Laurent asked about the Scholarship Program.

"It's interesting getting to know the high school kids. Becka Douglas is doing her senior project on feral cats. It's called Trap-Neuter-Return and when I heard about it, I took her up to the Animal Rescue League. They're neutering for free and she's getting people to be colony caretakers, giving feral cats food and water and supervising them when it's cold."

At the end of the main street, they looked back.

"Do you miss Brooklyn, Laurent?"

"It seems like I've always lived here."

"Sometimes I feel that way, too. Especially when I hear the seagulls."

They crossed the street to a verdant and peaceful parklet, an escape from the shops and busy harbor. Ferns added definition to colorful bushes and trees dipped down and soared upward with masses of reds, yellows and oranges. A small fountain created glittering rings of beady pearls along the surface of a small pond.

Their next stop was Walt Harris's Barber Shop. Bronwyn poked her head in to say hello and noticed Walt clipping a boy, happily seated in a red toy car.

"Hello," she said to the boy, as the door closed behind them. "I like your car."

He beamed with pride of ownership.

"This is a great idea, Walt," Bronwyn said, examining the car, raised on a lift to the appropriate hair cutting height.

"Laura Storey found it for me," Walt said.

After Bronwyn said goodbye, they continued on.

"Laura has done such a great job," she shared. "I only hear good things."

A shopkeeper was sweeping leaves from the sidewalk of her pottery gallery. They waited, nodded hello and walked around her.

Of all the shops in town, Laurent had to say he wasn't fond of the Azalea Dress Shop on the corner. It was the color of Pepto Bismol. The wooden exterior was attractive enough, with pillars and interesting molding, if only they'd painted it taupe or cream. Next door was the knitting shop, where Laurent was a reluctant, regular patron, buying yarn for his mother and grandmother.

Bronwyn must have known, since she asked, "Need anything in there, today?"

It seemed like she knew everyone. Bronwyn either said hello, or bent her left wrist in little waves as they passed by. One older gent was holding a Jack Russell terrier. Bronwyn let the dog sniff the back of her hand and then slowly patted his forehead. Before long, she was holding the little fellow and he seemed content, with his legs leisurely crossed.

"Who was that?" Laurent asked when they moved on, and was surprised when she shrugged.

"Oh look," Bronwyn said, reading a sign in a window. "The First Presbyterian is having a church supper on Saturday. Chowdah," she said with a smile, "rolls, salads, lemon meringue pie…"

"You don't like lemon meringue pie."

"I know, but it sounds like fun, doesn't it?"

Laurent had to agree. It did.

"One of the best things I ever did was hiring Laura Storey. The town was decorated so beautifully last Christmas."

"I remember – it was festive. Even the harbor."

"Makes me excited to see what she comes up with, this Christmas. I'm meeting with her mom at 4:00; maybe she knows what Laura has planned."

"Ah oh," Bronwyn said as they approached Jordan's Jolly Candy Shoppe. "I'm going in."

Three pounds of candy later, they continued on.

"Why don't we have an early dinner together? The Sea Shanty? Or the Lobster Claw? You choose," Laurent suggested.

"Really? Don't you need to go home?"

"I'm sure Kristine and the girls can make supper without me."

"Why don't we all go? It would be fun to eat out with the girls."

"Test their etiquette."

"No, silly. Let me know. I should be back by five, after seeing Margo. If not, I'll just have soup at home."

Laurent dropped Bronwyn off at Margo Storey's house and she knocked at the door. Mr. Storey greeted her and Bronwyn detected a quiet detachment about the man. Perhaps they'd just had a disagreement.

Margo was frowning, and barefoot, with her feet perched upon a little stool under her desk.

"Anything wrong?" Bronwyn asked, as Margo took her hands away from the computer.

Margo sighed. "Have a seat, Bronwyn."

Bronwyn's radar went up.

"What's wrong?" She repeated.

"I think you've been pleased with Laura's work," Margo began.

Bronwyn reassured her. "Like mother, like daughter. It amazes me there's so much creative brain power between the two of you. I'm really lucky, Margo. She's doing a great job."

Margo looked doubtful, so Bronwyn continued. "Just this afternoon, Laurent and I were walking downtown and saying what a great job Laura did over the holidays. And really, Margo, the storefronts look wonderful – except for the Pepto store, and that's not Laura's fault. I like the new signs, especially the carved ones. The new shopping bags at Jordan's Jolly Candy Shoppe are a great design."

"She's quitting, Bronwyn. She's gotten another offer."

As quick as a wink, Bronwyn swung from being stunned to tasting the bile of anger. She had no idea how much she valued loyalty until that moment. Her face betrayed all of it; she didn't have guile enough to cover her emotion.

"Don't be angry, Bronwyn. Please. She believes in herself; she's confident. We can't fault her for that, can we? Bronwyn?"

"What's the job?" Bronwyn said, in a flat tone.

"Well, they offered her a job in Tylerboro. Bringing in new business, promoting the town, revamping the businesses. Basically what she's done, here."

"That's only thirty miles away. Is she going to commute from your house, or get a place in Tylerboro?"

Margo looked uncomfortable. "No, she's staying in the apartment. Her apartment, above the theater."

Bronwyn was silent.

"You could charge her rent, of course. I'm sure she intends to pay you rent. Honestly, I hadn't thought of it. She's so excited, I'm sure she'll be in touch with you about rent."

"She won't be living above the theater."

Both women stared at each other and the silence was uncomfortable, even for Mr. Storey who'd been listening around the corner. Mr. Storey wasn't at all surprised at Bronwyn's reaction. He'd warned his wife, but she was as blithely optimistic as his daughter.

"I see."

Bronwyn rose. "She'll want to polish her skills for grant writing. You might want to mention that to her, Margo. We know each other well enough for me to be honest. When I met Laura, I was impressed with her enthusiasm, her ideas, and her optimism. She's very special. The merchants will be sorry to see her go. She's their lifeline, at least they think she is. I think she is. Has been. But her real success is because of my money. Tylerboro isn't going to see the success we have here because she'll be working without my money. It's as simple as that."

Margo spoke, quietly. "I think she brings a lot to the table. And, if you think about it Bronwyn, once you get over your disappointment, you might want to improve Tylerboro. It would be satisfying I think. They're good people, just like here."

So, Laura expected she could access Bronwyn's money on her way to success.

"I don't live in Tylerboro", Bronwyn said in a monotone, essentially closing off the possibility. "I'm surprised she didn't use me as a reference. That's almost laughable, isn't it? I'm surprised she didn't tell me she was job hunting."

Margo started to interrupt, but Bronwyn lifted her hand. "And, I am incredibly disappointed she asked her mother to tell me. You know Jim Phipps is putting together a business etiquette class. I guess it's not soon enough."

Although Bronwyn knew she didn't want to lose two Storeys in one afternoon, she felt the power of her money and the rightness of her fury. Margo was starkly aware she was just as replaceable as her daughter. With that in mind, both women were angry, disappointed, uncomfortable, but neither was willing to end the meeting without some rapprochement. There was really only one thing Margo could say, and she knew it must be heartfelt.

When she was ready, she said it. "I'm sorry, Bronwyn," and waited anxiously for her response. Only a few years ago, Margo was toiling as the business manager for the school district, a low-paying job fraught with politics and back-biting.

Margo recalled the letters they exchanged back in 1998. Those letters began a real friendship and Margo was reminded of Bronwyn's potent love for the town before she ever moved to Maine. Those memories made Margo genuinely regretful and she repeated, "I'm so sorry, Bronwyn."

Bronwyn crossed over, lightly hugging Margo and murmuring, "It's okay" at the same time Margo was saying, "I can talk to her. Maybe she can back out of the job."

"No, no, Margo. I hope she takes it and it brings her fulfillment. They're lucky to have her. Thanks for letting me know."

Bronwyn bent over and picked up her jacket, grasping it in the middle of the collar with her right hand, placing her left arm delicately in the left sleeve, lifting the jacket slightly from her left shoulder as her right hand sought the right sleeve behind her back, placing her right arm through the sleeve and bringing it up in one smooth motion, as she learned long ago, in etiquette class.

"Do you think she can keep the apartment?"

Lightly laughing, Bronwyn said, "No," and waved goodbye.

CHAPTER EIGHTEEN

CLIVE AT THE LOGGIA
2003

The Animal Rescue League was an adoption center, providing veterinary care, and animal welfare advocacy. Bronwyn gave substantial funds to upgrade and expand the center, adding staff, and creating an attractive environment for both workers and animals.

She popped over at least once a week to play with the animals and chat with the workers. This evening, the staff seemed anxious when she arrived.

In hushed tones, they told her a man named Donald Harper was looking at dogs. He'd taken a white mixed breed puppy two weeks earlier and they'd been unable to schedule a home visit. With his return, they checked the computer to schedule a visit, but he said he no longer had the dog, saying, "I'm done with that one."

The staff was deciding how to respond. They'd sent him back to the dogs, buying time. One of the veterinarians had been briefed and was walking through the lobby as Bronwyn announced, "I'll go back."

"I'm going with you, Bronwyn. The guy might be a wacko."

Bronwyn hoped it was just a misunderstanding, but she had a bad feeling.

"Excuse me. Are you the man who adopted the white puppy two weeks ago? Don Harper?"

"You work here?"

"I do," said the veterinarian, mild-mannered and bespectacled.

Ignoring Bronwyn, Harper said, "I'm here for a dog."

The man's suit was meant to impress, but Bronwyn noticed his shoes were scuffed. Judge Wheeler, Jeeves, Graeme Woods – all had said men were judged by the shine of their shoes. Harper had lousy looking shoes. When she lifted her gaze, he was watching her.

"Dr. Marshall, would you excuse us?"

The vet withdrew, but ducked into an empty kennel.

Bronwyn spoke over the din of barking dogs. "I want to know what happened to that white dog."

Harper's laugh had a maniacal twang. "No you don't."

"You can't have another one. You signed an agreement when you took the dog, permitting a home visit for suitability."

"The dog was definitely suitable."

"Then why did you say you don't have it?"

Harper walked around Bronwyn, headed back the way he'd come. Knowing she'd be gutless, he leaned in and whispered.

She was stunned into silence. He got halfway down the aisle before she came after him, grasping his suit jacket and yanking him to his knees so violently, his kneecaps could have cracked on the concrete.

Dr. Marshall reached Bronwyn at the same time Officer Gary Grande grabbed Harper and stood between them.

"Whoa. Bronwyn you stay here. I'm walking this guy out."

"No, Gary. Hang onto him."

"Stay here, Bronwyn."

Harper turned and sneered at Bronwyn. "No one'll believe you, chickie. You're one of those 'save the whales' loonies."

Officer Grande escorted him to his car, just as Jeeves pulled into the lot.

Harper drove off.

In the employee lounge, Bronwyn was visibly upset, but she wouldn't share what Harper said to her.

"Miss, do you prefer to speak with Officer Grande? I'll be outside if you'd rather."

She looked thoroughly miserable and shrugged. "Maybe I'll write it."

But Bronwyn couldn't make herself write it any more than she could say it. She put her head in her hands. The words were sinking in and she felt more sickened with every passing minute.

Jeeves lifted her chin and looked into her eyes. "Just tell us."

Even then, she couldn't. Finally she said, "Get the vet."

Officer Grande and Jeeves waited outside the door, neglecting to confirm their next poker game; shuffling their feet, instead.

Jeeves drove her back to the estate, and Bronwyn agreed to spend the night in his spare bedroom. He poured brandy, and solicitous Edgar brought over clam chowder and hot biscuits. They sat with her at Jeeves' kitchen table and he patted her hand. "Everything will be fine, Miss. I promise you. Do you believe me?"

Bronwyn looked at him and then at Edgar, with haunted eyes.

"Believe him, Bronwyn. Jeeves'll take care of you. He'll take care of everything."

"Miss. Look at me, please. I will. I promise you."

"Thank you, Jeeves," she answered softly.

Respectfully, Bronwyn always called Moss's wife, 'Mrs. Mastrofrancesco'. Although they were friendly, she had never asked Bronwyn to call her Susan, and had rarely phoned her. So, Bronwyn was surprised when Mrs. Mastrofrancesco invited her for a visit.

On the flight to New York, Bronwyn focused her thoughts on the Mastrofrancesco's large bathroom. It was like an oasis with rich green glazed tiles and a private balcony overlooking Central Park. The green floor tiles were alleviated with white here and there, but the wall tiles were an expanse of garden green shades. She knew if Oré hadn't made the choices for her forgotten master bath, she'd have wanted one exactly like the Mastrofrancesco's.

When she arrived, Bronwyn mused over her first visit at nineteen, preparing to photograph Susie and Allison. Those large black and white photographs still dominated the graceful foyer. One revealed Susie seated at tea at The Plaza. In the other, Allison was stroking a horse's muzzle in Central Park. The black and white portraits forced the viewer to assess the unique beauty of the girls, without artifice or distraction. Both photographs were straightforward. It was amazing to see the young women they'd become, with every clue residing in their faces at such a young age.

The Mastrofrancesco penthouse was grand, with

breathtaking views of Central Park. In daylight, Bronwyn thought the acres of looping greenery bisecting the city's upper east and west sides looked benignly peaceful. But at dusk, as the lights began to glow from a deep wall of beaconing skyscrapers, in a lacy overlay of illumination, she was reminded what a pulsating, stimulating life the city led. Gazing at its night glory, one could forget about angst on the streets and exhaustion permeating the subways. Visiting the celestial Mastrofrancesco penthouse was the ultimate infusion of high-end, glittering New York City.

Bronwyn climbed the stainless steel staircase and dropped her bag in the guest room, where single beds sat beneath a tailored canopy. Glossy black headboards and footboards accentuated stark white bed linens. Only a vase of lilacs broke the black and white scheme.

She felt uneasy, and reviewed her arrival, trying to glean the source of her anxiety. Bronwyn had felt fine in the elevator, then greeting the maid, but now she felt a bit queasy. The photographs. Something about the photographs.

Although she'd visited the Mastrofrancescos, this was the first time in six years that she had contemplated Susie and Allison's portraits, rather than stride past them. Bronwyn's instinct with her work had always been to cup photographs as if they held a rounded significance. She nodded slightly, as her mind reached for the truth her heart had apparently latched onto.

She could almost hear the trilling giggles of Susie and Allison as she worked with them, spinning them into the light. Yes, she thought, the 'why' is getting closer. She imagined feeling Susie's pointed chin in the palm of her hand.

Over the years, Bronwyn protected her brittle vulnerability and loneliness, wrapping it in shy layers. Sometimes she came close to shattering like plates at a Greek wedding, no matter how strong Jeeves supposed she was.

Not much for introspection, Bronwyn nonetheless felt compelled to sort out her emotions. She recognized she no longer created atmosphere, preserving the moment, sharing her sight. In fact, she'd let photography fall away the instant Moss had offered to replace her equipment. And yet, gazing at the portraits, she'd felt the old pride. The stark contrast was what she strived for, echoing the way 'white' flowed from the hands of John Singer Sargent..

Bronwyn walked to the window, looking out with unseeing eyes. 'No more photography' wasn't an act of defiance. It wasn't an angry response to losing her photographs in the ransacked aftermath of Samuel and Paul's kidnapping. Not anger. More like resolve.

She felt revelation within her grasp. Why had she obstinately turned away from her analytical eye and her heart's embrace of her view? Bronwyn was in every photograph she'd ever taken, as surely as if she draped her arm around her subject. She bent the light, she was the one who saw and then revealed and…why had she abandoned her expression of life?

If she were back in the Chelsea gallery a dozen years ago, holding little Allison, she would whisper, 'see what I see, now and forever'. Unending moments. Without expiration.

Bronwyn walked to the bathroom and splashed cold water on her face. Why had she given up the most meaningful thing she'd found? She wished she'd simply walked through the foyer like always, without looking at the portraits.

When she lifted her eyes to the mirror, she smiled. Ah, yes.

After the kidnapping, it had been an instinctive vow to tread more lightly on the earth, to leave it unmarked by her presence, to glide around without taking a toehold, making a perch, revealing her heart or showing her path. She meant to barely glimpse an earth she had intensely viewed. The photograph showed the photographer, and she meant now to be invisible.

Her anxiety dissipated and Bronwyn went to the library. She found comfort in the circular balcony with its skylight, and the cream leather furniture seemed the height of luxury.

The library was where Mrs. Mastrofrancesco found her.

"Bronwyn. I'm glad you came. I have a situation I thought you might help me with."

"Really? What is it, Mrs. Mastrofrancesco?"

"Call me Susan."

Bronwyn girded herself.

"What's the situation, Susan?"

"Well, Bronwyn. Some of my friends are more societal acquaintances, than actual friends. Would you like some tea?"

"No thanks, Susan." She waited for her to begin again. It wouldn't matter to Bronwyn what Moss's wife might be involved in – she was ready to help.

"Go on."

"Well, I'm ashamed to say, one of my so-called friends is behaving abysmally. She has the most gentile butler, named Joseph. Well, her daughter is," Susan searched for the word, "wild. I guess that's one way of saying it. She left her lover, a French painter, and turned to poor Joseph. She should have known better, but she convinced Joseph to keep their relationship quiet, and he thought it was a secret, romantic love. Of course she got pregnant." Susan stopped.

"Would you like a glass of wine, Bronwyn?"

"I will, if you will."

"That's what I was hoping you'd say. This is so difficult."

Susan rang the bell and two glasses of chilled white wine were poured.

"There. That's better, I think."

"Okay. So, Joseph is the father, or the painter?"

"Definitely Joseph. They did a paternity test. If you met him, Bronwyn, you'd see he is the epitome of a gentleman. Gentile, beautifully dressed, exquisite manners. He's in his late forties, and has blonde hair waving back from his face. It's quite extraordinary." She lowered her voice. "I think he's a dream butler. I'd want him for my own, if it wouldn't cause unrest here."

Bronwyn took a sip of morning wine and settled back into the couch.

"Here's the thing. As soon as Trinity had the baby, she ran off to France. I wouldn't expect the painter to want her, but he did. Which leaves Joseph. Alone."

The story stalled. If Susan was hoping Bronwyn could guess the next part, she couldn't.

"Joseph lost his position. My so-called friend and I have had a few discussions and the last one rather damaged our relationship. Her husband is a client of Stanley's firm, so I'm trying to make amends although my heart is truly not in it. I wouldn't care if I never spoke to her again."

"Why have you argued?"

"It's dreadfully unfair of her to sack the poor man. And worse, he's so sensitive. He's been so despondent that my friend allowed him to stay in his quarters, but now she says she can't bear to see him; he reminds her of the mess."

"So, where will he go?"

"I was hoping – I was hoping you might take him on."

Bronwyn lifted her eyebrows and drummed her fingers against her two front teeth.

"Bronwyn, you know Jeeves is no butler. Wouldn't it be nice to have a real butler? You'd adore him. He's ever so special. And, if you didn't want him staying in your house, you have that little cottage beside the loggia."

"Knowing Jeeves, he'd be affronted, but maybe it could work. I don't think I have much call for a butler, but," Bronwyn thought of something. "What about the baby?"

"A little girl. She's three now."

"Three? You mean they've kept him on for three years and suddenly they sack him?"

"That's why I'm angry. It's so unfair and he's taking it dreadfully."

"But, why now? Why decide he has to go now?"

Susan looked embarrassed. "Because he wants to be part of his daughter's life. He's asked Stanley to represent him."

"And Moss won't do it?"

She shook her head and Bronwyn figured this was the source of the problem. Susan would expect Moss to help, and he must have a conflict of interest.

"It might work. Do you think I could meet him?"

"I was hoping you'd say that. He's coming for lunch." That made them both laugh.

Joseph was everything Susan had said, so Bronwyn returned to Maine and readied the cottage. It was charming, but hadn't been occupied. Bronwyn approved of the exterior with its colonial blue paint, black shutters and red door, but the interior was stark. Linda was a whirling dervish, selecting comfortable bedding, towels, kitchenware and dishes, while Edgar stocked the pantry.

Jeeves seemed not to mind her acquisition of a butler,

and actually seemed to approve when Bronwyn told him he was too good a friend and protector to ever do butler service. All the while, she was thinking he'd never done butler service, no matter what Jeeves told himself.

As Joseph began his duties, he was apologetic and gracious toward Bronwyn, and she found the best way to defuse his self-conscious gratitude was to keep him busy. Fortunately, Edgar and Linda had several suggestions, so The Silk Club's silver was polished, the linens properly pressed, and the pots and pans scoured. Joseph took to it with a quiet zeal and his spirits improved.

However, his nights were difficult. He was haunted knowing his daughter was somewhere in France, beyond his reach. He'd been emotionally crippled by her mother and devastated by her callous disposal of him, after the baby was born. He didn't understand it. He was at a loss, no matter how much time went by. They'd planned a future and Trinity ripped it from his heart, taking his daughter away. Only sleeping pills made it fade into nothingness. Until the next day. Until the next night.

Susan had warned Bronwyn of Joseph's sleeping pill habit, so Bronwyn consulted Doc Larchmont, who prescribed one pill each night, until Joseph adjusted to his new home. Jeeves was the dispenser and walked over to the cottage each evening, waiting with Joseph until the emotionally crippled manservant fell asleep.

Bronwyn hoped Jeeves would be sympathetic and make Joseph a friend. How could anyone not sympathize with him? He seemed like an angel with his quiet good manners, perplexed by the nastiness of the world. .

It became a pleasure having the elegant gentleman attending to her. Joseph ran her bath, gently awakened her with a gradual unveiling of the drapes, cracked the top off her egg-in-a-cup, presented her mail on a silver salver, made a charming spectacle of her daily tea, and even presented a freshly bathed Snooks Von Krinkles on one of her overnight visits, amazing Gus.

Everyone instantly took to the man. Everyone but Jeeves. When Joseph arrived, Jeeves circled him as if he were prey. He was barely courteous, but eventually concluded Joseph wasn't taking advantage of Bronwyn. There was as much room for him on the estate, as anyone else. His coming late to the party didn't really rile Jeeves. Until the music.

One day, when Bronwyn was shopping with Grace Cloud, Jeeves was reading the paper and heard someone vocalizing in The Silk Club. Joseph had been polishing the silver coffee pots, so Jeeves wasn't surprised to see him standing on the riser beside the grand piano. Joseph's back was turned, facing the expanse of lawn beyond the window. He began to sing again. Jeeves doused the kitchen lights and settled in the dark warming room.

Joseph had a beautiful tenor, Jeeves discovered. His voice was strong and resonant and Jeeves admired beautiful singing. Joseph launched into *Con Te Partiro*, a real favorite of Jeeves'. He was just about to consider Joseph for poker membership when he glanced through the doorway and saw Bronwyn standing back in the dark kitchen with tears wetting her face, exquisitely moved by Joseph's astounding voice. Jeeves hadn't seen her cry like that since she'd learned Oliver Silkowski had died. It was like watching her thaw, and seeing Joseph could evoke this gut-wrenched reaction from her was stunning. Jeeves tortured himself by watching Bronwyn cry. She turned and left, without seeing him or his palpable envy.

A week later, everything started coming up roses for Joseph. Jeeves found a way to stun Bronwyn, happily enlisting the aid of a top-notch custody attorney, at Jeeves' expense. Once Trinity realized she was about to lose custody of her daughter, due to the revelation of some surprising photographs, she began to remember what a fine man Joseph was. True, she'd been blackmailed by Jeeves into giving up her French lover, but she was ready to leave him anyway.

Bronwyn was impressed. Jeeves might have worked his magic over several months, but to gain such results in only a few weeks was stunning.

Before Joseph left for Connecticut, happily engaged to run the country household of Trinity's parents, Bronwyn spoke with him. Realizing he answered her cautions with only a beatific smile, she resigned herself to making him promise to call if he needed anything.

Once Joseph was gone, Bronwyn made an effort to spend time with Jeeves, so he wouldn't know how deeply sorry she was to see Joseph go. She was proud of Jeeves. She hadn't realized he could be so generous and selfless.

"I'm afraid Clara's a might suspicious, Jeeves. She's wondering why you won't let Linda clean and why I keep coming over here to make your meals, when she knows you're eating with Bronwyn."

The two men stared at each other. Edgar avoided crossing Jeeves, but dealing with Clara was no picnic. He'd held her off as long as he could, but she was ready to march into Jeeves' flat if Edgar didn't give her some answers.

"I suppose she can be trusted?"

"Of course. No one's more trustworthy than my Clara. She'll not breathe a word."

"Well, our friend's about to leave. He'll be gone tonight. Perhaps he could spend an hour with Clara and give Linda an opportunity to tidy up as usual. Might our Clara be persuaded to open the door to no one?"

"Yes. I promise you that. She'll appreciate being brought into your confidence, Jeeves. She'll respect your privacy."

Edgar warned Clara that Jeeves' houseguest wouldn't be sharing his name or any personal information. He set two places at the table in her sewing room and Clara went to change.

It was quite theatrical, she thought, as she sat in the sunny sewing room, waiting for her mystery guest. Edgar ushered in the gentleman, but she thought there must be some mistake. She'd expected an older gentleman, assuming he might be Jeeves' lover since he was so secretive. But this young man, perhaps thirty five or so, was a bracing force of energy – not anything like she'd anticipated.

"Hullo, I'm Clive," he said, taking her hand. Edgar raised his eyebrows. He expected Jeeve's Clive would use a different name or just sit in silence. It was obvious that Clara intended to get to know the boy, so Edgar gave up and returned to the kitchen, preparing their breakfast.

Clara couldn't take her eyes away from Clive. She was a bit excited by the secretive nature of his visit, and found him very attractive. He was certainly handsome, but not in the traditional sense. With bold features, everything about him was squared and seemed vibrant. Even his nose seemed to square off, as did his eyes, his shoulders and certainly his jaw. Those eyes of his seemed to crackle when he gazed into the sunlight, filtering in through the blinds.

"Would you like me to close the blinds? The sun is in your eyes, Clive."

"No, actually, sometimes I don't see much of the sun. I quite enjoy it."

He had an unusual, mournful tone. Once he was seated, he seemed very still; observant without moving. Clara knew Jeeves was part of a security force, and this friend of his seemed just the type. There was a manly beauty about him. His hair was wavy and tousled, brushed back from his forehead. And what long eyelashes he has, Clara thought.

There was a knock at the front door and Clara could hear Edgar, who'd been standing guard as they began their breakfast. She listened and realized Bronwyn intended to come back to visit. She patted Clive's knee and went down the hallway, finding Bronwyn just inside the front door.

"Hi, Clara. Believe it or not, I baked muffins this morning. Thought you'd like some. I'm headed over to Valli's."

"Oh, for any sakes. They smell wonderful. Hmmmmm. Give her my love and take care going down the hill." They hugged goodbye and Clara watched as she walked across the pavers, toward Oz Valley.

While Clara stood with Edgar, making certain Bronwyn didn't return, Clive peered through the mini blind slats. So that was Bronwyn McCall, all hidden and tucked away from him. She wore corduroys and a field jacket, and as she walked away, her hair sprung to life with every step. She put her basket down and for some inexplicable reason, dropped to her knees. He was tempted to race through the house to see what was wrong, but just then a Newfoundland dog bounded up the hill and bowled her over.

Bronwyn was laughing hard, hugging the dog as he bounded in and out from her grasp. A tall man came over the slope and made the dog stand still. That would be Alex Oz King, Clive decided. With both hands firmly under her arms, he picked Bronwyn up and righted her. Clive sensed it wasn't the first time the three of them had done this trick. The man kissed the top of her head and kept walking, with the dog running ahead. Before Bronwyn continued on her way, she turned. It seemed she was looking right at Clive. He jerked away, but moved back. He wanted to see her. And then she was gone.

There were times when Bronwyn felt manipulated. She knew Jeeves had his secret things; Van, too. But she wished Jeeves would accept her need for solitude with the same grace he expected from her. Tonight was one of those nights. Van Tsang took her to dinner and walked her home, inquiring about her plans. Normally, with a chilly evening, they'd use the tunnel. She found it suspicious to walk outside. Jeeves had come for breakfast and tea, but he'd been slightly pre-occupied and Bronwyn could count on one hand the times Van took her to dinner in town. She wondered what was going on.

They seldom saw each other around bedtime, but if Jeeves was at the estate, he called. Tonight the call was brief and he unbelievably said, "night luv" before hanging up.

That made her radar surge. Her Jeeves would never, ever, call her 'luv' – not under any circumstances. She removed her locator bracelet to walk undetected through her house. Grabbing a hooded sweatshirt, she slipped into moccasins. Once downstairs, she opened the kitchen drawer that housed her binoculars and undid the alarms for The Silk Club. Padding across the dark wooded floor, she was anxious to scan Jeeves' flat to see what she could make of things.

Lifting her binoculars, Jeeves' kitchen light was on and she saw figures inside, although his fenced patio had too many shrubs for a good look. She wondered if she should go outside, but moved through The Silk Club to the deepest corner, lifting her binoculars, again.

There. There it was. A tall man was with Jeeves, near his kitchen doorway. They were embracing. He kissed Jeeves' cheeks and then when he pulled away, Jeeves drew him back in, embracing him. Bronwyn's eyebrows rose. Obviously, Jeeves was distracted by the man when he'd called her 'luv'.

The man had already faded into the dark moonless night, but Bronwyn kept her binoculars trained to Jeeves' flat. The kitchen lights went out, the upper level lights went on, and five minutes later she watched as Jeeves' flat went dark. Jeeves moved toward his bed; if he was reading, there'd be a light. No, he was in bed. Ready to sleep. This was a surprise. Whoever had been there must have given Jeeves peace of mind.

Bronwyn flew through The Silk Club, reset the alarm, grabbed a warmer jacket from the hall closet, and sat for a moment. She guessed where the man would go. He'd taken a few steps toward her house before he disappeared. She left the binoculars on the table, turned off the alarm, and walked into the night.

She could have made an effort to walk soundlessly, but she wanted the man to know she was coming. If he had somewhere to go, he'd have gone through Jeeves' front door and into the garage. Coming her direction meant he had time to kill.

She cleared her throat.

"I know you're here. I saw you at Ernest Rose's flat. I'm not leaving until I see you."

When she said it, she wondered if she'd made an insane move. She didn't know this man, she'd left her alarm bracelet inside, and it was too cold for a stand-off.

Then she remembered she belonged; he did not. Her nerve returned.

She stood at the foot of the steps, leading up to the loggia and its secretive corners of chaises and tables. She realized he could see her, faintly. There was just enough light shimmering off the water, reflected from security lights along the edge. "I'm not leaving."

Clive watched her. He'd learned more about Bronwyn from Clara in an hour, than from Ernest in three days. Once he'd seen her with the dog, he couldn't let it go. He had to find out about her. Although Clara didn't name names, she'd even told him the part about her saving two boys. Didn't mention they were Prime Minister Abraham's boys, but she was proud of Bronwyn, proud of her courage.

But this was foolish. Not courageous. He knew he must send her away, but he didn't want her to move an inch. She was good at the silent part; he'd give her that. Ten minutes passed with Bronwyn gazing slightly to his right, unwilling to shift her gaze from the spot. Pretty good guess, he smiled approvingly. Of the few things Ernest had shared, he said she had good instincts. Remarkably, he thought.

Bronwyn heard him shift, knowing he'd done it deliberately. At least he'd seen her gazing *almost* at him. "So, does he have a voice?"

"You need to go back inside, Bronwyn."

She was surprised at the depth of his tone. He was whispering, but it was deep.

He waited to hear her reaction, that he knew her name.

"I'm not going anywhere until I see you."

"Unwise. Do you get that? You don't know me. You haven't a clue who I am or anything about me. I could hurt you, kill you, throw you down over the rocks."

His voice had an even delivery. Yet he was slightly menacing and his words were effective. She didn't doubt for a minute he was a dangerous man. If he'd been safe, she would have met him.

"I saw you with Ernest and we both know he'd hunt you down if anything happened to me."

"You're not wearing your bracelet."

"So, how do you know Ernest Rose?"

He didn't answer her. She knew he could dissolve into the shadows if he hadn't already. She walked up the steps with deliberation, and over to where she'd heard his voice, realizing how perfectly in the shadows he stood. He was leaning back on a glass table, against the outdoor kitchen's wall.

She allowed her sigh to be audible. At least he hadn't moved.

"What do you look like, Ernest's friend?"

"What do you look like, Bronwyn McCall?" He took her breath away. The way he said it, was almost a growl. Resonating. He was in total control. He'd have disappeared without her ever finding him if that's what he wanted. It was a moment laced with vulnerability and power, but she was drawn to him and unafraid. She reached down and found his hand, pulling his index finger and bringing it up near her face.

"Here. This is what I look like. This is my father, Bobby McCall, right here where the length of my nose meets the turned up part." She placed his finger at that very point where bone meets flesh and he allowed her to move his finger slightly, along the bloom of her small nose.

For years to come, Clive would look back on that moment, knowing he fell in love with her right then. In corners of the world, he would try to recreate the moment, but his own nose was a poor substitute. It had its own meandering path, thanks to a few punches thrown, but it simply couldn't bring forth the passionate punctuation he felt when she chose to show herself as her father's daughter.

"Do you feel it? Right there. That's who I am. Who are you?" He held his finger there, lightly, and then dropped his arm. She waited, hoping he'd play the game. Minutes went by and she couldn't hear his breath; only her own. She still wasn't going anywhere.

Bronwyn brought her right hand slowly upward, waiting for it to find berth on the side of his face, discovering it was remarkably warm, protected by manly stubble. Her touch was light and he seemed willing. He had no idea that as a photographer, she could stake out the planes of a face more easily than a surveyor could mark land. Her fingers made back-and-forth paths, almost hovering without landing, delicately finding a slight crease delineating the cheek, rising past the bottom point of his nose. She moved to his ear and found a large squared earlobe. The ear was nicely large; the better to hear with, she thought. Her palm gently caressed his cheek and then she lightly traced his nose. She brushed across it with fairy wings, waiting to see if he'd allow her to search, further. When it appeared he wasn't going to snap off her wrist, she traced his nose until she had some sense of its size and shape. The eyebrows were simply full and straight; his forehead gliding slightly inward at the temple, hair brushed back from a slight widow's peak. He wasn't startled. He didn't seem to mind. In fact, he seemed mesmerized. Like making circles on a dog's chest.

An artist knows the left side and right side of faces aren't symmetrical, so she very lightly ran her left hand across his right cheek, earlobe, and forehead. She tenderly cupped the right side of his face, not wanting to break the spell. While she cradled his face with her left hand, her right forefinger traced a path from his strong chin up to his lips. She moved left and right, judging the width of his mouth, wondering if it would widen into a smile, when those lips sailed across the twelve inch space, taking her own lips into his.

His lack of breath was no more. She heard his breath, felt him exhale into her, knew she was swept into every bad place he'd ever been. She felt him exploring her lips and mouth and she ran her tongue along his teeth, trying to judge the size and shape of them. Then she was swept into the tumult of two desperately lonely people. She met his heavy breath with her own. She didn't feel cold anymore, shocked that he could generate so much heat. He tested to see if she could hold her own, finding she threw herself into his need as much as he drew her in. She didn't want it to end. Just as he'd forced his own breath of life through her lips, and she'd taken it for her own, Ernest Rose seemed to come between them. The man held her to his body, clutching her. He was gaining control of himself, while at the same time possessing her. It seemed an eternity. Bronwyn wondered if he was going to let her go. She gave his back a little squeeze. And then, a little pat. She nestled her head into his shoulder, knowing precisely the size and shape of the chin that rested upon the back of her head.

"Go back, Bronwyn. Get warm in your bed. I'll watch the balcony off your bedroom. Turn your light on and off, twice, and I'll know you're right as rain. Can you do that for me?"

"Are you going to tell me who you are?" She stood back and waited, but she knew he wasn't going to answer. He'd come to the loggia, waiting for something. There'd be no point in deterring him.

She stood back, and Clive could see her silhouette. Bronwyn's eyes had gotten used to the dark, or perhaps his kisses infused her with super-human powers, but now she could see the outline of his head, the shape of his shoulders. More than he would want her to know.

"I'll go, if that's what you want."

"Good night, sweet Bronwyn," he whispered, huskily.

She sighed, then stepped back into the pocket of emotion, took his face in her hands and urged, "Come back to me," kissing him goodbye, as sweetly as she could manage.

Clive watched her walk through the covered walkway, over to the huge lobby doors. He knew how long it would take to walk through the lobby, then the hallway, turn and mount the stairs, walk through the hall and past the bed to the balcony.

She did the light switching as he'd asked, but once in bed, her mind replayed each moment from hearing Jeeves say 'luv' to the final request that this man come back to her. Play and rewind. Over and over. Beginning with 'luv'. Believing they'd meet again. She would see his face just as he would see hers.

It might have been a dream, if Bronwyn's cheek hadn't been raw from the man's stubble; her lips still bruised from his kisses. She knew he was gone. It had certainly seemed like a 'goodbye' at Jeeves' doorstep.

Jeeves. Yes, a good morning to go to the diner.

Ordering their usual breakfasts, Bronwyn looked for something different about Jeeves. He definitely seemed happier, she'd give him that.

Officer Grande often joined them for breakfast, and she was glad to see him striding through the door. While he talked to Jeeves, she could drift off to daydreamland.

The police officer ordered the daily special and tapped the Formica table in front of Bronwyn.

"Guess what? Your troublemaker's gone. Bit the dust."

"Who's that?"

"You know…your animal guy. The bad guy." He waited for it to register. He hated to be explicit. She was so sensitive.

Her surprise was evident. "You mean Harper? At the Animal Shelter? The one with the white puppy?"

"Yep."

"What happened? Did he move away? Far away?"

Jeeves finally spoke. "I believe Officer Grande said he, 'bit the dust'. Meaning he's deceased?"

"Yeah. Car wreck, heart attack. Drunk. All of the above."

"Was anyone else hurt?"

Grande shook his head.

Bronwyn cut a bite from her omelette and then glanced up and murmured, "I'd like to say 'too bad', but I won't. He looked too healthy for a heart attack."

"Well, Bronwyn, you never know. Not everyone eats the syrupy pancake mountain like I do!"

Bronwyn gave a little smile, but Grande knew she was still thinking.

"Maybe he died fast."

"Maybe. You'll never guess what he did for a living. Go ahead, Bronwyn. Guess."

She thought. "I hope he wasn't a cop."

"Worse. A lawyer."

"You're kidding."

"He was out of town. Up on Route One."

Bronwyn sensed Grande wanted to tell Jeeves something. "What were you going to say?"

He measured his words, while the waitress refilled their coffee.

"I made a couple of calls. The guy lived alone. They found all kinds of things in his house. They're digging up the yard, now. You were right, Bronwyn. He was a bad character. And when people hurt animals, they often graduate to people."

More than Bronwyn wanted to know. Her face was pale and Jeeves urged her to have some water, making eye contact with the policeman.

"Gee, Bronwyn, I'm sorry. I knew better. I did. Are you okay?"

She nodded, halfheartedly.

Two days later, Bronwyn and Jeeves were at McDonald's for breakfast, on the way to Freeport to shop.

Bronwyn saw one of the Scholarship Program boys, ordering take-out.

"Hey, Theran," she called over to him, when he'd paid. "How are you? No school, today?"

"Nah. Guess you didn't hear. Lisa's dad died. She's all upset."

"Oh, I'm sorry Theran. I met him a few times. He was the nicest guy. Interested in Lisa's school work and so proud. You're going over to see her this morning?"

"Yeah. Her mom won't go up to the funeral home. Lisa's having a tough time about it. Do you think you could maybe go up there tonight? Since Lisa's mom won't go? You know Lisa really likes you, Bronwyn. She talks about you paying for college, all the time. It might help to see you, d'ya think you could go?"

"Sure, Theran. We'll go up tonight. Just let me know which funeral home. Okay? And, Theran, you and Lisa are earning your way into college. Don't forget that. I'm not doing the work. You are. I'll see you tonight then?"

As Theran waved goodbye, Bronwyn was uneasy. Oliver Silkowski's grandmother always said 'death comes in threes'. It made Bronwyn wonder where the third one would pop up.

That evening, it took almost forty minutes to drive to the funeral home for Lisa Luna's dad. It was a rare occasion for Bronwyn to go to a funeral home. She made it a point to stay out of 'the room'. If she got steered into 'the room', she concentrated on the flowers. She hoped she could visit with Lisa and Theran in the lobby. Or outside.

No such luck. Jeeves dropped her at the door, and Theran met her, looking dapper in a suit. Her heart went out to him as he tried to be the stable manly influence, for his grieving girlfriend.

Bronwyn glanced around, seeing Lisa standing beside the casket. As she looked for Jeeves, she did a double-take.

Grabbing Theran's elbow, she whispered, "I thought you said Lisa's dad passed away."

"That's right."

"Does he have a twin?" She was gesturing to a man who looked exactly like Mr. Luna.

"That's her step-dad. Well, actually he adopted her. But this is her real father. Her real dad died."

Bronwyn had a sick feeling. Lisa came out of the room and put her arms around Bronwyn, sobbing.

"It's okay, Lisa. It's okay," and she patted her as the sweet girl sobbed. Bronwyn could see straight into the room, but she wasn't looking at flowers. Lisa took her hand and led her in.

"This is my dad, Bronwyn. I know a lot of people didn't like him," she whispered. "My mom wouldn't even come, but he's my dad. You know?"

"Of course, Lisa. He's your dad." And he was a monster, too, she thought.

Back in the car, Bronwyn rested her elbow along the bottom of the window, holding her head. In times of need, she often pretended her hand was her mother's, and patted her own cheek. Her forefinger touched her nose and she thought of the man in the night.

She asked Jeeves if he minded stopping at Gus Townsend's house. She phoned ahead and Gus was happy to have unexpected company. As much as she loved Gus, he wasn't the one she wanted to see. It was Snooks Von Krinkles.

When they left Gus's place, Jeeves asked, "Are you sorry he's dead? Now that you know he was the girl's father?"

"No, I'm not sorry." She watched the houses zipping by and realized the man she'd seen at the loggia wasn't the real executioner. Not even Jeeves. She hadn't realized it at the time, but now she knew she signed Harper's death warrant the moment he told her about the white puppy. She felt powerful. But, she was concerned about the next time she wanted something fixed. Jeeves was a mighty weapon.

Chapter Nineteen

An Umbrella for Laura

When Bronwyn opened her eyes, there was Snooks Von Krinkles, snuggled in the bed linens, with only her head exposed. Bronwyn wanted Jeeves to see Snooks while she slept, but realized he'd be at his flat with Gus and Tiny; the aftermath of poker night.

It occurred to Bronwyn to try out her bracelet. The prime minister had authorized a tracking device implant for her, right after the kidnapping. But the tracking bracelet was an extra precaution and she'd never used it.

Jeeves had explained how pushing 'green' would beckon him or Van Tsang; the 'yellow' button signaled a problem; 'red' signified distress. When she sniffed at the simple color system, Jeeves had coolly informed her there could be circumstances where she'd be fortunate to comprehend the significance of 'color'. She'd been chastened by his serious tone.

With the green button pushed, it took Jeeves longer to appear than she expected. Even though it was 'green', supposedly a simple 'come see me', he looked worried.

"Shhhh. Look at her, Jeeves. Look at her little face."

"Miss. You've utilized the bracelet to fetch me for a peek at Snooks Von Krinkles?" He sneered the dog's name.

"Now we know it works. Look at her. Isn't she dear? Look how her eyes are squeezed shut. Little Spanish peanut head," she whispered.

"Quite." Jeeves moved to the other side of the bed and peered over Snooks. He lifted her flipped ear with the lightest touch, adjusting it slightly. Pulling the covers slightly upward, he bent over to watch as Snooks sighed with deep contentment.

Bronwyn caught his eye. They smiled and returned their gazes to Snooks. Eventually, Jeeves tip-toed around the bed.

"Should I wake her up? She might fall out, if I don't."

"Allow me to stand guard, Miss."

Jeeves was annoyed with himself. His reaction time was bloody pathetic. He hadn't asked much of himself, since he'd been with Bronwyn. If there had been a more crucial emergency than the observation of the darling dachshund, he'd be hard put to respond.

Bronwyn supported the town's fundraising activities. If she was in Maine, she seldom missed a church strawberry festival, pumpkin sale, or school carnival.

Organizations often held meetings on the Factory's fourth floor. It was an impressive atmosphere, with massive amounts of dark wood and thick carpets. Crystal chandeliers and inset lighting illuminated gallery displays of photographs and memorabilia from the Bayside Blanket and Toboggan Company. Mackintosh style balconies ringed the upper tier with a winding staircase of the same open woodwork linking the two levels. Near the ceiling, rectangles of stained glass lent a timeless feel, while a huge stained glass skylight hovered above. Its design featured a field of lime green and deep blue swirls, with a perimeter of aqua, gold and ivory discs. Unlike the rescued and reclaimed theme of the Factory, this piece of looming artwork was commissioned by Bronwyn, who sought a dynamic way to illuminate the space.

A museum design group showcased the Factory's history. Lining the walls were large photographs of the 1821 Breast shot water wheel, the portable steam engine in 1854, steam powered looms in 1858, the engine house and Calloway boiler in 1864, the power loom shed in 1865, the blanket finishing room, a sock knitting machine, spinning mules for carding and weaving, the warehouse where blankets were finished, and the certificate recording the 1907 *'Fleece to Blanket in 10 hours 32 minutes'*.

Several examples of woolen products were displayed, including a Wadmill, the rough cloth made to line collars and saddles of working horses in the late 1950's.

Company workers were highlighted in sepia toned exhibits with audio buttons for oral histories…foreman of the stockhouse, loom tuner who checked the weave and weight of blankets, weftman, weaver, manageress of the canteen, perchman who inspected blankets, console operator on fiberweaving lines, wool buyer, spinning manager, firemen, and works engineer. One of the oral histories spoke of the noise in the blanket finishing room, with loud *clang, clang, clangs*. Those workers developed special calls to get each other's attention.

Two old toboggans rested within glass cases; both made of Northern Hardwood Maple. They could accommodate loads of a thousand pounds, and the steel bridging and sled rail attachments resulted in very little drag and minimal friction. The toboggan operation had been housed in the valley where Alex Oz King lived.

However, Bronwyn's Silk Club was seldom open to the public, so invitations were eagerly anticipated. Grace helped organize Silk Club dinner dances for the Scholarship Program. The dressed-to-the-nines high school students and guests posed for photographs to mark the occasion, and the following week, Bronwyn would host a luncheon for them and their senior partners, with laughter, applause, and spontaneous tributes shaking the walls.

Margo Storey should have handled all donation and funding requests, so Grace was wary when the school board invited Bronwyn to a board meeting. Margo offered to accompany Bronwyn, but she declined. Bronwyn was curious; it must be a huge request, if they were bypassing Margo and heading straight to her.

As it turned out, the school board's president simply didn't care about the usual protocol of dealing with Margo Storey. He wanted Bronwyn to know they were cutting funding for the arts. She listened halfheartedly. Although she believed schools had an obligation to teach art and music, her Arts Center in the old bank building offered free classes. She wasn't inclined to make a comment or a commitment. Seated near the back, she quietly left at the first opportunity.

It was raining hard and Bronwyn realized she'd left her umbrella. As she neared the boardroom door, she overheard two women gossiping inside.

"I don't know what her problem is."

"I don't know, either. I hear Bronwyn McCall buys everything and anything she wants. Have you heard about that place of hers? Too bad we can't all inherit money. Too bad some of us have to work for a living."

"She does help the nursing home, don't get me wrong. And I heard she bought three more plows for the road department."

"But, this is about our precious children. She's so detached. Did you see her? Bored to tears, couldn't care less. Probably because she doesn't have children."

"She's probably too busy spending money to want children tying her down. Doesn't have a man either, I hear. Never see her with one. Have you?"

"Haven't. What's up with that?"

Bronwyn could hear snickering.

"I don't get it. But, let's face it. She's a walking wallet."

Several people laughed loudly.

"A walking wallet and it's a slap in our faces if she doesn't help out. It's…"

Bronwyn turned away, unseen, without retrieving the umbrella. She was as stunned as if she'd been the one slapped in the face. She ran through the rain to her car and started the engine, anxious to get behind her stone wall.

In her bedroom, she called Margo and asked her to inquire about the arts programs. Margo thought Bronwyn sounded tired, but she knew how wearying those board meetings could be.

Bronwyn couldn't sleep. She'd never heard anyone talk behind her back, even when she was a child. She'd led a secluded life with Oliver Silkowski as her only real friend. It was a terrible novelty to be on the receiving end of gossip and speculation. The hot flush of her embarrassment didn't subside. She felt wounded, then vengeful and wounded again.

She checked the time. She'd spent an hour frazzled with ugly thoughts. The television offered no distraction. She considered staying behind her stone wall, and not going into town for a very long time. Bronwyn could have Jeeves investigate who was gossiping about her, but she couldn't imagine him not taking some tasty revenge on her behalf, so she disregarded the idea. Unhappiness had grabbed her before, but this was different. The money felt like a weighty sack of gold and for the first time, it threw her in the hot glare of attention. It was depressing and unnerving.

Finally, it was 1:00 AM. Her feet were cold and she put on a second pair of socks. Nevertheless, the heat of embarrassment was still a furnace on her face. Bronwyn watched each minute click by for another half hour and then she called Conor Frost at his Paris flat, hoping he'd answer, rather than Nova.

Conor assured her that he was ready for the day, always the early riser. He listened to her tale of woe and regretfully felt the miles between them. Explaining the transient ignorance and jealous nature of people, he assured her the women only spoke behind her back to amuse one another at her expense; that not a word would have crossed their lips had they known she was there. Conor made her laugh with numerous vengeful suggestions, and when they finally ended their chat, she felt a little better.

As the day unfolded, Bronwyn seemed noticeably preoccupied. Edgar treated her gently and Jeeves avoided her. The day was agonizingly long, and she couldn't focus her thoughts anywhere but in obsessively reliving the catty words and laughter she'd overheard. Every minute, seeming an hour.

Charlie came over to the house in late afternoon, inviting Bronwyn for a cookout in the garage. With his thumb hooked through a belt loop, and his baseball mitt tucked under one arm, he said Edgar had planned a 'really fun' meal with long tables. Bronwyn agreed, too fond of Charlie to say anything but 'yes'.

She dragged herself to the garage, and saw Edgar had made a rainy day picnic. She sat near the end of the table, beside Jeeves. Bronwyn cradled her head in her hand, responding with 'a hamburger' as Charlie took orders. He was hopping around while his dad grilled burgers and steaks. Charlie called her name and she offered him a feeble smile. He moved farther down the table and called to her again. She glanced at him and absentmindedly waved. What a happy ten year old boy, she thought.

Finally, Charlie stood between Bronwyn and Jeeves and gently lifted her chin with his long fingers. She saw his imploring eyes and smiled tenderly at him.

"Bronwyn," he said firmly. "Bronwyn. You should look at me."

Her eyes followed him as he hopped and teetered around Jeeves, around the end of the table, past Edgar and Clara, past Augie and Jen, past…

Conor.

Bronwyn didn't react, at first. Surely he was just a figment of her imagination. How could she possibly believe Conor was there, beside happy hopping Charlie, when she'd just spoken to him hours before? In Paris?

Conor rose and walked around the table. As he approached her chair, Bronwyn pushed it back and put her arms around his waist, staying there so long that everyone realized something was wrong.

Happily, when she unburied her face from his shirt front, she was a revived soul. 'How did it happen' she wanted to know. 'The Concorde' he'd said. 'They haven't stopped flying yet'. And Bronwyn tossed her angst away. No one at that stupid school board meeting would have a friend so wonderful, that he would drop everything and rush to her side, as fast as humanly possible. They were right about one thing. With Conor on her side, Bronwyn was indeed richer than those women.

"She's getting fired."

"You're kidding."

"It's true," Grace replied, watching to see Bronwyn's reaction.

"What do you think happened?"

For an instant, Grace thought Bronwyn might be playing coy, but then she realized Bronwyn had faith in Laura Storey's talent and hadn't foreseen the outcome.

"Well, her one year contract was up. Their council meets tonight."

"I wonder how she's taking it. She must be disappointed."

"She shouldn't be too surprised. She just didn't make anything happen. You know how it goes, with councils and budgets. No one can make a decision, and everyone's out for themselves."

Bronwyn nodded.

"Her office should have given her a clue," Grace shared.

"Why's that?"

"She just had a desk in the fire station."

Her surprise was obvious and Grace thought she looked a little pale.

Two days later, Bronwyn and Grace Cloud were sipping lattés in front of the Euro Bakery.

"Ready, then?"

"I could call, Bronwyn. I could let Margo know we're stopping by."

"No. You're sure Laura's home?"

"It didn't sound like she'd be going anywhere for awhile. Holed up like her father."

Grace was sorry she mentioned Mr. Storey; she knew Bronwyn was fond of him. She veered the discussion to the newspaper. "Margo should have warned her they'd cover it in the paper."

"I know it's embarrassing for her. For all of them," Bronwyn sighed.

She was thinking about Laura as they tramped through crunchy autumn leaves to Margo Storey's house. Laura had never spoken to Bronwyn about leaving. In fact, Bronwyn hadn't heard from Laura at all for the past year. She was obviously the kind of girl who let her mother do the tough stuff, and now she couldn't avoid the tough stuff. It was splashed on the front page of the local paper.

"Margo said she's staying in bed. Crying." Grace wanted to warn her that the odds of seeing Laura Storey were slim.

Neither spoke as they climbed the stone steps, but Bronwyn was annoyed. Mr. Storey had a breathing problem. She wondered why Margo had insisted on buying a house with so many steps.

"Oh, hello Grace. Bronwyn. I didn't know you were coming," Margo blocked the doorway. Grace said hello, but Bronwyn was silent. After a moment's hesitation, Margo stood aside and let them in the house.

"I suppose you've come because of the article. That's kind of you. She's hanging in there. It's difficult, but she'll get through it."

"I'd like to see her."

"I don't think that's possible today, Bronwyn."

Mr. Storey was hovering near the living room and Bronwyn turned to him. "I'd like to see Laura."

Knowing Mr. Storey was unlikely to take the stairs, she expected he'd call up to his daughter, but he took Bronwyn's elbow and walked slowly up the stairs, beside her.

A quick rap at the door elicited, "I don't want to see her, Daddy."

He whispered to Bronwyn, "I don't know if she's decent," but Bronwyn just smiled. The utter kindness of that smile set any fears Mr. Storey had, to rest.

She turned the doorknob and caught Laura by surprise.

Balled up Kleenex were everywhere. The room actually seemed a bit humid, from all the crying. Laura's back was turned and it amused Bronwyn that she didn't pull herself together. Rather, she seemed to think Bronwyn might disappear if she waited long enough.

Slipping her jacket off, Bronwyn placed it on the unmade bed and sat.

"Sit here, Laura. Beside me," she said patting the bed, insistently. "Come on. Right here."

Laura reluctantly backed over and sat, without looking at her. Bronwyn expected Laura would be unsettled, backward, despairing. She had her MBA and she had the respect and affection of the entire town, but Laura Storey was someone who basked in the upbeat moments of each day. She didn't cope with disappointment.

At least Laura accepted her presence, however reluctantly. Laura was a large girl, gregarious with a winning personality. People often commented on her appealing smile and Bronwyn admired her oomph, not to mention, her auburn hair.

"You've highlighted your hair. I like it. Kind of

butterscotchey," Bronwyn said. A tiny smile crossed Laura's face. She couldn't help herself.

"Please don't say 'I told you so'," Laura pleaded, close to tears.

"Stop. That's all done," Bronwyn stood and lifted Laura's chin. "Look up, Laura. Look up and look ahead. Lift your eyes."

She cast her eyes downward and jammed her chin against Bronwyn's attempt to keep it up. Bronwyn smiled. She was only four years older than Laura, but Laura was such a child. Bronwyn felt like the girl's wise old granny.

"Your apartment is waiting for you. Hasn't changed at all. Just as you left it."

"Mom said you rented it."

"I didn't."

"She said there were Christmas lights in the windows. And I'm sure she said she's seen people there."

"Just the cleaning crew. We put Christmas lights in the windows for the movie goers. It was nice to look up and see some sparkle."

"Mom said you insisted on renting the apartment."

"She misunderstood. The apartment went with the job. That's all."

"Why didn't you hire someone to replace me? You made Mom pick up the slack. Why did you punish Mom, just because I left?"

"I wasn't punishing your mother. She was just maintaining what you'd already done, two days a week. Maybe your mother didn't know it, but she was just holding your place for you."

"I don't understand. You didn't know I'd come back. I haven't even said I want to come back."

"I kept your job open, but I did it for myself," Bronwyn

admitted, sitting back down. "The merchants thought it must be my fault that you left. No one said anything, but I could tell." Laura glanced at her, stricken. "They thought I must have given you good reason to leave because you seemed happy here, and then you left so suddenly."

"I'm sorry, Bronwyn. That wasn't it at all." Laura remembered the emotional high she'd felt, leaving town for something better.

"So, I decided leaving your position unfilled would prove it was you and about you, all the time. It wasn't a job; it was Laura."

"I don't understand."

"We either have you, or we have nothing."

"You want me back," Laura said, almost to herself.

"Well, I'm thinking we should expand your job. You did a great job in town, and maybe you should hire an assistant. There's plenty of room for two in your office."

Laura's back was straightening and she looked a degree brighter.

"We can put together an evaluation system. Travel around Maine, find places you think are worth helping. Dairies, farms, cafes, any independent family owned business. The islands, too. You compile your data and if you think they're worthy, let Grace know."

"All over Maine? Bronwyn, I couldn't even function in Tylerboro. The only reason I accomplished anything here is because it's my hometown."

"Wrong, Laura. Wrong. Tylerboro was just taking advantage of you. They thought you'd bring them easy money and they wouldn't have to cooperate or make an effort. They didn't plan to work with you or they wouldn't have stashed you in the fire department."

Laura considered this. "How would I get to know towns if I've never been there, and how would I find people out in the woods or in the country? Or, all those islands? I mean, there might be a great diner in the mountains, but I'd never know about it."

"You'll have to travel around, Laura. You're the most likeable person I know. When you see places that charm you or places you think need help, chat them up a bit, give them your business card and ask them to call if they find themselves in trouble. Taxes, replacing equipment, polishing their appearance, you know the drill."

"And you think, like three years from now, when they need me, they'll even remember me? They'll have my card?"

"Make it a spectacular business card, Laura. You're good at that. And give them a roll of Lifesavers."

Laura giggled and Bronwyn saw she was coming back to life.

"You'll need a car. I'm thinking a Land Rover. Come down to the Factory and Van Tsang will let you drive his. See what you think. You need a substantial car for the mountains of Maine. You can still bike around town. People have missed that. I've missed that."

Touching Bronwyn's knee, Laura looked around her room. "I'm sorry for the mess, Bronwyn." Then she said, "I'm sorry for everything."

"Seems like you never left. We'll just think like that, okay?"

"Well, one thing's for sure. I won't be stopping in Tylerboro to see what they need."

"I'm surprised you'd say that, Laura. It should be your first stop."

"You're kidding, right? Like that would ever happen."

"Laura, don't trip on your pride. You know that town

now, like the back of your hand. Surely there are things you'd like to do. Awnings, an art walk, holiday decorations. Is there any outdoor dining?"

"There's an Italian place a block up from the main street. They have a little patio in the back yard."

"What about heating lanterns for cooler weather? And outdoor music piped in?"

Laura's brain was clicking into gear.

"I'm gonna go, Laura. Stop and see the Range Rover. I'll tell Van Tsang. Maybe your dad will go to some dealerships with you. Van Tsang and Ernest Rose will have some good car suggestions, or the four of you can go together. I'll leave your apartment keys. I'll put them here on your dresser."

Bronwyn gave her a solid hug and went into the hallway, where she found Mr. Storey.

"Thank you, Bronwyn," he said and was rewarded by a light kiss on his cheek. Bronwyn wished she had a dad who would listen at the door.

Laura was practically waltzing around the room, thinking about designing a new business card, a spectacular business card. She could hardly wait to grab her mom and go clothes shopping. Some serious suits would be a good idea, a suede coat with Sherpa lining, maybe a cocktail dress or two. She'd be meeting all kinds of people...Maine was a big place. She caught her reflection in the mirror, happy to see the person she always thought she was. Laura crossed the room, made her bed, scooped up her piles of Kleenex and deposited them in the wastebasket. Then her eyes alighted on the keys to her beloved apartment, under a shiny roll of Lifesavers.

CHAPTER TWENTY

GUS AND SNOOKS, TINY AND LUKE
2004

When Gus complained he was out of breath, Bronwyn sent Doc Larchmont to take a look. It was downhill from that point on.

Within days, Gus was in the hospital with Bronwyn sleeping in a chair in his room. Clara sent Edgar over with instructions to bring her home, if only for a night, but he only succeeded in dropping off food that she didn't eat.

Bronwyn called Luke's staff, and finally his wife at the Blaine House, leaving urgent messages for him to come down from Augusta and see Gus in the hospital. When she finally convinced his chief of staff to put Luke on the phone, she made her plea in no uncertain terms. Gus was failing. Luke needed to come home. He spoke to her is if she were a child, reminding her patronizingly of his duties as governor; he had no time to indulge in personal matters.

Furious, Bronwyn made it clear to Jeeves that Luke must come to the hospital, but despite Jeeves' solemn nods, he had no intention of intervening. He was fond of Gus, but if the governor wanted to dismiss his father, Jeeves was glad to let him fall out of Bronwyn's favor.

A revolving troupe made regular visits to Tiny, including Van Tsang, Teddy, and even Officer Grande. Tiny knew Gus was ill, but no one had the heart to tell him how dire the situation was. Snooks stayed with Tiny, and everyone agreed she was a good distraction for him.

When Doc Larchmont said the time was near, he volunteered to let the governor know. Doc never let on that Luke was unmoved. Bronwyn expected him to walk through the door at any moment, and reassured a comatose Gus that Luke was coming.

Gus died a quiet death as Bronwyn held his hand, and she entered the netherworld of grief and bereavement. When Jeeves informed her that the governor was still in Augusta, Bronwyn called the Nash Funeral Home, and then went straight to Clara and Edgar's and curled up on the couch, letting them fuss over her.

That evening, Van Tsang came over, followed by Jeeves.

"I hate to tell you this, Bronwyn, but they took Tiny to the hospital late this afternoon. He's stable. He had chest pains, but they think it's just angina."

The words were a severe blow. The one thing Gus would expect from her was to make sure Tiny and Snooks were okay.

"Where's Snooks?"

"The governor got here this afternoon. He took Snooks back to Gus's house."

Bronwyn's eyes narrowed. Van Tsang was hiding something. "Did Luke see Tiny? Is that why Tiny had chest pains? You were with him and you told him about Gus, right? He was okay then, wasn't he? That's what you said," Bronwyn challenged him.

"Tiny seemed okay. We'd been preparing him, right Edgar? I told him to pack a bag and I'd be back for him and Snooks. He was excited to stay with me. When I drove over a half hour later, the ambulance was leaving his house."

No one liked the look on Bronwyn's face. "What did Luke do?"

Van Tsang didn't answer. Bronwyn crossed the room and put her face within inches.

"What did he do?"

"I talked with Grande and he said Luke told Tiny he'd have to move. Luke's selling the house...both of the houses. Tiny's, too."

She was stunned.

"And did he take Snooks away before or after Tiny had chest pains?"

No one was surprised she cut to the heart of it. "Before."

Bronwyn was heartsick. She could barely form a plan. How to fix this. How to make things better for Tiny and Snooks.

She looked up at Jeeves, distress apparent on her face. In all their time together, he hadn't seen such fresh hopelessness and despair. Even leaving the hospital, she'd been brave.

The phone rang and Bronwyn jumped. Clara took the call and Bronwyn was sorry she had. Clara looked like she'd been through the ringer, as she motioned for Jeeves.

"Is it Tiny? Is Tiny all right? Snooks? Is she okay?"

"Yes dear, yes, yes. I'm sorry. It's a small matter, that's all."

"What?" Bronwyn inquired reluctantly.

Jeeves didn't answer, so Clara said, "Well, that was Officer Grande. He wanted to let us know the viewing is tomorrow and the funeral is Thursday." Bronwyn sighed with relief. "It's the funeral home out of town, up the highway. The new one."

Bronwyn was amazed. Luke was absent at the end, but now he took control, moving Gus. The Nash Funeral Home was owned by close friends of Gus; it never occurred to Bronwyn that Gus would be anywhere else.

Bronwyn stayed at Edgar and Clara's and barely slept. Each time she opened her eyes, she found truth sitting on the bed, a sentry whispering 'he's gone', over and over. The sobs gagged her and the tears flowed and she cried so much that her chest was like an accordion with its air squeezed out – until she slept, and found truth ready to pronounce, 'he's gone', again. Not a dream, but harsh truth.

At breakfast she pushed her food around the plate. When she rose, the weight of her grief was enormous. It seemed barely possible to endure Gus being gone.

She was relieved when Doc said Tiny was coming home. The hospitalization had been a precaution; the event was apparently stress-related. Teddy and Charlie volunteered to stay at Tiny's for a few days, uncertain what measures Luke might take. Officer Grande promised to keep an eye on the house, disgusted by Luke's plans.

Bronwyn asked Teddy to drop her off at the funeral home's afternoon viewing and told Jeeves to ask people at the estate to wait until evening. She didn't want an audience in case things were chilly with Luke.

Chilly didn't begin to describe it. The governor's people blocked Bronwyn at the entrance. Despite her vow to be calm, she made enough noise that someone fetched Luke and his wife. The governor's wife watched from the steps, as Luke approached Bronwyn. She walked toward the cars, aware people were watching. When she turned around, he was at her heels.

"I'm sorry, Luke." He looked at her, impassively. "About Gus."

"Of course. About Gus."

"Your people wouldn't let me in."

"My orders."

Bronwyn stepped forward with only electrified space separating them. "Are you kidding me? Why?"

"I think it's time his family was with him, Bronwyn. You had your time."

Luke was ready for a fight. Aching for one. He could turn and go back to his wife and the funeral home of his choosing, gleaming and brand new. Or, he could flip some verbal venom through the air.

"It's sad, really. You tried so hard, Bronwyn." She was a diminishing target, walking down the highway shoulder. "You tried to make him your family, just like you've tried to buy your own."

He jogged through the cars. "You tried to buy yourself a family and buy yourself friends." he shouted. "Admit it, Bronwyn; you're all alone in this world." And when he turned back from yelling at the top of his voice, people looked away. Reverence for the governor of the great state of Maine, or shame at witnessing some personal battle. Either way, he walked proudly into the building, taking his rightful place beside his father.

It didn't take long for word to spread. Luke lost some votes that day. Of course he hadn't carried his home district in the last election, but he always chalked that up to sour grapes. Local boy makes good. Some people just can't stand that, he always rationalized.

Word got back to the estate before Bronwyn reached the Bergamot Country Club. Van Tsang drove up for her, making it in record time. Jeeves was going, but Van hadn't liked the look in his eye.

When Van arrived, he found Bronwyn sitting with Laura Larchmont, having a glass of wine. He wanted to go over and speak to the governor, but she said no. Van agreed Luke wasn't worth it, but a part of him wanted everyone to see what he could do to the man.

Bronwyn hung out at Clara's, shaken, more than angry. Embarrassed that Luke may have been right, she considered the charge; perhaps she had bought herself friends. But she remembered she had good friends like Graeme Woods, Conor Frost, and Sebastian Hughes, before the money. She was certain they genuinely liked her. She just wanted to lie on Clara's couch and lick her wounds. She even let Edgar make her a grilled cheese sandwich and chocolate milk.

At the evening viewing, people from the estate made an appearance. If they could manage to avoid Luke, they did, and if their paths crossed, they gave brief condolences.

Dr. Larchmont, always a gentleman, informed Luke of Bronwyn's devotion at the hospital. Luke was squirming to get away, but when Luke began to dismiss him, Doc took his elbow and flooded him with a wash of hospital reality.

None of Bronwyn's people felt welcome at the funeral home, but they commiserated afterward at the Bergamot Country Club. Returning to the estate that night, several stopped in at Clara's and Bronwyn warmly thanked them for representing her, passing off the Luke clash as a display of grief.

Afterward, Van Tsang and Jeeves seemed almost cheerful,

carrying two dark duffel bags. Clara and Edgar went into the kitchen while the men moved chairs to sit across from Bronwyn, knees to knees.

"We're undertaking a covert operation, Bronwyn. We thought you might like to join us," Van offered.

Without knowing what they were planning, Bronwyn nodded 'yes'.

Van opened a bag and pulled out camouflage gear, while Jeeves lifted her chin and began blackening her face.

"We're about to liberate Snooks Von Krinkles."

"You mean she's still in the house? All alone? Luke wouldn't be staying at Gus's; he'd want something grand, right?"

"She's alone in the house, but they've changed the locks and hired guards."

"For Snooks? They're keeping Snooks a prisoner instead of taking care of her?"

"According to Officer Grande, she's a prisoner. He can hear her howling whenever she's not crying. He asked the guards if he could take her home, so unfortunately, he'll be suspect. We're keeping him out front with the guards, so he has an alibi of sorts," Van continued.

"Jeez. What are we going to do?" It was a lot of information for Bronwyn to absorb.

"Taking you with us isn't wise, Miss, but Snooks will be too busy giving you kisses to raise a ruckus. Think you can do everything, just as we say?"

Jeeves and Van Tsang were glad to give Bronwyn an opportunity to strike back at Luke, but both yearned to take more satisfying revenge. Earlier, as they made their plan, Jeeves reminded Van about the price they must pay to have a home. Striking and disappearing was the life they'd always led. But a life of normalcy came at the cost of suppressing their savagery.

It was 1:15 AM and Bronwyn had forgotten about the other tunnel beneath the Factory, leading to the water. When she'd first heard about the tunnel, she assumed it was impassable, but now they walked along its pale green tiled walls and beneath its sparsely lit ceiling, to wooden stairs and a concealed dock.

They motored across the bay in a small boat, until Van Tsang cut the motor. He checked his watch and began silently rowing to Gus's dock. Van stayed with the boat and Bronwyn was surprised how nimble Jeeves was. She saw the whites of his eyes but not much else, as the small sliver of moon slipped behind clouds. Her heart was pounding. There was muted conversation at the front of Gus's house. She knew Officer Grande was supposed to be having coffee and jelly doughnuts with the three guards.

Jeeves got past the door's new locks, silently opening the door with ease. He'd worried about the dog, but Bronwyn assured him if anything went wrong, it wouldn't be because of Snookie. She hoped she was right. Not knowing if Snooks would be caged in the house, the dog surprised them by click click clicking into the kitchen to greet them. Bronwyn scooped her up, placed her in the baby sling Van had borrowed from expectant Katrin, and gave her bits of filet mignon, courtesy of Edgar, while Snooks struggled to lick her. Bronwyn zipped her inside her camo jacket, exposing her nose to the air.

Thrilled to have the prize in hand, Bronwyn was anxious to escape, but she saw Jeeves take the 'Dogs Playing Poker' print from the wall and snatch Gus's jacket from the kitchen peg. On their way out, Jeeves silently pointed the path. She turned and waved, confounding Jeeves, but there was Charlie waving from a second floor window at Tiny's house. Jeeves shook his finger in her face, and they hotfooted it to the boat. Bronwyn imagined the satisfying vision the boat made for Charlie. Hopefully, no one would question him about what might have happened in the middle of the night. She didn't want Charlie to lie. The truth wouldn't hurt her. It was just a dachshund. Some poker playing dogs. And a jacket. She knew Jeeves would stash the picture and jacket somewhere safe until everything blew over, and no one was going to take Snooks Von Krinkles from her. No one.

The day of the funeral passed quietly. Bronwyn enjoyed having Snooks at her house. She'd visited many times before and Bronwyn was glad to share her bed with the dear dog. She was a good diversion from the grief that weighed so heavily on Bronwyn. Warm and cozy, wiggling and happy, Snooks was blissfully unaware that Gus wasn't coming to get her.

Van Tsang moved Tiny into his house, while carpentry adjustments were made to the cottage next door, soon to become Tiny's home. They were adding a second fence so Snooks could run freely without Tiny worrying, and enlarging the doorways for him.

Bronwyn consulted her attorneys and decided not to fight Luke on Tiny's behalf. If she gave up that battle, she expected he'd give up Snooks. It all made her very sad. She knew Gus wanted Tiny to stay in the house he'd grown up in, and would have wanted Snooks to live with Tiny, right there. Luke knew it too, she was certain.

People reacted differently to grief, but she was disgusted that the governor was acting like a petulant six year old. Not only had she been generous financially, she'd provided some Hollywood star power for his campaign fundraising.

Luke was planning a run for the U.S. Senate. What was Luke thinking? He'd act like a creep and expect her to support his campaign?

Jeeves' cell rang that evening as he and Bronwyn were upstairs, sharing their supper with Snooks Von Krinkles.

Jeeves cranked into gear.

"Get downstairs. Luke is coming with State Police. I'll take Snooks. Act normally. When you bring them upstairs for the search, make certain they all come with you. Go! Now!" There was pounding at the door.

Bronwyn opened the front door and saw Luke with a State Policeman. Two more stood on the lawn and Officer Grande was with them, looking sheepish.

"Let us in, Bronwyn, we know you have the dog. We have a warrant."

"What are you talking about, Luke? Come in." Only Luke and the State Policeman entered; the others waited outside.

Bronwyn stood in the foyer and Jeeves came downstairs, without Snooks Von Krinkles.

"Here, Snooks," Luke shouted.

"What are you doing, Luke?"

"We have a warrant. We're searching everything."

"How could you get a warrant?"

"People heard you threaten me yesterday, at the funeral home," he lied.

Her beating heart didn't betray her. She looked calmly at Luke, while Jeeves wondered if she had threatened him. He rather hoped it was true.

"I know you stole the jewelry. It's missing from the house. All of my mother's jewelry. It's part of the search. Even if you didn't take it yesterday when you got the dog,

I know you convinced my father to give it all to you, taking advantage of a dying man. You'd do that," he said with disgust.

Bronwyn's face was pink. She looked at Jeeves who impassively returned her gaze. "Go on, Luke, toss my bedroom."

"I'll make some tea, Miss. You seem upset. May I?" Jeeves asked in a most subservient manner, bowing slightly. The State Policeman nodded.

Jeeves opened and closed the kitchen's heavy leaded glass door, glad to have the privacy it afforded. Knowing Bronwyn's disgust over a jewelry accusation would buy sufficient time; he walked into the kitchen, opened the dumbwaiter and reached in, pulling Snooks to his chest and patting her gently. "Good girl, Snookie, good girl," he cooed quietly.

He crossed the kitchen and rapidly descended the steps, opening the cellar's hidden pathway to the Factory. Snooks Von Krinkle's ears flew behind her, such was the speed of Jeeves on the run. He crossed the basement and called the freight elevator down, placing the dog inside its cavernous interior. Instructing Snooks to 'Be good' in his most commanding voice, he put the elevator on hold, yanking the door shut.

Van Tsang's call had warned Jeeves everyone was evacuated from the Factory, awaiting Luke's search for the dog, while twenty State Police were searching each of the estate homes. Warrants included the Island House and even tree houses, garages, greenhouses, outbuildings and the horse stable. It was a massive operation.

Jeeves used the scooter to traverse the tunnel, emerging into the kitchen to snatch the kettle as it began to whistle.

Carrying a cup of tea, he heard Bronwyn saying, "Ask Judy. Call her."

"What are you talking about?"

"Just call her."

"Don't try to distract me. Search for the dog," he snapped at the frowning State Policeman who turned to enter the library.

When the trooper emerged, he handed his cell phone to Luke. "You should take this. It's your daughter."

Luke's eyes narrowed and he snatched the phone, "Jude. What's up?"

He sounded nervous. "Oh. You didn't tell me. Yeah. I guess that was nice. When was that? Okay, yeah. It was a nice service. I'll talk to you later. Bye."

Bronwyn cocked her head. "She wasn't at the funeral?"

And with that, Mrs. Townsend's jewelry wasn't mentioned again. Months ago, Gus had asked Bronwyn to mail the jewelry to his granddaughter Judy, and they'd sent pertinent notes and stories about each jewelry piece. Bronwyn had the signature confirmation, so she knew Judy received them.

Hearing Bronwyn question Judy's absence at her grandfather's funeral lit a new fire under Luke. He could hardly wait to reprimand Pomeroy for having the audacity to make the call behind his back.

"The dog's not here. You'd better tell me where she is, Bronwyn. We're dropping her at a shelter far away from here, once I find her." He knew that would get Bronwyn's attention and was rewarded with her look of panic. Satisfied, he led the way outside. Bronwyn grabbed a jacket and followed him.

"Okay, follow me, men. We're searching the Factory."

"I'll go," said Officer Grande.

"No," Luke answered him. "Or you, either. You're staying here," he said to Jeeves, who had donned Gus's jacket.

"If Jeeves isn't going, then neither are you," Bronwyn told Luke. He wheeled around and stood a crackling two feet from her. The State Police and bodyguards moved to the covered stone walkway. Jeeves decided she looked furious enough to take care of herself, so he joined them. Luke and Bronwyn glared at each other, setting their jaws. Bronwyn was thinking how his eyes were all lively for the voters, and dead for her.

In the cold air, he was seething. With a harsh guttural whisper, he gestured to his squad of uniformed and ear-pieced men. "This is what power brings, Bronwyn." He laid his palm out. "It's what I have and you don't. Power." Bronwyn recognized his theatrical sneering; she'd seen it in movies. "Feel yourself bouncing along on my string?"

She closed so much space between them that her jacket rustled against his, as she brought her mouth to his neck and hissed, "And this is what money brings. You've no idea how well-funded your opposition is about to become. If you didn't have my money, that would hurt. But if he gets it, that's kind of double trouble, isn't it?"

She didn't give a damn if he was grieving. She could see her people shivering in front of the Factory. Biding their time…yanked by his string.

Luke walked over to the squad. "Make sure she calls out the dog's name. That dog can't resist her. Make sure she goes in every apartment. Clap your hands. The dog'll bark. Keep it simple. Pomeroy, you go in with her."

"It's just us then."

"That's not what I said, Pomeroy."

"It's just us then. It's a damn dog, for chrissake," he snapped.

All eyes were on Bronwyn. She gazed evenly over all

of them, looking to see if Jeeves had any signal for her. He didn't. She wasn't surprised.

As Pomeroy and Bronwyn began to walk around the front of the Factory, Luke called out.

"Pomeroy! Use the steps, outside. I want to see that you go up every floor. No shortcuts!"

The governor had no idea how much Pomeroy hated being ordered around.

Bronwyn took Pomeroy to the basement and quietly called, "Snookie". She showed him the gym, boxing ring, and weight room. They mounted the steps over the racquetball courts and surveyed the space. He nodded, admiringly. They returned to the garage level, where Pomeroy made a cursory glance here and there. He whistled under his breath when they entered Jeeves' flat, but Bronwyn's call to Snooks went unanswered and they left. They did the same at Edgar and Clara's.

As they walked up the glassed stairwell, they were lit like a Christmas tree, for the observant figures below.

Pomeroy was appreciative of Linda and Matthew Brodie's apartment, and walked out to the balcony. "I could live here. Just my style." Bronwyn started to smile but changed her mind. Pomeroy wasn't exactly friendly. They crossed over to Katrin's and did the usual call to Snooks.

Reentering the stairwell, Pomeroy grunted as he mounted the steps.

"It's not fun being watched, is it?" Bronwyn asked, getting no response.

"This is a guest floor," Bronwyn explained, when they emerged into the enormous space of the third floor. "Guest rooms on the left, three suites on the right, with a soda fountain dividing them. There's a model train room, doll room, and craft room at the end, past the guest rooms. Did you want to go in every room?"

They were standing halfway into the living space, with conversation pits beside them. Pomeroy hadn't made a decision about which rooms to search, when they heard the freight elevator move up to their floor, and stop. It was about thirty five yards from where they were standing. They'd both had the impression the entire Factory was empty, so they were surprised to hear any sound other than their own. The huge door rolled open and they gazed at a completely empty, enormous freight elevator save for the little red dachshund sitting right smack in the middle of its floor. They looked at Snooks; Snooks looked at them. They didn't move; she didn't move. Bronwyn held her breath. It seemed like an hour passed, everyone frozen in place. Then, the door slowly rolled closed, without Snooks moving a hair.

Bronwyn was afraid to breathe. She stole a glance at Pomeroy who hadn't said a word. Bronwyn's heart was thudding horribly.

"Well, let's try the fourth floor," he said gruffly. "This is getting to be a royal waste of time."

Bronwyn couldn't believe her ears, but caught up to Pomeroy, headed for the door. They mounted the final flight of stairs, glancing at the black shapes far beneath them on the ground. Bronwyn and Pomeroy stood silently inside the fourth floor, letting a few minutes pass before reentering the stairs.

"Do you want to go up to the rooftop pool?"

"Better, Miss McCall. We want to do a thorough job."

Bronwyn turned the lights on when they got there, and Pomeroy snapped them back off.

"Let's call it a night," he said, brusquely.

Luke was thinking more about his Senate campaign, than Snooks Von Krinkles. Officer Grande asked if he wanted the police to keep their eye out for Snooks, but Luke just muttered a profanity under his breath.

Bronwyn sat in Clara's living room, worrying about Snooks, when Jeeves entered with the dachshund pressed snugly against him.

"This little girl deserves an ice lolly, Edgar. What say you? Have you any?" Edgar left to retrieve a cherry popsicle and cut it into bite-sized pieces on a little plate.

"She was such a good girl, staying nice and safe in the freight lift. That's where I tucked, her. Would you have guessed, Miss?"

And Bronwyn told them the tale of Snooks Von Krinkles and the freight elevator, riding without benefit of reaching the buttons.

CHAPTER TWENTY ONE

SICK IN BED
2005

*I*ndestructible seemed to be Jeeves' middle name, but the flu felled him in the spring. It was a sudden blow, for which he was unprepared, and Bronwyn stayed with him while he slept. She wanted him to know she was there, just as he'd been at her side when she first met him.

In the midst of his fever, Jeeves arose from sleeping, eyes wider than Bronwyn had ever seen them, and distinctly uttered, "There's nothing quite like blood on snow."

"You're just dreaming Jeeves, it's alright."

But he'd have none of it, lying back and nodding sagely.

"It's not crystallized or sugary or sparkly the way we like to see snow. No, it's like seeing smooth and velvety rose petals. But they're not rose petals. No my dear, they're not rose petals like we hope they'll be. If you look closely and kick at the snow a bit, you'll see it separate into thick clumps of orangey red snow. Vivid red. Vivid blood. It becomes not snow and not really blood at all. It's altogether different."

"Shhh."

"People think he'll set things right eventually, but he won't. He longs for death, to ease his guilt."

"Jeeves," Bronwyn murmured soothingly. "It's a dream. It's okay. I'll read you a story and you just close your eyes and think sweet thoughts."

Bronwyn's eyes sought a stack of magazines, wondering what quiet and calm thing she could find to read aloud, when Jeeves took her forearm and met her eyes with great sadness.

"I hope you'll never see such blood on snow, Bronwyn. It isn't right I tell you. It looks quite interesting until you think about it. Until you know all about it."

Bronwyn gave Jeeves a sip of water, adjusted his bed covers and talked quietly of Maine restaurants, recalling their visits to Cook's Lobster House and how they must go to Mt. Desert Island Ice Cream for stout and fudge ice cream. When Jeeves smiled slightly, Bronwyn reminded him how he'd tried the grapefruit tarragon sorbet while still managing to snag most of her zabaglione and raisin ice cream. She patted his forehead with a damp washcloth and as Jeeves drifted off, she promised him a quick trip to Jordan Pond for popovers. Even though she thought he was sleeping, she nattered on about their recent visit to McKay's in Bar Harbor and how they'd ordered the *Pub Fondue for Two* – a deception for the waiter's benefit, as it was all for Jeeves. Before long, as she whispered about stopping at Rockland for a lobster club sandwich at the Brass Compass, Bronwyn closed her own eyes and drifted off, a victim of her own luscious lullaby.

"I don't think he's alright," she told Doc that evening.

"He's fine, Bronwyn. He had a fever and it's broken. He just needs some rest."

"I don't think so. It's the way he was talking." She bit her bottom lip.

"It's natural you'd be worried, losing Gus so recently."

"He never says much, you know? And this afternoon he talked on and on and I think he was worried about something."

Doc gave her a brotherly hug. "He won't even remember it, Bronwyn."

And happily, Jeeves didn't seem to, although she didn't forget. Whatever had haunted Jeeves had cast a chilling wave over her.

Never one to make demands, she surprised Edgar with numerous suggestions for soups and puddings for her Jeeves. Linda discovered Bronwyn had strict expectations for cool and refreshing bed linens and changed his bedding twice a day. Tom 'learned' the temperature in Jeeves' flat fluctuated, so when he wasn't stoking the fireplace flames, he was adjusting the thermostat. Van had no idea Bronwyn knew so much about western collectible magazines and antique car publications, and he was dispatched daily to find new ones in Portland.

For his part, Jeeves was pleasantly surprised at Bronwyn's intense devotion. She seemed to be there whenever he opened his eyes. Bronwyn fed him chicken broth when he was well able to do it himself, and he enjoyed her solicitude. She tucked velvet haps around him, polished his reading glasses, bent his straw. She crumpled saltines into his tomato soup. Jeeves felt loved.

Finally, as he was nearing good health, he inquired, "Miss, what has caused this devotion?"

"You'd do the same for me, Jeeves."

"In fact, I have not."

"Well, I say you have. And, it's easier for girls. You should have had a daughter. I'll be your daughter when you're sick."

"I'll not forget this, Miss."

"There, there Jeeves. Of course you will. The world seems so fragile when you're not feeling well, but you'll be strong and able in a day or so. It'll be a distant memory."

"You've been very kind, Miss. I couldn't have a better daughter."

Bronwyn wanted to return the compliment, but Jeeves was nothing like her father. Instead, she bent down and gently kissed the top of his head. "Have a sleep, Jeeves. Have a sleep."

When he was back on his feet two days later, a hearty cheer went up in houses across the land. At least, across the estate.

Bronwyn wasn't motivated to meet with Grace Cloud, but there were issues that needed attention.

Well aware that Grace's assistant would be dressed professionally, and knowing Grace was a clotheshorse without rein, Bronwyn stood in her closet and mused over outfits. It seemed unnecessary to dress for the meeting, but Bronwyn decided she should make the effort. Still weary from her 'Jeeves attentiveness' of the past week, she chose a boldly striped navy and white turtleneck, a white cotton skirt, and a navy tissue faille trench. She swept raspberry lip gloss across her lips, hoping it would zap her with oomph, and wondered what springish ensemble the women had chosen.

The sky was brooding and the air smelled of impending rain. Riding the Factory elevator, she tried to get in a 'meeting' frame of mind, but felt beleaguered. She reminded herself there was very little day-to-day work required of her. A meeting here and there wasn't much to ask.

"Here you go, Bronwyn," Sam Brown said, placing a large café au lait in front of her. "Grace."

Grace Cloud accepted an espresso. She nodded to Sam, who left the women alone at the long mahogany conference table. Grace glanced at her legal pad.

"No agenda?" Bronwyn asked.

"No, I thought we could wing it. First, I think it's great how well Laura's done. She's stepped in like she was never gone."

"Good." Bronwyn wondered if Grace had doubted Laura.

"Your forgiveness reminds me of Luke Townsend. None of us believed you'd give him a penny after he tried to take Snooks."

The first time Bronwyn had gone to the cemetery, she'd planned to tell Gus the shocking tale of Luke, Tiny, and Snooks. But when she'd stood there, it flew from her mind. She was wracked with grief and remembered how proud Gus was when Luke ran for governor. She could only imagine his pride, having Luke in the Senate.

"I got over it," was all Bronwyn said.

"Well, I think it's great you gave Laura a second chance."

"It's more like a gap. She was here, she left, and she's back. It's up to Laura to make of it whatever she can."

Bronwyn sat with her back to the window, facing the doorway. Lately, she didn't like having her back to God knows what.

"I have an updated listing of Laura's projects if you'd like to review it."

"Any problem?"

"No, but it's scattered across the state. I wasn't certain how you felt about the island projects. Small populations, you know." Bronwyn was silent, so Grace understood she had no objection. "If you have lunch at a little restaurant in Calais, they might want to thank you for their new freezer."

"We're buying a freezer in Calais?"

Grace laughed and nodded, happy to see her friend's lopsided grin.

Bronwyn waited for the next order of business.

"The family of that LifeFlighted island boy wants to thank you."

Bronwyn frowned. "He's doing better?"

"He is. Much better."

"They could write a thank you note."

"I don't think that's what they're hoping for. The Lewiston hospital says you donated the helicopter and deserve the thanks. And the family wants you to meet their boy." Bronwyn was still frowning. "I know you want to remain anonymous in these things, but it would mean so much to them."

"You go. Let me know how he is," Bronwyn said with finality.

"Do you want to renew your donations to these charities? The same amounts?" Grace handed her a preliminary list, indicating the Mario Lemieux Foundation, The Prince's Trust, Hole in the Wall Gang, the Old Friends retired thoroughbreds, and Last Chance Ranch Animal Rescue.

"Graeme said he'll match my donation to The Prince's Trust, so let's double it this year," Bronwyn suggested.

"Sneaky."

"Grace, have you seen the book *Stuart: A Life Backwards*?" She shook her head.

"I could lend you mine. It's a unique perspective about homelessness in Cambridge. It's very warm, but also distressing – a roller coaster."

"Sounds depressing."

"It reminds us that everyone matters. There's a charity attached to it – Willow Walker. It's to become FLACK in the near future. Their magazine has brilliant stories. Here's Kirsten Laver's number – give her a call. See what they need."

"The book has moved you."

"Truly."

Grace glanced up as she shifted her papers. It was obvious that Bronwyn wasn't herself.

"You know what I hate, Grace? I hate when they get you in their database, not these groups, but others, and they pressure you to continue donating, as if it's no longer a choice. As if you're in the system and of course you'll donate and how much more will you give this year? I realize they feel pressure to increase donations, but to me it's the old 'beat yesterday' book. I'm a one time donor, even if I donate four years in a row. Don't expect it of me. I can't stand the pressure."

"Bronwyn. None of that should reach you. You shouldn't be aware of foundation requests."

Grace was appalled that Bronwyn felt any pressure to donate. She was the kindest, most generous person she'd ever met, but looking at her, Grace was struck for the first time by her vulnerability. Usually plucky, dry-witted, and resilient, it was evident Bronwyn was excessively burdened.

Bronwyn felt anxious and hadn't meant to blurt out her feelings. She pressed both hands flat upon the table and her knuckles were white. "Margo mentioned some of the local groups pressuring her. There are times I feel like so many people have their hands out, and it's hard because I do definitely have money..." she trailed off.

Tilting her legal pad upward, Grace wrote surreptitiously, *Margo*, and circled it. There wasn't much Bronwyn missed, and Grace hid her intention to lay into Margo with a fury.

Behind her, Bronwyn sensed gloom descending outside the tall windows. There was a perpetual hush in this room, with windows soaring two stories, much like a library. The walls were sponged in a creamy Tuscan antique wash, a suitable backdrop to old photographs. An Oriental carpet anchored the space and hovering over the table were antique brass chandeliers sporting tiers of crystal lights. The conference room seemed dim beneath them and Bronwyn heard the distant rumble of thunder. She put the heel of her right hand on her temple and gently patted her head with her finger tips. To anyone else, it would seem an absent-minded gesture, but Bronwyn was seeking invisible comfort.

"What's the date today, Grace?"

"The twenty-eighth."

Grace waited for her to reengage.

Yes, yes, Bronwyn thought. It's amazing how deep in your subconscious rests a clock, counting back the moments of your life, while you are unaware. Ringing the faint alarm so constantly that you can't dismiss it. You can't quite hear it, you can't quite place it, but it rings. All day long. You might think you forget, but the core of you always remembers. Sneaking up on you.

Grace took the list from Bronwyn. "You've said it yourself. Giving should always feel good, Bronwyn. If it doesn't, we've failed you, but that's going to change. We'll take a break after this round." She hoped Bronwyn might perk up at the thought of a break. "You've helped people so often, instead of faceless bureaucratic groups, and I haven't given you enough credit for that. All the snow removal equipment, fire trucks, those two LifeFlight helicopters, the canine unit dogs, the Business Assistance Group."

Bronwyn was reflecting. Now that she knew the cause of her private unrest, her anxiety was gently quelled. "I'm thinking I'd like to give gift cards for the Book Nook... hundred dollar ones to high school seniors and I think, fifty dollar ones to first and fifth graders. We might need to help Jane Jackson pump up her inventory, though. She'll like an excuse to buy new books."

"I went into the Book Nook this week and saw Jane recovered the balcony sofas and chairs. They look lovely."

"They're cozier than new ones would have been," Bronwyn admitted.

"I think it's nice how Jess Jackson has free York Peppermint Patties at the register, and books behind his wrapping station at the Men's Store. I bought myself a grilling book and a golf tip book when I got that hoodie, and Jess was trying to figure out what other books to bring over from Jane's. He said he only expected guys to buy them," Grace chuckled.

Bronwyn offered a small smile.

"Why don't we trip around some farms and dairies this week and lift our spirits? They're always glad to see you. No need for anonymity. They're your peeps," Grace suggested.

Bronwyn seemed brighter. "Okay. We'll do a farm market tour."

Grace rose, saying, "I'll be right back."

Gazing about the room, Bronwyn wondered if it needed cheering, rather than herself. Perhaps Jen should bring fresh flowers. For some reason, the place seemed old and stale. Distant thunder reminded her it was the day becoming dreary, not the room. Years ago, the estate and Factory projects had given her the giddy sensation of bolts popping and shackles falling off, but perhaps it had been freedom that had always been her problem. The moment her family had died, she was free as a balloon, released to the winds.

Hearing a trilling bird outside, Bronwyn focused on its song.

Grace returned and sipped her espresso. "My toenails are changing."

"Pardon?"

"They're not the same anymore, Bronwyn. They're getting thicker. They're not as pretty."

"Is it drastic, or just in your head?"

Grace was thoughtful. "Probably in my head."

"Well, don't show Linda or she'll tell you they're yellowing into a rigid plastic."

Grace laughed.

"Did you decide to sponsor a Little League team this year?"

Bronwyn nodded.

"Clara seems to think she's going to make their uniforms. Since Charlie and Augie are going to play," Grace shared.

"Maybe she should do a prototype and they could use them as practice uniforms."

"Don't you think they might look, I don't know, maybe delicate, wearing homemade uniforms? Even if they are just for practice?"

Bronwyn guffawed. "Delicate?"

"Shades of my mother, I guess."

"Well, let's ask Teddy what he thinks."

"The league needs the team name, Bronwyn."

"That's easy. Factory Pirates. I have to honor my Buccos." Bronwyn waited to see what was next.

Grace toyed with her espresso cup.

"I was thinking about our last meeting. Remember how we talked about *Queen for a Day?*" Bronwyn nodded. "Well, I asked my Mother and she used to watch it, too. I guess that's why I was laughing about a freezer."

"But, when you really need a freezer, you really need one," Bronwyn declared.

Sam knocked at the doorway, telling Grace she had a phone call. Sam's pink boucle suit set off her blonde hair and of course she was wearing black stilettos. It pleased Bronwyn to have an air of elegance on the fourth floor.

"Does Jozie still love everything 'Princess'?" Bronwyn asked.

Sam took a seat and crossed her legs, glad for the break. "She is. And Elijah's still into science and biology."

"Has Charlie shown him his telescope?"

"Elijah loves that telescope. He thinks Charlie is the luckiest kid in the world. They had a sleepover last month. Did you hear? And, Charlie let him light the weather tower over at Splash Flanagan's. Elijah talks about it all the time."

Grace came back and Sam returned to her office.

"Since Margo is only handling Laura's local projects, maybe you should bring in another assistant, Grace, for state projects."

"I don't think we need anyone else, but Sam could take on more responsibility. I'll ask her what she thinks."

"It's your call, but I feel badly, giving you new projects."

"Don't. It's invigorating." Grace assured her.

Van and Edgar peeked around the corner. Bronwyn was surprised, as she hadn't heard the elevator. They were carrying trays and placed them at the far end of the table. Grace must have called Edgar when she interrupted their meeting. Three miniature cheeseburgers were lined up on each narrow plate, with two brown paper sacks of handcut French fries and two milkshakes; strawberry for Grace and caramel for Bronwyn.

"Join us," Bronwyn urged the men.

"No, thanks. I can't spoil my dinner with Clara," Edgar declared, but Van wavered.

"Have one of my burgers, Van."

"And one of mine," Grace said, plopping one of her burgers on Bronwyn's long plate, and sliding the remaining pair in front of Van.

His dimples appeared as he grinned from ear to ear. "If you insist."

Edgar fetched a root beer for Van and sat companionably with the three burger fiends. It did his heart good to see Bronwyn eating. He caught Grace's eye and winked, eliciting a vibrant smile from her.

When they were finished, the men excused themselves and the women resumed their meeting.

"Bronwyn, the therapy dog program is taking off. The League wants to implement it throughout the state. I'm considering a vehicle for travel and they'd like another trainer."

"Sounds good. Did you know Charlie's Muffin has gone over to Pine Manor? She's a big hit. Coolidge is going over next time." Bronwyn said proudly. "Did you compile the list yet for canine unit grants?"

"Yes, but we're waiting for two more responses from police departments. I don't have their paperwork yet. You want to do $15,000 for each? Two dogs?"

"Yes, I'd rather do two now, than wait and add another."

With a deep sigh of her own, Grace announced, "My mother's coming to visit."

"It'll be okay," Bronwyn said reassuringly. "She'll be impressed."

Grace had something on her mind, and Bronwyn assumed it was about her mother. Giving her a moment, Bronwyn gathered their cups.

"Susie took the jet back to New York."

"I'm sorry, Grace, but you're going to have to tell her, it's not her personal taxi."

"They're having problems."

Bronwyn sadly nodded with comprehension.

Reading her exhaustion, Grace ended their meeting. "Leave the cups. Let's have dinner tomorrow, after the farms. My treat. The Lobster Pound."

Grace gave her a monster hug, soundly conveying her affection.

Before she stepped on the elevator, Bronwyn crossed to the windows. She only had a view of sloping woods past the Island House, but she suspected Alex Oz King would be home.

When the elevator reached the third floor, she sat in the nearest chair. She couldn't help but glance down to the end of the Factory, to Susie and Allison's suite. It occurred to Bronwyn to go over and poke around. Perhaps she could find some clue to explain how Susie had gone from her little pal, to the unexpected bride of Alex Oz King.

As much as she missed Samuel and Paul, Susie and Allison, she didn't look around their rooms; never breathed in their scent on the pillows, never stroked the books they'd opened. Now she imagined 'Susie + Alex' on ski posters or some such nonsense. If there'd ever been clues, Bronwyn had missed them.

She slid back against the soft cushions and absorbed the length of the building.

It was Allison who called Bronwyn three months ago. Moss, his wife, and Allison were the only witnesses to the wedding of Susie Mastrofrancesco and Alex Ozwald King, in the mayor's office in New York City. A family wedding luncheon at Tavern on the Green did little to dispel Mrs. Mastrofrancesco's disappointment. Now it was Allison's destiny to one day star in the lavish wedding production befitting the family.

Allison had filled in the silent gaps created by shock; hadn't Bronwyn noticed how often Alex and Susie went skiing together? Didn't she know how Alex visited Susie in New York, when she was home? Didn't Bronwyn think they made a handsome couple?

Bronwyn had no defense. She always gave Alex Oz King the widest berth because they had so much in common. They were both loners, or so she thought. She'd promised Alex freedom, and that's what she gave him. They were always pleased to run into each other, and Duchess and Newfie were exuberant to see her, but no, Bronwyn hadn't placed Alex with Susie, in her thoughts. Not even in the same phrase.

Well, Allison happily assured her, it was because Susie so much wanted to live on the estate. At least that's what Allison thought.

But, in the months since the surprise marriage, Bronwyn had only seen Susie once, from a distance. The newlyweds took a honeymoon to Florence, returned for a few weeks, left for the Riviera, and then returned for a week before Susie flew back to New York, without Alex. Since then, she only seemed to visit for a few days before returning to spend most of her time in New York.

Obviously he had reached for a greater happiness and dreamed he'd found it with the young lady Bronwyn had invited to the estate, year after year. Now he was sitting rejected and desolate, much like he'd been on the Hampton beach.

Bronwyn tried to remember Susie's youth. Who was the girl she thought she knew so well? Who was the girl who hid her romance, who never breathed a word of it to Bronwyn?

Allison, wise beyond her years, said Susie had tested Alex. She made him promise to say nothing of their relationship to Bronwyn, to judge his faithfulness. Alex's silence wasn't hard to understand. Bronwyn couldn't imagine Hughie or Conor being in love, facing such a choice, and not agreeing.

At least she could walk over to the suites, she decided. When she reached the door of Susie and Allison's, she raised her hands and pressed them against the wood. She could almost see the sisters sunbathing and dashing over to the soda fountain for an icy drink. Susie had dearly loved the estate; of that, Bronwyn was certain.

As she crossed the common area, Bronwyn got an idea, and by the time the elevator was descending, it took full form.

It was always a little dicey, walking down the hillside to Oz Valley. The steps tended to be covered with nature… slippery moss, wet leaves, twigs. She made her way down, like a careful, elderly creature. At the bridge leading to the elevated loggia, Bronwyn regained some energy. Rapping at the door, the dogs barked and Alex Oz King emerged.

He looked embarrassed. "Hello, Bronwyn. Susie's not here."

That was an odd thing to say; Bronwyn hadn't been to the house since their marriage. Maybe he was just confessing the truth. Susie wasn't there.

They sat outside, suspended above the stream. Newfie sat beside her and Bronwyn was thinking what a perfect dog the Newfoundland was for Alex Oz King. Large but sweet-dispositioned, she was devoted and loved the land as much as splashing in the stream. She had dignity and carried her head proudly, but she was such a sweet dog, with enormous snow feet. Bronwyn patted Newfie's head as amiable Duchess scratched at the door. Alex let her out and she immediately dropped at his feet and tucked her head in for a snooze. Bronwyn bent over and gave her a solid pat as the Dalmatian sighed.

It was quiet and still, except for the sounds of birds and water. Crocus and tulips were popping up amidst budding bushes and Bronwyn thoroughly enjoyed the atmosphere. A thick column of iris emerged from the large gray stones managing storm water runoff. Bronwyn was happy she'd come armed with an idea; without it, she was certain none of nature's early show would catch her senses.

"I'm afraid she thinks she's made a mistake."

"Well, not about you, I'm certain of that."

"Why?"

Bronwyn smiled as if he were a little dimwitted.

"What does Susie say when she goes to New York?"

Alex pursed his lips. "She says it's not what she expected. Maine. She says she misses the excitement of New York."

"Bennington wasn't a metropolis," Bronwyn let her ire surface.

An odd feeling swept through Bronwyn. She didn't exactly envy Alex Oz King's house, but she appreciated it.

Their tastes were similar and she could name a hundred things he'd done with his two million dollars that she admired. Birch slat ceilings, the walk-in fieldstone shower with its vaulted ceiling...the beautiful engineering of the timber-framed loggia, springing from stone pillars in swoops and pitches, broad beams and peaks. Alex Oz King was brave enough to give himself the home of his dreams.

Bronwyn had deliberately created spaces in her home to resurrect the past. She tried to touch the people who had gone; hoped to feel their presence in her rooms. She remembered Mama Lou telling her 'honey, your Mama and Papa would just love this suite you've set me in. I know you done it up for them; don't be tellin' me no. They'd be proud o' you, baby.' When Mama Lou had said that, Bronwyn remembered holding back tears. It made her see her house in a new light. Mama Lou was right. And now Bronwyn's eyes were filling again, with the memory.

She discretely wiped her tears. It annoyed her that Susie wasn't enjoying every aspect of Alex's house.

"When Susie gets back, have Katrin make her favorite cake. It's a dark chocolate crepe cake we've had in New York. They're chocolate crepes with hazelnut filling between. Then, chocolate glaze and candied hazelnuts. Probably 50 crepes stacked together. Susie loves it."

Alex pursed his lips and nodded slightly. "I've been thinking she might like new ski clothes. I know she wants to ski in Gstaad. Still. With me. I just don't know why she's not as interested in being here."

Bronwyn wanted to launch into her idea, but was diverted by Susie's immaturity.

"Allison starting at Bates College should help Susie's attitude about Maine, and I know she's always loved the estate."

Alex was looking more miserable by the minute. Bronwyn thought about those Hollywood marriages that lasted weeks or months. She never pictured knowing someone in that situation.

"Have you been building any furniture, Alex?"

"I have been, quite a lot, actually. I've started making sleds and sleighs, too."

"That's a great idea. Because of the toboggan factory?"

"Exactly. Perhaps the Gods will favor me, if I do the work the place was meant to do."

She saw tears in his eyes and was almost sorry she'd come into his valley.

"I'm nearly twenty years older, Bronwyn. She must think she made a mistake."

"You're a prize. Don't think for a moment, that you're not."

"That's what I'm afraid of. I think she wanted to win me. That sounds egotistical, but she wanted to shock her parents, and she definitely wanted to keep our relationship a secret from you. After she got her wedding, it's as if she had no interest in being married."

Bronwyn thought there might be truth to his fears.

"I know you. I know the essence of you, don't I?" He nodded. "And, I've known Susie since she was six years old. I think there isn't anyone from the outside who could better picture you together, than me. You make a good couple. Your personalities compliment each other. My opinion, without speaking to Susie, is that she just doesn't think she fits here, on the estate. You've been happy when you've traveled, haven't you?"

He nodded.

"Well, she must feel this is your place; not hers. And, since she hasn't come over to see me, maybe she's embarrassed. Your secret romance was fine, until she found herself here."

"She's jealous of you," he said regretfully.

"Really?" Bronwyn was dumbfounded. "Really? She thinks there's something between us?"

"Everyone you've brought to the estate has a bond with you. Susie would realize that if she'd just live here."

"I came down because I have an idea."

He instantly brightened.

"Susie did ceramics and sculpture at Bennington. Why don't you put an artist studio, above the garage? You're just storing furniture you've made, right? And lumber?"

He was thoughtful. "I could definitely do that. Her own work space. The second floor is huge."

"And, you could sell your furniture along with her art pieces in town, or maybe up on Exchange Street in the Old Port."

"I think you're dead right, Bronwyn. She needs to feel she has her own life, and she did always say she loved Maine."

"Susie could still spend time in New York. So could you. And, travel. Travel as much as you like. Life's short. You should see everything you ever wanted to see. But you need to get in a groove, here. I know you'd make her a fabulous studio," she said emphatically.

"Yes," he said with an exhausted smile that showed his dimples. "I'm actually feeling better. I'll ring her tonight and see what she thinks."

"Call Allison first. She's such a positive person, and she's always adored you."

Alex Oz King nodded, as his mind raced. "Let's go check out the space."

"No, you go ahead and start planning." Bronwyn was thinking the less she was involved, the better. "Tell Susie I'll send the jet whenever she's ready to come back, okay?"

She gave him a quick hug and crossed the bridge.

The last order of business would be to phone Grace Cloud and tell her the jet was available for a one way ticket. One last time. If it didn't work out, Susie could 'Greyhound-bus-it' back to the Big Apple.

After Bronwyn called Grace, she changed into casual clothes, donning a hooded wax jacket and Wellies. She made her way in the misty drizzle along the stone wall, past Van Tsang's security post and beyond the ivy-covered bricks, encircling the Factory visitor parking lot. She approached Squirrel Hill, threading her way through the greenhouses and corral.

Farther up the hill, little bird graves were marked along the left, with small stakes indicating 'Robin', 'Little Sparrow', 'Lady Cardinal' and the like. Another section was reserved for small animals and she always marked their place with an engraved stone, indicating 'Chipmunk', 'Squirrel', 'Bunny', and occasionally marked by more specific identifiers like 'Bunny by My House' and 'Favorite Little Red Squirrel'.

Clara was so used to Bronwyn's request for velvet, that she kept bolts of different colors. When she saw how tenderly Bronwyn fingered the fabric, all the while knowing the little animal was lying somewhere nearby, to be gently placed by Bronwyn, Clara began to pleat the fabric and make more of it. Finally, Bronwyn could simply ask Clara for small, medium or large velvet blankets. As time went by, Clara was happy to lift Bronwyn's sadness with embellishments on the velvet squares and for the rabbits, a heraldic arms crest stitched to the center. It got so Clara actually anticipated the next opportunity to show off her new and improved death buntings. In fact, she had a double blanket padded with thermal insulation and stitched with braiding, awaiting the next fallen bird destined to reside on Squirrel Hill.

It wasn't winter anymore, but it wasn't the full blown beauty of spring, yet. Mud season was in full swing. Bronwyn stood at an angle at the top of the hill, looking particularly insignificant and small along the rise.

The word went out. Bronwyn didn't cross King Street without the silent sirens of estate women going off. Jen noticed first and called Valli. Valli got on the phone to Edgar to see what he knew about Bronwyn 'wandering about'. Edgar called Jeeves, and before long, Bronwyn found Jeeves at her elbow.

"Evening, Miss."

She turned with a perplexed look. How did Jeeves seem to appear out of thin air, so often?

"It's a titch rainy for a stroll." He had donned a wax jacket of his own, boots and a tweed cap. When Bronwyn glanced at him, she noticed he still looked pale from his recent illness.

She turned her neck left and right, as if it was stiff. They stood in silence for several minutes, neither desirous of conversation. Bronwyn seemed to forget he was there. Jeeves appreciated the opportunity to observe her. She stood long enough to apparently satisfy her mission and when Bronwyn turned, it was obvious she was taken aback to see him there.

"May I ask, Miss, the nature of your business? You seem actively still."

Bronwyn was thrown by his astute observation, so she rewarded him not with an answer, but with *the* answer.

"I'm reaching across the ocean, Jeeves. It calls to me sometimes, and I'm reaching out as mentally hard as I can to bridge the gap."

It was no surprise when he asked, "and the rest?"

She could choose to answer or not, but she was tired of her day's isolation and melancholy.

"Today is my sister's birthday. She was four when she died, four years younger than I was." Her voice was so quiet it seemed to carry on the wind, rather than emanate from Bronwyn. "I hardly remember her."

After a bit, she added, "But I remember envying Claire her red hair."

It was apparent how weary Bronwyn was; she hadn't asked for any deeply buried secret of his, in exchange.

"I see, Miss," he answered in a reassuring voice. "Are we done now? Might we have some chowder for supper? Edgar advised me he's made it just for us."

Bronwyn was glad to walk over with Jeeves. It gave the day a nicer ending than she'd have anticipated. They had lovely hot chowder, warm crusty bread with cold butter, and Chardonnay, while Bronwyn listened raptly to all that Edgar and Clara said, relieved to lose herself in the convivial atmosphere. Clara plopped down a plate of warm chocolate chip cookies and was rewarded with the newly recovered Jeeves' enthusiastic swoop of three, while Bronwyn grinned and ate one, with chocolate melting just a bit on her lower lip.

Warmed and renewed, Bronwyn walked with Jeeves

through the tunnel to her house. He made certain she was settled upstairs and Bronwyn shared Grace's plans for the next day. Perhaps a farm stand and dairy visit, but definitely, dinner at the Lobster Pound together.

As Jeeves turned to leave, Bronwyn said, "I'm glad you're feeling better, Jeeves. You should think about a little trip – somewhere warm."

"Perhaps we should visit Menke, Miss."

"Then you probably want to visit The Franklin Fountain."

"I'd not be averse, Miss. I've a yen for The Stock Market Crunch."

"And I wouldn't mind having at least one Southern Sympathizer. I love that place. It's the soda fountain of my dreams. And we could bring back some homemade marshmallows."

Jeeves' face softened and he uncharacteristically opened his mouth and then shut it. He meant to say he was sorry about Bronwyn's little sister Claire, but he said nothing more and headed down the staircase.

Before he reached the bottom, Bronwyn called to him. Without a word, she pointed her index finger straight at him. In kind, Jeeves made the same gesture back and his sly wink made her laugh.

Jeeves left; satisfied her spirits were sufficiently lifted. It had been a worry when Edgar shared Grace's concern from earlier in the afternoon.

Bronwyn would sleep better that night, but the night didn't bring sleep for Jeeves. After midnight, he mounted Squirrel Hill with his laptop and vectors. He stood precisely where Bronwyn had stood and entered the coordinates; in fact he could see her boot prints in the goopy mud. She had been standing, not toward water's edge, which to most people would signify the watery expanse of which she'd spoken; instead, she faced solid woods well back from the granite cliffs. He wasn't surprised to see the line on his laptop connecting to the precise point in France, over which her family's plane had exploded, raining down the remnants of her shredded life.

CHAPTER TWENTY TWO

GRACE

*I*t was difficult having Bella Cloud as your mother. Grace told Bronwyn often enough, but it wasn't until Bella visited that Bronwyn finally understood.

From the moment they walked Bella to Grace's guest room, Bronwyn felt rumblings. The three women gazed from the balcony to the first level. A beautifully rendered mural of the Maine coast stretched behind them. Sweeping staircases were like elegant parentheses, punctuated on either side by pedestals topped with lavish floral arrangements. The view from the balcony was glitteringly impressive as the hallway ran the Factory's length, with dark tones of Indonesian hardwood on ceiling and walls, studded with a long row of twelve glittering crystal chandeliers.

Bella made no comment, except to groan about her room's location. Bronwyn gasped when she complained, "My, it's small. I thought you'd at least have a house, Grace." Bronwyn always considered Grace's space to be the most elegant of all the estate homes and apartments.

Grace returned to her apartment for a final once-over, while Bronwyn helped Bella unpack. She could barely cope with the clothes Bella draped over her outstretched arms, as if she were a pack mule. Bronwyn hoped Bella would be impressed by the walk-in closet, with every luxury option available. Surely she would delight in the rotating carousels. Perhaps she packed a hat to place in one of the Italian linen hat boxes. Surely she'd realize how important Grace was, if Bella pulled out sweater shelves and noticed how thick the glass was, how polished the edges. She could sit on the cream velvet bench and marvel at Grace's collection of floor to ceiling shoe cabinets

Silent Bella left the plush dressing area and Bronwyn looked around the guest room, trying to take it in from Bella's perspective. The bed had a large nineteenth century French glass mirror as its grand headboard and was generously dressed in toile, stripes, and florals, all in cream tones highlighted by raspberry red. The rug and French bedside table were pale gray-blue and the French armoire from the 1800's held a collection of antique quilts. All in all, Bronwyn was certain it was a lovely guest room, full of personality and warmth, despite Bella's mutterings. Bronwyn regretted taking Bella back to Grace's apartment. Only ten minutes had gone by; Grace was in for a very long visit.

As they sat in the living area, Grace's frozen smile was drawn in a straight line. One of the declared reasons for installing her mother in the guest room was so she wouldn't have to deal with Dudley and Frog, Grace's French bulldogs. Even that backfired when Bella had an instant affinity for the dogs. Dudley's lips were perpetually drawn up in a constant smile which elicited a similar expression from Bella. And Frog's seriously huge eyes and bat-like ears won Bella over, as she lifted the little black dog onto her lap.

"He looks like he's wearing a tuxedo," she cooed over his white chest and front paws.

Every aspect of Grace's home was dignified and sumptuous, Bronwyn reminded herself. Bella was sitting on a custom couch in cream velvet, while Grace and Bronwyn faced her on a long chocolate sofa. An enormous square coffee table divided them, holding books and a crystal vase filled with white hydrangeas. Grace chose a seat behind the flowers, unable to see her mother. White carpet covered much of the marble floor, and the walls were intricately framed by dimensional carvings. Bronwyn tried to view it with fresh eyes; getting no response from Bella was unnerving her.

The staircase leading to Grace's bedroom seemed to lift into the air, with glass sides and only a bright silver banister pointing the way. Tray ceilings were subtly aglow with recessed lighting, fabulous twig and crystal chandeliers, and a 1950's capiz shell lighting fixture.

While Bella occupied herself with the blessed dogs, Bronwyn tilted her head to the dining room and Grace followed her.

They stood by the bar area with its deep backsplash of mini mirror tiles and Bronwyn tinkered with the coffee/espresso machine, having no idea how to make it work.

"How long is she staying, Grace?"

"You're joking. This was your idea."

"I know. We can make it work." Grace gave her a dirty look. "Why don't I call Katrin or Edgar and get some food up here?"

"Bronwyn, we're set for lunch in two hours. Don't you think we can at least wait till then?"

They stared at each other until Grace muttered, "Do you want to call Edgar, or shall I?"

Bronwyn asked Bella to join her on the balcony. She shrugged and Bronwyn held the door for her, as Dudley and Frog followed adoringly behind Bella.

The balcony had a spectacular raised fire and water feature, perched in a protected corner and surrounded by large slate tiles. Bronwyn fired it up. In fact, she turned on all the outdoor lighting, trying to get as much ooh and ahh factor as she could at ten thirty in the morning. Dudley and Frog were frolicking in their patch of fresh grass, fronting a line of white wooden chaises. Bronwyn pointed out the southern exposure to Bella, explaining how the grass was easy to tend on the top floor of the Factory; then gestured to a slender tool shed with lawn equipment. She was about to show her the lawn mower, when Bella put her hand on the bronze spiral staircase rising from the balcony to Grace's bedroom suite.

It shouldn't have surprised Bronwyn that Bella said she was going up. When she suggested they wait for Grace, Bella gave her a stern look.

"Really. I think my daughter won't mind showing off her bedroom. It's not as if she has a man hidden there." Bronwyn didn't like her tone and gave her an analytical once-over. Her gray hair was cut into a beautiful swinging bob. She wore high-waisted charcoal tweed pants, gray stiletto heels, a charcoal blouse, tons of distinctive silver jewelry and a pricey man's watch. She knew where Grace got her fashion sense.

Maybe Grace would understand how Bronwyn couldn't stop her, she thought dejectedly.

"We need to put the dogs in before we go up." She abruptly handed Frog to Bella and gave her a cloth to wipe his feet while she did the same for Dudley. Bella tossed Frog inside and headed for the staircase. Bronwyn thought it would be funny if Bella yanked on the door and it was locked, but after she put Dudley inside and mounted the stairs behind her, Bella was already walking in.

"What do you think, Mom?"

"Yes. Yes. It's lovely, Grace."

The glazed sliding doors provided access to the bedroom's balcony and when Bronwyn closed them, it seemed a transparent and open space. Grace's pale carpet was etched in a subtle pattern and velvet curtains were drawn back. The bed faced the bay, backed by cream leather built-in units spanning the width of the room. Bella peeked into the bathroom with its satin panels and mirrored walls. She touched the taffeta curtains and custom moiré wall coverings, and then sat at the mirrored dressing table with its silver candlesticks and fresh white flowers. Her head swiveled to the reflected wall sconces and crystal chandelier.

"Yes, Grace. Quite nice."

"Bronwyn, you can go. Come back for lunch."

"Okay, Grace. I'll see you soon, Mrs. Cloud."

As Bronwyn picked up her jacket, she heard Bella say, "I thought you'd at least have a house." Bronwyn walked away, making what Jeeves called her 'rat face' by screwing her mouth up in an unattractive way.

Once Bronwyn got back to her house, she called Linda and asked her to prepare the Carnegie Suite. Grace meant too much to Bronwyn to have her endure Bella, especially when it had been Bronwyn's idea to invite her. Linda was game, arriving within minutes and bustling through the suite. Bronwyn had never seen Matthew enlisted to duty, but Linda had her husband vacuuming. Evidently, Linda knew the angst a mother could bring.

Next, Bronwyn got on the phone. Bella had given her an idea.

Having guests could be difficult. Bronwyn remembered Jeeves asking why she had never invited Sebastian Hughes to Maine. She wasn't proud of herself, but she had told Jeeves if Hughie came to visit, she didn't think he'd ever leave – not with a crowbar. Not with a tow truck.

It hadn't taken much to move Bella to Bronwyn's house. As a testament to their affection for Grace, Edgar and Linda shared the burden of entertaining Bella. For her part, Bella enjoyed the beautiful suite and the enormity of Bronwyn's lobby.

Bronwyn used her formal dining room for meals with her, but she didn't use her tea room. Afternoon tea was too special to share with Bella. Coping and entertaining were two different things.

When it became difficult to enlist dinner companions on the estate, Bronwyn invited her neighbors, the Todds and Masons. Outnumbering Bella seemed a good thing and the evening went well. Bronwyn didn't mind if Grace didn't join them for meals and Bella didn't mind either. It seemed Grace's flat was becoming smaller in Bella's eyes with each day she spent at Bronwyn's.

Toward the end of Bella's visit, Bronwyn had movie night in her upstairs theater. It was one of Hughie's most irresistible romantic comedies, and Bella laughed in all the right places, beaming afterward.

"What a charming man that Sebastian Hughes is. Just charming."

Bronwyn agreed.

The next morning she suggested that they go over to Grace's and surprise her with muffins and croissants. Bella reluctantly trotted along behind her.

They walked through the lavish public area of the fourth floor. Bronwyn knocked lightly at Grace's flat and walked in.

There, in pajamas and robe, was Sebastian Hughes.

"Hughie. I didn't realize you were here this weekend."

"Just snuck up to spend some time with Grace, Bronwyn. You must be Bella."

Bella was a polished, elegant woman, but her mouth was gaping open.

Grace came down the floating staircase and wrapped her arms around Hughie, kissing his neck. "Hi, Mom. Hi, Bronwyn."

Now it was Bronwyn's turn to gape. There was no mistaking their familiarity.

"Hughie, may I speak to you a moment?" He looked confused. "In the kitchen? Just for a moment?"

When they walked through the dining area into the kitchen with its pure 'white as the driven snow' bead board, Bronwyn grabbed his elbow. "Where did you sleep?"

Hughie's eyes were big, wondering why dear Bronwyn seemed upset. "Here. You know. As you asked." He leaned back against the granite countertop, finding it incredibly cold through his thin robe.

"You mean you slept with her?"

Hughie looked around and found nothing to save him. "I quite like her. She's brilliant, wicked amusing and we got on right from the start. I'm actually dead struck by her."

"You slept with her."

"You'll not hear her complaining."

Bronwyn made for Hughie and grasped his forearm, squeezing it. "If you hurt her, if you break her heart…" she gave a pinch, in warning.

Hughie trusted Bronwyn not to hurt him, at least in this demonstration phase.

"Bronwyn let go. I'm quite taken with her. And, the place of course. It's splendid. Everything about it. And, the doggies quite like me as well. Not to worry."

Bronwyn was angry at herself for setting the scenario into motion.

Hughie turned serious. "I wouldn't say this to just anyone. In fact, I've never said it to anyone. Charlotte took the stuffing from me. It's taken awhile, but it seems like Grace Cloud has been waiting for someone just like me. Even her name, Bronwyn…Grace…Cloud."

"Don't get carried away, Hughie. It's just been a night."

"You underestimate yourself Bronwyn. Grace told me how you've brought all these people together. Now, it's me."

Bronwyn suppressed a grin and said, "Get dressed."

It was easy having Hughie on the estate when he wasn't filming. An old friend amidst new ones was comforting.

Early one morning, Valli asked permission to use one of the King Street cottages. Her sister was coming for a visit and Valli seemed troubled.

"Of course you can use the cottages. You don't need to ask."

"Thanks, Bronwyn. Linda said she'd get one ready for me. Then Tom said he'd do it, but it should be me," her voice trailed off.

Bronwyn sat beside her on the back porch, watching the

miniature horses in the corral. They had spare bedrooms, so Valli must not want her sister staying with them.

"I haven't said this Valli, and I should have. You should be so proud of yourself, moving to Maine. It's a huge accomplishment." Bronwyn patted her arm. "Huge".

"Oh, it isn't anything to be proud of. My sister finally got me to admit I haven't left the house. I could hear how disappointed she was."

"Valli, you left everything that was familiar, and you've made a good life here. New friends. And you're a very active friend, and that's rare. You've added a lot to my life, you know."

"Oh, Bronwyn. You've made it so easy. You've been so kind. Dr. Larchmont comes to me and Vicki comes over to do my hair. Then the Mobile Dental Unit showed up at my door."

Bronwyn grinned. "I do actually think that was brilliant. Not just for you, Valli. They zip around town to people who can't make it to the dentist office. Everyone seems to love it. We might add another one."

Valli sighed. "I know how disappointed my sister will be with me."

"She hasn't been here before?"

Valli shook her head.

"Then, I'm guessing she's going to be impressed with the fine life you've built."

Bronwyn was stroking Snowball the cat.

"Tom says he told you to take Snowball home with you."

Now it was Bronwyn's turn to be uncomfortable.

"I couldn't do that, Valli." Bronwyn stroked the cat's white fur and watched her black tail swishing around. Two large black spots gave her a Dalmatian look.

"Take her. She'll be good company for you. As soon as she saw you, she came charging over from the barn."

"I couldn't."

"We'll get another cat, Bronwyn. Maybe two. The horses like having cats around. Take her," Valli urged. "Go on."

It didn't seem right to sit beside Valli's open vulnerability and share nothing of her own, so Bronwyn finally said, "I'm afraid Snowball would get lost in the house. You know I close off the Silk Club and the lobby. Maybe she'd be in the Carnegie Suite and I wouldn't know and we'd just keep missing each other. It's just too big."

"I think she'd stick close to you, Bronwyn. And she'll come to the kitchen for food. She'll find you, don't worry about that. It wouldn't be hard. I can see how much you like her."

"Well, she gives me a good reason to visit you."

Valli clucked. "You shouldn't be lonely, Bronwyn."

Bronwyn leaned over, kissed her cheek and resolved to impress Valli's sister with the good life Valli was living. Bronwyn wryly thought how her world was often smaller than Valli's.

It seemed ironic that Bronwyn pictured the estate as one big happy family, and yet she avoided the Palimores. She saw Charlie often enough, but she rarely walked by his house. She heard Charlie pounding the pavement with his basketball and decided to swing by his outdoor basketball court.

"Hey, Charlie." Bronwyn was rewarded with a huge grin. He spun around and showed off several dribbling moves before shooting. He tried to look nonchalant, but there was no mistaking his urge to impress.

Charlie wanted to show Bronwyn his school projects,

so she gathered her nerve and went in the house. Vicki had a mug of coffee waiting for her. She realized Vicki could see the basketball court clearly, despite the crush of new outdoor furniture, fountains and statuary in the courtyard.

When Charlie tugged at her to see his room, both women were glad for the interruption.

His room hadn't changed, although Bronwyn figured Teddy's room would be unrecognizable. Bronwyn felt a pang of shame and decided she should ask Vicki to tea – someday.

"Bronwyn. Are you listening to me?"

"I'm sorry, Charlie. That's great. What did you use to make the moon?"

"It's a plastic golf ball."

"These wires are practically invisible. You know, at first I thought they were fishing line, but they're too strong."

"Tom gave me special wire."

"So, you like your room?" Bronwyn said, looking around.

"Yeah. It's cool. Mom says I should change it. Paint it, but I don't want to."

The boy seemed troubled by something and was swinging his legs while sitting on his bed. His frisky beagle trotted in and Bronwyn reached down to pet her.

"Something on your mind, Charlie?"

He spoke quietly. "Mom says you have a lot of money."

"Hmmmm. I have some money. I guess the point is I have enough money. Some people don't. So, it's a good idea to help those people. And help animals that need help, too."

"Mom said you can never have enough money."

"Do you think she meant 'me' or people in general?"

"I think people. I think Mom thinks you have enough money."

Bronwyn suppressed a smile.

"Well, you know how we've gone to Cracker Barrel? They have a sign in their restaurants that says something like 'genuine goodness and honest hospitality'. You know how it's fun to go in there and hear the music and it's relaxed?"

"Yeah, it feels happy. I like being there."

"Well, I think it's homey. And I think all anyone really needs in life is genuine goodness, honest hospitality, friends, someone to love, like you love Muffin and you love your mom and dad. None of that is about money."

Charlie was nodding his head, but still thinking. "So you don't think it's true about never having enough money?"

"Having a whole lot of 'stuff' doesn't make you as happy as just having something that's special to you."

"So, you don't think it's true about never having enough money?"

"Nope. At least not for me. It's not about money. Some people would say I'm just saying that because I have money. But I know people who have a good life and don't have much money," she rattled on.

"You know, Charlie, we're trying to make the town more green."

"Environmental, right?"

"Yep. We're painting the roofs of buildings white, or putting solar panels in. Some people are planting roof gardens. It saves on heating."

"Cool." He was thoughtfully gazing around his room. "Dad says you have school kids helping old people."

"High school kids can sign up and they take an older person as their partner. The students pick up their groceries and do yard work, shovel snow, check on them. They become friends, and I'm guessing a lot of them might stay friends forever."

Charlie's head lifted and his chest puffed out. "I want to do it. Dad told me they don't get any money, though."

"No, they get money for college or school."

"Then, I want to do it."

"Why don't you ask your dad and mom if you could help the Todds or the Masons, across the street? You could rake leaves, shovel their walks. I bet they'd like having you for a partner."

Charlie was antsy to find his mother and ask permission, but first they checked out the bedroom treasures he wanted to show her.

It seemed a muddy mess, this talk of money. She followed Charlie and Muffin into the kitchen and before she could stop herself, she blurted, "Vicki, why don't you come over to my house, for tea?"

After she heard the words in the air, for just the briefest of moments, Bronwyn hoped it had only been a thought, a reverie.

"When?" Vicki asked, with a skeptical look.

Ah, then. I did invite her, Bronwyn thought.

"Today. Is 3:00 okay?"

The more it seemed Vicki was considering a way to side-step the invitation, the more Bronwyn warmed to the idea.

"Bring Charlie." Bronwyn turned to Charlie, who was buzzing the living room, "Would you bring your mother over to tea, today? At my house?"

"Sure. What's tee?"

"It's fun, Charlie, you'll like it," Bronwyn assured him, turning to Vicki. "You'll like it, Vicki and you don't have to stay long. A quick cup of tea, some pastries and mini sandwiches. It'll be fun."

As Vicki mulled over the offer, Bronwyn tried to picture it. Forget that Vicki already thought she had too much money and now Bronwyn was inviting her over to see her private world. It was just tea. How hard could that be?

"What would I wear?" Vicki asked, suspiciously.

"Just wear exactly what you have on. I will, too. We can talk about Charlie, or not talk at all. Deal?" Bronwyn stuck her hand out and Vicki took just the tips of Bronwyn's fingers in a dismal little shake.

"3:00. See you then."

Bronwyn dashed over to Edgar's, checking on her pantry supplies. They agreed she could make cucumber and asparagus sandwiches, pimento cheese on wheat, and diamond-shaped sandwiches with ham, orange marmalade, and crumbled bacon. Katrin popped down to Edgar's and assured Bronwyn she'd make scones, lemon tarts, and chocolate dipped strawberries, all in Bronwyn's kitchen so her house would smell lovely.

Bronwyn called up to Linda's and asked her advice on table linens. She wasn't surprised that three fourths of their conversation was taken up with Linda's astonished 'are you sure you want to do this?' second-guessing.

Back at her house, Bronwyn leaned against her kitchen counter and Katrin was as good as her word. The house was filled with luscious baking aromas.

"I called Vicki. She says she'll have whatever tea you're drinking."

"Do you think she'll like Earl Grey? Should we try a pot of something else?"

"I think we'll take her at her word." Katrin looked as if something was on her mind.

"Something wrong?"

"I was just wondering. You said you're not changing clothes, and you told her not to, but what if she does?"

"Oh, she won't."

While she dusted the brownies with powdered sugar, Bronwyn heard Katrin on the phone saying, "...have Jeeves keep them for ten minutes," in a firm voice.

"What's wrong, Katrin?"

"Jen called. She saw Vicki walking over. She's wearing a dress."

"Drat! Drat!" and Bronwyn flew out the kitchen doorway and up the stairs, angry with herself that she hadn't planned something special to wear, just in case.

Jeeves didn't mind detaining Charlie and Vicki. He warmed to the entire idea of Vicki coming to tea. It was a disaster in the making. Some days were just chock full of fun.

Charlie brought his mother inside and they said their hellos to Katrin. Vicki's head was spinning this way and that, taking in as much as possible.

In the tea room, Katrin smiled approvingly at Bronwyn. She'd split the difference between jeans and an organdy pinafore, by wearing an aqua turtleneck, dark brown flannel slacks, and a chunky necklace of turquoise.

"I thought you weren't going to change," Vicki said accusingly.

"I thought you might change your mind, so I took a chance," Bronwyn answered kindly, amazed to see Vicki was wearing a loud pink, black and white flowered sundress with a hot pink linen bolero, despite the breezy fall weather. Charlie's hair was damp, and featured a novel side part.

"Charlie. Would you like some hot cider with cinnamon sticks?"

"Yeah."

"Yes," corrected his mother.

Katrin brought in three bowls of pumpkin squash soup, garnished with a swirl of cream and toasted pumpkin seeds, courtesy of Edgar.

"Ahhh, Katrin, this looks great," Bronwyn enthused.

Leave it to Edgar, to come up with a surprise.

"Your Uncle Mark is envious, Charlie. He's never been to a proper tea before. He wants you to stop over and tell him all about it," Katrin informed him.

He gave his aunt a worldly nod and spied a tiered tray of desserts on the table, beside scones and finger sandwiches.

"Mom, can I have a brownie, now?"

"No, Charlie. I've never been to tea. We're going to do everything the way Bronwyn says we should."

Both women had promised themselves to eat fast and get it over with, but the repast went surprisingly well. There was more to talk about than either would have guessed, and the subject wasn't always Charlie. They talked about the weather, segueing into Katrin and Mark's baby girl, Charlie and Augie's first attempt at playing golf, Vicki's plans for Halloween decorations, the latest hair coloring trends, Teddy's building projects, and before they knew it, they'd poured a second cup of tea and were sampling the desserts.

Bronwyn caught Vicki's eye and nodded toward Charlie, who was carefully sipping his hot cider from a tea cup. He'd thoroughly enjoyed his miniature sandwiches, and decided his scones were perfect, piled with Devonshire cream, smeared with strawberry jam, slathered again with Devonshire cream and garnished with yet another teaspoon of jam. He ate four of them, amazing his audience.

When they rose to leave, Charlie made a bee-line for the snuggery.

"Here, Mom. Check this out. This is the bathroom I always use. See? It has a silver bowl. Cool, huh?"

Vicki was taking in the chintz phantasmagoria, and then poked her head into the bathroom.

"Charlie, why don't you turn on the library lights for your mom?" Bronwyn suggested.

"Look, Mom. Come here. Over here. Look." He threw the switch for the Dickens houses.

"It's not Christmas. You keep this up, all year long?"

Before Bronwyn could answer, Charlie said with slight disdain, "It's a *town*, Mom. A town."

"But, it has snow," Vicki insisted.

With authority, Charlie flipped the sound effects switch and stood reverently as the whistles blew, the birds called, and the townspeople chattered.

"Your rooms are small, Bronwyn."

"Thanks," Bronwyn answered earnestly, thinking it was a complement.

Both women looked perplexed, not certain what to say.

Charlie drew the metal sheath around the display and triumphantly informed his mother that no dust could get in.

Bronwyn put her hand on Charlie's shoulder, still surprised at how tall he was, and steered him to the front door. Giving him a hug, she nodded goodbye to Vicki.

Mother and son walked to the Factory, talking animatedly together. Bronwyn was ready to wave, but they were too engrossed to turn around. Waiting until they'd gotten as far as the gatehouse, Bronwyn was just about to go inside, when Charlie turned and waved his arm with a swoop worthy of an Indy 500 finish-line flag. With a wistful gaze, she thought how dear Charlie was to her.

CHAPTER TWENTY THREE

SOLEIL
2006

Graeme Woods' *Henry VIII* film was nominated for a Golden Globe, and Bronwyn was touched that Graeme wanted her at his table.

Keiran Kish sat three tables over, with a beautiful blonde actress named Heaven, and his girls, Chelsea and Monterey. He was surprisingly attentive to Heaven – a marshmallow-like confection, in her wisp of a blood red Zac Posen gown. Bronwyn was surprised to see a new look about Keiran's eyes. She wondered if he'd scored his new arm candy before or after he'd had his eyelids lifted.

After the Actor in a Supporting Role Motion Picture was announced, Monterey Kish passed a note to actor Jack McClean's table, whispering "Graeme Woods". McClean saw the words 'meet us at the *In Style* party.' He looked at Monterey and Chelsea and whispered, 'But I hardly know you girls'. Monterey giggled but Chelsea flushed, whispering fiercely, 'No – the Graeme Woods table!' and fluttered her hand in a pushing motion.

The note made its way to Bronwyn, who leaned back and nodded to the girls.

Jack took a long look at Graeme's table girl. There was something camouflage-like about her. Certainly no one in the room was wearing brown. The name of this game was glitz, glow, cinch, pinch, and flash the veneers. Her hair was what he'd call a 'good cut', quite unlike the Taj Mahal styles at his table. She looked like a studio executive or producer, stepping back to let the star power shine. Then again, when she'd turned toward the girls, loads of turquoise swung around her neck, a bit of flash after all. He'd seen 'Bron' on the flap of the note. That sounded familiar. He turned to his table, but his mind wasn't on the amusing mutterings of his mates.

Then he remembered. When he and Graeme had filmed in Poland, he heard Bronwyn McCall was visiting the set. He'd intended to stop by Graeme's trailer, but got side-tracked. Ever since Mike Veneti told him how Bronwyn McCall transformed his character in twenty minutes on a driveway in the Napa Valley, Jack had hoped to cross paths with her. Veneti nearly wept with adoration for her. Bronwyn was his talisman. Mike recounted how he'd threatened to walk-off the sequel to his first Oscar winning role, unable to believe the character, the script, or himself. She righted him, infusing him with the character he'd once known so well. According to Veneti, she breathed a new Oscar into his soul. Intrigued, Jack asked him about it. Apparently she ran through a short scene with him from the original film, and Veneti said when she looked into his eyes, his character, dormant for 20 years, was reborn. 'This little nobody knows my freakin' character better than I know myself,' Veneti marveled. 'Twenty minutes.'

Jack had asked Graeme about her and he remembered Graeme saying she grasped inner landscapes of character, sensing rhythm in scenes that others didn't hear. Graeme had a twinkle in his eye though, and said she only sprinkled the fairy dust upon her friends...Sir Winston Watkins, Conor Frost, and Sebastian Hughes. Like a secret club. Funny how they keep racking up awards, Jack thought with a pang, realizing that he'd probably go home empty-handed tonight. Even if they weren't often box office, those blokes were brilliant. He wondered if any of that was due to Bronwyn McCall and vowed to speak to her tonight. She seemed to like the English boys. Hopefully she wouldn't mind some Irish mixed in.

Jack McClean detested these after-parties; all the more if you got all worked up and then lost. Time spent with his pals was one thing, but this was for tofs. Nevertheless, after he passed the note between Kish's girls and Bronwyn McCall, he decided to maneuver his way into the *In Style* bash. He hadn't passed a note since grammar, so he took it as a sign.

He spent almost an hour watching the Woods table, all the while fending off his actress-of-the-evening, anxious for him to realize she was falling out of her dress. He questioned his acting ability when she didn't seem to comprehend his disinterest. No wonder he lost tonight.

Not wanting to waste a round of Botox and newly plumped lips, she focused her attentions elsewhere after breathing a profanity into his ear.

Jack would make his way over to Graeme, but was spurred to visit the loo first. Usually the Ladies had the long line, but tonight the Gents did as well, so he did the easy thing and went out the door and round the corner. He zipped up behind a fair-sized shrub and lit a cigarette. Leaning against the wall, Jack breathed in the night air and pretended for a moment he was home.

He heard voices and ducked deeper into the shadows. Not the time to be caught behind a bush. His publicist would string him up.

"He's probably just around the corner, Monty. Sit down and I'll be right back," and Bronwyn gestured to a bench, not far from Jack. Her other hand carried a plate of food. He field-stripped his cigarette and jerked to the ground, in complete shadow. Jack's tux was getting damp and dirty, but he hoped they'd stay long enough to make it interesting. He settled in to get an unguarded view of the mysterious Miss McCall.

Bronwyn faced Kish's daughter, less than eight feet away. What fun to be a voyeur. If only he'd brought along some Chivas.

"I love your necklace, Bronnie. Where did you find it?"

"SoHo," she answered as her fingers rose to her neck. Sniffing the wind, she asked, "You aren't smoking, are you? I smell smoke."

"No," she laughed. "Maybe it's the drivers. I bet yours was glad you took him some food. Dad would never do that. We can't wait for New York. Chelsea is so psyched."

The seat of Jack's pants was getting damper by the minute. Oh, to light another cigarette would be sweet bliss. And, his legs were getting cramped. He'd just focus on Bronwyn, since it was the perfect opportunity to see her. Better than around a banquette with six of her best clubby friends.

"I'll tell you a secret Monterey, if you'll tell me one."

Monterey seemed to consider this.

"Something you don't want anyone to know."

Jack's attention was piqued.

"I don't know what you mean," Monterey finally answered.

"I have a secret. Don't you? If you tell me and I think it's your big secret, I'll give you my necklace." Bronwyn reached behind her neck to unfasten it and Jack's heart leapt forth at the sight of Bronwyn so momentarily vulnerable. The play was heating up.

Bronwyn put the necklace around Monterey's neck and Monterey fingered it. "I love it. But, we don't have to tell secrets."

"But, you have one, don't you Monty?"

Jack wondered if Bronwyn was prepared for a secret. She probably knew what she wanted to hear, but damn, she might find out the girl shot heroin or slept with a dolly grip. Watch what you wish for Bronwyn, he thought. He didn't even notice his wet seat anymore.

Standing in front of Kish's daughter, Bronwyn began in a soft voice. Jack had to strain a little to hear; then knowing no one could see him do his old-man bit, cupped his hand to force every word into his ear.

"I made a movie, once."

Monterey sounded surprised. "I never knew you made a movie. Dad never said."

"Your dad doesn't know. Hardly anyone does."

"It wasn't released?"

Bronwyn smiled. "No, it was released and it was a good movie. I'm just mostly on the cutting room floor."

"Is that your secret?"

"Yes – not even Jeeves knows."

"Wow," Monterey breathed. "Was it a sex tape?"

Bronwyn sputtered, "No. Why would you think that?"

"It was a long time ago, right?"

"Yes, but absolutely not a sex tape," Bronwyn shivered. "Your turn."

"I'm still thinking about yours."

"Well, stop thinking and spill. I want to hear your secret."

"I know it's not nice to say, Bronwyn, but if Dad knew you had a sex tape, I bet he'd dump Heaven for you."

Bronwyn gave a little laugh.

"I don't believe you, though. Sorry. If you made a movie, I'd know about it."

Jack didn't really care what Monterey's big secret was. He was trying to think of a film he'd seen Bronwyn in, and was coming up empty. Had he seen her face on film? Heard her voice?

"...breaking into homes. I told him I hate it. It makes me so nervous, but I don't want him to be mad at me or tell everyone I'm a baby."

"You know we can fix this. Your dad will send you to another school. Those kids aren't your friends. Tell me how I can help and I'll talk to your dad."

"Monterey," her father called to her. She gave Bronwyn a hug and dashed back into the restaurant.

Kish walked over to Bronwyn.

"You were right, Keiran. Monterey admitted she's been breaking into houses with that boy. I think she should change schools." Jack could see her profile as she looked up.

He nodded. "I need you to tell the girls you're not going to New York."

"Why would I do that?"

"Because Heaven and I are going. They need to like Heaven."

Bronwyn settled back into the bench, looking straight ahead.

Keiran strolled back to the restaurant. "No more of that old Algonquin for the girls." He reached the end of the hedge and turned. "You tell them Bronwyn. You can't make it."

Bronwyn didn't answer.

"Heaven and I are having a baby. If it's a boy, we're naming him Brentwood," Keiran laughed, lightly. "You tell the girls...New York is off." And he went back inside.

Jack heard her soft pronouncement, "Perfect."

Inside the restaurant, Jack ordered a whiskey. He glanced over at Graeme Woods' table as Bronwyn slid into her seat.

Gray Willingham and his girlfriend were there with the director, Billy Foster, Foster's wife, Graeme and his wife.

Gray's girlfriend was catty and obnoxious and Bronwyn couldn't imagine what wonderful attributes she could possibly have to land Gray. On the other hand, despite his outstanding good looks, she knew his age was worrying him...he was getting old for his Superhero sequels.

The girlfriend's nonstop chatter was white noise gone bad. Bronwyn didn't remember the names of Gray's girlfriends. They came and went, so why should she bother? Graeme rose to get Bronwyn coffee, and Gray's girlfriend watched Jack greet him at the bar.

"Oh God, there's Jack McClean. He deserved to lose tonight. Did you hear what he did at that premiere party?" No one responded. "You didn't hear what he did to that girl in the bathroom?" Again, they ignored her, but were tired and couldn't manage conversation to drown her out.

Finally, Bronwyn interrupted her with, "That girl got

exactly what she was after and it wasn't Jack McClean. She wanted publicity and she got it in spades." Gray's girlfriend was unmoved. Bronwyn leaned into the table, glaring at her. "I don't believe for a minute that he forced her to do anything," she hissed. "You know how girls can be."

This was not a fun evening, Bronwyn thought. It was especially irksome because Jack McClean was one of her favorite actors and Graeme was fond of him. The girl veered into another gossipy tirade; then she yelped.

They turned to see Graeme walking to the table with Jack.

"Everyone...you all know Jack McClean?"

Bronwyn stood and took Jack's hand.

"No, we haven't met. How are you, Jack? I'm Bronwyn McCall."

He beamed at Bronwyn, but the girl shrieked, "You're not welcome at our table."

Neighboring tables went silent. Bronwyn's eyes narrowed at Gray. "Of course he's welcome here. Have a seat, Jack," and Billy Foster and his wife scooted over.

The girl half rose and leaned over the table, pointing at him with her arm dangerously over the candles. "I know what you did to that girl in the bathroom."

Bronwyn didn't look at Jack. She sighed and said, "I'm leaving."

Unfortunately for Bronwyn, Gray's girl wasn't finished. "Just you be careful, Jack McClean. Bronwyn got millions from Oakley Forse. Sexual harassment. You better watch yourself." And she turned her back to them and snuggled against Gray. She was smart enough to know there'd be a return volley. She hadn't gone from Homecoming Queen to Drama Queen for nothing.

No one dared look at Bronwyn.

Calmly, but with red heat rising on her face, she asked, "Where did you hear a lie, like that?"

"From Gray, of course," she said defensively. "And, The Boys. They told me."

Graeme started to stand, but Bronwyn firmly pushed down on his shoulder. She looked at Gray's girl and snarled, "Believe me; I like Oakley Forse just fine. He's always been a gentleman and a friend of mine. It's none of your business, but I inherited my money the old-fashioned way." She looked at the girl, hoping it was sinking in. She wanted to bore a hole in her head and pour the words in. "I should feel sorry for you. They lie to you because it shows you're a fool and it brightens their day."

Jack followed Bronwyn to the lobby, but got hung up in the partying crowd and lost track of her. Deciding she might be in the Ladies, he waited, watching women come and go. Then, he noticed a phone being handed to the coat check girl, who turned into the recesses of the room with it. It was dark with wraps and topcoats, but he found Bronwyn sitting in the back, with her head down.

"Can I help?"

Bronwyn was tucked into a mass of coats, with Jack McClean at her elbow. Dread was crowding out any niceties. She might never leave this dark womb of cashmere and fur, but she was embarrassed to have Jack fall into her rabbit hole. She took his hand for a moment and pressed it to her cheek. It wasn't the warmth that struck her, but rather the human touch itself. He was real.

"How can I help?"

He motioned for the coat check girl, "Bring me a brandy, would you luv?" and a waiter was dispatched.

Bronwyn took a sip and called Moss.

❧

Jack was surprised to see four men meeting their limo, after the short trip to the Beverly Soleil Hotel. Three surrounded Bronwyn as they swept her toward the doors, but she paused and took Jack's hand and they were led to a private mezzanine room. Jack took a seat as the night manager handed Bronwyn a change of clothes. She told Jack she'd be right back.

Settling into the leather sofa, he watched as hot hors d'oeuvres were placed on the marble credenza. "What would you care to drink, sir?" asked the white coated boy.

"Iced tea, I think," replied Jack.

The coterie of hotel staff was most impressive. Candles were lit and the recessed lights flicked off. She must have called her fairy godmother.

When Bronwyn returned, she seemed more relaxed. Soft knit pants and a gray cashmere pullover suited her. Seating herself beside Jack, she kicked her moccasins off and tucked her legs beneath her.

"I spoke with my attorney. His name is Moss. I just have to wait here for a bit, until one of his people shows up. But," she sighed, "I'm feeling better."

"Perhaps I shouldn't ask, but is this about Forse?"

"There was never any sexual harassment or anything like that. I hardly know him. I just don't want him to think I'm defaming him, you know? I'd never say anything like that about him."

Jack nodded. "So, he never sexually harassed you. He's a big guy, Bronwyn; I'm sure he deals with gossip all the time."

There was a moment of awkwardness as Bronwyn thought of Jack's recent moment in the blinding spotlight of gossip. She moved closer to him, touched by his attempt at reassurance. After a few moments, she moved to the credenza.

"Let's see what we have," and they nibbled on Dungeness crab cakes, beef sliders, and crispy pizza wedges topped with mushrooms and Fontina. His iced tea came and they brought hot chocolate with whipped cream and chocolate curls on top for Bronwyn. It made Jack smile.

"They'll make one for you, would you like one?"

Jack shook his head. She was no novice, as she lifted one curl at a time and then spooned the whipped cream little by little, finally drinking it down.

Bronwyn was reluctant to take a good look at Jack McClean. She'd already logged the bow of his mouth, the curve of his smile, the bruised smudges under his eyes, the flush at the top of his cheekbones, the squareness of his jaw, the thickness of his neck. Her years of photography had given her an ability to analyze the topography of a face. She seldom looked at people, really looked at people, unless she could capture their face in the camera lens. When she most needed to possess them through her eye, she felt an exquisite pain. Without photography, she suffered more than frustration. Like losing an appendage, she could still feel the weight of the camera in her hand. There was anguish in the photo untaken.

She knew the regret of losing Jack's face without capturing it would cause her to build parts to some semblance of whole, over and over again. She dreaded the moment he'd be gone. No Jack in the three dimension and no Jack in the two dimension. This was someone she'd never made an effort to meet because he was someone who'd taken her breath away on huge screens. She closed her eyes.

It was late and Jack thought Bronwyn was getting sleepy. Surely the meeting could wait until morning, but when he suggested it, Bronwyn said no. He coaxed her to snuggle against him and sang softly to her.

She sat straight up. "That's one of my favorite songs. Scarlet Pimpernel, '*Where's the Girl*'," she marveled.

"Saw it on Broadway."

"I saw it, too. I wonder if we were at the same show. I didn't know you could sing," she said, amazed.

Jack's smile crinkled and the candlelight reflected sparkles in his large eyes. Bronwyn gently turned his face to hers, peering into his eyes with a solemn expression.

"Sing it again, please."

"You sound like Oliver Twist, 'More please'." He wended his way through the verses and couldn't imagine a more satisfying audience than this soft girl tucked under his wing.

The Moss associate arrived; he and Bronwyn spoke quietly for a few moments. All in all, not worth waiting up for, Jack thought.

Bronwyn thanked Jack, went down to the lobby with him, kissed his cheeks at the elevator door, and said goodbye.

Letting one elevator come and go, she watched him as he walked through the lobby. As the second elevator door opened, she turned away from it and went outside. Looking down the street, she couldn't see Jack. She hopped up on a large circular planter, at some expense to the shrubbery. Standing on her tiptoes, she raked the street for sight of him. Bright lights confounded her, even as they illuminated the sidewalk and cars. Angry with herself for letting him go, she turned to find Harold the doorman with his arm out to assist her.

"Looking for something, Miss McCall?" he inquired as she turned, sat and as gracefully as possible, pushed off for landing.

She shrugged.

"I think it might just be over there."

Bronwyn's eyes followed his gesture and saw Jack smoking against the wall. He dropped his cigarette and gave her a big, loopy grin. She was glad he didn't tease her; well aware he'd have seen her leaning like a ship's figurehead for sight of him.

When they got to her room, Jack used the bathroom and came out to find Bronwyn in the same cozy clothes she'd changed into, but with a soft flannel robe on for good measure. "Are you going to wear all those clothes to sleep in?" he asked.

"I'm not going to sleep." He gave her a look that made her back-step. "I'm going to watch you sleep. I have to be the luckiest girl in the world to watch Jack McClean sleep." His eyebrows lifted in slow motion, but she vowed, "I'm not gonna miss it."

He'd left his trousers on, but was shirtless and barefoot. They piled extra pillows at the top of the bed, climbed in and settled side by side. Bronwyn stroked his arm.

"You'd best not do that if you think I'm just going to sleep," Jack warned. She stopped, but rested her hand on his chest.

As if breaking a vow of silence, they became founts of chatter. She began a progressive tale of her early life and told him about her family, losing them in France, over-hearing Judge Wheeler argue with his wife about taking her in. Jack told her about losing his dog. She explained how she came to live at the William Penn Hotel...he told her about being bullied as an artistic boy. She explained about finding photography and losing photography. He recounted his first time on stage. She told him about Ellis Fielding. Jack told her about his first time. She told him about the city Christmases of her youth, with stores and sidewalks crowded with excitement, and how she spent most Christmases alone. He told her about his father losing his job. Then he launched into tales that made her giggle and laugh. Bronwyn found herself falling into his big life.

She told him how The Boys envied Jack his hair and called him Samson behind his back. Bronwyn analyzed how producers must hire his hair first, Jack second, because it was beyond chameleon-line. She said his hair was more expressive and evocative than most actors. Jack roared with laughter. She said if The Boys knew she was there with him, there'd be 100,000 pounds in it for her to cut his hair and divvy it up amongst them. They hated it long, short, highlighted, chestnut, blonde, wavy or buzzed. Jack's entire body shook with amusement. She said when The Boys watched his films together, they'd moan in unison 'That hair'. Jack was still shaking with delight. Bronwyn asked him what his hair was like as a boy, and when he said 'auburn', she stared hard at him. He shifted his eyes from her as she seemed uncomfortably interested in oh-God, his hair.

"How is it that you tan?"

Jack smiled at the odd question. "Some of us do."

"Some of us. Hmmmm. I have the pale skin you should have and you have the hair that I should have."

"But, we both have the green eyes." They laid back, quiet and content. Bronwyn broke the silence. She detailed his incomparable ease with dialect and how he was an historian, skipping from century to century and taking audiences with him. It was obvious to Jack that she was a student of his work, having studied nuances that even his parents had surely missed, perhaps even he had missed, and her grasp of lighting and cinematic choices impressed him deeply.

Jack asked her why his recent contemporary film had tanked. She whispered that it had been horribly miscast... except for him. He laughed, but she looked at him and said, "I'm serious." And, for a moment he decided he *had* been surrounded by ineffective miscreants. She also pointed out if Jack would watch the DVD extras, he'd see the director's thoughts on the film didn't match the reality. She gave specifics. Jack looked at her as she spoke and was stricken with the knowledge he'd now have a difficult time working with the bloke, ever again.

She told him about meeting Snooks Von Krinkles. Animals had always been a big part of Jack's life, especially his childhood. He liked Bronwyn's intense connection to animals. He told her they must plan a trip to see unusual animals all over the world, and was pleased she liked the idea.

Bronwyn asked for more stories about his parents. As he spoke, she watched his pride and sincere affection. She tried to imagine how those people had formed the boy to man.

She told him about the Betsy McCall dolls, her mother's goodbye at the airport, and Bronwyn's aversion to France.

"I must show you Paris one day. You'd love the lights... and the food." He waited for her reaction.

She murmured wistfully, "Laduree," and they both said "Macarons!" at the same time.

Jack sensed it was rare for her to share small stories and memories. It seemed she'd opened the Book of Bronwyn and spilled the words across the bed. He loved how beautifully orchestrated they were together, spawning laughter, intriguing each other, creating warmth, and sharing sadness. It seemed equal revelations between them, but Bronwyn could not have guessed how Jack's heart was breaking, learning the extent of her orphaned loneliness.

He turned on his side and slid his hand under her robe. She stopped his progress.

"Sorry."

"It's just that I have a lot of scars," she whispered. "I was in an accident. I can't have children because of it. I wish I'd had a baby before it all happened."

"It's a terrible disappointment, I know," Jack responded, as he lay back down.

"You do?"

"I'd have been a Dad at six, if I'd had the foresight. The balls met the wicked end of a cricket bat."

"You're serious,"

Jack solemnly nodded. "No children for me."

Bronwyn gently kissed him. Jack nearly swooned and jumped out of bed.

He excused himself to regroup in the bathroom, returning to pour glasses of water. "Green eyes and no children. Aren't we a pair, darlin' Bronwyn?"

Jack motioned for her to sit and she lifted his hand and kissed the inside of his wrist. In the near darkness, she still hadn't made the effort to fully memorize his face. Skip that part, she thought. Leap. Just jump. And she pulled his face down to hers and kissed him with the full measure of warmth she felt for him. She appreciated his gentle restraint. It allowed her to push in small doses until he met her kisses with an open desire. It wasn't long before Jack launched himself back into the bathroom.

They laughed and shook their heads. Bronwyn fluffed the pillows and ushered Jack into bed. She stood before him and recounted her memories of his films. The first viewing, she'd watch the film. If it spoke to her, she returned, focusing on his role. If it continued to stay with her, she watched it again. He was fascinated and like any actor, adored her adoration. She pushed her sleeves up and held her arms in front of her, vulnerable side up. She said his films instilled a need to be filled through her eyes, ears, veins. "More please."

Third visit to the bathroom. When he came out, his hair damp once again, Bronwyn was tinkering in the mini kitchen. "I'm making coffee for us. I'm guessing those are cold showers?"

"It isn't funny, Bronwyn," he said dolefully. She stepped back, laughing, appreciating his seriousness but not sharing it.

"Bronwyn, are we going to make love? In this lifetime?"

She was surprised her heart had cracked open. She'd felt isolated, contained and in control of her feelings, for as long as she could remember. Their conversation had seemed a lifeline to her and she had no intention of walking away.

"I'm not very good at wanting something enough to make it happen. But I can't think of anything in this world I would ever want more than you."

Jack was touched. He made the decision to invest in this girl. When he suggested they sleep, Bronwyn was insistent to know more stories about him, but Jack shook his head.

She hadn't shared the violent episodes of her life, acquiring the estate, her wealth, or her home. But she'd exposed the silent path of her life that truly mattered – private hidden bits of herself. It wasn't so much the physical closeness or the shared tales in Room 1110, but rather the prying open of each of their hearts, letting the other in.

Spooned in warmth, they fell asleep for almost four hours. When the wake-up call for Bronwyn's meeting came through, they made a quick plan. She got dressed and returned to the private mezzanine room to meet with the attorneys.

The meeting went smoothly. Oakley's attorneys said Forse was disinterested in idle gossip, confident that Miss McCall would not violate the terms of their agreement or jeopardize her settlement, and apparently wished her well. Her attorneys were satisfied, as was Moss, via conference call.

Relieved, she turned her thoughts to Jack as she rode the elevator to the eleventh floor. He was unlike other men she'd been attracted to. He was tall and well-proportioned, but not slim. He added and subtracted weight for roles, but in person he was a large presence. She'd always admired hands, but his were meaty, not slender and artistic. She was pleased with herself for liking him so much, even with substantial hands. They were *kind* hands; in fact everything about him seemed kind. She had fallen for him, but most of all she felt safe.

When she knocked softly at the door, she found him freshly suited and shaved, courtesy of his personal assistant's emergency delivery.

They ran into Jack's assistant on their way to breakfast.

"Bronwyn, I'd like you to meet Dick Domitrovich. Dick, this is Bronwyn Dai McCall."

She insisted Dick join them for breakfast. Jack found he couldn't quite say 'No' to the idea, without being rude.

When Dick asked where she lived, Jack realized he didn't know and was surprised when she vaguely answered, "over East."

Bronwyn discovered Dick was from Cleveland and giggled, "Well, I believe we are honor-bound to hate each other, then. I'm from Pittsburgh."

They laughed. It turned out that Dick had relatives in the Pittsburgh area and they chatted about Stouffer's, PNC Park, and Isaly's skyscraper cones. Jack thought he'd resent not having Bronwyn to himself at breakfast, but he enjoyed seeing her easy animation as she talked about her hometown.

From that breakfast onward, Bronwyn and Dick were 'Pittsburgh' and 'Cleveland' to each other.

Dick was impeccably dressed, well-mannered, slender, gap-toothed, and with short white hair combed straight back from a widow's peak. He had a perpetual smile and an air of optimism. She was happy to discover they'd been together for twelve years.

It was time to leave. Dick excused himself and Jack was hurt when Bronwyn declined to give him her home address or phone number. Communication with Bronwyn was to go through her attorney. She explained it was a security issue, but seeing his disappointment, she assured him Moss would be the perfect, trusted go-between. In fact, she urged Jack to meet Moss in New York, anytime Jack was in the city. Suddenly, Jack was mentally rearranging his next two weeks to make meeting Stanley Mastrofrancesco his priority.

Bronwyn was due at the airport, and their goodbyes were cordial. Only the fierceness and duration of their embrace betrayed their emotion. As Bronwyn's car pulled away, Jack waved with a lovely smile and Bronwyn knew that would be the 'Jack' vision she'd see each night before falling asleep.

CHAPTER TWENTY FOUR

ON LOCATION

Exchanging letters with Jack, Bronwyn was intrigued to learn his next filming location – Israel. She decided to get permission from Prime Minister Abraham to visit with Samuel and Paul, and then surprise Jack on his set. Asking Moss to intervene with the prime minister, and secretly working with Jack's assistant, she set the plan in motion.

Moss said the prime minister was allowing her only ten hours in the country, from 6:00 AM to 4:00 PM and had given permission to meet the boys at an orphanage near the movie location. Bronwyn vowed to make her time count. She hoped Bram would make an appearance at the orphanage, since it had been ten years since she'd seen him.

Because there had been rumors years ago about Jack McClean and his co-star, Ann Toth, Bronwyn contacted Ann's husband, Donald Hunt, to see if he'd like her to deliver anything to his wife. She figured it wouldn't hurt to remind Ann Toth about her family.

Donald Hunt was on his Sante Fe ranch when Bronwyn arrived. He'd been uneasy about his wife's filming with McClean and had jumped at Bronwyn's offer to play courier.

When Hunt planned to send along a new photograph of himself and their son, Bronwyn surprised herself by borrowing equipment and offering to take their portrait – the first photograph she'd taken in a decade.

Bronwyn walked with Hunt to his barn, explaining what she'd like to do.

Placing extra hay beneath the hay loft opening, Bronwyn asked ranch hands to stand on a sturdy board above, with the free end extending out. Hunt edged his way across the plank with his hands, as two workers anchored his feet. At Bronwyn's direction, he laid his chest upon the board and buttoned his jacket over it. Extending his arms, he appeared to be flying. Bronwyn shot from beneath. A slight wind ruffled his hair, the sky was robin's egg blue with fluffy cotton clouds, and the board wasn't evident. She maneuvered the shot from below, while keeping Hunt's head back. If she didn't get it right, the dreaded jowls would show. There was authenticity in the shot, as Hunt had no visible means of support. Thrilled with the concept, Hunt talked his six year old son onto the board. He hovered over the boy, creating a convincing flying shot.

Bronwyn promised to deliver the finished photo to Ann Toth and said goodbye to Hunt and his brave son, calling them The Flying Wallendas.

Bronwyn wanted her visit to the orphanage to be a rewarding time for Samuel and Paul. Her local Book Nook ordered one hundred copies of the latest Harry Potter boxed set, and art sets in wooden cases. While she was gathering the gifts, the brothers worked on distribution specifics from their end.

What to give Jack was a puzzle. She asked Dick Domitrovich to contact Jack's parents, and settled on a family photo album and a horse blanket from their farm with its evocative smells. The tight time frame worried Mr. and Mrs. McClean, but Bronwyn sent Van Tsang as her courier.

Bronwyn decided to buy some of her favorite books for Jack, and hoped he'd do the same for her someday. She gathered *The Vegetable Thieves; Moe the Dog in Tropical Paradise; Kitchen Fun* (her Mom had a copy as a child); *Carl Goes Shopping; Roadfood; Paris Boulangerie-Patisserie; Dachshunds – Lightweights Littermates*; and mysteries by PD James and Charles Todd.

Jeeves had not been happy about their trip to Israel and it was disconcerting seeing a wary Jeeves. Their flight was late arriving; the books and art supplies were opened for close inspection. Ten hours were quickly becoming seven hours.

It was delightful to see Samuel and Paul at the orphanage, and hallway tables were set up for distribution. Bronwyn enjoyed the orphans' enthusiasm as the boys made bookplates for each Harry Potter book and affixed brass nameplates to the art boxes. The smiles were contagious.

Bronwyn kept her eye out for the prime minister, unaware that he had come to look at her. With arms crossed and narrowed eyes, Bram watched from behind a specially darkened window, with the rapt observation he'd had when she was fighting for her life in the hospital. If he'd forgotten how close Samuel and Paul were to Bronwyn, he was acutely reminded. His quiet and laconic boys were sprung to life around her. Laughing, nudging, buoyant. He owed so much to Bronwyn. Bram saw evidence of what the boys had sparingly shared with him. His dynastic desires could better be quelled, seeing their simple act of 'being' – Samuel's desire to become a veterinary surgeon and Paul's happiness working with horses seemed, for the first time, to suit them. Bram remembered what it was like to be a young man, free, safe and anonymous in America. Some of his happiest times had been in Maine with his parents and David, and at University with Moss.

Plans were made for the boys to visit Bronwyn in December and they said their goodbyes. Bronwyn and Jeeves left for the short ride to the movie set.

Jack's lunch break was nearly over and Dick Domitrovich was waiting for her. Bronwyn was beside herself with giddy anticipation.

First, she put the 'Flying' portrait in Ann Toth's trailer. Then, she placed her bundle of books, the small photo album and horse blanket in Jack's trailer with a note of apology that she couldn't stay longer. Knowing Jack was nearby made her feel tingly and she was secure in the certainty of seeing him. It was as if the clock had stopped ticking and she had all the time in the world.

Dick pointed to Jack, sitting just beyond the craft services table. Wending her way through long tables, she approached him and tapped his right shoulder while leaning in to whisper in his left ear..."I'm really here." The look on his face was priceless; not just for her, but for Dick and everyone sitting nearby.

He swooped her up and kissed her and looked at her and looked at her again, as if she might be an apparition. He pulled her to a corner and they marveled at the sight of one another. Fifteen minutes later, Jack was called to set. Bronwyn said she had to leave, but Jack jabbed a finger in Dick's chest and warned, "She'd best be here when I get back."

That was the high point for Jeeves, who'd stayed in the background. Knowing Jack McClean would be angry upon discovering Bronwyn was gone, was a rich delight.

What Jeeves didn't realize was Bronwyn's thought-fulness had impact. Each time Jack looked at the books, he'd feel close to her. A note inside each book explained its significance in her life. As Jack held each one, he was charmed. He was as pleased and happy with all those gifts, as he was perplexed by his invitation to dine that night with the Prime Minister of Israel and his family. The invitation was extended to Ann Toth and to the director, but it was meant most of all for Jack McClean.

When Jack, Ann Toth, and their director were ushered into the prime minister's living room, introductions were made. Ann Toth was certain the dinner had been arranged so the family could meet her. The director was equally certain dinner had been planned to acknowledge his directorial achievements and perhaps encourage future filming in the country. Jack's only certainty was that he had no idea why he was there, especially when he'd tried to bow out.

The prime minister and his wife were seated across from the director and Ann Toth. Jack stood near the fireplace, thinking both women had gone all-out in the wardrobe department. The prime minister's wife was dressed in an ice blue satin suit. The actress had pulled out the big guns, wearing a dress with sheer black lace revealing skin in all the right places. Or, perhaps wrong places, Jack wasn't sure, given the solemnity of the occasion. He hadn't managed to wear a tie, but was glad he settled on a blazer. At least he wasn't wearing jeans and a Boston Red Sox ball cap, as the director opted to wear. Just then, Paul took Jack's arm and guided him into another room.

The other son, Samuel, followed. They gestured for Jack

to sit, but as he did, Samuel stood over him and Paul wandered around the room. As Samuel came around to sit across from Jack, Paul joined him and the interrogation began.

"We saw Bronwyn today."

Jack's eyebrows shot up. "You know Bronwyn, then?"

"We know Bronwyn a lot better than you do," Samuel answered quietly.

Paul regarded Jack, "We brought you here tonight because she likes you and we want to see if you're good enough." They watched for his reaction.

Jack rubbed the stubble along his cheek, but his eyes went from Samuel to Paul and back again. Surely this dinner wasn't about Bronwyn. Bronwyn, who was already on a plane back home, just a few hours after seeing him.

"Has Bronwyn been in the country for awhile then?" Jack asked.

"No, she just came today to see us and surprise you," Paul said.

"She told you she planned to surprise me?"

It became evident the boys weren't there to fill gaps for Jack. In symmetry, they leaned forward, with their arms across their knees.

"How well do you know, Bronwyn?" Paul asked. He was the younger of the two boys, but was serious with his questions.

"I suppose we know each other quite well, for not having spent much time together. We've talked of course, and we've both taken to letter writing." Jack stopped to see if his answer was sufficient.

"Tell us something Bronwyn told you, that hardly anyone would know."

Jack smiled slightly. He could go for a drink. Even water.

This was turning into a game and he wasn't sure how to play. He walked around the room a bit. His interrogators remained seated and impassive; he assumed they were waiting for a winning response.

"I know Bronwyn only drives Ford cars because she and her father visited a Ford museum right before he died." The boys exchanged looks. Samuel shrugged at Paul. "Something else."

Jack thought that tidbit was obscure enough to prove he and Bronwyn shared a trusting bond. Now, he really did sit and ponder. He folded his arms across his chest, sunk back in the soft cushions, and tilted his head back as if to see an anecdote floating by.

It occurred to him that he didn't know Bronwyn's address, phone number, or even what state she lived in. He felt he knew the heart of her, but factually he was bereft. He should have examined those books she'd given him. Surely they weren't a part of this inquiry. Surely she hadn't asked these boys to grill him – the prime minister wouldn't be part of that, would he?

"How do you boys know Bronwyn?" was asked in futility. They just looked at him. Jack wondered if dinner wasn't to be served until he satisfied the boys' curiosity. Or, worse still, was he missing dinner? He was starving.

Jack sorted through his memory.

"Bronwyn was in a movie once."

The boys looked at each other and shook their heads with derision. "You don't know her at all," said Samuel. "We've known Bronwyn for ten years and she's never been in a movie. You're just guessing, trying to impress us."

Jack feared he may have betrayed Bronwyn. "No, sorry, I was thinking of something else." The boys stared at him. Ten years would have made the boys maybe four and seven. He looked at their tall, thin bodies and realized they had known Bronwyn a long time.

"Is it important, then? Is it important that I tell you something rare about her?"

Samuel answered, "Is it important that you have Bronwyn in your life?"

"'Tis."

"Then, think of something," encouraged Paul.

Jack sighed. It was time to get into the game. What was it the boys wanted? Something rare. Something that spoke to Bronwyn, the Bronwyn these boys knew. What kind of a girl had she always been? Jack leaned forward and put his head in his hands, closing his eyes. He let himself think of Bronwyn. The girl at the Beverly Soleil. The girl lying beside him, revealing her soul.

"When Bronwyn sees a dead animal on the road, she silently prays 'Please receive it into heaven, dear Lord, amen'."

Both boys stood, neither looking at the other. Without knowing it, Jack had placed a key in the lock of their traumatic memories. Neither boy knew Bronwyn said that prayer, but both boys instantly knew it was true. Jack McClean knew something about her that they didn't know, and that made him genuine, proving how Bronwyn felt about him.

Samuel took a seat to the left of Jack and Paul seated himself to his right, nudging Jack over a bit. Each boy slanted himself slightly toward him, so they could look at each other as they spoke.

"Bronwyn saved our lives," Samuel began. "We were little, shopping with our mother, when we were kidnapped. Papa told us Bronwyn had seen our photos in the anteroom…"

Paul cut in. "She was supposed to photograph Papa, so she'd just met with him."

"She thought something wasn't right. The men were carrying us. We went up the escalator and Bronwyn looked at me. She put her finger to her lips for me to be quiet and then gave me thumbs up."

Paul looked at Samuel and took up the story. "I remember she yelled 'Mickey Mouse' and 'Donald Duck' really loudly and we were outside, at the car."

"They put Paul down, and I wet myself. On purpose." Samuel looked sharply at Paul to see if he was going to tease him, but Paul was solemn. Samuel went on. "The man dropped me, really angry, and I grabbed Paul and ran for Bronwyn."

They didn't look at Jack. They were telling the story in fits and starts, and Jack was sitting very still. He remembered Bronwyn's scars. He dreaded hearing any more.

The boys were quiet and Samuel reached over to touch Paul's hand. Giving it a pat, Samuel continued. "I remember her whirling us around. It was so fast, my legs swung out. I could see Paul...she had us both up in her arms. I don't remember anything except the whirling, until we were inside."

Paul nodded. "I remember the whirling and how tightly Bronwyn held me. It made me feel safe, like she was going to save us." Paul bit his lower lip. "Papa told me that it was because she held me so tightly, that she lived. Even when we were inside, under the desk, she held me tight. I guess I kept her from bleeding so badly. That's what Papa said."

Samuel stood up and Paul followed his lead, but seeming burdened, Samuel sat back down and so did his brother. With a sigh, Samuel said, "Bronwyn is one of those people who came back from the dead. Papa was there at hospital when she died, and when she lived again."

Paul waited for his brother to go on, but took up the

lead when he seemed lost in thought. "Bronwyn lost everything because of us. People didn't trust she was innocent, so they went to her home and destroyed everything, looking for evidence that she knew the kidnappers. We don't know what happened, but Papa believed she was innocent, but it was too late."

With a hard look at Jack, Samuel said, "She can't have children you know."

Jack found his voice. "Yes, I know. We've talked about it."

"Because of us," Paul said wearily.

Jack felt close to these boys, their vulnerabilities so near the surface, their lives touched so poignantly by Bronwyn. "That's not true. I'm sure she doesn't feel that way at all."

"It is true. It certainly is true," Samuel opined. "Bronwyn said you don't know where she lives. Papa is always worried about her safety. But Papa said we can tell you that our family gave her a home in Maine. In the States."

Paul perked up, looking angelic and blissful. "We go there loads of times. It's splendid. There's no where on earth better than at Bronwyn's place."

Putting his hand on big Jack McClean's shoulder, Samuel gently told him, "I bet you'll get there one day."

"What's it like?"

The boys considered his question, not certain how much their father would want them to disclose.

"She has horses," Samuel said. For some reason, Paul giggled.

"Yes, she has horses. Several of them." Samuel seemed to be enjoying this exchange. Their moods had brightened. "Three of them are named after the first three great thoroughbred lines, right, Paul?"

"Godolphin, Darley, and Byerley," Paul shared with a grin.

"Well then, if you're right and I get there one day, I imagine she'll let me ride them," Jack said confidently.

"Sorry, friend, but she will never, ever, let you ride her horses."

"But, she's let you ride them?"

They nodded, yes. "It's been awhile, but yes, we've ridden them."

"Why are you so certain she'll not let me?"

They shook their heads, suppressing grins, and despite all the years gone by, Jack felt he was the unpopular school mate, and it cut him.

"Forget it friend, it will never happen. Ever. But take heart, we know she does like you," Samuel said, sympathetically.

As they rose to join the others, Samuel asked Jack for his silence about all they'd discussed. They had their father's permission to get him up to speed, but it was confidential information that could one day jeopardize Bronwyn's safety.

Dinner was a quiet affair, by comparison. Jack tried to glean how the prime minister fit into it all. He'd expect the prime minister to tell him about the kidnapping. Entrusting his sons to judge Jack's fitness showed the prime minister respected them. Watching them at dinner revealed he was a man who also loved his sons.

That observation made the little digs directed at Jack not so hard to bear. If the prime minister was playing the role of 'cautious father' on Bronwyn's behalf, he was doing a damn good job. He evidently didn't have much time for actors. One thing was apparent. The prime minister was not devoid of feeling where Bronwyn was concerned.

His wife tried to keep up with Ann Toth, chatting about Paris runway fashion and the latest handbag craze. But

Jack didn't miss it when she sharply referred to Bronwyn as 'Saint Bronwyn'.

Ann Toth was telling them about the remarkable photograph Bronwyn had taken of Donald Hunt and her son.

"I didn't realize she was taking photographs again," the prime minister wondered aloud in his deep voice. He looked questioningly at the boys, who shrugged.

The evening ended with formal good wishes. Jack stayed behind the others, kissing both boys as he shook their hands. "I love her," he whispered. "I truly do."

CHAPTER TWENTY FIVE

DINNER AT NUIT

Visiting New York in March, Bronwyn and Jeeves planned to shop and see Broadway plays. Bronwyn chose the Inn at Irving Place near Gramercy Park. It had only twelve rooms and was a quaint little brownstone tucked into 1830's townhouses, but Lady Mendl's five course tea was the main attraction.

Their first full day was a shopping excursion. Jeeves ordered custom-made shirts from Frank Rostron. Rostron made periodic visits from Manchester, England to see his New York customers and somehow Jeeves always knew when. Jeeves assured Bronwyn the shirts were just a fraction of the price of most custom-made shirts. Then it was time for shoe shopping, Jeeves-style. He bought Tod's patent leather shoes for the play that night, while Bronwyn was thinking her shoes had only cost $65. Jeeves moved on to a pair of handmade Berluti lace-ups at Barneys. Bronwyn admired how plain they were, but was stunned that they were over $1,000. She was in for a greater shock when he ordered made-to-measure shoes for $3,000 from Ermenegildo Zegna's new line. Bronwyn observed him as if he were a specimen she'd never seen. Somehow her Jeeves had become a shoe freak. Did Manolo Blahnik and Jimmy Choo make men's shoes? She shuddered to think.

All those times when Jeeves sat bored in Saks Fifth Avenue while Bronwyn shopped, she assumed he was disinterested. Now, she realized he'd been jumping out of his skin to move uptown for his own material obsessions. Bronwyn realized she hadn't shopped with Jeeves when he was buying his gentlemanly attire. Sometimes they'd browse together, with Jeeves giving hints as to what he liked. But this was eye-opening. Jeeves was used to the best of everything, but just because a person *could* have something didn't mean they *should* have something

The next day, Bronwyn met with Zuleika at Moss's offices. Trusting her fortune to Zuleika was easy for Bronwyn. She could meet a thousand people and not trust them with twenty dollars. But fate had brought them together; Bronwyn had found Moss and Moss had found Zuleika. All their lives had changed a great deal since then, including Jeeves who'd left Florsheim shoes far behind him.

Zuleika said Jean Luc had made reservations at a new French restaurant. Bronwyn and Jeeves were to join Moss, his wife and the Zanninis. When Bronwyn was leaving the offices, Moss handed her an envelope of mail. Delighted, she saved it to read later that night.

Arriving at Nuit, Bronwyn reviewed the menu. She wasn't surprised there were traditional French selections, as Jean Luc had chosen the restaurant, but her heart fell when she saw foie gras. Jean Luc was aware how she felt about foie gras; she'd asked him to remove it from his menus.

Bronwyn hoped no one would order it. She chose roasted beet salad, as did the other women. Moss had the onion soup gratinee, and Jeeves knew better than to even consider foie gras. However, for some insane reason, Jean Luc ordered it. Bronwyn's face went slack. Not wanting to ruin the meal, Bronwyn decided she'd concentrate on how amusing Jeeves and Moss were, struggling with the cheese atop their soup. She and Jeeves agreed to have Plats Pour Deux...Cote de Boeuf with frites and haricots verts.

Everything was delicious and Jeeves was already thinking about dessert. Unlike Bronwyn, he had dined at Nuit and enjoyed Profiteroles with ice cream and hot fudge sauce. Then again, there was Strawberry Tart with white chocolate pistachio ice cream and strawberry coulis. Yes, that would do nicely, he mused contentedly.

As they were eating, Bronwyn told Zuleika about the play they'd seen. Over the din, Zuleika's husband was laughing. Moss lifted a finger and shook it at Jean Luc. All eyes were on Bronwyn, as she caught Jean Luc talking about horsemeat. Horsemeat that he'd had in France and what a delicacy it could be if properly cooked. Bronwyn listened long enough to make certain she wasn't misunderstanding, put her fork down, and left. She was at the door before anyone could react.

Zuleika ordered Jeeves to go after her. Unconcerned, he shrugged and continued eating his utterly delicious meal. He never minded when so-called friends of Bronwyn got themselves into hot water.

Zuleika wove her way through the tables and called to Bronwyn, headed down the street. Bronwyn stopped her march, spun around and waited for Zuleika. Just as Zuleika's mouth opened, Bronwyn gave her a scathing look, silencing her. Bronwyn headed back down the street.

In her hotel room, Bronwyn opened Jack's letter and

marveled that her heartbeat slowed and the world seemed more welcoming.

7 *March*

Dearest Dai,

I know I told you in the last letter, but I must do it again. Thank you so much for flying halfway around the world to surprise me, love. What I would give to hold you in my arms, just now.

I've been reading the books. I can see why your mother would have loved Kitchen Fun *– even I could manage to make penuche! I'm going to show my Mum – I know she'll love it. Wonder if they had it in Ireland when she was a little lass? You know, with metrics and all. I'm going to be thinking of my favorite books, for you. I want to give you a Hemingway book, as I've started to do my research for the next one. Do you think I can manage it? Be up to playing the great man? We're filming in Key West. Would you like to join me? We'd have to take care that you not burn. I'm reminded how you pointed out your fairness. I'll carry your parasol, if you'll just say "yes"!*

Roadfood…I had no idea what culinary delights I've been missing. Let's use the Sterns' book and cross them off. Wouldn't that be wicked good, traveling together?

I'm off to do press for the "thriller" I filmed a year and a half ago. I hope there are some thrills in it (haven't seen it yet) or it's bound to

*make the 500 press interviews grind to a halt.
Didn't actually get along with my co-star (no
names!) so that should make the press junket go
splendidly.*

*I can honestly say, I can't remember when
you weren't in my life. These letters make an
extraordinary courtship. I read your letters over
and over and carry them with me, read them
when I go to bed and read them again when I
wake up. I look at your writing and imagine
your hand gliding across that very page.*

*My day is defined by thoughts of you. To
know that I matter to you, takes my breath away.*

*Every time I call Mum and Pap, they ask
about you. What an impression you've made
on them. They didn't know what a courier was,
until your friend came to their door for my
horse blanket! I hope to meet your friend Van
one day, and needless to say, the folks are keen
to see you! Think we can manage it?*

*I close this letter with dear and precious
thoughts of you. As I embark on this press tour,
my mind will turn to you and those thoughts will
save me from utter boredom, answering the same
questions a thousand times. I will try to stay semi-
alert, in case someone asks me, "Who do you
love, old boy?" You and I both know the answer to
that. Jack loves Bronwyn. With all his heart.*

*Sleep well, my dearest.
Your Wren*

She knew just what Jack meant about her hand gliding across her letters. She imagined his 'kind' hands doing the same. They'd started using their middle names, as if that would throw anyone off who might find their letters. Bronwyn didn't know why her middle name was Dai, but Jack's parents had named him 'Wren' after Christopher Wren, the architect. It was yet another reason she thought his parents were very interesting people.

There was another letter, post-marked Malibu, but it wasn't the handwriting of Graeme, Roddy or their wives. Her brow knitted as she wondered who else she knew in Malibu.

The next morning, Bronwyn agreed to meet with Jean Luc at the Central Park horse-drawn carriage station, across from The Plaza Hotel.

Jean Luc crossed the street to find Bronwyn waiting. Her hands in her pockets, she stood beside a gray horse, harnessed to a carriage. Jeeves observed from The Plaza Hotel and watched Jean Luc lean in and kiss her cheeks, one, the other, and back again in his customary greeting. He yearned to see how Jean Luc's froggy attitude would stand up to Bronwyn's wrath.

"I fear you are angry with me. And, with Zuleika. There is much worry in our house today."

"I'm not angry with Zuleika. And, you know how fond I am of you, Jean Luc."

Bronwyn's eyes were still hard, but Jean Luc took her words as forgiveness and hugged her tightly. When he released his grip, he peered into her eyes, and their hardness had their intended effect.

"Bronwyn, cherie, I want you to know that I have eliminated all foie gras from the menus of my restaurants. As soon as new ones are printed."

She realized Jean Luc was perfectly aware that she'd been upset with his ordering fois gras.

"That makes me happy, Jean Luc," although Bronwyn didn't look happy. "But, I also want you to influence restaurants in France to stop serving horsemeat."

Jean Luc's eyes grew big. "Cherie, you ask too much. It is the culture. You understand. One cannot dictate culture."

Bronwyn smiled at him. "Zuleika is wealthy because of me. This is something I want you to do."

Jean Luc looked stricken. The Bronwyn he knew was a nice, quiet girl, who never made requests, never seemed aware of her wealth, and certainly never held it over people. "It cannot be done. The foie gras I can do, in my restaurants. And, I can try to influence others. I can try. For you, dear Bronwyn. For you."

"The horses, Jean Luc."

"I am only one man."

Bronwyn put her arm around his shoulder. "Jamie Oliver is just one man, but he's changed school lunches in England. Just one man." She squeezed his shoulder and reached into her pocket.

"Here, Jean Luc, for the horse," and she pressed sugar cubes onto his palm, bending his hand back and placing it under the horse's velvety muzzle. As the horse bared his enormous teeth and took aim, she repeated, "For the horse."

CHAPTER TWENTY SIX

THE CHARITY EVENT

*R*eviewing the charity invitation, Bronwyn told the limo driver she'd call for the trip back from Malibu. As she walked the path to Ann Toth's door, she realized she only did this sort of thing if Jeeves wasn't around. Accepting Ann's Malibu invitation felt weird. She had been lured by the 'charity' aspect, but she and the actress weren't friends. Bronwyn wouldn't tell Jeeves and she wouldn't be telling Jack, either.

Greeting Bronwyn with over-familiarity, and wearing a tiny bikini, Ann said it would be just the two of them prepping for the next day's charity fashion show. Her note had said wear 'work clothes', but Bronwyn knew there'd be very little work done in that bikini. She was sorry she'd let the limo go.

At least Donald Hunt was there. They greeted each other and walked around the pool area, noting the changing tent. Donald took Bronwyn upstairs and showed her where the 'Flying Portrait' was hung. She complimented their beach house and raved about the ocean view.

Things went downhill when Ann gave her a bucket, rags, and toothbrush. Bronwyn had never seen a bathroom so filthy and when she took a sweaty break from latrine duty, Ann was reading a magazine by the pool. Bronwyn silently berated herself for being dense. For whatever reason, Ann had found a way to humiliate her. Maybe she thought there was something between Bronwyn and Donald. Or, maybe she was jealous that she and Jack were getting close. Bronwyn decided she wouldn't give her the satisfaction and returned to the task.

Surely Donald Hunt knew what his wife was up to, Bronwyn thought angrily. Closing the bathroom door made it hot, but she didn't want them watching her work.

After forty minutes of cleaning ground-in crud, the door suddenly opened, spilling the bucket of filthy water across the floor and soaking Bronwyn. Before she could turn around, it went dark and the door slammed shut. A large body was lifting her off the floor, holding her roughly. Her voice strangled in her throat. The hulking man held her tightly and his whiskey breath was on her face. She struggled, kicking his leg with all her might, ducking and squeezing past him. Her right hipbone cracked against the sink and the pain drove her to the left. She knew every inch of the damnable bathroom and didn't need light to know her advantage. His arm went for her waist as she reached the doorknob. Bronwyn elbowed him as hard as she could, and got the door open.

With every intention of fleeing as fast as she could, she stopped dead in her tracks. There on the sofa, were undressed and active Ann Toth and Donald Hunt. Laughing, they came apart and Donald cackled, "Am I next, Jack?"

Bronwyn turned and to her horror, saw Jack McClean standing in the bathroom doorway. She grabbed her satchel, ran out the door and down the path. Catching her breath, she saw a gardener and borrowed his cell phone. Bronwyn waited behind a shrub for the limo.

Jack's heart was pounding like a blacksmith's anvil and his insides were feeling the brunt of the hammering. He replayed each moment…where he'd put his hand, where he'd moved to the left, how she'd pushed against him, how she'd thrust past him, how her face shown horror. The whiskey wasn't helping him find clarity or escape. It had all gone so horribly wrong. He'd been made a fool, but what mattered was that Bronwyn misunderstood it all. And that realization refueled his despair.

He'd had his moment with Ann, and yes, she orchestrated everything to messily flaunt her husband; as if Jack hadn't been through with her for years. But most of all, she wanted to hurt Bronwyn. And the look of that laughing husband of hers was a roaring nightmare.

Jack played, rewound, and replayed each part of the afternoon, wanting to change everything. It seemed he kept walking into the middle of a scene. He couldn't imagine how Ann had lured Bronwyn to her house, much less into the bathroom and it seemed Bronwyn was on the floor looking for something. Had the toilet overflowed? He remembered the water. Jack hadn't even known it was a bathroom – he just knew Bronwyn was supposed to be behind the door. He shuddered. What a brute he'd been. He should have been happy to see her, in a light and charming way. But knowing Bronwyn was there, he just wanted…what? To grab her? To have her? To possess her? The light in the room had been dim, before Ann must have turned it off. Bronwyn probably had no idea it was him.

He'd left the press tour to surprise Bronwyn, but she

wouldn't know that, he reminded himself. The evening light would be pouring through the windows and he'd have been silhouetted. A hulk. A brute. Everything he hated being accused of, he had been. And worse still, to the person he treasured as a gentle, fragile discovery. He'd accosted her and held tight, making certain she wouldn't escape. Having his arms around her was satisfying, rewarding. Of course she misunderstood; anyone would have misunderstood. Jack took a breath, gulped more whiskey, pondered the back-lighting and began again. Each replay was the same, except he felt more fractured and the whiskey line was going down.

Jack swayed a bit as he splashed cold water on his face. Think. Think again. Ann had called and told him Bronwyn was coming to her house. He'd taken the bait, drank shots with Hunt while he waited and at some point Ann took him to the pool house, pointing to the door. He was wild with excitement to have Bronwyn so close. They'd have left Ann's house. Of course they'd have done. He was sick at heart that Ann Toth knew he'd grab the girl. She knew there'd be nothing gentlemanly about Jack McClean.

Moving to the toilet, he vomited. Contemplating a face that shouldn't see the light of day, he brushed his teeth furiously and returned to the edge of his bed. His face in his hands, he made a guttural sound and rocked back and forth.

He lay back on the bed and moved to a fetal position. He was still for several minutes, but it wasn't sleep he found. Clarity took hold of him. Jack decided on a plan of action. The clock showed 3:42 AM. Grabbing his sweats, he was out the door in ten minutes.

Harold the doorman was on duty, as Jack had fervently hoped. Pleading 'love sickness' and looking like 'love death', Jack gathered forces at the Beverly Soleil Hotel. His dutiful soldiers, perhaps bored with night duty, were willing to come to his rescue. He holed up in the mezzanine meeting room and the word went out to detain Bronwyn whenever she left her room, requesting that she meet Jack McClean if she'd be so kind.

Jack had rightly guessed she'd be at the Beverly Soleil – maybe even room 1110 – but he didn't make things worse by knocking at that door, or persuading the staff to reveal her room number. He was a gentleman and waited, determinedly hopeful.

Jack pictured her sleeping, waking, dressing and emerging. He began this fantasy scenario around 5:10 AM and pathetically repeated it until he thought he'd go mad. It reminded him of measuring kilometers on childhood road trips, three or four power poles at a time. Always wrong. Always too soon, no matter how much patience he tried to muster.

The staff brought a coffee carafe, orange juice, and a pastry basket. He was pleased to see a raisin brioche as it reminded him of Bronwyn. He remembered how kind the staff had been, bringing hot food when he'd been in this very room with Bronwyn, after the Golden Globes. Remarkably, the little repast made a half hour go by and the time was 7:20 AM.

He wished he knew more about Bronwyn's habits. Would he be waiting all morning? Would she even agree to see him? Knowing she was a breakfast lover of the first order, he thought she wouldn't miss coming down for breakfast. If she'd ordered room service instead, his spies would surely let him know. The door opened and Bronwyn walked in, smiling.

Praise all that's holy, he thought.

Bronwyn was taken aback. "Wow, you look really bad, Jack." She smiled more broadly. Jack felt his left eye twitching.

They sat side by side and Bronwyn was asked if she'd like breakfast. She glanced at the credenza and requested a mushroom omelette and hash browns.

Jack looked ashamed. "I ate your raisin brioche."

Bronwyn added a raisin brioche to her order and then said, "Two."

If Jack had known Bronwyn well, he'd have taken it as a very good sign that she was ordering breakfast. When Bronwyn was most upset with life, she couldn't eat.

Jack began his apologies. Bronwyn had never seen anyone so miserable about his behavior.

Since leaving Malibu, she'd been afraid, angry, disappointed, resigned. It didn't take long to realize Jack had been set-up by Ann Toth, and Bronwyn couldn't comprehend Donald Hunt being the same man she'd photographed with his son. She doubted Ann had been driven by jealousy, but she couldn't fathom her motivation. Bronwyn decided they were just sickos and resolved to avoid Los Angeles, for a very long time.

Bronwyn held Jack's hands, which made him believe everything would be all right, but it wouldn't be all right; not the way he was hoping.

In her sleepless hours, Bronwyn had analyzed her fear. Ten years before, during Samuel and Paul's kidnapping, she'd been focused on saving the boys. It happened so fast, she hadn't thought about being wounded or killed. When Oakley Forse shot her, even she couldn't explain why she wasn't afraid when he pointed the gun to her head, or when he pulled the trigger. She knew that was the pivotal moment sealing her connection to Oakley Forse, but she didn't understand it. She wondered if the prime minister's brother inhabited her being, and perhaps his courage and bravery infused her. Saving Oré's daughter on the roof had taken courage, but it was a matter of overcoming her fear of height. And when Oakley Forse had wielded the sock, they'd looked in each other's eyes and shared the blame. She'd had no fear, just shame.

She sometimes suspected Jeeves had instigated that beating, seven years ago. His laptop would have shown the 'Oakley' tracking dot in Beverly Hills, surely merging with the dot marked 'Bronwyn'...how could Jeeves not have known? Maybe he suggested Oakley dangle the tease about Graeme Woods, luring her to the office. And, the sock filled with a few coins seemed to be Jeeves' style; insane Oakley was capable of worse. Had Jeeves sworn to protect her and done the opposite? To insure an unholy fortune?

If Jeeves had been involved, if he'd guessed the beating and the money would kick her off the starting blocks, it had. Yet she still didn't fear Jeeves. She carried a lifetime of dismal anguish and she could rise with a dragon's fire if she needed to.

Yet, how could she ignore Jeeves' possible sin/probable sin and feel afraid of Jack? She was abidingly fond of Jeeves; he had always been her someone, when she had no one. But, she was guarded with Jeeves. With Jack, she was vulnerable. She wanted to feel safe with Jack and was weary of being cautious.

Bronwyn had replayed being accosted and her ice cold dread and primal panic. The hulking danger with liquor on his breath was smothering her, blocking her escape. Bronwyn wished she could get over it, but it chilled her to the bone. A part of her doubted Jack. She'd defended him against gossip about forcing himself on a young actress in a bathroom. It was clever of Ann Toth to recreate the scenario. Brilliant.

Realizing the time had come to write Jack McClean off, she didn't expect he'd find her and apologize. It was what Bronwyn would have done, and it mattered.

Bronwyn halted Jack's apologies. She said she understood how Ann Toth had made fools of them both and reassured him as they ate their breakfast. They felt a small sense of relief and gently regarded each other.

With regret, Bronwyn checked her watch. She was going to have to state her case in the next half hour, and be gone.

She took Jack's large hands in her own.

"I love you, Jack. I always will."

Jack looked stricken.

"I forgive you. I know it was a mistake, a misunderstanding. Truly. But, I can't get over the fear I felt and I'm sorry for that because I know, I really know it was the last thing you wanted to do…to frighten me. But, there it is."

"What are you saying?"

"I'd like to keep writing to each other. Not to see you or talk on the phone. I couldn't bear to hear your voice. But it would mean a lot to read your letters and share our days. Maybe it's ridiculous, but I have to tell you, it's because you came here this morning."

"Yes."

"Don't just say 'yes'. You can say 'forget it'. I just think I might be able to put this behind me, someday. If I know you better."

"Absolutely, yes."

"Well, good then. I mean great. Are you sure?"

Jack nodded and his big, square eyes regarded her. "I need something from you, Bronwyn."

"What?"

"I don't know...something. Anything. Something of yours that I can hold and know I have a small part of you."

Bronwyn thought. Everything was packed and waiting downstairs. Even her handbag didn't have anything she could spare. "I'll write my perfume name. I don't wear perfume often, but it's the only one I wear." Bronwyn began to write 'Calandre – Paco Rabanne'.

"What's wrong? Bronwyn, what's wrong?"

Tears welled in her eyes and spilled down her cheeks.

"Bronwyn. Bronwyn," Jack implored, cupping her face between his hands as she closed her eyes.

She looked down at the word 'Calandre' and said, haltingly, "It has bergamot, then rose with geranium and hyacinth and then musk."

Taking a deep breath, she said softly, "It's a quiet scent."

"What's wrong, Bronwyn? What have I done?" He was near tears, himself.

"It's just that you wanted something from me. Anything." Bronwyn looked thoroughly miserable. "And you already had it."

Jack waited.

"My heart."

Bronwyn gave him a drenched-in-tears smile, shrugging. "There you go."

Jack promised to write that very day. Bronwyn apologized to him for her feelings, while he admonished her. They agreed they were both pathetic, conceded each loved the other, made promises to take good care of themselves, and moved toward the reality of regret.

CHAPTER TWENTY SEVEN

SAVING PRODUCTIONS

*B*efore Bronwyn received Jack's latest letter, she had an odd dream.

Jack was leading men the wrong way across the Fort Pitt Bridge, toward the exiting portal of the Fort Pitt Tunnel. Bronwyn could see Station Square to her left, and she warned him he was headed the wrong direction, bound to get mowed down by cars at any moment. He said he was playing Henry VIII, but something about him wasn't right. Actor Jack rallied troops, while she appraised his appearance. The costumers had him in white tights with a linen shirt, a brocade doublet, and an ecru jerkin. But just as he was breaching the tunnel, Bronwyn realized what was wrong. The costumers and makeup people had made a mistake and Jack looked like Old King Cole. His hair was in a horrid Prince Valiant style with straight bangs and a curled under pageboy. *They have the wrong king*, she wanted to shout, but it was too late. And then she woke up.

The dream made Bronwyn even more concerned about Jack's letter. Before starting his Ernest Hemingway film, he had squeezed in a small film about a head chef and his sous chef. Jack was worried. Shooting had begun and it seemed to be nothing more than a showcase for the R&B singer, Bebe. It would be difficult to not think of it as stunt casting. The odds were against it being a Frank Sinatra in *From Here to Eternity* success.

She didn't know if Jack was normally miserable during filming, but Bronwyn called Dick Domitrovich and made arrangements to read the script on the sly. They were filming in Brooklyn, so she flew to New York with Van Tsang and invited Dick to her hotel. The first read-through, she wondered what had drawn Jack to the project. The director must have done a great pitch. The more she read, the more she understood his concerns. The script focused on Bebe's character and there wasn't much substance. She knew even the best actors had duds in their filmographies, but she vowed this wouldn't be one of them. Not for Jack.

It was great to see 'Cleveland' Dick, but time was slipping away; she handed him the script, said good night and called her director friend, Billy Foster. Billy called Jack's director, Trudale Smith, and set up a breakfast meeting between Smith and Bronwyn.

Trudale Smith didn't mind being rescued. Jack McClean wasn't pleased with his co-star and vocally doubted the film's direction on a daily basis. The project seemed destined to fail. When Billy Foster told him Bronwyn had helped Foster on his own films, Trudale was willing to listen. He had nothing to lose.

Bronwyn and Trudale sipped their coffee. Without saying the script was sloppy, she suggested the movie needed a frame around it. She had an idea for the opening and closing, and thought Jack's character having failing eyesight would be an intriguing element.

Trudale shared that Bebe's dream was to be accepted as a serious actor, yet he wanted his music in the film, to hedge his bets. Bronwyn said it was a ruinous idea.

She described her idea for an opening – a dramatically scored verbal kitchen dual between the two chefs, and only instrumental songs on the soundtrack. Most importantly, she wanted the composer to work with the writer creating non-musical beats and rhythms for the first scene. Only a composer could create music from words and sounds.

Staccato had to match staccato; long vowel sounds must have the same beats and similar long vowel sounds. Four syllables against four syllables. Three, a pause and two. Versus three, a pause and two. A dual. Meat cleaver for emphasis, matching meat cleaver for emphasis. That sort of thing. Bronwyn suggested trying Marco Beltrami and before the meeting was over, the concierge dropped off Beltrami soundtrack CD's. Bronwyn urged Trudale to get the opening choreographed and filmed as soon as possible, to create new vigor for both Jack and Bebe.

Trudale was glad he'd taken Billy Foster's call. He was seeing good flesh on the bones of his movie, knew there was a ferocity added from the non-musical set piece, recognized that McClean should stretch and felt reassured that Bebe's character could be framed by more maturity. He also realized Bebe's role would shrink, but that might be a relief. The pressure seemed to be getting to the singer.

Anticipating a grand vision to end the film, Trudale was almost greedy. "And, the end?"

Bronwyn simply said, "Tear Soup." He studied her and slowly nodded. Bebe cries into his soup, and those salty tears give it the taste of humanity. Jack's character could catch

Bebe's daughter's tears in a jar...a tear jar. They exchanged ideas, shaping the pathos.

Bronwyn had a few ideas about the cinematography. She urged him to make an effort to showcase food, filming it with reverence for its natural beauty, hearing its sounds, watching it transform, making food an essential character. The sparkle of sugar...refracted light...a shimmering atmosphere. The sound of a cracked crème brulee with caramel iceberg shards descending into the creamy thick sea.

Trudale listened and thought he'd never really eaten food before. How was it that he was making a movie about two chefs, but had little patience with the food stylists?

He'd been seduced with the idea of bringing Bebe into film. But it wasn't too late. Not too late at all.

"Tell me."

"I'm sorry, Miss. Tell you, in what context?"

"You lifted your eyebrow." Spending so much time with a man of very few words, Bronwyn was adept at reading Jeeves' subtleties.

"My eyebrows are in complete repose."

"Come off it, Jeeves. You think I shouldn't keep paying for the soda fountain."

Jeeves chose not to speak freely and disturb the carefully constructed persona he offered to Bronwyn. He hadn't spent three weeks at the International Guild of Professional Butlers for nothing.

"I'm simply concerned, Miss, that it's nearly a matter of extortion."

Bronwyn made a face and Jeeves waited for her response. With a sigh, Jeeves continued. "I'm afraid Mort's son is taking advantage of your generosity. If you call his bluff and he eliminates the lunch counter, well Que Sera, Sera."

Bronwyn was amused at his unexpected Doris Day moment, then annoyed.

"If it wasn't for the soda fountain, we might not even be here, Jeeves. It was because of our lovely lunch here that I loved the town. Remember, grilled cheese sandwiches and chocolate frappes? Remember?"

"I was under the impression that Snooks Von Krinkles was the determining factor."

Bronwyn gave him a dark look. "I'd want to live in any town with a soda fountain, and a drugstore with one is even better."

"There's a reason they're a dying breed, Miss."

Triumphantly, Bronwyn retorted, "My point, exactly."

The next few moments were silent.

"I don't mind paying him, Jeeves. It's a subsidy. It's important to keep the soda fountain and lunch counter. Don't forget the high school kids who work there."

Bronwyn felt the chill in the air and knew she could frost their days, two times over.

It was more than days, actually. Bronwyn and Jeeves avoided each other and barely spoke when their paths crossed. It rattled Grace, Edgar, and Van Tsang, who interacted daily with the pair. They compared notes and wondered how to spark a turnaround.

Grace popped in to see Clara and Edgar, bringing surprising news. Zuleika Zannini was making an unexpected visit. Alone, without Jean Luc. Grace reported that Zuleika hinted it was a personal matter with Bronwyn, and because the only Bronwyn issue seemed to be Jeeves, they were brimming with curiosity.

Bronwyn didn't like being second-guessed and decided to teach Jeeves a lesson, despite his being more than thirty years her senior. She authorized Zuleika to reserve $500,000 for Jeeves' use. He had three weeks to spend the money in a manner he saw fit. At the end of three weeks, if he didn't spend the money it would go into his personal account. Zuleika was appalled. She did everything she could to persuade Bronwyn to change her mind.

Bronwyn was adamant. If Jeeves was going to question how she spent her money, he could discover it wasn't easy deciding where money should go. Zuleika railed that Jeeves would know exactly where the money should go. Bronwyn wouldn't agree, although privately she knew there was a chance Jeeves would keep the money. Bronwyn planned it so he could do so while saving face. He could always say the three weeks wasn't sufficient, that he simply could not winnow the options. But Bronwyn was confident he'd find the money a trial, and that was her point. She wanted the money to weigh around his neck, with the myriad of options, even selfish options, becoming a burden.

Bronwyn told Zuleika she didn't want to know the outcome. But Zuleika vowed to tell Bronwyn the moment the three weeks were up. She had no doubt the money would revert to his account, headed for a selfish spending spree.

Watching Jeeves was amusing. Bronwyn thought he might mention her intriguing experiment, but when he didn't, she wasn't surprised. Almost immediately his brows were knit and his forehead furrowed, analyzing options. She enjoyed observing him and he didn't have the luxury of protesting.

When the three weeks expired, Zuleika was so softspoken revealing the result, Bronwyn knew Jeeves had done something 'good' as opposed to 'bad'.

Zuleika wasn't impressed with his choice. If Jeeves' goal had been to impress Bronwyn, he should have made a huge donation to relief funds or animal sanctuaries. That would have made Bronwyn happy. Zuleika didn't foresee Bronwyn's satisfaction; she never expected Bronwyn to squeal with delight.

Edgar was the one who saw Bronwyn dashing to the Factory. He knew Jeeves was reading the newspaper in the Orangerie and watched Jeeves watch Bronwyn, as she darted into his kitchen. The Orangerie was Bronwyn's next guess and she found Jeeves sitting there. Ready to hug Jeeves, his stern expression stopped her.

"Good choice, Jeeves."

"Thank you, Miss."

She resisted the urge to say, 'so it's not so easy having money, is it'? She already knew it was a lesson learned.

"Are we going every night?"

"Would you enjoy that, Miss?"

"I would."

And the chill in the air was gone, much to the relief of their friends.

Three weeks later, Bronwyn and Jeeves spent a week and a half in New York City, seeing the Broadway musical Jeeves had bankrolled for ten extra days, before it closed. Once in the city, Bronwyn and Jeeves asked their maids, doormen, and wait staff if they had a free afternoon or evening. If so, they gifted them with tickets and gift cards for dinner in the Theatre District.

Plays and musicals were a joy both Bronwyn and Jeeves shared, eager to immerse themselves in the magical feeling of being transported within suspended time. Their joy was compounded by watching those special seats fill and seeing the people whispering, sensing their anticipation, watching their reactions.

Bronwyn and Jeeves applauded every matinee and evening performance as if they were proud parents and she marveled that he had learned from the Production Office of the show's financial troubles. Bronwyn urged Jeeves to go backstage and reveal himself as their angel, but he never did.

The only show they didn't attend was the final night's performance. Bronwyn knew money didn't forestall the end. This time Jeeves realized it, as well. Neither could bear to see the final curtain.

CHAPTER TWENTY EIGHT

THE RETURN

Clive Grove's return to the estate had never been a consideration. Jeeves was satisfied to see him occasionally in Europe, and bringing him to the property seemed risky at best. Until now. Jeeves discussed the idea with Van Tsang, suggesting Clive come in October for a few months. Van wondered if Jeeves was mellowing. His desire to spend time with Clive seemed distinctly out of character.

Jeeves didn't know Clive had seen Bronwyn, three years before. He didn't know he'd watched Bronwyn get bowled over by the Newfoundland dog. If he'd known Bronwyn had kissed Clive, he wouldn't have considered inviting him back. But, if he'd known how Clive had never forgotten the kiss, regardless of the disparate circumstances he'd found himself in over the years, Jeeves would have invited him sooner. Jeeves could always find a way to exploit emotion.

In truth, Bronwyn often thought of Clive. Not knowing his name, she thought of him as the man in the night. She knew he'd chosen a moonless night with darkness obscuring his face, but she'd relied on touch and instinct to broach the distance between them. She remembered his voice and its resonance, and although he'd spoken softly, she hadn't forgotten. Knowing Jeeves, she was certain the man in the night wouldn't be returning, but she suspected Jeeves kept in touch with him. Their embrace at his doorway that night had been emotional. In the years since, she hadn't known Jeeves to turn out his light and go to sleep at a normal hour. Only that night. Only the night he'd embraced the man in the night, and felt safe enough to sleep.

Tuesday evening, the men were playing poker at Jeeves'. Bronwyn had gone to the Chowder Box with Grace and was about to settle in, when she decided to visit Linda at the Island House for a quick cup of tea. Popping over to Jeeves' flat to let him know, she saw Coolidge sitting sweetly in the hallway. She walked past the doorway, casually updating Jeeves as she walked by. Coolidge looked solemn and cocked his head to the side. She stopped. Turning her own head to the side, the Scottie straightened his, she did the same, and then Coolidge cocked his, again. With eyebrows raised, Bronwyn walked into the library.

"Matthew, I'm taking Coolidge with me to the Island House." She was surprised the room was so dark. She'd stopped in on poker night, before. Had it been this dark? This smoky with cigars?

"Okay, Bronwyn. Thanks," Matthew said distractedly, intent on his hand.

Bronwyn was nearly out the library door when she stood straighter and her shoulders settled down. She smiled as she turned. She knew. She just somehow knew. Jeeves watched her, not with disappointment, but with pride. Bronwyn had great instincts. She walked straight to the table and looked Clive squarely in the eye. He'd been hunkered down between Edgar and Officer Grande, but she'd caught the height of his torso. He smiled with delight.

Her eyes took him in. The harsh overhead lighting cast deep shadows over a face that was chiseled and broad. Cheekbones high and hollowed, jaw line strong and shoulders wide, those were things she well remembered, having drawn her fingers across his face and felt the width of him. It was his eyes sparkling in the dark room that surprised her. Memories of the man in the night were devoid of eyes, and as a photographer she knew they completed the picture. The thought occurred to her that those eyes could never render him anonymous and nondescript. In his line of work, those eyes would catch attention, anywhere. She wondered how he coped with such easy betrayal.

"I don't believe we've met," Bronwyn said, turning questioningly to Jeeves.

"This is Clive Grove, Miss. Friend of mine and Van's. Clive, this is Miss Bronwyn Dai McCall."

"Owner of all," Matthew laughed.

Clive stood and kissed her in greeting. His breath fell upon each of her cheeks before his lips landed. She didn't know if Jeeves had intended to hide him, but he'd be hidden no more.

"Are you staying with us, Mr. Grove?"

"Clive, Miss. Ernest has invited me to visit."

Bronwyn turned to Jeeves. "He's staying awhile?"

"If you don't mind, Miss. Perhaps through the holidays."

None of the poker players could miss Bronwyn's happy smile and excitement. "Through the holidays. Perfect. We can shop at Freeport, Clive."

The entire poker table groaned, as Clive stood happily nodding.

After scooting Coolidge over to Linda's, Bronwyn returned to her house. She wasn't certain what magic Clive worked, but she fell happily, instantly to sleep just as she imagined Jeeves had done, all those years before.

As the weeks went by, Bronwyn and Clive became great friends. She thought it a blessing that neither of them was looking for a romantic relationship. Bronwyn treasured Jack McClean's letters and mentally traveled through his days. She didn't mention Jack to Clive, but she suspected he knew.

One day, they walked past the loggia and Bronwyn explained how she'd kissed him to bring him back. Clive assured her he knew what it meant and he'd always intended to return. He had to fight the urge to take her in his arms and reenact the moment. Perhaps it was best to avoid the loggia, he thought.

Bronwyn enjoyed showing her estate to him, pointing out the small details she loved so much. It was satisfying to show the pride she usually kept hidden. Her reliance on the visual was something he shared. He wouldn't be worth much in MI6, if he wasn't visual. So, the things she'd planned and chosen, planted and unearthed were mutually explored.

Clive spent the better part of each day at Bronwyn's, relaxing, chatting, and sharing household chores. They competitively raked leaves, and then shared hot apple cider with cinnamon sticks on the stone patio. They baked cookies together, punctuated by Clive's uproarious laughter and his impatience as the oven did its eighteen minute work. Bronwyn could count on Clive wearing bits of the cookies. She told him no one was going to take his cookies away, but he just grinned and ate.

Sometimes they didn't speak at all, good friends enjoying a companionable silence. She taught him to play racquetball and he was dumbfounded when she won. It was a game that suited her. Quickness in a confined atmosphere. They crashed into each other, but she was resilient.

He hadn't expected Bronwyn to be so lonely and ready for play. He blamed Ernest for that. It was obvious the estate residents enjoyed their lives with very little interaction with her.

Clive gathered information about her missed opportunities. Every romantic entanglement had apparently been doomed to failure. Clara and Valli were particularly fond of Oré Diaz Dominguez, but there was some messiness over his wife's pregnancy and it was over when Ernest drove Oré to Bar Harbor to meet with Bronwyn. They'd all hoped for reconciliation, but instead, it was over.

When Bronwyn and Grace flew to New York, Clive spent two days with Anna "Menke" Black. He wanted to gain perspective on the early days of Bronwyn and Ernest Rose. Menke professed some disappointment in Rose's oversight, wishing Bronwyn had found a husband by now. She feared Ernest was lining his pockets and hoped Bronwyn wasn't being generous to ensure his staying. Before Clive left, Menke had a weak moment and mentioned she'd always hoped Bronwyn would eventually be with her son, the prime minister. She clucked and shook her head, saying it was a foolish thought. Taking Clive's hand, she looked him in the eye and pronounced, "His boys are like her very own. That never changes."

A quick call to Samuel and Paul seemed in order, and

they told him about Jack McClean. Both boys were in favor of the match, although neither knew where things stood.

The women on the Factory fourth floor, Grace and Sam exchanged glances when asked about Jack McClean. Jack's letters were the highlights of Bronwyn's days, they informed him.

Clive hadn't discovered why Ernest invited him back, but he was determined to take advantage of it. He'd teach Bronwyn to defend herself, and he planned to ensure Bronwyn would have a partner to love and protect her.

Bronwyn was delighted that Clive appreciated her home. When Graeme visited, he was used to beautiful things and simply accepted the surroundings. Mama Lou's family visited, but Mama Lou was content in the Carnegie Suite, while her son and grandson, Ernie and Ernest, enjoyed the Factory's third floor. This was so much better.

Clive watched her point and gesture. She lifted objects and placed them in his hand for his reaction. It seemed there were a hundred things to discover every day. All the fittings were from a slower place in time, pieces of vintage art. Several lighting fixtures were rescued, and Bronwyn had a touching appreciation for their histories. All the flooring had been reclaimed from European farmhouses, castles, and hotels.

She'd gathered some long-forgotten things like a framed tintype of a white dog with one black ear, begging on a wooden chair. A cloth drape on the chair came up to the back of the dog's neck. The chair was sitting on grass; wash was hanging in the background, its shadows falling on a stable. The dog's little black eyes, black nose and straight mouth made for a solemn and timeless pose, much like the people of the era. He seemed as still as if he'd been sitting up for an hour, patiently waiting to be photographed. His hind feet were supporting him even as they were obviously on a very shiny, polished wood. The photograph was probably circa 1900, and Bronwyn's affection for it made Clive love it as well. She touched the frame with gentleness and said she'd give anything to be able to reach through time and pet the dog's head. She said as long as the photo had place of honor in her library, the dog would live forever.

Even as Clive listened and watched, he was taken with how huge Bronwyn's green eyes were. Beneath pale eyebrows, they were wide with wonderment as Bronwyn reviewed, inspected, and rediscovered the things she loved. She assumed he was listening, but he was observing her pupils sitting above the whites of her eyes, as if the green orbs floated. He'd never seen such large, black pupils unless he was looking into drugged eyes, yet beautiful green rimmed the black. Something about Bronwyn made her invisible; a defensive demeanor she'd developed. But, seeing those eyes, noting the bowed curve of her lips and their fullness, how could she ever fall into the background? She talked; he analyzed. Bronwyn kept in the shadows, kept her head down, stayed away. But, if she looked at you, that made the difference.

He wondered if her life had been different, would those huge eyes have noticed less, each day? Would her smile have dominated her face? Would she sport even more freckles, facing sunny southern days instead of northern mists? Would her hands caress her children instead of the objects she loved? We all travel different paths, he decided, grateful his path had crossed with hers.

In her Secret Garden, Bronwyn said there was power to a garden's entrance and the door had been obscured by overgrowth. Now, the heavy dark green door swung easily open. Inside, flowers and plants ran along the walls, but Clive was surprised to find lines for hanging laundry, and a badminton net. A bench here and there made it a quiet place for contemplation, but there wasn't much garden in her Secret Garden. The place reminded Bronwyn of a quote she'd read of George Eliot..."Delicious Autumn! My very soul is wedded to it, and if I were a bird I would fly about the earth seeking the successive autumns." Several trees overhung the garden, with birds zipping about. "George Eliot must have been thinking of Maine," she said.

When they exited the garden, Clive had a different vantage point for her tea room. He'd sat inside, having tea and scones and appreciating the window with thirty or so leaded panes of glass, but the exterior reminded him of England. Painted a deep forest green, it featured gold lettering, 'Ollie & Co. Tea Room'.

They walked across the stone patio and into the dining room with its dark shuttered windows, twin chandeliers, and club atmosphere. Eight chairs lined each side of the long table. At one end was a floor to ceiling display of oyster plates. He asked where she got the idea to glass-in both the dining room and kitchen.

He was perplexed when her answer was the movie, *Gosford Park*.

They crossed into the kitchen for a cup of tea. As Bronwyn filled the kettle, Clive looked at the dark coffered ceiling, huge archways, paned windows, dark moldings, and immense clock from an Irish hotel. He was struck with how masculine it looked, compared with Ernest Rose's cheerful white kitchen with roses and cherries on the walls, straight from the fifties. He asked Bronwyn about her inspiration and she said she'd gotten used to hotels and wanted something massive. She gestured to the gilt bronze chandelier above the work island, with several alabaster shades, made in 1910 and shipped from a French hotel.

Seemingly out of place was an incredible work surface. They leaned over it as she explained.

"It's called semiprecious surfacing. They take large semiprecious stones and join them with a mineral binder. I'd never heard of it before. This is turquoise, here is carnelian, this is jasper," she pointed to each, "and mother of pearl. They're sliced and I love how huge they are. It's like looking into a sea shell."

"I believe it's my favorite thing so far," Clive said, his hand moving over the smooth, cold surface.

Another day, she invited him upstairs. Her office, atop the tea room, featured a walnut and burl desk, made in the mid 19th century. She purchased it from a grocer in Bar Harbor whose grandfather had managed the grocery from his glass-enclosed office, situated in the store. The enormous desk had been on one side of the office; a roaring fireplace on the other.

"I like to think his grandfather would be glad I have his desk because I love it. I told his grandson he could come any time and see it. That made him happy."

An old Royal typewriter was on one of the cabinets as well as some old cameras...a Seagull Twin Lens Reflex Camera from the 1930's and a Hasselblad 1600F Camera from 1948. She began to tell him more about the cameras, but stopped herself.

They walked down the paneled hallway to the bathroom. Handrails with hidden lights were integrated into the corridor walls. Entering the bathroom, she admitted Oré Diaz Dominguez had designed it and Clive judged it with a different eye. An enormous bathtub sat in the center of the room, beneath two crystal chandeliers with dangling amber pears. Art Deco vanities flanked the doorway, with mirrored chests of drawers. He approved the separation. It was satisfying knowing they hadn't been elbow to elbow. There were definitely too many mirrors. It was creamy and sensual and soft, and he hated it.

Shrugging off the bathroom, she said she usually used the smaller one, beside the second bedroom. Now that one, Clive liked. It was small, just right for one. Glass mosaic tiles gave a magical mirrored effect. He appreciated the radiant floor heating and was pleased to see a tiny shower stall at one end, and seating for one on an iron chair. That chair would be uncomfortable; no one would be resting there while someone was in the bathtub. Yes, he liked this bathroom. This was the bathroom she should always use.

In the bedroom, Clive admired the chocolate and mocha tones in the seating area and rich polished wood. Discomfited by her carved and well-turned four poster bed, he didn't want to linger. On this side of her Maine wall, he was almost an innocent.

It was puzzling to see that her bedroom had no doors. Two openings on either side of the floor-to-ceiling bookcase, allowed complete access. What had she been thinking? Did she think Dominguez wouldn't have wanted privacy? What was Ernest thinking? Why would she be more vulnerable than the average person? French doors opened onto a long balcony, hovering over the hotel-style lobby at the back of the house. It was as if she were a jewel in a box…a box, easily opened.

Bronwyn showed Clive the butler's pantry. "See the dumbwaiter? That's where Jeeves saved Snooks Von Krinkles from a fate worse than death." Her eyes were as big as her smile. The floor was covered by traditional black and white diamond flooring. Honey-toned cabinets were outfitted with retro hardware, and paned cabinetry had black and white checked curtains behind the glass. Extravagant crown moldings added stateliness.

When Bronwyn walked him through her dressing room, the uncompromising dark cabinetry was stunning and masculine. It reminded him of Jeeves' flat. He asked about the black and white family photos on display, and she proudly told how each Christmas, Jeeves gifted her with one of his family photos. It was the tradition that most meant 'Christmas' to her. She took Clive's elbow and they went through the door, settling into the dark brown loveseat.

"The thing I most regret after losing my family was losing the family photographs. My Dad's great aunt let them all go at auction...I was just eight." Bronwyn looked ahead, not seeing the four poster bed with its dark velvet linens. She was gazing into the past. Sometimes she jerked her head just a little; sometimes her mouth parted, to speak. Eventually, she began again.

"That's why I took up photography." She turned to look at him. "Did you know that? Did you know I was a photographer?" He didn't reply and she was reminded if it was intel about her, he wouldn't say one way or another.

"I can't tell you how much photography means to me." She looked at him and gave a shrug. "I really, can't. But it meant everything to me. If you lose your photographs, you lose your life. It's as if you had no family, no friends." Her voice was hushed and they sat in silence for a long while. "It's as if you never lived, at all."

Clive stood over Jeeves, in his kitchen. "Bloody hell, Ernest. What are you playing at?"

Jeeves didn't expect every day of Clive's visit to go smooth as silk. He'd anticipated an explosion from time to time. After all, Clive was the most murderous man he knew, save one.

Seeing that Ernest wasn't going to make inquiry, Clive got angrier. "The pictures. The bloody photographs." Clive spit out the word 'photographs'.

Ernest looked questioningly at Clive and then said, "You mean in her dressing room."

"Yes, you old twit. Her dressing room. What are you playing at?"

Jeeves was calm. "They mean a great deal to her."

"Bloody bloomin' hell they do. They mean everythin' to her. Where did you get them?" Clive thundered and grabbed Ernest's collar, slamming him against the refrigerator. "Where?"

"Portobello Road. Easy enough."

Clive shook his head with disgust and stormed out to the garage, no doubt headed for Van Tsang's.

Two days later, Clive asked Bronwyn to go upstairs with him, to her dressing room. Carefully, he lifted each of the framed photographs and piled them up.

"I'm bloody sorry, Bronwyn. These photographs are fake. They aren't photos of Ernest's family," he said gently. "He was trying to please you, I expect. He probably thought it dangerous to give you real photos. Security, right?"

Bronwyn didn't seem disturbed. In fact, she smiled. "Well, that was a nice gesture, wasn't it?"

"I'll just take them away. But I do have something for you.

This is a true photo of his wife." He reached in his pocket and pulled out a small 4x6 frame. "You can put this one up."

"He doesn't know you've brought it here, does he?"

Clive shook his head.

"Thank you." She brought it up to her eyes and peered intently. "She's lovely. Just lovely. Look at her golden hair. And, her sweet smile. I'll treasure it."

Clive was surprised when she opened a drawer and lifted its bottom panel. Bronwyn placed the photo of Ernest's wife on top of numerous letters, tied with ribbon. "This is my secret stash. Even Jeeves doesn't know about it." She kissed Clive's cheek and smiled. "You're so sweet to bring me this picture."

She began putting back the Portobello Road anonymous photos.

"No need for that, Bronwyn. I've called him on it. He'll not expect to see them."

Bronwyn smiled sweetly. "That's all right, Clive. Photographs capture a moment in time. These people were loved by someone. I'll always treasure these photos. I hope someone, somewhere has my family photos and honors them. They were probably thrown away or destroyed. But I won't do that to these. These people mean a lot to me, whoever they are."

Clive wrapped his arms around her and held tight.

It was an early November day, and Bronwyn had been eagerly anticipating the arrival of Clive's friend, Jamie Donald. There was a chance he'd upset the dynamic they enjoyed, but Clive said they'd have twice the fun and she trusted him.

Crossing the sloping lawn and stepping over her narrow serpentine watercourse, she saw them sitting on the dark green Adirondack chairs overlooking the water. She loved the evocative look of Adirondack chairs but found them uncomfortable. She thought it amusing they'd be settled into them. Walking around Clive's chair, she asked, "So, has this become a home for wayward boys?"

As Jamie Donald rose, much more lithely than she could have managed, she drew a breath. Not traditionally handsome, he had quite an aura. Bronwyn understood this, being with actors so often. It was a charismatic, only-man-in-the-room thing. Clive was sitting back with great amusement.

He patted his lap and Bronwyn sat with her legs dangling over his chair's arm, looking at Jamie. She couldn't have related any of the conversation. She just took in the vision of Jamie Donald. When he had no expression, he had meanness, a no-nonsense coil of aggression just beneath the surface. But, when he smiled, and Clive could certainly make him smile, he had the most intriguing look. Bronwyn knew the lines of a face, but she'd never seen such curves and depressions and wrinkles. Jamie Donald looked like an elf when he smiled. An elfin elf. Whew, she thought. That's a dichotomy. Killer and elf.

Clive was tall and had long muscles. He was agile playing racquetball and graceful, even walking. But Jamie Donald seemed to be a hairbreadth from explosive. His trim and tailored clothing seemed to barely contain his muscles and although he wasn't as tall as Clive, violence would never be a surprise, coming from Jamie. When Clive said his name, Bronwyn heard 'Jimey' instead of 'Jamie' so that's what she called him. 'Jimey'.

CHAPTER TWENTY NINE

JAMIE
2006-2007

So much of Bronwyn's life had been without friends. It seemed an embarrassment of riches, having two special ones at once. Surprisingly, Bronwyn found an even stronger connection with Jamie, than with Clive.

As a boy, Clive had enjoyed a loving upbringing, raised by maternal grandparents in Ireland. His father left home and his mother had died a tragic, early death, but he assured Bronwyn he was always loved and happy. Clive's career path seemed something he chose to do, given his particular strengths. She suspected Jamie Donald's early life might have mirrored her own. She imagined Jamie fell into MI6; perhaps falling on that side as easily as he could have fallen on the other.

At the estate, Jamie and Clive balanced athletic endeavor with quiet times. Sometimes they convinced Bronwyn to join them in the gym, and even took turns playfully sparring with her in the boxing ring. However, when she saw them fight each other, she jumped into the ring and stopped it, pronto, placing herself between them. It had frightened her to see there was nothing playful when they put on the gloves. They adored her for caring; ignoring the fact she'd separated and berated them both, equally.

Clive warned Jamie about her racquetball prowess and he was suitably impressed. They took turns playing against her, while the other cheered from the observation box. Other times the three played together. Edgar slipped in for a quick peek, and usually had a snack and beverage waiting in the Orangerie. The glass house would all but shake, as the men would one-up each other telling tales of glory, tales of shame. Seeing Bronwyn's face light up and nose crinkle lightened Edgar's heart. He decided Clive and Jamie were worth their weight in gold.

One morning, Bronwyn came upon Clara and Linda giggling, and they gestured for her to join them. Linda opened her mouth to speak, and then dissolved in a fit of giggles. Clara made an attempt and fell into a convulsive, shaking, laughing state. They finally composed themselves.

"Have you seen him?" Clara asked, with her face flushed.

"Seen who?" asked Bronwyn.

Linda clutched her blouse, pulling it into a bunch and catching part of her neck. "Jamie Donald, that's who."

"I see him every day."

The women exchanged glances, stifling giggles. Clara shifted her body away from Linda, fearing she'd fall apart if she looked at her.

"Bronwyn, dear. You know how I've been doing my laps, for my heart." She waited for Bronwyn's acknowledgement. "Well, one morning, Jamie Donald came up to the pool and," she glanced quickly at Linda, "he has the most fit body I've ever seen. Anywhere. Even in *People Magazine's* Sexiest Man."

Linda vigorously nodded. "Honestly, Bronwyn, maybe you've seen him. We don't mean to sound like you don't already know. But omigod, is that man built. Muscle on muscle. Not an ounce of fat. The perfect six pack. And arm muscles, just perfect. Not bulging, just solid and curved. And, no body hair, smooth as silk. And tan. A golden, caramel color. And, then, when he lifts his head out of the water, you see those blue eyes. Like Paul Newman's blue eyes…they're marine blue."

"Aquatic blue," Clara murmured dreamily.

Bronwyn looked at her quizzically. "That impressive, Clara?"

She nodded.

"Linda, since when were you up there swimming?"

"I don't have to swim. We all go, just to watch."

"We?"

"Grace, Sam, Clara, me, Kristine, Jen. We haven't told Vicki. We knew you wouldn't like her looking at him."

"Looking at him? That's what you do?" There was no mistaking that Clara and Linda were in a state of bliss; cats who'd had their fill of cream. "He doesn't notice?"

They shrugged. Bronwyn smiled with the realization the ladies knew more than she did. Even playing racquetball, Jamie wore sweatshirts or long sleeved tees, just as Clive did. Good for the ladies. Maybe Jamie actually thought the ladies had some business up there. Good for him.

Curious about the portraits throughout Bronwyn's lobby, Jamie listened as Bronwyn told him about Milton Hershey, Andrew Carnegie, Vernon Stouffer, Henry Ford, Roberto Clemente, and Teddy Roosevelt. Jamie declared Milton Hershey was his favorite, for the chocolate, and Jamie's love of chocolate was becoming more evident each time they went to Ogunquit and brought back chocolates and Caramallows from Harbor Candy. However, Bronwyn suspected his admiration might be because of the Milton Hershey School, founded in 1910 for 'poor and healthy boys'. Jamie's interest was piqued when she told him how Hershey gave his entire fortune to the school, as well as controlling interest in the company, when he died.

She reverently described The Hotel Hershey, explaining how Milton Hershey built the hotel during the Great Depression, employing his town's 600 construction workers in dire times. Hershey had shown his architect a postcard of his favorite hotel, the Heliopolis Hotel in Cairo, and a facsimile was built. She told Jamie they must dine in the Circular Dining Room. Not only was it elegant, but the shape was unique because Milton Hershey's circular design treated every diner equally. He and his wife Catherine kept notes on their travels and put a Spanish patio, tile floors, and a stunning fountain in the hotel lobby. Her enthusiasm was contagious. Jamie looked around Bronwyn's lobby and saw it in a new light. When others were distracted, Bronwyn observed, and being alone since eight gave her hungry observation skills and a distinct appreciation.

That night, Jamie lay awake in Ernest Rose's alcove bed. Jamie didn't tell Bronwyn he was familiar with her Heliopolis Palace Hotel. It had been turned into the Federation of Arab Republics headquarters in 1972 and later became a presidential palace under Mubarak. He suspected Milton Hershey would be disappointed; surely Bronwyn would be as well.

His thoughts drifted to a small town in Pennsylvania with streetlamps shaped like Hershey kisses and chocolate wafting in the air, as he fell asleep.

Samuel and Paul arrived for their December visit. They enjoyed being with Clive and Jamie, and Bronwyn spent much of her time watching the young boys take on the old boys. They played racquetball, ran snowy foot races, and even managed two golf games at the Bergamot Nine, while Bronwyn trudged along, hauling thermoses of hot cider.

A wicked winter volleyball match was played in the Secret Garden and Bronwyn and Edgar cheered from the narrow balcony just off her office. It was a good vantage point and Bronwyn and Edgar stayed warm beneath her down throws, and Edgar kept hot beverages and snacks coming from the butler's pantry.

Bronwyn ducked downstairs so the volleyball players could warm up with a shower. Samuel and Paul changed while Edgar went to Jeeves' flat, fetching dry clothes for Jamie and Clive. Bronwyn sat with Samuel and Paul downstairs, wondering what the ladies would give for a quick visit now, with Clive and Jamie waiting upstairs for their clothing.

As the weather turned much colder, the competitions turned to card games. Bronwyn watched their fierce Flinch, Rook, Canasta, and Pit battles. She wondered where Edgar had unearthed the games, but the old yellowed boxes held the key to joyful hours at Clara and Edgar's dining room table.

The heaviest snow came right before their departure, and Samuel and Paul were delighted. At the Secret Garden, they built a snowman holding a volleyball. Bronwyn added a red scarf, carrot nose, black stones gracefully curving into a smile, and two huge buttons for eyes. She mixed red food coloring and water, turned the plant mister to 'fine' and sprayed a lovely faint red blush on his cheeks. The boys ran inside, pushing to get through the dining room, to grab their digital cameras. It was a happy-faced snowman, but not as happy as the people who posed around him, especially the pair of six foot tall boys.

After Samuel and Paul went home, Jack McClean's bank heist movie was opening, and Bronwyn had an early copy of the Chef/Sous Chef film. She decided to show the chef movie upstairs, so Clive and Jamie could eagerly anticipate the other one at The Roxy.

Clive and Jamie didn't seem excited, so she asked Edgar and Matthew to kick off movie night with diner food in the Factory's soda fountain.

Spirits lifted when they'd had their fill of Vermont cheddar cheeseburgers, hand-cut fries, tempura onion rings and milkshakes, accompanied by Gay Nineties music. Bronwyn was a little surprised when Matthew kept pouring shots of Kahlua into Clive and Jamie's shakes, since hers tasted fine, just as it was.

The night was cold, so the three moviegoers walked back through the tunnel. Emerging into the house, they smelled freshly popped popcorn. Bronwyn led the way to the third floor, up the staircase of macassar ebony, with its narrow brass railings and footlights. Katrin had the popcorn waiting and stood behind the candy counter.

Clive and Jamie were stunned to see the authentic theatre entrance, and then realized of course Bronwyn would purchase a ticket booth and double doors from a sad theatre closing on Main Street somewhere. Mosaic flooring, neon bulbs, and globe lamps were breathtaking. Clive found himself reaching for his wallet as he perused the candy display. Jamie stopped him, grinning. That was the first time their eyes had met, and they smiled. This was a special place. All of it.

They followed a wooden parquet hallway, dotted with recessed lighting and ornately plastered walls featuring movie posters and another set of double doors. Inside, they should have been prepared for the authentic millwork, three levels of motion velvet chairs, and a fiber optic ceiling. But they weren't; they were still in a state of surprise. Bronwyn pulled up the drop-down food trays for their popcorn, motioned to their cup holders and dimmed the lights.

When the movie was over, Bronwyn couldn't help herself. She was delighted with the movie's opening. Jack had written to say he was re-invigorated filming the sound dual with Bebe. Bronwyn knew the reviews at Sundance had been great. It was a little movie, but a movie that didn't diminish Jack's film accomplishments.

Bronwyn allowed a few moments for the movie to sink-in, and then turned the lights slowly up with her remote control. She turned to Jamie and Clive who looked alarmingly sleepy, and said, "Ta Dah!"

No response.

Bronwyn stood before them, lifted both arms and shook them, as a conductor might do.

Clive looked at Jamie. Jamie looked at Clive.

"Darlin'," moaned Clive. "He was wielding a saucepan." Afraid to hold Bronwyn's gaze, he turned to Jamie for help.

Jamie shrugged. "It was a gentle movie. Not to worry Bronwyn, we know you find him fetching."

That gave Clive more courage. "That's right, luv, you like him. You bloody well love him. To you, it was probably an action-packed load of, I don't know, oven action."

Jamie crumpled with laughter, laughing so hard he

cried. He wiped the tears from his eyes, but one glance at Clive started the heaving fits of jollity all over again.

Bronwyn stood between them, leaned down and kissed the tops of both their heads. "It's okay. You'll like his bank heist movie, better."

Jamie stopped laughing.

Shopping was something Jamie never imagined enjoying, but he was actually quite good at it. He could go into any store in Freeport and snag five things in a row that Bronwyn loved. They were in sync and the more on target he was, the more addictive her praise became. Clive's tolerance was minimal for the shopping bit, but he enjoyed the towns and the dining out. The three had a companionable time of it, every day, no matter what they did.

Clara told Bronwyn that Valli yearned to walk across the estate to the Factory and take the elevator to the roof pool, just to see Jamie Donald. Valli had confessed she couldn't do it, but Clara and Bronwyn marveled that she found the courage to imagine it.

When Bronwyn couldn't sleep at night, she devised ways to trick Jamie into taking his shirt off, so Valli could see what the ladies enjoyed. One scenario was spilling red wine on his shirt at Valli's and having a fresh shirt to hand him, all the while touting Valli's laundry prowess and shoving them into a room together for the shirt exchange. Another idea was giving him the gift of a massage, for some unknown reason, at Valli's. Why she would happen to be watching him was a problem, but then Bronwyn pictured the massage table in the tropical vertical garden, with Valli watching from her balcony. But, perhaps she wouldn't be able to see him as closely as all the ladies had, and that was the point, wasn't it? In eight years, Bronwyn had never known Valli to say she wished she could go somewhere and it was breaking Bronwyn's heart.

Finally, she decided to just ask Jamie to take his shirt off in front of Valli. It would be his problem how he'd manage it. Perhaps he'd be offended. *Probably*, he'd be offended. But Bronwyn knew he was fond of Tom and Valli and enjoyed spending time with them. He could figure something out. He was MI6.

She told Jamie her dilemma, and if he was incredulous to learn the women were vying for front row seats to watch him swim, while purporting to conduct knitting club meetings in the warm moist air, for Clara's health, he was kind enough not to show it. He smiled and assured Bronwyn he'd take care of it.

The next morning, Van Tsang was having coffee at the gatehouse with Clive and Bronwyn, when he got a call on his cell phone. "Got to get a medical kit," he said and they rode the Cushman over to the stable. Valli was waiting on the porch.

"What's wrong?" shouted Bronwyn, leaping off the back.

"It's Jamie. He's cut himself on a rusty nail." Valli was wringing her hands.

Jamie stepped onto the porch, buttoned his shirt, and briskly waved them off. He strode past Bronwyn, climbed aboard the Cushman and rode over to the Factory, ready for a cup of coffee.

Bronwyn went into the living room, to calm Valli down. "He seems okay, Val, really. What happened?"

"He was raking straw for the horses and bent over Godolphin's stall and scraped his stomach against a rusty nail."

The light dawned for Bronwyn, but she hoped he'd faked it with paint. "What did you do?"

"I washed it really well with soap and water, put Neosporin on and a gauze cloth with tape. I was so worried." She shuddered. "He said all his shots are up to date. I hope he was telling the truth and not trying to make me feel better."

Bronwyn cringed. "Was it deep?"

"It was, Bronwyn, really deep."

Bronwyn grimaced and her stomach lurched. He'd seemed okay, but according to the ladies Jamie had a flawless upper body. To think he might have sacrificed perfection... no, she decided it must have been realistic makeup. He was MI6 after all. She sat patting Valli's hand and told her she'd done a great job, everything right, had she been a nurse at one time, or just a good mother? When Valli calmed down, Bronwyn asked how Jamie looked with his shirt off.

"I don't know. I was busy taking care of him."

Clive and Jamie showed Bronwyn self defense techniques. She wasn't very good, but she tried. Jeeves was away, and they stepped-up their wide-ranging regimen. He'd be gone another week, so Bronwyn moved into Jeeves' flat, taking the alcove bed while Jamie moved into the big man's bedroom. They had a grand time, and Edgar upped the meal delights.

The empty school car park was perfect for them to teach Bronwyn some slick defensive driving techniques. They'd invited Officer Grande to join them, but Bronwyn was too afraid to try. When she explained she could only visit towns with angle parking, they shifted their focus to parallel parking, allowing Officer Grande to be the 'Dad in the car'. When that was a failure, they upgraded Officer Grande's skills.

He proved to be a quick learner and peppered them with questions about bodyguard work, envisioning a future with Hollywood starlets.

Toward the end of the week, Clive and Bronwyn put on boxing gloves with Jamie in Bronwyn's corner, encouraging her. They danced around the ring, lightly bobbing and weaving, with Jamie calling for Bronwyn to jab, hook, and launch an occasional uppercut. Enjoying his coaching role, he reminded her to keep her wrists straight and elbows close to her body. As Clive feigned recovery from blows, Jamie yipped at Bronwyn to keep her lead foot in line with the toes of her rear foot. She was listening to Jamie through the ear cut-outs of her soft helmet, trying to ignore her own puffing breath. Clive laughed as he danced and Jamie kept barking out orders, devoutly hoping Bronwyn would wallop him. Through all that, no one noticed Jeeves until he was surging across the gymnasium floor, cursing at Clive. Startled, Bronwyn moved into Clive's glove just as he turned, and his momentum dropped her to the floor. Jeeves swung a chair over his head toward Clive, and Bronwyn screamed, "Jimey".

Jamie snatched the chair with one hand and controlled Jeeves with the other. Clive checked on Bronwyn, lifted her to her feet and jumped out of the ring. In an instant, they were gone, leaving Jeeves and Bronwyn.

She knew Jeeves would ask if she was all right, but he didn't. He shook his head, glaring at her boxing gloves. She pulled them off and turned toward the locker room. When she came out, he was gone and Edgar was waiting for her. They rode the elevator up to the garage.

"I heard there was some excitement, Bronwyn. You're all right?"

"Yes. I'm fine, Edgar. Do you know where Clive and Jamie are?"

"I knew something was up. Saw them running like gazelles. Van Tsang said they're at his place...gonna stay there for a couple of days till Jeeves cools off."

"You're sure? Should I check with Van?"

She spoke with Clive and Jamie on Van's cell phone and they were as glad to hear from her as she was to hear their voices. She didn't understand why they were avoiding Jeeves, but as long as they promised to stay, it made sense they'd be at Van's. Clive admitted Jeeves didn't want her to box and they'd left so he wouldn't be angrier. She assured them she was okay and that things were fine with Jeeves.

Bronwyn asked Edgar where Jeeves was. He said Clara had taken a sandwich up to his room. It was dinnertime and Bronwyn assured Edgar she wasn't hungry. She planned to sit in Jeeves' kitchen until he came down. He nodded, and went to give Clara a report. It was a disturbing turn of events, having Jeeves on the outs with Clive and Jamie.

Clara couldn't help herself. She sat in the Orangerie with Edgar, having supper as a light snow fell. She could see Bronwyn seated at Jeeves' kitchen table.

The poor girl, thought Clara. Surely Jeeves knew she was down there, waiting. Well, if not, Clara would see that he did.

She grabbed her coat and left Edgar in the Orangerie despite his protests. It didn't take her long to walk the short distance, leaving stomped footprints in the skiff of snow.

"Hello, dear," she said loudly. Bronwyn suppressed a smile. It was obvious that Clara had had enough of this foolishness. "I'm going to fix you a nice cup of tea, and I'll make extra for when our man Jeeves comes down."

Surely Jeeves would hear Clara's racket, especially with his bedroom suite right above the kitchen.

Bronwyn thanked Clara for the tea and assured Clara that Jeeves would be down.

Edgar insisted his wife go to bed, but when she arose at 7:30 AM and saw Bronwyn still sitting in Jeeves' kitchen, she became nearly apoplectic. Edgar was just as angry and disappointed in Jeeves, but Clara was no match for him. She gave her husband a look that sent him into his seat, and he watched as Clara strode purposefully across the short path.

"No luck, dear?" Clara inquired, quietly.

"No."

The old woman nodded curtly, strode down the hallway, went up the steps more nimbly than Bronwyn could imagine, and stomped down the hall above her. Bronwyn wondered what state Clara might find Jeeves in, but she knew it wouldn't matter. Clara had a look in her eye that meant she'd take him by his ear even if he was in his drawers.

"You get down those stairs and see that girl. You know very well she's been waiting this whole night to apologize to you. I am ashamed to know you, this day. Ashamed."

Clara's voice had a mother's power. She came storming down the steps, more angry than when she'd mounted them, smiled sweetly to Bronwyn, patted her hand and quietly predicted, "I believe he'll be down, dear."

Bronwyn watched Clara return to the Orangerie, as Edgar joined her. When Bronwyn turned back, Jeeves was in the doorway. "You've come to apologize, Miss?"

Bronwyn stiffly rose, after thirteen stubborn hours in the chair. Jeeves turned to the stove, fussing with tea, while she waited for him to turn back. When he did, Bronwyn met him with a terrible gaze. He couldn't have imagined seeing such black fury on the girl. His mouth dropped slightly open, but she gave him one last withering look, turned and walked down the parquet hall, through his breathtaking living room, and out the door before slamming it shut.

It was almost an invasion of the neighborhood, across the estate. Bronwyn hadn't stayed at Van's since construction years before, and living next door to Tiny and Snooks Von Krinkles was delightful. Despite the cold weather, Clive sat on Tiny's porch, their feet propped up on the railing. Jamie loved Snooks and Bronwyn loved it all. She slept on one of Van's couches, Jamie had the other, and Clive took the spare room. Van utterly enjoyed having their visit and it was a week he would fondly remember into his old age.

Charlie decided to stage a King Street Holiday Basketball Tournament in his basement, and sold tickets. Even Snooks couldn't gain entry without a ticket. Bronwyn was glad she'd convinced Teddy to put in bleachers when they built his house. They were crammed with the ladies of the estate, as well as Tiny and Matthew. As Bronwyn sat, she hoped there wouldn't be a groaning bleacher collapse.

Earlier, Bronwyn had heard Jen and Kristine trying to convince Charlie to play shirts-and-skins, but as promoter he'd declared all team members must purchase t-shirts from Entrepreneur Augie. The Blue team was comprised of Charlie, Clive, Teddy, his brother Mark, and Hughie. Members of the Red team were Ken Cotton, his son Augie, Laurent, Jamie, and Officer Grande. Kristine's daughters, Nicole and Josselyn, were enthusiastic cheerleaders and Edgar created a tasty bill of fare for the refreshment bar...mini lobster rolls, nachos, white cheddar popcorn, homemade chips, and ice cream sandwiches rolled in sprinkles. The game was enthusiastically played, and Bronwyn was happy to see how Jamie and Clive sheltered Charlie and Augie. Luckily for the ladies, it was hot in the basement and t-shirts eventually clung to all of the men.

Tom and Valli's miniature horses were a big draw for Bronwyn and Jamie, and Squirrel Hill was their quiet meeting place, beyond the stables and greenhouses. Clive would join them to walk among the animal gravestones, gazing at the Factory and the sliver of Bronwyn's home, barely in view.

Jeeves and Clive finally reconciled. Bronwyn predicted they'd be sharing a bottle of wine from Jeeves' extensive wine cellar. She was correct about Clive going downstairs into the inner sanctum, but it was Jeeves' secret Operations Room, not the wine cellar. When Clive returned, he met privately with Jamie, and their unforgettable visit was winding to an end.

Edgar served Bronwyn lunch in the lobby. She was pleased to see Jamie, with an odd arrangement of food.

"I've a ploughman's lunch, Bronwyn. Would you care to partake?"

Bronwyn examined the large wedge of cheddar, pickled onions, piccalilli, a hunk of crusty bread, butter, and a Branston pickle, alongside a pint of Guinness. "No thanks," and Bronwyn glanced around. "Is no one else coming?"

"Just us."

Bronwyn sat beside him on the sofa, watching Jamie sip his brew as Edgar entered with a small tray of cheese, sesame crackers, grapes, chilled shrimp, and smoked almonds, setting it in front of Bronwyn. "Told you this was her speed," he said to Jamie.

Jamie smiled fondly at her.

Edgar cleared his throat. "We're having a light lunch, because Jeeves has a surprise for you this evening. Would you like dinner in the dining room or the Silk Club?"

"What do you think, Jimey? I expect you know the surprise."

"The dining room, I think."

Edgar nodded approvingly. "Would you like something special to drink, Bronwyn? A glass of wine?"

Bronwyn began to shake her head, but glancing at Jamie's pint of Guinness, decided to have a glass of Chablis.

She asked Jamie if he had a long history of ploughman's lunches, adding some of her shrimp to his plate. She told him about the Isaly's chipped ham sandwiches she used to have with chocolate milkshakes in Sewickley.

As they munched, Jamie commented on the red poinsettias on either side of the huge fireplace. They were strategically placed in tiers, as if suspended on a slope and Bronwyn was reminded of Pittsburgh's Phipps Conservatory. She told how her friend Oliver Silkowski and his mother always took a holiday cruise, certain she'd be spending the holiday with Judge Wheeler, her quasi-guardian. Judge Wheeler believed the Silkowskis took Bronwyn with them. Bronwyn's only problem was avoiding the hotel staff at the holiday. On Christmas Eve, she generally ate at Penn Avenue Stouffer's.

"Their menu changed daily, but they had potatoes hashed in cream, delmonico potatoes, duchesse potatoes, cottage potato cakes, French-fried cauliflower, carrots vichy, braised Swiss steak, Yankee pot roast, chicken fricassee over cornbread," Bronwyn drew her breath, thinking dreamily.

"Criss cross cherry pie, crêpes Suzette, and chocolate chip chiffon pie. And they always brought you a plate of assorted rolls like orange kuchen, coconut honey squares, rum raisin rolls, pumpkin muffins, cloverleaf rolls, parker house rolls. And, more than that. They had fabulous vegetables and they always served a vegetable plate and I'd order two potatoes and the waitresses would look at me and before they could say anything, I'd say 'yes, two potatoes'…and when you sat at the counter you'd hear the waitresses say to the cooks, 'May I call please?' and they couldn't say anything until the answer was 'yes'. When you ordered a hot fudge sundae, they served the hot fudge in little silver pots and you'd pour your own fudge on. Yourself! And there was a blue plaid room in the back, kind of like my warming room here and the other rooms were elegant and there was a Gentlemen's Dining Room off the lobby and a winding staircase up to an upstairs dining room with an iron railing, if it was really crowded. You'd see newscasters from KDKA sitting at the counter. I can still feel my hand on the revolving door, pushing through it." Bronwyn lifted her hand, in pantomime. "And Horne's Department Store connected through the parking garage, so if it was rainy or snowy you could eat at Stouffer's and go to Horne's and stay dry. And if you went that way, you were right in their candy department."

Jamie grinned. His head was spinning at her stream of consciousness.

"We'll go, Bronwyn. Straight away. Let's go tomorrow."

"Aw, Jimey, I'm sorry. It closed years ago."

Jamie was genuinely disappointed. She patted his hand and took up where she'd left off, a little more slowly.

"Christmas Eve, I'd sneak back into the William Penn and hope I could get in the hotel elevator and down the hall, without anyone noticing. I didn't mind being alone. There honestly wasn't anyone to be with. But if the hotel staff noticed I was alone and not with Judge Wheeler at Christmas, they might have made trouble. Never got caught, though. Early Christmas morning, I'd sneak out and go over to the big churches on Sixth Avenue, across from the Duquesne Club."

She asked Jamie if his family opened gifts on Christmas day or Christmas Eve. He didn't answer and Bronwyn hoped she hadn't made him sad. She told him on Christmas morning, she pretended everyone had already opened their presents the night before, although she was a firm believer in gifts-on-Christmas-morning.

Jamie's face was impassive, but he wanted to cover her mouth with his own and make her stop. He wanted to force every sad and solitary memory from her head, obliterate her desolation. His hands were itching to grab weaponry and unload, but she continued and he remained mute and stoic.

Taking his silence as interest, Bronwyn cheerfully described Pittsburgh at Christmas. Decorations couldn't come soon enough, and Bronwyn was a daily visitor to the department stores as they created their Santa Wonderlands and Secret Santa Shops for children. Shoppers anticipated the animated store windows; there was music in the streets and the excitement was constant from Thanksgiving until Christmas. Bronwyn's eyes sparkled as she spoke of the decorations and finery, getting swept along on the tide of memories. But, she said she was always relieved when Christmas day was over and being alone wasn't obvious. It was always a relief to know the Silkowskis thought she'd been with Judge Wheeler, he was certain she'd been with the Silkowskis, and the hotel staff was never suspicious.

Jamie realized Bronwyn didn't know he and Clive

would be gone before this Christmas. It was almost too much for him to bear. Her pale skin had a pink flush, either a remnant of her Stouffer high, or the heat of the fire. She looked exquisite and trusting. He started to feel warm and then a bit clammy.

Bronwyn asked, "What were you like as a boy, Jimey?" He looked stricken. Then the mask came back on, and he was furious with himself for being vulnerable with her.

She moved against him and softly declared, "I love you, Jimey." She took his face in her hands and kissed him gently and then more deeply. She wanted to distract him from what seemed a sad childhood and was sorry she'd brought it up. In a flash, he leaned over, entwining her hair with one hand and placing his other hand along the small of her back, sweeping her beneath him. She welcomed his long, sweet kisses, glad of the closeness that was overdue. It was thrilling to know he loved her, too. Suddenly, he stopped and sat upright.

"It's the wine, Bronwyn."

Her eyes widened. "I assure you, it's not."

He rose and walked to the windows facing the water, beyond the craggy rocks. She watched as he gazed outward, realizing she'd be content to watch him there, forever.

"It's not me you want, Bronwyn. It's your actor, Jack McClean."

She was taken aback. He was still looking out the window, and she had to raise her voice to be heard across the lobby. It echoed unnaturally. "You're asking me to choose?" Jamie didn't answer. "What if I choose you?"

Jamie walked to the chair where he'd laid his down jacket, and put it on. He went down the hall to her foyer closet and brought a warm jacket, slipping her into it. "Let's take a stroll, Bronwyn."

They found themselves standing at the Adirondack chairs. It was cold and windy and Bronwyn put her hands in her pockets, finding gloves. She wanted to feel hopeful, that she could steer this where she wanted it to go. But, one minute they were generating heat and passion and now here they were, shivering in the gray mist.

"Do you realize you've surrounded yourself with actors and MI6, Bronwyn? We're nearly the same, you know. Actors and operatives and agents. We each pretend. We can be anyone, at any time. The difference is Clive and I are dangerous people. You've no idea where I've been; you've no idea what I've done." He looked searchingly into her eyes. Without blinking, daring her to hold his gaze, he breathed, "It would chill your soul."

Bronwyn turned away, looking out beyond the rocky cliff protecting her estate. There was nothing welcoming about those huge rock formations, jagged and every shade of gray. But, the water was always beckoning.

"You know you're different here, Jimey. You know life on this side of the wall is different." She turned and smiled at him, without reservation. He basked in the warmth of her smile and might have given in, if he hadn't brought them out to the cold and chilly reality of the Maine coast in December.

When he didn't answer, she asked quietly, "Why do you think I should be with Jack? He's never been here. We're not together for a reason." She waited for him to say something. "Why would you think I'd choose him over you?"

Jamie was relieved to get an easy question. He practically beamed at her. "Because you stood and applauded at the end of his flick."

Expecting her to smile with realization, Jamie was alarmed to see her eyes filling with tears. She held them back when other girls would have blinked to send them tumbling, and Jamie felt his heart skip. "You mean because I clapped, we can't be together?"

Jamie realized that Bronwyn took single instances to have great import, and perhaps she was right. Maybe her world was laden with missteps and right steps. He took her hands in his and warned, "Bronwyn, if we were together today, and we can go back and be together, right now. But, if we were together today, I could never come back here." He shook his head as he said, "Never."

He watched as she weighed her options, not certain which answer he wanted to hear.

"You can be with Jack, and Clive and I could jolly well put up with your whisking, tea cozy actor. We don't have to lose what we've had, on this side of the wall." He stared into her eyes, drinking her in, and she thought she'd never see such unearthly blue eyes again. "We could always come back. I could come back."

He was imploring her and Bronwyn saw how much he appreciated the days they'd spent together. Those days were as potent for him, as they were to her. She nodded several times and turned back to the water. Jamie stood behind her and wrapped his arms around her like a bat, warming her with his body. He leaned into her hair as it blew in the wind and whispered, "I do love you, Bronwyn," his breath warm in her ear.

Clara wasn't the only one watching Jamie and Bronwyn. Jeeves was watching from his kitchen window, nodding and calculating. He heard Graeme's voice in the hallway as Van Tsang ushered him in.

"What a capital idea, Jeeves. Bronwyn doesn't know I've come?"

That evening, Graeme surprised Bronwyn while Edgar

presented a lavish pre-Christmas dinner for her with Clive, Jamie, Jeeves, and Clara.

Jen had decorated the long table with shimmering candelabra, and crystal vases filled with ruby red cranberries supporting beautiful cream roses. Small Christmas trees decorated each sideboard and a large Father Christmas figure stood sentry. The menu was traditionally English with prime rib, braised carrots, crispy potatoes, Yorkshire pudding, soul-satisfying wassail, and a flaming Yule log. There was plenty of laughter and fire-lit golden faces.

Unable to resist, Bronwyn and Jamie shyly exchanged glances whenever the table was most jolly and least likely to notice. They shared secret knowledge of the kisses that warmed their hearts.

Graeme announced he'd only come for the surprise and had to fly back to New York. He promised to be back soon for his usual Scotch eggs and jelly omelettes. Graeme kissed Bronwyn goodbye and walked to the Factory with Jamie and Clive.

"I saw the two of you at dinner, mate." He winked at Jamie. "Something going on between you and our Bronwyn?"

Jamie shook his head, but when Graeme had gone to the airstrip with Van, Clive was quick to pounce.

"So?"

Knowing there was no point in denying it, Jamie admitted, "I'm done for. She's kissed me."

Clive softly whistled and gave him an amiable hug. "Join the club. What do you think she meant by it? She wanted me to return."

"I'm certain that's it."

Clive detected a miserable note in Jamie's tone, but let it go.

The next morning, Bronwyn walked toward the Factory. She expected to see Jamie in sweats, but he was wearing a suit and an elegant topcoat.

Jamie's eyes were sad. "I have to leave, Bronwyn. Sorry."

Bronwyn halted.

Jamie came to her. "Let's be chipper, shall we? I've had a grand time."

"I thought you'd be here for Christmas." Her disappointment was evident.

"I'm so sorry…I've a job to do."

He wasn't prepared to see the joy drain out of her.

She remembered something and chirped, "Wait here. I have your Christmas present. Promise you'll be right here when I get back. Promise."

Jamie nodded. She kept turning as she walked back to her house, checking to see if he was still there. When she got to the door, she yelled, "Stay there. Promise." And Jamie was sadder than he could have imagined, that she would think he'd leave one moment sooner than he had to.

Once in the house, Bronwyn flew up the stairs to her dressing room. She already had his gifts ready, but looked inside to make sure all was in order. She snatched a note card, put extra lip-gloss on, kissed the card and quickly blotted it for permanence. Satisfied, she placed it in the bag and tied it shut. She ran down the long hallway to the bathroom and looked out the window making sure he was still there and then descended the stairs a little more slowly, knowing he had waited.

She handed him the bag. "Here you go, Jimey. Don't

open it until Christmas, okay? It has a timer on it, so I'll know if you cheated."

"A timer? With Matthew's assistance?"

Bronwyn laughed and shook her head. "Just kidding. I wanted you to think I'd learned some sneaky spy secrets."

Jamie examined the gift bag with its red dachshund dressed in a green sweater. His throat had a lump in it and he knew he'd never feel this way again. He hadn't lost his edge, he was certain of that. He'd use his hostility, anger, and disappointment to fuel him and be more controlled and capable than ever. His moments of indulgent vulnerability were about to end. He gripped the bag and turned away to the stone wall fronting the estate. It had indeed cast a certain magic, just as Clive promised it would. When Jamie glanced back, Bronwyn had gathered herself. She pulled his head firmly down and whispered in his ear, "Come back to me."

He unveiled his wide elfin smile, nodded and promised, "When you least expect it."

A little more than a week later, Clive was preparing to leave. He'd be gone before Christmas, but that didn't surprise Bronwyn. As soon as Jamie had gone, her expectations for a wonderful Christmas evaporated. She expected Clive would go.

They strolled the grounds, settling into the Adirondack chairs. Discussing love and life, hopes and dreams, Clive promised he'd return to live there every day if she had a place for him. Bronwyn pointed to Joseph's empty cottage beside the loggia, and suggested that would be a perfect home.

She urged Clive to leave MI6, but as much as she wanted

him to return to Maine, she said she didn't want to stand in the way of his happiness.

"I expect I'll be back within the year, Bronwyn, but no matter what, I plan to breathe my last breaths, here. At this very place. I'll get here eventually, I promise you that. This is the home I love."

"I'll be here, Clive." She left her chair and dropped into his lap, just as she'd done the day the other wayward boy arrived.

With the visitors gone, Van Tsang worried about Bronwyn, so he asked Katrin to prepare a holiday tea at his house. He hoped it wouldn't make Bronwyn's solitude worse, since memories of Clive and Jamie seemed to reverberate in his glass house.

Happily, she enjoyed reminiscing about the week they'd spent together at Van's. There was a serious moment, however, when Bronwyn implored Van to tell her if Clive and Jamie were safe.

"Of course, Bronwyn," he assured her earnestly. "Jeeves' strength was always in operations, planning. He was better suited to private protection. They're different. Clive is one of the best agents I've ever seen. He and Jamie know everything about weapons and they're killer fit. They're expert in survival, evasive driving, extrication, climbing, parachuting, explosives, combat, warfare in desert and snow. You've no reason to worry."

"You said Clive is one of the best. Jimey's not as good?"

Van looked down and spread his hands on his knees. Bronwyn expected Jamie was vulnerable in certain situations, and her heart sank. She waited to hear the words she knew were coming.

"I know you're fond of him, Bronwyn. When Ernest needed someone top shelf, he called on Clive. He always succeeded."

Van took a sip and drew a deep breath in, blowing it out. Bronwyn braced herself.

"Jamie's a killer, Bronwyn. An assassin when they need him to be. He's everything Clive is and more. Sometimes their assignments have nothing to do with kills, but if it does, he's ready. It's not as if Clive isn't an assassin, too, but Jamie is ruthless. Clive is one of the best, but Jamie is hands-down, the best I've ever known. If you're wondering if you should worry about either of them, don't. I'm not. They'll both be fine."

Van Tsang feared he'd changed her opinion about Clive and most of all, Jamie. Perhaps he'd betrayed them both. She looked nonplussed.

"Now I won't worry quite as much." She smiled sweetly at him. "You're sure they're that good?"

Van nodded. Bronwyn was gratefully reassured and they began another round of scones and Devonshire cream.

She'd brought Christmas gifts for Tiny and the children on King Street, and they went door to door, dropping them off. She was glad to have Van's company. Snooks and Tiny would be having Christmas Eve supper and Christmas dinner across the street at Tom and Valli's. Tiny was as content to stay near his new home as Valli was to remain in hers. Lucky for Snooks, they'd take her into the stable to visit the miniature horses. She loved being noisily, Queen of All She Surveys.

On Christmas Eve day, Sam brought over a heavy box from Moss, a gift from Graeme, boxes from Scotland and Ireland, packages from Samuel and Paul, and one from Mama Lou.

Bronwyn saved them all for Christmas morning, and put them at the foot of her bed, beside a tissue-wrapped ball of something from Tiny and Snooks Von Krinkles.

She filled a stocking, placing an orange in the toe, just as her mother had always done, a box of nonpareils, a small piece of jewelry, socks and lip-gloss. She always considered it a blessing that she could pretend to be surprised by her Santa stocking.

Bronwyn and Jeeves enjoyed oyster stew with Common Crackers floating on top. Edgar had made a crème caramel for dessert and it was all quite comforting. Back home, she settled in with popcorn and cashews to watch Jack's chef movie again, and fell asleep, trying to imagine where Jack, Clive and Jamie were this Christmas Eve.

Christmas morning, she tackled the packages and boxes. Snooks and Tiny were first. Tiny had given her a fuzzy purple scarf from Jackson's. That little dickens, Snooks Von Krinkles, had given her a dachshund calendar. Bronwyn was delighted with both gifts and called Tiny right away. He breathlessly giggled, telling her all about choosing her gifts. He said he was wearing green pants for Christmas dinner and Bronwyn thought how nice it was for Jess Jackson to order his size in green. Bronwyn wished Tiny a Happy Christmas, and she listened as he gave Snooks Von Krinkles a very loud and sloppy kiss for her.

Back to the boxes. Mama Lou sent homemade caramel fudge (Bronwyn's favorite), divinity, and a large tin of roasted pecans. Samuel sent three mysteries. Paul's gift was a beautiful equestrian scarf and a photo of the Secret Garden Snowman with Jamie, Clive, Bronwyn, and the boys kneeling in front. She gazed wistfully for several minutes.

Moss's heavy box held a collection of Bobbi Brown

makeup from Mrs. Mastrofrancesco, and a pink and turquoise majolica oyster plate from Moss. Inside was a package of books from Jack – *Watership Down, The Wind in the Willows, Irish Fairy Tales, Inside the All Blacks Rugby, Ernest Hemingway on Writing, Key West – a Tropical Lifestyle* and *Respect for Acting by Uta Hagen,* with notes in each.

Graeme's gift was an antique bowl with silver walnut feet and two silver squirrels perched on the handles, munching on silver nuts. It was exquisite.

Clive's small box, post-marked from Ireland, held a beautifully wrapped antique photo of a boy and his dog, much like the one she'd shown him in the library. She put it right beside her bed, and then opened the last box.

It was from Jamie. The box was broad, but lightweight, and when she opened it she recognized the bright plaid of her McCall tartan woven into a gorgeous throw. As she wrapped it around her, thinking of Jamie wrapping his arms around her down at the water, she saw a small photo album at the bottom of the box. Her eyes widened. Flipping it open, Bronwyn was stunned to see the first picture of Jamie, standing in front of The Hotel Hershey. The next photo was of Jamie in a handsome pin-striped suit, seated at a window table in the Circular Dining Room. The next photo was of his fabulous meal, set before him. The longer she studied the photo, she realized there were two potato selections on the plate, a whipped potato of some kind and a potato hash. She shook her head, lovingly. Then he was standing in the snowy hotel gardens, like an adventurer in his hooded parka. The next showed him on the front steps of the Hershey School with Hershey bars fanned in his hands. Others showed him seated in the Chocolate World ride with two wary children, perched on a kiss shaped streetlamp, holding two gray wolf pups at the Hershey Zoo, and standing amidst the twinkle lights at Candylane. The last showed Jamie surrounded by poinsettias at the tile fountain of the famous lobby, wearing a red sweater and his elfin grin.

It was almost an O. Henry moment. Her gifts to Jamie were a four-pound box of Harbor Candy from Ogunquit, and after much persuasion and a large monetary donation, Milton Hershey's wrist watch, engraved with Milton Snavely Hershey on the back.

It was a winter of contemplation and reflection. Bronwyn missed Clive and Jamie, but found solace in the hope of seeing them again.

She enjoyed Jack McClean's current film project, vicariously. He wrote in great detail about Ernest Hemingway, and was meticulously doing the work to bring life to the film.

The co-star playing Hadley had inspired Jack mightily, and Bronwyn was relieved to know Kate was happily married. However, the actress playing Mary Hemingway was difficult for him to work with.

He wrote that Bronwyn's letters helped him find balance in his days. She eagerly anticipated every letter, and read the most recent one in her snuggery.

25 Feb

Dearest Dai,

I was laughing so hard when you told me Ginger/Mary Ann, you choose Ginger. I had to ask Able Assistant Dick what you were talking about! When he explained it to me and you wrote F. Scott/Ernest and you 'used' to choose the Gatsby himself but were now embracing Good Old Ernest, I was deeelighted. I hope you're not the only one I convert.

Oh, my love, Sarah is no Sarah Bernhardt. She's driving me barking mad. Why she thinks showing up is sufficient, I'll never know, but I fear my ugly old monster has been rearing up from time to time. I can't bear it. She's physically uncoordinated and obsessed with looking the 'Elle' version of Mary Hemingway. For chrissakes, it's not a photo shoot, it's a bloody film. She has no focus or attention to mechanical details. Yet she's quick to tell me she has a People's Choice. A what?

Well, I've had my share of face time with Mr. Director and he assures me she won't drag the film down. Honestly my love, I think it may well be a very good film. And, happily, shooting with silly Sarah is done as of tomorrow. I must admit, I have mixed feelings about our shooting the end of Ernest, so near the end of filming. I'd give anything, anything if I could somehow change history and take that gun away from his head. I'm inordinately fond of the man.

I enjoyed your tale of Tiny and

Snooks Von Krinkles. I hope I can come for a visit sometime and see Snookie get the better of him. She sounds brilliant and from the little photo you sent of her in her red-haired glory, she looks a fine bit of stuff.

I'm glad you're still enjoying the books. Mum says she's made six recipes from your little Kitchen Fun *book. Do you think for even a moment, that I parted with it? Never!!! I copied the pages and posted them to her. You've bedazzled her, Bronwyn, absobloominlutely bedazzled her. And her son.*

I've a script to study, but know that I love you every moment of every day, dear one.

Your Wren

"Well, that's that. It's official. I'll tell her, Jeeves," Moss said, when the waiting was over for CNN to announce the news.

"I'm happy to do it."

"I'm aware of that, Jeeves. Does she know I've been here?"

"No, shall I tell her you're coming over, Moss?" asked Van Tsang.

"Let's wait a few minutes. I'll have another drink."

"Hello, Bronwyn," Moss said, as he entered her snuggery. Bronwyn put Jack's letter on the table.

"Hi, Moss! I didn't know you were here. You're visiting Susie and Oz?"

"A short visit. I was hungry for lobster."

"That's nice. Do you have plans? Shall I check with Edgar and see about dinner? Oh, I know. Let's go up to Lewiston and surprise Allison. Jeeves and I took her to Fuel for dinner last month; it was terrific. Or we could go to Duckfat in Portland."

"Bronwyn," Moss began, tentatively.

"You should have seen Jeeves last time. He actually slurped his Moxie Float – you could hear him! I was much better behaved with my Sea Salt Caramel Milkshake. And of course we had Paninis and Belgian fries. We brought churros and beignets home."

Moss opened his mouth, but nothing came out.

"Oh, and I picked up a cashmere cloche for Allison with a velvet band. From the Queen of Hats shop in Portland. If you go up, you could give it to her."

When he lifted his eyes, Bronwyn saw he was troubled.

"What's wrong?"

"You know, when I was in prep school, my favorite teacher was my biology instructor. Years later, he got his Ph.D. and became a university chancellor."

"And you kept in touch with him."

"I did. Off and on. But the odd thing is, he retired a few years ago and the newspaper article talked about his love of turtles."

"Turtles."

"Yes, he collected turtles of all kinds, plush toys, marble, ceramic, jade. And he had turtles at home – something called red-eared sliders."

"Neat."

"But, the turtles were the story. More than his work as chancellor, I'm afraid."

"He probably liked sharing the turtles."

"I wonder what I'll be remembered for, Bronwyn." It wasn't a question, it was a sad reflection.

Bronwyn waited.

"I've just learned some news Bronwyn, and I'm afraid it might be upsetting. Or, perhaps a relief, I don't know." He took her hand.

"What is it?"

"Oakley Forse died on a ski slope in Vail. Heart attack."

Chapter Thirty

The Fox
2007

$\mathcal{C}$harlie watched a fox weave its way through the lush spring growth of Oz valley. Although there were plenty of squirrels, chipmunks, and rabbits, he'd never seen a fox before – not even up on Squirrel Hill. He walked along the bike path and waited until it crossed the stream. Then he leaped across. There was something odd about the fox; he seemed a little wobbly. Charlie didn't know if seeing a fox in the middle of the day was a bad thing, so he gave it a wide berth, just in case.

If Alex Oz King's dogs were out, this slow fox might have a hard time staying out of their way. Newfie would outrun him for sure and although Duchess was slower, even she might get him. Charlie listened for the dogs. When he turned back to see the fox, he was surprised to see it had climbed the long hill and emerged beyond the Island House.

Bronwyn was sitting in front of the Adirondack chairs when she saw the fox. She didn't question that he was headed straight for her. His breathing was labored as he crawled into her lap and laid his head down, just as a dog would do. She marveled at the look of him and felt a groundswell of emotion, reassuring him and holding him gently as he died.

Charlie ran up, shouting, "Bronwyn, get away. Get away from him. He probably has rabies!"

But Bronwyn cradled the fox and didn't look at Charlie.

He came closer, more anxious. "Is he dead? Bronwyn, is that fox dead? You've gotta leave him and come with me. He probably has rabies."

Bronwyn looked stern. "Go away, Charlie. I'm fine. Just go away."

Charlie ran for the Island House, called his dad at Clara's and ran over, filling them in. "Dad, Bronwyn looked at me, mean. She never does that. Maybe she already has rabies. Maybe the fox bit her."

Teddy ran down the lawn, stopping several feet from Bronwyn, taking in the scene. Something about her stillness stopped him; he knew how she felt about animals. Clara caught up with tears in her eyes.

"Oh dear."

Teddy approached Bronwyn.

"Hey, Bronwyn. See you have a little fox there. Why don't you let me take him, maybe I can help."

Bronwyn shook her head.

"He's dead." Her voice was low, almost a growl. "Go away."

Clara motioned to Teddy that she was going over.

"Oh dear, my dear. I'm so sorry. He's really lovely. Let Teddy have him, Bronwyn. Let Teddy take him away."

Bronwyn turned with a meanness that surprised Clara.

"Leave us," Bronwyn barked.

Charlie lingered around the back of the Island House,

watching. His father backed up toward the Factory, taking Clara by the elbow, and called Jeeves.

A few minutes later, Teddy walked the same path as before, addressing Bronwyn, while Jeeves moved stealthily behind her, laying her backward when the injection had done its work.

Alex Oz King came up the hill and carried her limp body back home while Teddy gathered the dead fox for its ride to the clinic, hoping it wouldn't test positive for rabies.

A cautious Doc Larchmont treated Bronwyn. She'd been furious when she awakened in her bed and refused to speak to Jeeves or Teddy, after warning Teddy to keep Charlie away. When Clara haltingly mounted the stairs to Bronwyn's bedroom, Bronwyn stopped her from speaking when she brought up the fox.

Each time Bronwyn awakened, she could still feel the fox in her arms. She knew the look in his glittering black and gold eyes as he crawled onto her lap, the feel of his beautiful red fur beneath her hand, the shudder of his body as he drew his last breath. Nothing would have made her give the fox up, and because she knew that to be true, she realized Jeeves had to do his sneaky best. The secret needle. The injection ploy. The 'distract Bronwyn and we'll tranquilize her trick'. She hated them for it. She'd had a sense of utter peace as that fox crawled into her lap. She wasn't surprised to see him; he wasn't surprised to see her. The fox walked over and she welcomed him and no one should have taken him away. It was a profound sadness that she would have to overcome, but she felt the same fury for Charlie, Teddy, Clara, and Jeeves every day, undiminished.

The tests were back. The fox didn't have rabies.

Bronwyn stayed in her room. Doc read quietly on her balcony most afternoons, hoping he was company for her. Grace and the other women had heard what a foul mood Bronwyn was in, so they decided to delay visiting until she cheered up.

After a week, Jeeves asked her to come downstairs as Teddy had come by for coffee. They expected Bronwyn to reject the invitation, but she was tired of the same four walls. Jeeves heard her moving around and they waited in the kitchen, watching the bottom of the staircase. When Bronwyn reached the bottom, she disappeared from view and Jeeves smirked at Teddy. He'd told him she had great instincts. They left the kitchen and looked in the library. She was on her knees at the fireplace. Jeeves cleared his voice and Bronwyn stood, with a broad smile on her face and the preserved fox at her feet.

Teddy had taken the fox to the taxidermist to be freeze-dried, when it was released from animal control.

Bronwyn hugged Teddy. "I'm so glad he's here. Thank you," she said, warmly.

"Can I send Charlie over to see him, Bronwyn? He tracked him, you know. He was amazed to see a fox on our land. He'll be really surprised to see him, and he'll be happy for you."

"Sure, Teddy. I need to tell him I'm sorry."

And with that, Teddy left to track down Charlie.

"He's a fine looking creature, Miss."

If Jeeves was waiting for an apology, it wasn't forthcoming.

"You should know what this fox means to me, Jeeves," she challenged him.

"Really, Miss?" Jeeves stood with his legs apart and his arms folded, reflecting. "Nothing comes to mind. Our paths have yet to cross with a fox."

"I assumed you'd read my file," she answered, sitting beside her beloved fox, stroking his head and touching its ears, not knowing if Jeeves had a file on her, but suspecting he did.

Jeeves returned to his flat and walked downstairs to his Operations Room. He needed to get his hands on her file. As he read, nothing struck him, but when he closed and reopened it, he saw it. Her mother's maiden name was Fox. Maggie Fox McCall.

"So, you believe your mother became reincarnated as this fox? Twenty eight years later?"

"No, Jeeves, I'm saying my mother sent this fox as a sign that she knows where I am and that she's with me."

Jeeves nodded, with a patronizing half smile. It was the first time he regarded her as an eccentric millionaire. He hoped it wasn't the start of things to come.

"I've waited all my life for some sign from my family, that they're with me. I've waited since I was eight years old. When that fox walked up the hill, he knew me and I knew him. It was the same feeling you have with family, with someone you love."

Bronwyn wanted him gone, so she said, "Thank you, Jeeves. I know you had something to do with this, too. It makes all the difference, having him here with me."

She gave Jeeves a bright, yet insincere smile. He nodded curtly, and left. They both knew injecting her had been an unforgivable offense.

Bronwyn had never told Jeeves about her near-death experience and seeing the prime minister's brother, David. She'd always been angry that none of her own family had been there to meet her. Why had David and the dog named Pal been there, and not her mother or her father? But now she had a sense of peace, with the fox. She wasn't so alone anymore.

Back at the flat, Jeeves made a notation in his log about the taxidermist's delivery. Flipping the pages to review the past two weeks, he realized it had been difficult, waiting for Bronwyn to right herself.

Bronwyn and the women of the estate planned a Ladies' Sleepover in the Factory's third floor. It had been a long time since they'd had one, and Bronwyn wanted to show the ladies she was fine, and that she was sorry. She invited Vicki, and Charlie was so delighted that he'd carried her bag. He lingered so long that Bronwyn was tempted to make it a 'Ladies and *Charlie* Sleepover'.

The women staked out their sleeping quarters. Climbing the loft stairs, Linda and Vicki leaned over the ornate iron balcony. Their larger bedrooms had exposed-brick and were perched atop three bedrooms with false-front shop windows. They waved and called to Sam and Jen, while Bronwyn and Grace were deep in conversation beside the nostalgic soda fountain.

Gathering around the fireplace and lounging on various couches, the ladies began their gabfest.

"Why does a yellow traffic light mean 'go'?" Katrin asked the others.

"Haven't you ever noticed how if you go through as it's turning red, two more cars are right behind you?" Linda complained. "It's like, if they see any movement at all, they just keep going. They don't even look at the light."

Clara nibbled chocolate chip cookies. "And, why do they keep adding so much seasoning to food? Don't tell Edgar I said so, but I'm an old woman. I don't want so many flavors."

They giggled, glad Edgar wasn't around. Linda nodded toward Jeeves, hovering behind the kitchen area. "I can get rid of him. Watch," she whispered.

"And what's with those tampons? I mean they say cardboard applicators, plastic applicators, but it's all the same. It's three inches of..." Linda trailed off and then cackled as Jeeves entered the elevator.

Katrin took crêpe orders.

"Did you notice how I'm fading?" Linda asked.

The women prepared to hear a litany of examples.

"Everything about me. I'm just disappearing. I see gray hairs in the rear view mirror and pull them out and let them flutter out the window and some poor guy behind me wonders why it's raining gray hair. My feet are longer, my earlobes keep dropping. My earlobes are going to reach my shoulders. And my lips have fallen into my mouth. Did you know that? Your lips don't get thin; they fall into your mouth just like gravity makes everything else fall." They nodded, but crêpe-making Katrin couldn't have played along as she was too young for gravity issues.

Vicki jumped in. "I'd like to know what kind of meeting people had when cell phones were invented. Did someone say people could die if they're using their phone while driving? And did they say who cares?" Vicki was good at the rants. "No one would ever text and drive at the same time, and did someone say who cares? I wish I'd been at those meetings."

Sam Brown asked, "If walking is so good for you, why

aren't all women golfers skinny? No one walks more than they do."

"I know! I think of that when Edgar has the golf on. Even some of those men golfers are quite stout," Clara said, shaking her head.

Katrin passed the crêpes.

"Has anyone else noticed how pie crust mixes don't work the way they used to?" Kristine asked. There was general agreement, although Katrin looked perplexed.

Linda was still musing about the effects of getting old. "One day, out of the blue, I found two bristly hairs sprouting from my chin. I'm not kidding," she assured them.

"I shave them off with a little mini shaver, but once, I got out the tweezers and plucked them. It was bad after the first one, but after the second one I dropped to my knees from the pain and begged myself for mercy." Linda shuddered with the memory. "Do you girls realize how much time I used to spend, shaving my legs? I mean, every time I went to the pool..."

Grace interrupted. "I thought you didn't swim."

"I didn't swim, but I still bought the cutest bathing suit I could find every summer. Anyway, I spent half my life shaving away and guess what?"

Clara predicted, "I know what you're going to say."

"It's like I don't have any hair on my legs, at all. Really. Feel..."

Jen ventured over as Linda lifted her pant leg.

"She's right. Smooth as silk. That's weird."

Linda cocked her head, feeling old.

"I've been thinking. America should halt the space program and use that money for the hungry and homeless," Bronwyn suggested.

"I don't think Charlie would agree, Bronwyn. You know he's obsessed with outer space," Vicki reminded her.

Bronwyn smiled. "Only Charlie could put me on the fence about world hunger. But space exploration is a luxury – especially with the state of the world."

Linda raised her fork, hesitated, and put it down. "I can't believe my reflection when I pass store windows. I'm dumpy."

Bronwyn immediately protested, "You are absolutely not dumpy. You carry yourself so well, and no one has glossier hair."

The women jumped in, offering their own compliments.

"You're all just being kind."

"I mean it, Linda," Bronwyn assured her. "And, anyway, is there a better moment than in *Bridget Jones's Diary* when Darcy says he likes her just as she is? We should all like ourselves, just as we are."

"Well I don't think Mr. Darcy would like me just as I am, if he caught sight of my jiggly underarms. It looks like frozen peas swinging inside. It's horrible."

Katrin rose to make another round of crêpes.

A moment later Bronwyn asked, "Do you think Chap-Stick is addictive? I can't go to sleep if I don't put ChapStick on. I mean, I lie there and it calls to me."

The crêpes were ready, but the evening's conversation continued. Later, the women interrupted their thoughts on the world, for toasted almond ice cream sundaes. Nothing got resolved, but their bonds were strengthened by laughter and sharing.

A week later, Jeeves received a call from John Joseph. Jeeves didn't expect anyone from MI6 to visit him in Maine. Nevertheless, he and Van Tsang prepared for the meeting.

After greeting one another, MI6 Director John Joseph nodded to Van, who made himself scarce. The soft-spoken man watched Ernest Rose carefully, as he told him of Clive Grove's recent death in an IRA bombing. Ernest seemed to take the news in stride, and John Joseph wasn't surprised. Rose was an inscrutable man. He handed him a small box of Clive's remains and a wristwatch, surprisingly intact. Ernest turned it over and saw 'DA' engraved on the back. His eyes closed, just briefly.

Van returned to the room, carrying a tray of glasses and two bottles of whiskey. Edgar delivered Dagwood sandwiches and the three men from MI6 settled into a game of poker. Swapping tales well into the night, they shared a warm camaraderie.

Laughing about their time together in Columbia, John Joseph pointed at Jeeves. "You and Clive were such a pair on that mission, Ernest."

"I didn't have much faith in you, to tell the truth," Van said, laughing merrily. "So reserved."

"When Clive got that girl with the long legs involved…"

"He was so bold. You were tight Ernest, no other way to say it. We called you 'the Box'. You were so closed, and Clive was so wily and clever. The box and the fox, both deft in your own ways, approaching everything so differently. But, the outcome was always there. A good team, Ernest. A good team. Did you ever work together, again?" asked John Joseph.

"Just twice more. But not as jolly as Columbia. That girl with the legs…no one can forget her."

"Amen."

John Joseph stayed with Van Tsang that night. Jeeves made motions of going home, but he walked back to King Street, and threaded his way to Squirrel Hill. He stopped at the tool shed for a shovel, and despite wearing one of his beautiful David Chu Bespoke suits, he dug a small grave for Clive's remains. Jeeves' eyes were moist as he turned the watch over in his hands; it shined brightly in the moonlight. An IRA bomb had taken every bit of the Clive he knew and loved, but here was his watch. To bury it, or keep it. He turned it over and over and over. Finally, he took his pocket square and gently folded it around the watch, placing it on top of the small box and covered them with dirt. He placed a stone, six inches across, atop the grave. If he left it unmarked, someone would bury an animal there one day. This would warn anyone away from it. Already taken. Already filled with a life once lived.

Feeling every one of his sixty six years, Jeeves went down to his secret Operations Room and took his seat. He recalled the last time he sat there with Clive.

"The prime minister says to me, 'why does this man live?' and Clive, I can't tell him. I can't answer."

"Why not?"

"Because when I posed it to Bronwyn, she said, 'is there ever enough money? Is there ever enough?'"

It was a necessary lie. Bronwyn's disinterest in money plagued Jeeves.

If only Clive hadn't returned to Ireland one last time, he mused. Jeeves took out his log and flipped through the pages, reliving Clive's visit to Maine. He'd jotted *Bronwyn took C to L.L. Bean; C has his first clam bake; C and J beat S and P at racquetball; C and E have Lazy Man's Lobster at*

Splash's. Jeeves walked through the door to his wine cellar and opened an old burgundy. Pouring himself a glass, he went back to his desk and turned the pages of the log, then closed it. With a deep sigh, he opened it again, turning back to April 5, steeling himself to write *'C dies'* beneath another entry. He wrote *'C dies'* before he glanced up to see he'd already written *Bronwyn's fox dies* on that date.

"I'll type the letter, Van, but I rather think the envelope should have Clive's handwriting. Can you manage it? These are letters he wrote to me."

"I'll write the letter, no problem. Come back this afternoon. Are we going to have it posted from London?"

"No, you'll see Dublin should do."

Van Tsang put his hand on Ernest's shoulder, and then watched him walk down the street, turning up to Squirrel Hill. Ernest had already asked Jen to put miniature rose bushes on the animal graves; that much Van knew. He was touched by Ernest's sentimentality...not that Clive didn't mean the world to Ernest. Van noted where Ernest's path led him. He would make his own trek up there, as soon as he forged the letter.

Dear Bronwyn,

I hope this letter won't come as a shock to you, but I know you'll be happy for me. I have found my childhood sweetheart, and I've been able to change my identity and begin a new life. I know you've always wanted me to be happy, just as I've wanted you to be happy. I hope you are. It seems a grand life in Maine.

We had a small wedding and we've settled in a very remote part of Ireland. It's a beautiful place.

I wish I could say we could see each other again, but it's not possible. It's not safe for me and my new family. Not an option. You wouldn't even recognize me, anyway. New face. Even a new voice. Amazing what they can do.

Promise me that you will take great care of yourself. You know what you mean to me. Think of all the chats we've had and you'll know how much I truly thank you – ever so much – for showing me the way to a new life.

Being with you was one of the very best things that ever happened to me. Say hello to Samuel and Paul when you get a chance. I won't forget all the moments we've shared, Bronwyn. I hope you will remember them, too.

Fondly,
Clive

Van had made a few changes to Jeeves' script, and when he was done, Jeeves couldn't challenge him. The handwriting was masterful. They reviewed the letter, slipped it into Van's envelope and made arrangements for its posting.

A week later, they began to worry about Bronwyn's reaction. When 'Clive's' letter arrived, they hovered in Jeeves' flat, peering out the triple glazed glass windows. It seemed ironic they'd be doing surveillance behind windows patterned after 'Legoland' – the Secret Intelligence Service's building. It heightened the tension. Did they expect to see a puff of smoke? A prostrate Bronwyn, falling out her front door? Hear a scream?

Edgar asked Van if he was joining Bronwyn and Jeeves for lunch. Van hesitated. Would it seem unusual? They decided to risk it; both concerned about her reaction. Lunch in the Orangerie, and hopefully, Bronwyn would come over. Neither held out much hope for her appetite. Jeeves requested Lobster Club Sandwiches. If anything could tempt Bronwyn, it was always lobster.

They needn't have worried. She seemed fine, handing Clive's letter to them as they ate.

"I suspect you already know this, Jeeves," she said with a smile. "I'm glad. Do you know the girl?"

"I'm afraid not, Miss, but he sounds pleased I think, don't you Van?"

"He does. I hope you're not too disappointed, Bronwyn."

"I'm happy for him. Truly. Right before he left, I told Clive to come back if he wanted to, but the important thing was to leave service and be safe." Bronwyn had a bite of mango flan with coconut and caramel. "Anyway, he told me no matter what he decided to do, he'd come back at the end. He promised he'd come back to die here. I know he'll get back eventually."

Jeeves stared at her.

"It's okay, Jeeves. Really. I adore Clive. I want him to be happy." She looked intently at Jeeves. "You're probably disappointed, too. You think he is really underground? Surely, you'll be in touch with him, Jeeves?"

"Not once he's gone under, Miss. He's on his own, now,"

Jeeves had a sad expression. "But he's safe. No harm can come to him now."

Van looked away. It was difficult closing the chapter on Clive. Just like the other MI6 expatriates, Van was reminded how vulnerable to sentiment they were, behind Bronwyn's stone wall.

Bronwyn nudged Jeeves. "I've an idea. I think it will cheer us up."

"Tell us," encouraged Van Tsang, always happy to hear Bronwyn's ideas.

"I want to have an 'in absentia' wedding reception for him…at the Silk Club. We'll invite everyone from the estate, Splash Flanagan's family, Jess and Jane Jackson, the people over at Bergamot, Graeme, Officer Grande and his wife, our neighbors."

She noted that Jeeves looked less than enthusiastic, but that was his normal demeanor.

"Jeeves, we can have Guinness. And, we'll bring in an Irish group to play music and I might even dance! It'll be a celebration. We'll have a wedding cake and a chocolate groom's cake and we'll hire a photographer. Maybe you can find where to send him the pictures. It'll be great."

As plans were made and the day approached, Bronwyn took Grace to Lancaster. She'd spent an enormous sum to have an Amish quilt made on short notice for Clive and his bride – hand quilted navy and burgundy velvet.

Bronwyn ordered Waterford Crystal goblets, and netted Jordan almonds were attached assembly-line style by Linda and the ladies. It was surprising how much fun the event was becoming without the angst of a bride.

The bands were staying on the Factory third floor, and once Graeme and his wife were invited, he arranged to bring Conor Frost's family as a surprise. Bronwyn hoped Jeeves could find Jamie Donald somewhere in the world, but even Jeeves couldn't pull that off. Jamie was deep in an operation; so deep that Jeeves feared Van Tsang would be forging another letter.

The Silk Club was dressed in white dotted Swiss and white organdy. Tartan plaids festooned the beams and draped the tables as runners. Flowers were everywhere. Older varieties of peonies were showcased in the Silk Club's lobby, a voluptuous hint of things to come. Large vases of hyacinths, hellebores, sweet peas and black parrot tulips adorned the food tables. Each female guest was given a demure pansy nosegay, their stems wrapped tightly in silk and beribboned with antique grosgrain. Amaranths decorated the stage around the Irish and Celtic bands in Victorian style arrangements and dahlias of every color were gathered in lavish centerpieces at each table.

The food was utterly delectable, but the big hit was Katrin's cookie table. Bronwyn wanted a Pittsburgh cookie table with tiers of dozens and dozens of cookies – Kourabiedes, Baklava, Pizzelles, Russian Tea Cakes, Seven Layer Cookies, Miniature Cherry Cheesecakes, Lemon Bars, Macarons, Florentines, Peanut Butter Blossoms, Lady Locks, Nut Horns, Pecan Tassies, and Thumbprints, supplemented with Katrin's usually seductive confections. Bronwyn provided pretty take-home boxes at the end of the table; an improvement over the surreptitious napkin-in-the-handbag.

The Irish and Celtic bands provided constant music. Conor's son, little Luca, danced and romped with Sam Brown's children, Elijah and Jozie. Seeing their inspired jigs was a highlight for everyone. It was a wonderful mix of people and none meant more to Bronwyn than the shopkeepers, neighbors, and restaurant owners who'd become Clive's friends. They understood Clive and his new bride couldn't make it back to the States and no one was surprised that Bronwyn honored her dear Clive with a loud bash that might just echo across the Atlantic.

Even Jeeves seemed to enjoy himself, and Bronwyn was immensely delighted to see he'd moved her fox from the library, into the Silk Club. Children took turns petting it and Charlie and Bronwyn went over together, for a nice pat on its head. Bronwyn kissed its nose and smiled brightly at Jeeves, squeezing his shoulder as she moved on.

True to her word, with a little white zinfandel courage, Bronwyn danced a jig with Charlie. Conor swung her around in a fashion, two self-professed non-dancers caught up in the revelry. It was the kind of evening where everyone danced, man and child, bookstore owner and movie star.

The band quieted.

"May I have your attention, please? Fill your glasses; I'd like to make a toast." Bronwyn took center stage.

"We've all come to say 'Good Luck', 'Bonne Chance', 'Mazal Tov', 'Buona Fortuna', 'Buena Suerte', 'Viel Gluck' and as Katrin would say, 'Lycka Till' to my dear friend Clive Grove and his new wife in Ireland. I'd like to thank each of you as well, for making this such a wonderful party." The crowd burst into applause, warmth permeating their hearts as the glow of friendship surrounded them. "Clive and I had a few good talks together, and we spoke of the wonderful life in Maine. He told me he never felt more alive than here on the bay. We talked about future hopes and dreams, and he hoped he could find a way to feel this Maine vigor, this Maine friendship, this Maine feeling of being alive for the rest of his life. I'm happy for him; join me in wishing them well. Lift your glasses, I ask you, and join with me in a toast. To Clive who's alive!"

The next morning, when Bronwyn handed the boxed velvet quilt to Jeeves, he warned her once more that he wasn't at all certain he could find Clive.

"I know you can do anything, Jeeves." Her sincerity was quite apparent.

Jeeves couldn't help himself; he puffed out like a peacock and accepted the quilt.

Later that day, he took it to Clara when he was certain Edgar was otherwise occupied. Jeeves asked for her pledge of secrecy and directed her to cut off a six inch corner of the quilt. Clara implored Jeeves to allow her to cut and hem the other three corners for balance, but he refused.

Thanking her with a heartfelt gratitude that surprised Clara, Jeeves returned to his flat.

That afternoon, he boxed the quilt and addressed it to his own dear old Mam, in Ballinasloe, County Galway. He had no doubt his mother would be surprised and thrilled with the quilt. Ernest had to admit, it was a beauty. He drove to Portland to post it, and returned at dusk.

After a light supper with Bronwyn, he walked past the Factory, turning past Van Tsang's and crossing near the miniature horses. In the encroaching darkness, he buried the six inch piece of quilt, giving it to Clive, as promised.

CHAPTER THIRTY ONE

JACK'S LETTER

Although Bronwyn was genuinely happy for Clive, she missed him and missed Jamie, every day. Jack McClean's letters made her feel less lonely and she wrestled with the idea of surprising Jack on location.

Sam felt directly responsible for Bronwyn's happiness whenever she delivered a Priority Mail envelope from Moss, as it evoked a pleased 'It's a letter from Jack!' response. This time, Jozie accompanied her mother, with Jozie the bearer of Jack Tidings.

When Sam said her children were staying all day, Bronwyn arranged for lunch in the soda fountain. Jozie trotted off with her Mom, and Bronwyn opened Jack's letter in the snuggery.

5 July

Dearest Dai,

You'll never guess who I ran into in New York! Our friend Graeme. It was great luck. I was only there for a read-through.

Graeme was on a press tour for his Dickens flick. We met for dinner and dearest, it made my weekend. Nothing like the Union Square Café!

So here's the scoop – we both ordered Lobster Shepherd's Pie because it's the Monday special and leave it to Graeme to know these things. Outstanding. I can taste it now, as I write. It had mushrooms and carrots, and spinach with the mashed potato top. For dessert (you didn't think we'd miss dessert, did you?) I had Meyer Lemon pot au crème with an almond tuile. I actually know pot au crème and I've helped my Mum roll tuiles around her rolling pin. Now you know. I'm a closet apron-wearer. Graeme had brioche French toast with apples. He said it was sublime. Looked it.

Well, dearest love, beyond reliving my delicious meal, I'm anxious to share something. I know you and Graeme are great friends, so I'm sure you've seen his film Find Me.

Bronwyn held her breath.

Graeme told me to watch it again, because he was certain I'd find something fresh and new. What a kind friend he is. Of course I've watched it several times – his portrayal of widower's angst is powerful and he more than earned his Oscar.

*Darling girl, I'm sure he was being a
good teacher to this hungry student. But
there's something you must see.*

Bronwyn relaxed. Jack must think the unseen wife's
hand looked like hers. Not much else of Bronwyn showed
in the cut. It was her hand, her arm, even her walk, but
she was younger then and walked with an exuberance she
hadn't felt in years. Maybe someday Jack would realize the
girl portraying Graeme's wife didn't just look like Bronwyn,
it was Bronwyn.

*Here's the part I want you to watch
carefully, Bronwyn. When the young wife
climbs the fire escape and drops the little
girl into the open window, the murderer
climbs up after her, unaware the girl isn't
with her.*

Bronwyn thought it was sweet how Jack would describe
the film in case she hadn't seen it before.

*He stabs the young wife, she falls over
the fire escape, he flees, but she knows
she must leave a message for the police
inspector (her husband), to identify the
murderer and convey her love, as she lay
dying. I never gave the message much
thought when I'd watched it before. Like
most audiences, the first time, I didn't get
the clue at all. Watch what she writes, with
her own blood.*

Bronwyn was well aware of the blood message she'd drawn in the exhausted, expiring manner of someone dying with purpose.

Look at it carefully. At first you think she was trying to write I Love you. Of course, as the movie goes on, you know she was writing "One Eye" and then "love you". (Spoiler: it's the one-eyed neighborhood dry cleaner.) But it's more than that for us – as she's writing, it looks like 1110 before she finishes.

I do try to soldier it, but I wish I could call and talk to you. Well, now I fear I've ruined the letter with pathetic whining. I can't wait for you to see Hemingway when it's done. I'm quite proud. But you never know how they'll put things together. The premiere is set for the Odeon on Leicester Square. Grand and glorious.

Please keep writing. I ache to see you, read your letters, kiss your lips. Well, I'm done for, aren't I? Hopelessly in love with you. I can hear my father saying, well if you're going for it, be bold. I love you, Bronwyn.

With all my hopeless, Shepherd's Pie and Tuile, heart.

Wren

Bronwyn fast-forwarded her DVD and there it was. If you didn't know what the wife was trying to write, you would see a clearly scarlet '1' and a small 'i' with a faint dot above it. Then, the forefinger and middle finger swiped fresher, richer blood and a small 'L' beneath the other two letters and a well-closed 'O'. If that was all you saw, you might think she'd written '1 1 1 O' – Bronwyn and Jack's room number at the Beverly Soleil Hotel. The next letter was a 'v' – then, in new gushing blood, 'u' before the wife died.

She found herself watching more of the movie, always surprised at the enhanced color of the flashbacks, showing the full richness of Graeme's character before he moved through life alone, in muted tones.

In late July, Jeeves asked Bronwyn if she felt like crab cakes, and Bronwyn knew what he meant. Andora road trip. It had been awhile since their last visit to Pittsburgh. They'd been quieter than usual, each missing Clive, but neither mentioning him.

Bronwyn had rarely ventured to Jeeves' flat since the wayward boys left in December, but the road trip was a good excuse for them to gather and plot their path. She took a legal pad and wrote all the places they didn't want to miss, deciding the length of the trip according to their meals. Ham Bar B Q's at Bert's…dinner at the Grand Concourse with Charlie's Chowder, of course…a jaunt up route 228 to The Johnston House for elegant tea and shopping…brown sugar and banana French toast at the Original Pancake House… grilled cheese and peppered bacon sandwiches with tomato dill soup at The Sewickley Café…Devonshires and steak salads at JW Hall's, with turtle sundaes at Bruster's across the road...Breakfast Smiles and strawberry pie at Eat'n Park...crab cakes at Andora without a doubt...Mitchell's Fish Market at the Galleria and time reserved for buying cigars at Jernigan's Tobacco Village...Six Penn Kitchen's lobster mac and cheese, but as Bronwyn jotted it down, Jeeves slapped his knee and yelped 'coffee frites' so she marked it with a 'two' so they could indulge in brunch – maybe a crab frittata with grilled asparagus.

Jeeves reminded her about the Mike Ditka restaurant for serious steaks. And they'd spend an afternoon at Soergel Orchards, looking at Amish furniture, the farm animals, nursery, gift barn, and garden shop. The Soergel staff was always the absolute nicest, so they weren't about to miss a visit. They'd stay at The Priory Hotel on the North Side and have dinner at least once at Max's Allegheny Tavern. Two weeks should do it.

When they returned home, they brought Isaly's chipped ham, Reymer's Lemon Blennd, twenty four loaves of Jenny Lee Raisin Bread, and Sidney Crosby jerseys. Bronwyn gave Clara a Jojo Crow Primitives one-of-a-kind doll. It wasn't the first time she surprised Clara with a folk art doll from Joann Miller...and this one had such a delicate vintage fabric, stunning blue eyes, and carried a ratty little dog as her 'needful thing'.

Jeeves was anxious to unpack his heavy box from Soergel's. But first, he sat with Bronwyn as they sorted their mail. His interest was piqued when he noticed Priority Mail envelopes from Moss.

"They're letters from Jack," she said a bit defiantly. Jeeves' calm exterior belied the lurch of his stomach. He thought that ship had sailed.

CHAPTER THIRTY TWO

THANKSGIVING

As Edgar discussed the Thanksgiving menu with Bronwyn, Jamie Donald was pulling into the Factory's circular driveway. Van Tsang leaned into the car's window and shook Jamie's hand.

"Welcome back. So, it's done then?" Van asked. Jamie nodded. "Ernest is in the study."

Van took the silver Mercedes onto the turntable, as Jamie headed toward the entryway. He leaned against the stone wall, watching Van unpack the boot. As their eyes met, Van stacked the luggage and returned to the gatehouse.

Driving to Maine, Jamie's senses had been heightened by the chill air and crunch of long-fallen autumn leaves along the roads. He wanted to fill himself with this New England. It reminded him of home...that faraway place he vaguely remembered. Or, was it imagined? The boats, woolen sweaters, foggy mists of morning, blueberries and lobster – those things that drew Bronwyn to this place were about to ensnare him as well.

The return wasn't quite as he'd pictured. Ernest Rose was now off the prime minister's payroll and Jamie was on.

And he was most unhappy that Ernest had concocted a tale about dead Clive changing his identity, marrying, and living in Ireland. He resented having to perpetuate the lie with Samuel and Paul, and dreaded lying to Bronwyn.

The prime minister made it clear that Jamie was the one who could protect Bronwyn better than Ernest Rose had ever done. Surely Ernest was aware of his failings. Everything that befell Bronwyn had happened on his watch, when she was alone. Clive had known. The change of power began before their trip to Vail.

Jamie had an undeniable connection to Bronwyn and she was as fond of him, as he was of her. He tried not to think of it as love. Given his MI6 assignments, he was overqualified for the position, but so was Ernest. How could protecting one young woman be more difficult than the heart-stopping assignments they'd had, from one dangerous corner of the world to another? Jamie vowed he wouldn't underestimate their surroundings, no matter how much laughter and lobster might cushion their days.

After leaving Clive in Vail, Jamie had finished his MI6 career with an incendiary bang.

Clive had planned to spend the rest of his days on the Maine coast with Ernest and Bronwyn, and had very nearly done so. Now Jamie gladly stepped in for his friend. The time he'd spent in Maine had been a joy. Clive promised him a grand respite and it had been all that. Aye, all that and Bronwyn to laugh with, dine with, and shop for Wellies with. Mother of God, he had been happy in this place, while the rest of the world spun its web, just beyond. They'd be sheltered. He'd always be ready. This would be the life he'd lead.

He glanced at the bluestone archway, leading to Ernest

Rose's flat. Bronwyn had spared no expense where Ernest was concerned. The entrance was remarkable, a mix of outdoors and indoors. Small river stones made a satisfying crunch leading to the stairway and arched entrance. A reclaimed trough hung on one stone wall as did ancient wooden chests. Lighting was effective but nicely tucked away, lending a caramel wash to it all. Intriguing as it was, no one would guess at the baronial sanctum, just steps away.

Jamie continued to muse about what brought him back. It was unusual for the best to leave service, but MI6 had stamped him unfit, deciding he'd had more than his share of psychotropic and torturous drugs. It was their lingering essence, ensuring his escape to this good and simple life. Drugged to freedom. So be it.

Discharged from service just three months ago, he had been summoned by Prime Minister Abraham. It was so soon after his discharge, he suspected the prime minister's involvement in his dismissal. After that intense meeting, Jamie had flown to the states to meet with Samuel at university, Paul at the horse farm, and then Moss.

The boys were of a mind – they hadn't known Bronwyn to be truly happy, and they expected Jamie to change that. Samuel said she was lonely; Paul said she was sad. Both boys happily shared her likes and dislikes with him, noting how she created happiness for others. They recounted childhood days watching the estate coming together, pitching in with chores, nestling in their Factory suite. Paul was certain Bronwyn was charmed. Perhaps the boy had some Irish blood in him, Jamie thought with a smile. They mentioned Jack McClean and wondered why he wasn't with her.

Each boy told his tale of being rescued by Bronwyn. Remembering how placid and languid they were a year ago, he noted the tumble of words, increasing agitation, and definitive hand gestures each used in recalling that day. Even though he'd spoken to them a week apart, they had few variations in the telling. He realized why the boys were so easy with Bronwyn last December. People on the estate kept a physical distance; friendly enough, but with a barrier. Conversely, the boys were relaxed and puppy-like with her. After questioning them, he recognized the intensity and ferocious jointure that was forged between them and Bronwyn. Forever linked by fear and reclamation.

Jamie acted as courier for Samuel, delivering CD's to Paul. He was fond of the boys and realized he already had ties to this new life. Perhaps that's where Clive had gone wrong. He'd relaxed before he got behind the Maine wall.

Moss was nearly as adamant about Bronwyn's protection as the prime minister had been. Jamie learned how serious her injuries had been during the kidnapping in '97. It was easy to view her as a healthy young woman, laughing and whacking at racquetball. Now he knew the reality of her trauma.

There'd been no exit wound when she'd been shot, and she was sedated and medically paralyzed. The X-ray showed fragments scattered as if a small grenade had exploded. She'd been put on a ventilator, forcing air into one injured lung; a chest tube was inserted and three intravenous lines were run. Slight damage was done to her spleen. Surgeons cleared blood around the left lung, knowing her young, healthy lung had a good chance of healing itself. The diaphragm had a small hole. Surgeons removed shards of bullet fragments and removed the uterus and one ovary. Her liver was slightly torn, but they meticulously stitched it up, salvaging it; end result was the liver regenerated itself. Bronwyn regenerated herself.

Samuel said their father had been at hospital when she came back from the dead. Nearly giving her life for the boys explained the family's Maine estate as her reward. Losing her best friend on the same day was a red flag, but Oliver Silkowski's hypertrophic cardiomyopathy was well documented, and a link seemed unlikely. Aware that Ernest Rose became 'Jeeves' to orphan Bronwyn during her long recovery, Jamie understood her dependence on him.

During the past month, Jamie had immersed himself in Bronwyn's medical records and confidential files. Moss had shown him the kidnap footage, the Palm Springs shooting at Sir Winston's, the Oakley Forse beating, and the roof rescue of Dominguez's girl. Jamie hadn't quite reconciled the Bronwyn who showed such bravery, with the amusing Maine girl he'd shared sundaes with. He found it curious that the stunning footage showed extraordinary passivity under fire alone, but remarkable courage, strength, and timing, saving the children. The plight of the orphan, gone to extreme, he feared. His mission was that she be safe, but also happy. It was long overdue, and each of them – the prime minister, Moss, Samuel and Paul – each had reason to suspect Ernest was to blame for her stranded state.

Jamie sighed, and with his hand on the door, turned to peer into the enormous garage. He'd been so deep in thought that he hadn't noticed the damnable Wells Fargo stage coach, hermetically sealed for Ernest Rose in a museum glass box of enormous proportions. Close by were Ernest's red Alfa Romeo Spider Veloce, red Triumph Spitfire MK III, and, of course, the indigo Jaguar XK.

Jamie gave an imperceptible nod to the specter of Clive hovering round the corner of his mind.

Just then, Jeeves opened the heavy wooden door and reached his hand out. "Well, it's all good then, Jamie."

"A team, Ernest. You know that. Bronwyn expects you to be there for her, and I expect we can bloody well give her that, don't you?"

The older man smiled slightly. He led the way down the hall, into his richly decorated library. "This is all yours then, unless you're to move into the house? Or, a cottage?"

Jeeves looked slightly embarrassed, having tipped his hand showing his fear of losing the home that meant so much. He knew again that he was getting older, for his brooding was too near the surface.

"If it's all the same to you, Ernest, I'd like to Artful Dodger, just as before. You have everything we need, and I don't expect Bronwyn would open her home to me, anymore than she did to you."

Jeeves felt the sting of the words, but said nothing. Jamie seated himself upon the tufted leather couch, easing against red plaid pillows, and Jeeves was grateful to take his usual chair. Perhaps things wouldn't change as much as he feared. Much of the past month had been spent wondering how he'd come to cling to this magnificent flat. He'd pondered if there was anything he could do to maintain position and save face. It was unseemly to have become so desperate, but there it was.

"Well, Jamie, I suppose we'd best get down below and make some changes. I'll ring Matthew. And, the next order of business will be how to surprise our Bronwyn. The return of her darlin' Jimey."

Jamie hadn't really taken in the elegance of Ernest's flat, the year before. Perhaps he was too busy enjoying Clive and Bronwyn's company and dashing in and out of the home for sport and recreation, camaraderie and discovery. Now as he settled in, he was taken with the whole effect. The living room was the perfect stage to unveil an enormous balcony leading to Ernest's suite and spare bedroom. Beautiful mahogany wainscoting propped up the balustrades of the balcony; the stairs were covered in fabulously plush dark green carpet with brass stair rods; the whole effect enhanced by enormous English portraits adorning the wall, two stories high. Persian carpets, brass and ebony tables, and deep navy walls were lit by Baccarat chandeliers, all adding to the swanky, private club effect. One might expect a wall of something tasteful at the top of the stair, but it revealed stacks of custom made dress shirts in niches, an unsettling spectacle that Jamie did remember. He and Clive had rolled their eyes at that.

Off to the side of the living room was an exposed circular stair, beautifully varnished and elegantly curved. It wrapped around lighted shadow boxes, stacked in a six foot square, showcasing collectibles. Among them were hood ornaments, including a Rene Lalique 'Fox' from the 1930's, an 'Airline' Jaguar from the 1930's, a solid silver Rolls-Royce 'Spirit of Ecstasy', and a 1920's 'Spirit of Triumph' for Isotta Fraschini. Jamie read the engraved nameplates, and then went up the stair to his nook.

He could sleep in the spare bedroom, but he chose the alcove bed. Its canopy was custom-made to fill the alcove's arch. Sconces lit the bed and a small painting in a gilded frame filled the space between them. He used the spare room for dressing, but the alcove bed was perfectly placed, affording Jamie a view of Ernest's hallway as well as the lower level.

Walking around the estate last December, Jamie had learned how Bronwyn planned the building of each home, as well as the Factory. She was obviously a brilliant visionary, but upon reflection, Jamie decided her master stroke was building this posh home for Ernest and keeping him out of her own.

Thanksgiving dinner was, by all accounts, wonderful. Bronwyn felt the familiar, rich fullness Thanksgiving brought to her heart. The anticipation of the holiday season was launched with that fizzy feeling in her stomach and when Bronwyn knew Jamie would be there, she tweaked the menu twice more with Edgar.

Clara and Edgar, Laurent's family, Van Tsang, Jeeves, Jamie and Bronwyn began their Thanksgiving meal with homemade crackers, cherry cheese spread, roasted pecans and holiday punch at Edgar and Clara's. Kristine's girls snatched the pewter spreaders and volunteered to keep the crackers fully loaded and ready to go.

After the munchies, they moved into the Orangerie, sun dappled against the chill air. Jen had decorated with corn stocks and red berried bittersweet, and the glass house came to life. Edgar placed the platter of turkey on a long table with triple cranberry sauce alongside bowls of cranberry wild rice stuffing and bacon stuffing balls. Laurent wheeled in green beans with pecans, sautéed Brussels sprouts with toasted hazelnuts, glazed carrots, sweet potatoes dotted with marshmallows, and potato gratin. Kristine and the girls carried baskets of johnnycakes, warm dinner rolls, and steaming banana bread.

Jamie enjoyed it so much that Bronwyn called him Pilgrim Jamie and was rewarded with his elfin smile.

Jeeves was getting older and, for some reason, more distant. Bronwyn was undeniably pleased to have Jamie protecting her and the estate, and now that Clive had gone to start a new life, she was hopeful Jamie would stay and call *this* his new life. She'd asked Jamie as much and he assured her he was staying. Her heart sang when she noticed he wore his Milton Hershey watch.

Talk turned to football games and holiday shopping. The men were going over to Tom and Valli's to watch the games. Bronwyn and Clara wrapped some of the apple cake with caramel sauce, as well as pumpkin pie with pecan crust, for Tom and Valli. They warned the men off the extra desserts, shaking their fingers at them, and settled on Nicole and Josselyn as trusted messengers.

That evening, Jeeves sat with Bronwyn and broached going to New York City the next week. They'd meet with Moss and Zuleika, see some Broadway shows, and do holiday shopping. Bronwyn was suspicious about meeting with Moss. They could meet at the estate, and Moss and his wife would be coming to see Susie and Oz sometime before Christmas. She didn't admit it, but Bronwyn had an uneasy feeling.

This worry was intensified by sadness, not hearing from Jack McClean for over two months. She supposed he was busy filming, but they'd written almost every week, sometimes more often. Not hearing from him inflicted a terrible longing. His letters were like islands she swam to, and his silence was deafening.

Before they left for New York, Bronwyn called Zuleika and asked what she knew about the meeting. The conversation didn't bolster Bronwyn; Zuleika was evasive. It affected Bronwyn's packing. She packed black.

Bronwyn hadn't stayed at The Lowell before. Moss had chosen the hotel for its close proximity to his offices. It had an understated elegance that Bronwyn deeply appreciated. Jamie noticed she smiled and spoke to everyone she encountered – the doorman, desk clerk, bellman, and the maid down the hallway from their rooms.

The men went through to their adjoining room as Bronwyn admired the taupe silks of her bed, pulled the taffeta drapes back to look out the window and peeked into the enormous marble bathroom. She felt like a wide-eyed child. There was muted refinement everywhere she looked, and she found it to be familiar and calming...the hotel life she knew so well.

Jeeves entered her room with Jamie. "It's time for a switch, Miss. Our Jamie will be your New York mate this trip."

Surprised, she simply nodded.

"I'll be off, then."

Bronwyn felt slightly chilled at the subterfuge. This meeting with Moss and Zuleika had the earmark of something bad.

Fortunately, Bronwyn always enjoyed having Jamie at her side. When they walked around the East Side that afternoon, he draped his arm over her shoulder. It was a familiarity she never had with Jeeves and it began to feel much like being in NYC with Oliver Silkowski, her childhood friend.

She took Jamie to Tender Buttons, where they scoured the floor to ceiling bins, buying dozens of wonderful buttons for Clara. At Laguiole, she found a classic corkscrew made of olive wood, for Jeeves. Jamie was an easy shopping companion, as always. If she hadn't been so nervous about the meeting, she'd have shown him dozens of favorite places. But, she felt an undercurrent of dread.

They had tea at 5:00 PM in the serene Pembroke Room, and that sufficed for the evening meal. Bronwyn hoped nibbling finger sandwiches would mask her lack of appetite.

Back in her room, she held a book, but didn't bother seeing words or turning pages. The television was on, more for a sense of normalcy than anything else. She finally called Moss and he was offhand, saying there were a few things they needed to review. It was late, but she called Zuleika, asking if there was a problem with the money and accounts. When she hesitated, Bronwyn thought about Oakley Forse's death and decided he must be the root of the meeting. A black cloud gripped her heart and squeezed. Of course Oakley would reach from the grave to get her attention. Why wouldn't he? Could the money already be gone? She was pacing across the plush carpet. Was all of it valid, only if Oakley lived? Was that possible? She began to feel light-headed and sat down at the desk. She crossed her arms and laid her head upon them, closing her eyes. Her thoughts were racing, her ears ringing. So many lives depended on her having the money. She remembered Oakley Forse saying she wouldn't want to know where the bad money came from. Did all those second chances she'd given hang so tenuously by the thread of her ill-begotten wealth? She shuddered as she thought of each family, the town projects, the Scholarship Program, the animal shelter, charities, all of it, with each thought delivering a crushing blow. She began again, mentally listing each of them. Again. And then, again.

Jamie rapped lightly on her door.

"Anything I can do, Bronwyn?"

She offered a wan smile, looking deathly white.

Jamie took her hands and peered into her eyes.

"I'm just sick with worry." It came out with a little moan.

He urged, "Can you tell me why?"

She shook her head, repeating, "I'm just sick with worry."

Jamie promised her the meeting was nothing to be concerned about as he poured her a sip of brandy. He felt guilty as he suspected only good news would come from the meeting. He'd be shocked if there was a twist. More than shocked.

When she had more color and seemed steady, he dropped Bronwyn's arms into her jacket, and made the next half hour pass with a stroll down Madison Avenue, under its starry winter sky. Clutching his arm made Bronwyn feel not-so-alone, and her spirits revived in the cold air. He seemed to be utterly confident about the meeting's agenda and she decided to believe him. They swung back to the hotel and agreed to pop into the Post House. It was a steak and chop house of the first order, with parquet floors, leather armchairs, and beautiful tables decorated in burnt sienna and tan. They ordered comfort food that comforted, and her spirits were noticeably lifted, as were his.

Back in her room, Jamie deliberated about placing a sleeping potion in her water. He decided he would, just a pinch, and it did the trick. He folded her gray flannel robe across a chair and watched her sleep. How vulnerable and childlike she looked. He watched her with a Goodall intensity, overwhelmed with the dear sleeping creature he'd promised to protect. He held her hand for hours, until he fell asleep in the chair beside her bed.

The next morning, he was pleased to see she greeted him with a smile.

"Are you up for any brekkies this morning, Bronwyn?"

"I'm always up for breakfast," and she realized it was the waiting that unnerved her. Now that the day was here, she no longer had to wait for the other shoe to drop.

Dressed in a black turtleneck and flannel slacks, Bronwyn walked with Jamie to the elevator and complimented him on his charcoal cashmere sweater, saying, "You tog up well."

He seemed slightly embarrassed, and she was delighted to see his smile lasting six descending floors. He wouldn't look at her, but he was beaming.

They strode into the Pembroke and noticed a spectacular gingerbread house on display, having missed seeing it before. Bronwyn oohed and aahed over it with two little boys.

She turned her attention to Jamie as he ordered the full English breakfast. Bronwyn never tired of admiring the fare at dining establishments; all the better if they were hotels. Jamie was happy when she ordered a croissant with her eggs and Virginia ham. Good girl.

"My Dad always said to order Virginia ham if it's offered, instead of bacon or sausage"

"My Gran always said to drink carrot juice, so I'll keep my eyesight," he responded, lifting his glass.

And with that, they enjoyed each other's company and briefly suspended thoughts of the Moss meeting.

Six attorneys for the estate of Oakley Forse gathered around the conference table of Attorney Stanley Mastrofrancesco, as Zuleika, Moss, and Bronwyn took their seats. Jamie sat slightly behind.

Once Bronwyn realized her money wasn't going to disappear, she tuned out the legalese until the estate attorney asked for her attention. As the stipulated ten month waiting period had expired, the attorneys were directed, upon her reading of a final letter from Oakley Forse, to transfer his remaining Swiss account to Bronwyn Dai McCall's Swiss accounts. Even Moss visibly reacted when he heard the amount, but she focused on the idea of a letter.

The silver haired gentleman at the head of the table, Bronwyn hadn't caught his name, was handing her an ecru envelope with a gleaming gilded edge.

"Must I read it out loud?"

"No, Miss McCall. However, I'm afraid you must read it in my presence, before we can transfer the funds."

Her voice was tight and quiet. "I don't care about the money."

"Mr. Mastrofrancesco, perhaps you'd like a word with your client."

"I don't think my client should be subjected to whatever invective he's delivering, ten months after his death. I insist I be allowed to read it in advance of Miss McCall's reading."

"Mr. Forse's instructions are quite clear, I'm afraid. We are all here for you, Miss McCall. Perhaps if you just focus on the money."

Moss knelt to the right of Bronwyn, as Jamie leaned over her left side. Moss urged her to have a drink of water and reminded her she'd be reading it privately. As Moss stood over Bronwyn, the silver haired gentleman issued another warning.

"Miss McCall must read it alone, without interference or interruption. I must ask you gentlemen to take your seats."

Moss handed her a letter opener and regretted the whole business. He knew Jamie was ready to snatch the letter and throw it into the fireplace, letting the flames devour it.

Bronwyn took a deep breath, and gave Jamie a pathetic, small smile. She reminded herself that she knew Oakley Forse in a way the others did not. If he had a letter he wanted her to read, it was uncomfortable, but she could do it. She found it difficult though, having an audience.

She walked to the end of the table, tore the envelope open and gazed at an ecru card of heavy stock.

She stared at the note, long enough that observers thought it was a lengthy correspondence. She placed the card back into its envelope. Her lips quivered as emotion welled up. Tears came, sobs burbled, and even Bronwyn didn't know where the animal-like wailing was coming from. She fell apart to such a degree that everyone vacated the room, save Jamie. The attorneys moved into Zuleika's office to make the transfer of funds, while Moss returned to his office and poured himself a stiff drink.

Jamie stood fifteen feet away, immobile and confounded. The participants were sorry to be part of Oakley Forse's well orchestrated ending. Perhaps they'd seen Bronwyn's grief over a secret revealed. Perhaps it was misery over the resurrected violent encounters. Only Jamie recognized it for what it was; abject despair over the death of Oakley Forse.

Eventually, Moss and Zuleika came to the door. Bronwyn was still sobbing at the end of the table, and they retreated. Jamie realized he had no words to comfort her, but he was compelled to read the note. It sat to her side on the table, while her head nestled in her arms. With Bronwyn unaware, Jamie slid the card from its envelope and read, *You're welcome.*

CHAPTER THIRTY THREE

THE NEW COCOA

"Nicely done, old man." Jamie sat on a tufted leather chair, lifting his feet to an ottoman in Ernest Rose's library. He looked around the room, taking in the patina of distressed parquet floors, the polished mahogany bar with its beveled mirrors and cut glassware, the billiards table and mother of pearl inlaid games table, coffered ceiling, hunt paintings... extravagant in its masculinity. The room reeked of money and good taste. There wasn't an inch that wasn't worthy of the wealthiest of men.

Ernest assumed he was speaking of the room and its furnishings. If Jamie'd known he was thinking that, he'd have been even more angry.

"It went well, then? The reading?"

Jamie stared.

"And how was our Bronwyn? Pleased? Delighted? Oh, I wish Clive could see this day."

"It was brilliant, really. She grieved. Did you know that? Inconsolable." He watched Ernest carefully, trying to gauge his reaction. If he observed so much as a twitch, he might smash his face. "I'd not seen it coming. You've mapped her heart, well."

Ernest knew he'd never succeeded in mapping Bronwyn's heart. She twisted in inexplicable ways and he wondered at how evasive and wary she was by nature. There was much he didn't understand and couldn't predict about Bronwyn Dai McCall. He expected her to be thrilled with the enormous windfall. That she would cry for that gormless creature was yet another unnerving surprise.

"It's not surprising, really. When Forse's mum passed, he and Bronwyn oddly enough connected in some way. Didn't seem to matter when he pummeled her in Beverly Hills. Didn't seem to matter to either of them. But you know our Bronwyn." His eyes narrowed like a hawk's. "Always willing to forgive."

"Wasn't that a risk, old man?" Jamie's voice was harsh. "Sending Clive? I thought you'd made the match. She'd not have forgiven Clive, any more than you think she could forgive me." Ernest's face was inscrutable.

The two dangerous men, each having saved the life of the other over the years, contemplated the removal of the other. "She needs us both, Jamie. As you said."

Jamie stood and gazed out the window toward Bronwyn's house, then calmly left the flat and headed to the rooftop pool.

With each lap, he contented himself with his mind's acorn gathering. He wouldn't compound the sin. He knew Bronwyn was fond of her Jeeves.

Jamie had no doubt he could protect Bronwyn from outside and in. His thoughts turned to Clive. After all, Ernest had sent them to secure millions more for Bronwyn, before Clive killed Oakley Forse.

Clive had been an affable fellow when he was your mate, but Jamie knew the dispassionate, deadly side of him. They were much alike in their cool professionalism, and despite a certain rivalry, they were like brothers. He understood Clive's cold sizzle and motivation, after Moss showed the melee footage to Jamie. To anyone who cared for Bronwyn, seeing Forse spit on her in Los Angeles and then rub her bruised face until she lost consciousness, with Moss wildly flying over the conference table, was somehow worse than the beating. It was so bloody blatant. The puzzle was that Clive would have done the job, simply because Ernest asked. Jamie figured Ernest showed that tape to Clive for a reason. He wanted to ensure nothing would stop Clive from getting the money and killing Forse.

Jamie'd gone out a week sooner, setting the trap bringing Clive and Forse together. They discovered the producer had already changed his will two years earlier, gifting Bronwyn the remaining 489 million dollars in his Swiss Account, and dividing his offshore Cayman accounts among his cousins. Once Clive and Jamie verified the money and will, the timeline adjusted itself, and Forse was eliminated promptly.

Jamie'd already taken an assignment in Uganda. With extra time on his hands, Clive returned to Ireland for one last job before beginning his 'new life' in Maine…an assignment that placed him too close to an IRA bomb.

Watching Ernest now, Jamie decided he'd wanted Forse killed for whatever bond he shared with Bronwyn. The money was just a bonus, before the well was murdered dry.

Jamie missed his friend. If Clive hadn't been Ernest's son, Jamie would have wondered at his untimely death. He mused over how Clive would have handled his father.

Disgusted with Ernest's promotion of Bronwyn's loneliness and perceived helplessness, Clive had brought Jamie to the estate. She seemed woefully unequipped to protect herself, so they added self-defense to their friendly games of racquetball and badminton. It all seemed like good friends having a lark. Jamie thought Clive's moving to Maine was to take Bronwyn's loneliness away. Now Jamie thought it was more than that. It was to keep Ernest Rose away from Bronwyn.

Pulling himself out of the pool, he felt personal resolve. He'd set things right. He'd set everything right.

Katrin served Bronwyn's favorite scones and tea sandwiches. She didn't know why Jeeves had stopped joining Bronwyn for tea and she hadn't asked. Sometimes it was best, not knowing.

Katrin closed the heavy glass paned door of the dining room, and left.

Jamie nodded to her as their paths crossed, and Katrin said Bronwyn was having tea. Jamie smiled at his timing. He'd enjoy a cuppa. Taking a mug from the cupboard, he opened the dining room door.

"Hi, Jimey. I'm glad you came over," Bronwyn said enthusiastically. "Will an oyster plate do, or should I get a regular plate?"

"Oyster would be jolly."

She opened the lighted wall case and chose two of her favorite oyster plates.

"Perfect. Little indentations for everything," she said as she poured tea into her china cup for Jamie and took the mug for herself.

They split their warm scones and plied them with chilled

sweet butter and strawberry preserves. Jamie added a dollop of Devonshire cream, and then gazed out the windows with quiet contentment.

When they'd eaten everything on the tiered tray, Jamie settled back in the upholstered chintz chair. "Bronwyn, as I'm taking over, I'd like to do a sweep of the house."

"You don't think there are cameras in my bedroom or," she swallowed, "my bathroom do you?"

"If there are, you'll find Ernest permanently on Squirrel Hill."

Bronwyn saw the flash of his anger.

"Why don't you dash up to Freeport with Grace and stay at the Harraseeket. Do a little holiday shopping and when you come home tomorrow, you'll have a lovely clean house. Are you aware that we have thermo-imaging? It reveals body heat in the house. That should suffice."

"Like a Marauder's Map," Bronwyn grinned.

"Precisely, my little Hermione."

Bronwyn wasn't surprised to find Grace ready for the trip. After all, it hadn't really been a request from Jamie. She always suspected there were hidden cameras…she was used to them in her life. If there hadn't been hidden cameras, she'd be hundreds of millions of dollars poorer. But she felt exhilarated to think she might come home to privacy. Real privacy.

When Jamie entered Ernest's living room, Ernest was wielding a poker in the moss rock fireplace. It was lovely weather for a fire, but the older man was seldom in this room, usually holding court in his library. The air was redolent with aromatic wood, but like the fragrant layers of fine wine, there was just a hint of an acrid aroma. Suspicious, Jamie approached, watching the grate where small white bits of paper were being consumed by flames.

"How long have you been burning them?"

Ernest straightened and gathered himself before turning around, blankly.

"You should know, Jamie. Of course, you should know. I've been remiss. Sorry."

He gestured to a beautifully upholstered sofa and sat himself in an elegant wing chair. "I wasn't aware of their correspondence until I came upon McClean's letters to Bronwyn." His voice grew cold. "They've grown quite close."

"And the burn?"

"On the odd occasion, she might not receive one…lost in the post, you see. I'm afraid she must have made inquiry with Moss at some point; they've had a wax seal of late. As if…" He said this with a slight smile. "Anyway, the last few have been inappropriate."

"And, you've no idea what she writes to him?" Jamie asked to annoy him, even as he knew Ernest wouldn't betray his annoyance.

"She posts them herself," was all he said.

"Quite." Jamie rose and left for the rooftop pool, his usual escape.

Jeeves sat musing. He was certain Jamie understood the unsuitability of someone like Jack McClean, and undoubtedly wanted Bronwyn for himself. He wouldn't unsettle her with the truth and he couldn't stop what was in motion. Too late for that.

Taking the elevator upward, Jamie stopped at the fourth floor.

"Hello, Mr. Donald," Sam said politely. "Did you want to see Ms. Cloud?"

"I'd like to speak with you. How do you handle Bronwyn's mail?"

Sam felt herself becoming defensive. Jamie Donald's tone implied something was amiss, and she prided herself on every aspect of her job but none more than assisting Bronwyn. She regained her composure before speaking.

"Owen delivers the mail downstairs. I sort it and then I give Bronwyn's mail to Mr. Rose. He hand delivers it each day." She watched Jamie's face, but he just listened. "I used to deliver it myself. Mr. Mastrofrancesco spoke with Grace a few months ago, and apparently there were a few items Bronwyn felt were lost in the mail," she could feel her mouth tightening with those little lines she hated, "or mishandled."

Jamie nodded.

"I've always been extremely careful with Bronwyn's mail. If she didn't receive something, it *was* lost in the mail." He nodded, again. "Anyway, Grace spoke with Mr. Rose and they decided he would hand deliver everything after I sorted it. And, correspondence from Mr. Mastrofrancesco began arriving with a wax seal across it."

She seemed to think of something and looked uncomfortable.

"I should probably tell you. A few months ago, I went to Bronwyn and checked to make sure the seal was intact. That's probably why you're here. It's not that I didn't trust Mr. Rose. I just decided it was the professional thing to do."

She looked miserable.

"Would you invite Ms. Cloud to join us?"

Grace motioned Jamie into her office.

"In the future, Sam will deliver Bronwyn's mail to her. Not Mr. Rose, under any circumstances." Grace's eyes gave a flicker and Sam's jaw dropped.

"When the mail bag arrives, I want it placed in a safe that should be arriving tomorrow. Only the two of you will have the combination and sort it. I'll speak with Mr. Rose and you can expect he'll no longer offer to convey the mail."

Despite these efforts, and Sam's stringent adherence to the new rules, no letters from Jack would arrive for Bronwyn. Jack McClean was no longer writing to Bronwyn McCall.

Jamie sat glumly across from Jeeves. They'd had a contentious time of it, almost physical, but now that it was time to see Bronwyn, his anger dissipated.

"I'll be off, then."

Jeeves lifted his hand. "Check with Edgar. She'll do for a nice cup of cocoa, I think."

Although it was late, Jamie buzzed Edgar and was grateful he was awake. Once Edgar understood the situation, he quickly dressed and followed Jamie through the tunnel. It was a cold, drizzling December night so he appreciated the warm and bright underground path.

"I'll start the cocoa, Jamie. You'll be going up?"

"Actually, I was thinking, Edgar. Could you manage a new variety of cocoa? Displayed differently, I mean? Jeeves had his and now I'd like to offer 'mine'."

Edgar smiled warmly at him. "Certainly. Excellent idea." And he got busy finding ingredients, a whisk, and inspiration.

Jamie mounted the stairs. He knew where the squeaks were and deftly avoided them, but his eyes were lifted for sight of her. As he got near the top, he saw the flickering light from the television screen. There was no sound. As he reached the landing and turned into the open bedroom, prepared for he knew not what, Jamie saw Bronwyn propped up in the bed, raptly watching the screen.

He cleared his throat and she turned to him; her eyes were nearly swollen shut. He wasn't often faced with grief or crying or anguish. Seems he usually was gone by then. Bronwyn discreetly turned to wipe the wetness from her cheeks, and Jamie gathered up endless Kleenex scattered across the bed and fallen to the floor. Glancing at the big screen, he saw a silent Jack McClean miming a call to arms to his revolutionary comrades. Avoiding the raison d'être for a moment, Jamie silently cheered for the opposition. He left for a moment to bring her a new box of Kleenex and was pleased to see she'd straightened the bed and wore a cheery, empty smile.

"It's okay, Jimey." She sounded exhausted. Even saying his name seemed to take real effort. "I know. I check the Internet before I go to bed. Usually I look at Getty Images, to see what The Boys are up to…press conferences, photo calls. But I saw on CNN's site that Jack got married."

"What can I do?" Jamie sat beside her.

"We haven't been in touch for almost three months now. It's stupid, really. He owed me a letter and I didn't write back. I was waiting. When we were in New York, I checked with Moss to see if there were letters for me, but there weren't. I thought Jack was busy shooting…or, maybe was tired of me…but…I guess we know now," she said, haltingly, "he was busy."

Jamie looked at her with pity. She didn't expect his pity and he didn't know it existed within him. They were both somewhat surprised. She smiled weakly. "I should have written to him." She shook her head regretfully, and then shook it again.

"Read this," she finally said, handing him a tear-stained letter. "You'll see that he loved me."

Jamie shook his head. "I don't need to read it, Bronwyn. I know he loved you."

"Read it, Jimey. You can't really know if you don't see his words," she urged.

"I know, because you're you."

Bronwyn fell silent.

"She's gorgeous, you know. Truly. She's young and blonde and adorable," Bronwyn said in a sullen monotone. "And, British."

"She's scrawny with a potty mouth," Jamie retorted distastefully, and under his breath, he muttered "The git."

"Good one, Jamie," Bronwyn flashed a quick grin.

Edgar came around the bookcase divider with a tray. He approached with a cup of cocoa surrounded by an army of thirty or so silver Hershey kisses. Instead of marshmallows, it was crowned with whipped cream and chocolate shavings. "I've always liked whipped cream in it," and Edgar and Jamie exchanged smiles. Then, Edgar plopped a tiny truffle into the whipped cream and Bronwyn softly whispered, "Wow."

It occurred to Bronwyn that Jeeves hadn't come. "Where's Jeeves?"

"I offered to come straight away. I hope that's all right. I can ring him to come if you like," Jamie offered.

She shook her head, and thanked Edgar, telling him she was fine and to get back to Clara and his bed. Jamie walked him downstairs to the tunnel opening.

When Jamie returned to her bedroom, he sat cross-legged on the bed and took her hand in his own.

She looked at him with haunted eyes. "I'm glad he's all right. I know you think this is terrible news, but it would be terrible if he was sick or injured or worse. He's probably quite happy."

She waited for Jamie to say something. When he didn't, she pointed to the screen. "How lucky I am to have so many movies of his." She placed her hand on her heart. "It's very comforting – like he's here. It's a blessing, really."

Jamie couldn't imagine her looking or sounding more pathetic. He wanted to hold her tightly, but decided against it. "When you're ready to have him back, I'm at your service."

She looked at him with stunned surprise, mentally weighing the possibility of 'getting him back' and wondered aloud, "That easy? Nothing to it, but to do it?"

He nodded with great seriousness. Throwing caution and propriety to the wind, Jamie did embrace her. Rather than feeling comforted, Bronwyn was busy thinking. Would Jamie bring Jack to her, tied and in a cage? Would he bribe him to get a divorce and come back to her? Would he erase Jack's memory and let him discover Bronwyn all over again? The hug ended with Bronwyn still thinking and wondering.

Bronwyn sipped her cocoa and Jamie saw the shock of reality washing over her again. She bit her lip.

"The prime minister called Ernest, but Moss called me," he said simply.

"They're good friends. Bram and Moss are good friends. They would call each other."

"No, Bronwyn. The prime minister didn't call Moss. Your Jack McClean did."

Bronwyn was stunned. Jamie reached inside his pocket, called Moss and handed her his phone.

"Hi, Moss. I'm okay. Really. You talked to Jack? What did he say?"

Moss was relieved to hear her voice. "Jack said he

hoped this wouldn't hurt you, he hoped you were all right and that he'd be in touch."

Once she knew Jack had called Moss, she had high expectations. She expected something more. And yet, she hated to ask and bring finality to the hope she harbored. "That's all? Nothing else?"

"Yes, Bronwyn. He had a number code for you."

"A code? Jimey, I need a pen. Do you think it's a code for a box somewhere? He left me something?"

"He didn't say. Are you ready to write? Let me see. Here it is. One. One. One. Zero. Did you get that? One. One. One. Zero."

She had written the numbers on her arm, to Jamie's dismay, having handed her a pad of paper.

"Does it mean something to you?"

Jamie watched a blissful look cross her face. "It means he loves me."

CHAPTER THIRTY FOUR

TIFFANY
2007-2008

"Another Christmas, shot to hell," Bronwyn had told Jamie with a lighthearted laugh. He didn't buy her ready acceptance of Jack's marriage, but she was facing it with grace.

It had been all well and good, Jamie thought, to know McClean sent a message of love and affection or whatever the hell it was, with his little code. But the day after and the day after that, she faced the days knowing Jack had embarked on a new life.

One night, shortly after the wedding news broke, Bronwyn was in bed flipping through channels. She was distracted and lost these days, so after a hot bath and an attempt at sleep, she gave up and watched snippets of old movies and late night talk shows. She flipped past a shopping channel and dropped the remote. As if a crane had yanked her, she went forward onto her knees, turned back the channel and gaped at the screen.

"Hi there, so is this Wendy from Oklahoma? Where at in Oklahoma, Wendy? Oklahoma City? I know it well. Well,

welcome to the show, Wendy. Say hello to Ellis Fielding and his wife, Cheri."

So that was what sixteen years had done to Ellis, Bronwyn's long-ago fiancé. Ellis Fielding, CEO, art collector, and world traveler was hawking candles with his wife. On television.

"Well, Ellis, I am so glad to have you with us for this two hour Home Day special. And thank you for bringing your lovely wife."

"She's a keeper all right, Suzanne."

Bronwyn swallowed hard and hit 'mute'. She walked down the long hall to the bathroom. Her mouth was slack as she looked in the mirror. She returned to the bedroom and sidled up to the TV to see if she'd dreamed it.

"We wanted to bring you the best fragrances, the longest burn and it was Cheri's idea to get into soy. Look at all these flavors. Oh, I'm sorry. Here, I'll hold it still."

Bronwyn heard his laugh. She didn't know if it had always been hollow and fake, or if it was an affectation for the shill.

She changed the channel, but less than a minute later, she was compelled to go back. It was fifteen minutes into a two hour show. As bad as it was to see Ellis Fielding, did his wife need to be there?

She turned the TV off, punched the pillow, tossed it off the bed, and turned the TV back on.

"There's still time to get these for Christmas, but aren't they just the perfect go-to gift for the holidays? Get three and have them in a basket, ready for those unexpected guests who drop by."

"That's right, Suzanne, you are so right. They're just so perfect. And, how can you ever choose just one design? Butterflies are Cheri's favorites, but I like the bird."

Bronwyn hit mute, and called Jamie.

"Hi, Jimey. I'm fine. Could you stop over for a couple of minutes? No, I'm fine, really. Just, could I see you?"

And quicker than humanly possible, Jamie was standing in her bedroom.

Bronwyn told him about Ellis Fielding, gestured to the TV as exhibit A, and told how Ellis had asked her to wear a suit to their wedding, but her friend Oliver Silkowski dragged her to Kleinfeld's, and trying on wedding dresses with Ollie was the best day of her entire life. And how Ellis hadn't called to check on her, after his wedding announcement in the *New York Times*. How it felt seeing a photo in *Town and Country* of Ellis Fielding and his new wife Cheri in Tiffany, her Tiffany. Ellis would never even think of Tiffany, if it hadn't been for Bronwyn's reverence for the elegant store.

Jamie waited for her to take a breath, and steered her down the hall to the second bedroom. He told her to think of more Ellis Fielding stories while he legged it to the butler's pantry to make tea. He was more than happy to hit 'Power' and end the Ellis Fielding absurdity.

Bronwyn had her chance to tell more tales, but after several sips of warm tea, she fell contentedly to sleep, nestled beside Jamie.

Disturbed that Bronwyn had more than a few idiots in her life, Jamie vowed to make her holiday a lovely one.

He was angry about Jack McClean and spoke with Graeme, trying to suss out McClean's character. Graeme was sad to know Bronwyn's heart was broken; he hadn't been aware there was anything serious between Jack and Bronwyn. However, he did speak highly of McClean.

Graeme wondered aloud if Jeeves had any involvement, but Jamie knew quite well that Ernest Rose was to blame.

Jamie told Graeme he wanted to find something special to give Bronwyn at Christmas. Surprisingly, Graeme had an absolutely mighty idea, and promised him he'd do his bit on that end. Jamie was glad he'd brought him into his confidence.

For Graeme's part, he'd planned to give the gift to her himself, but he remembered the happy love he'd seen on Jamie and Bronwyn's faces at their Merrie Olde England dinner, and was delighted to play Cupid.

After talking to Graeme, Jamie decided he had two issues at hand. One was bringing McClean and Bronwyn together. They deserved a helping hand to undo some of Ernest's manky play.

Jamie flew with Grace to New York to deal with the other issue. He'd requested a financial analysis from Zuleika, but it revealed nothing untoward regarding Ernest Rose, and safeguards were implemented at Bronwyn's behest. If Ernest was to enjoy his life, it would be while she lived, and not after. He'd not benefit from her will, or insurance policy. Only Bronwyn could send requests to Grace or Zuleika for monetary gifts, and Ernest was handled no differently than anyone else on the estate. The Swiss funds were all in order and Jamie decided Bronwyn's generosity must have kept him satisfied.

As Jamie and Grace flew back to Maine, they were quiet. She was relieved Jamie requested the analysis. She felt uncomfortable around Jeeves and appreciated knowing his finances were in-line. Grace hadn't known about Bronwyn's beneficiaries, but on the flight Jamie said Ernest wasn't among them. Samuel and Paul would inherit the Factory, and the residents could continue to reside there as long as both boys agreed. If Ernest Rose did anything the boys didn't approve of, he'd no longer be living on the estate.

Grace closed her eyes and drifted off.

Jamie gazed into the inky night sky. What was it, about Ernest Rose? He imagined sitting with Clive and debating the ins and outs of it all. The best he could come up with was the simplest idea. Ernest loved his glorious life, and didn't want to lose it. There was something about Bronwyn that kept him from stealing from her. Perhaps he viewed her as a daughter, and been won over when she was at hospital, or perhaps he admired her courage. After all, it was Bronwyn who'd secured the estate and then the millions, save the last time. That had been Puppet Clive and Puppet Jamie as Ernest jerked their strings. Jamie craved answers, but he knew that sometimes there was no answer. All he could do was keep Ernest away from her money, and she had done a fine job of that, so far.

"Grace, do you have a number for Jack McClean's assistant?"

She smiled warmly, and Jamie had to admire her radiant smile. Ever the professional, she was good at looking stern. However, he knew a different side of Grace because she and her English actor, Hughie, spent time with Bronwyn. When they were all four together, it seemed the American girls got quite caught up by the English boys and it was great fun.

She watched Jamie's lips purse together, unaware he'd realized he was about to substitute the Great Jack McClean for himself at those little get-togethers. Grace didn't mind watching him sigh deeply…it brought his impeccably tailored shirt to its straining point, and then he exhaled and it was over.

"Would you like me to place the call for you?"

"No, I'll ring him from town."

Jamie drove to the Lobster Pound and asked Splash Flanagan if he could use his office phone. He pressed a fifty into Splash's hand and went through the door. He could sweep the phones at the estate, but it just seemed easier this way. Besides, he could reward himself with a little Lazy Man's Lobster after he was done.

"Dick Domitrovich, speaking."

"Good afternoon, Mr. Domitrovich. Jamie Donald here, attached to Bronwyn McCall. Have you a moment to chat?"

"I do. How is she? Jack's in the next room. Shall I get him?"

"No, actually, I'd prefer speaking with you. To answer your inquiry, Bronwyn's doing as well as can be expected."

Dick lowered his voice. "Gee, I'm sorry to hear that. I love that girl, my little Pittsburgh girl. What can I do?"

"As it's nearly Christmas, you might mention to McClean that if he were to send Bronwyn a Christmas gift, I'd be certain she received it."

"I'm sure Jack's up for that." Dick was quiet, and Jamie waited. "You're not saying she hasn't received Jack's mail, are you?"

Jamie was glad to see Domitrovich was a bright chappie. Jamie let silence speak for him.

"Oh wow. You're kidding. Oh Lord…maybe that's what happened. I wondered why she wasn't writing. Why she'd moved on. Should I let Jack know?"

"That's not an issue at this point, Mr. Domitrovich. What's done is done. But, I do know Bronwyn might have a happier Christmas if she received a pleasant surprise."

"By 'surprise' do you mean Jack?"

"Not as long as he's wed to the Blue girl. I'm suggesting a gift would be a kind gesture. That's all."

"Forgive me, Jamie, but were you in favor of Jack with Bronwyn? Because after Thanksgiving, her man Jeeves showed up and said she'd changed her mind about Jack, and he was pretty brutal about it, if you know what I mean. Jack was devastated. I wouldn't want him to get his hopes up."

"All I can tell you, Mr. Domitrovich, is Bronwyn subjected me to a showing of McClean's chef flick, I sat through it and I'm still making the call."

Dick giggled. "Sorry, Jamie. You know, Jack doesn't have Bronwyn's address. Everything always went to Mastrofrancesco in New York. He doesn't have her phone number, either."

"Right. If Bronwyn didn't wish to speak to him before, I doubt that's changed, would you agree? I'll give you an address and I assure you she'll receive any parcels or letters from McClean."

"Would you like to join me, sending Samuel and Paul their gifts, Jimey?"

"What do we have, Bronwyn? Don't suppose you've found the boyos anything decent."

Bronwyn grinned and trotted upstairs.

"See for yourself," she said as she returned. "This is a 'Horsey' jacket. They designed these for the Italian Equestrian teams and you can button out the vest, see? It has what's supposed to be a 'Storm System' but I don't know if that means anything more than 'waterproof'. What do you think? For Paul."

"It's deadly cool, actually. He'll be beyond delighted."

"And I found this watch for Samuel."

"Not as grand as my watch, we know that, don't we now?"

"True." She walked over and patted his cheek, then took the watch from its box. "It's a rubber sports watch with two time zones, so one can be for his papa. And, it's waterproof, but the neat thing is it's supposed to reinforce the body's electromagnetic field and make you calm, relaxed, and enhances your performance."

"Does it now?" Jamie said, grinning from ear to ear. "Must be a good seller. Let's dash up to Freeport and then to Ogunquit and I'll get some sweets and things to toss in the boxes."

Bronwyn smiled. She was tired of being distracted by Jack McClean and Lara Blue. It wasn't so hard to shake off, once she realized she had Jamie with her this Christmas.

There was a time after McClean got married, when Jamie contemplated telling Bronwyn he loved her, and reaching for bliss he'd never considered. He waged a war with himself for a day or so, but he remembered the meeting he'd had with Bram, before returning to Maine. The prime minister told Jamie he always worried about Bronwyn's safety. If Bram's enemies knew how much she meant to him, they'd know he could be compromised. Jamie had seen it before. He was all too aware of today's tortures. What he didn't expect was the dispassionate way the prime minister said he wouldn't lift a finger to save her. Jamie could see Bram regretted it, even as he reminded Jamie to take every precaution and keep her safe, always. The burden was his, and Jamie was glad of it.

Reminding himself of that meeting, Jamie knew he must retain some detachment. It'd be a tightrope walk; he'd write the rules, but he was prepared to push them, just like the night Ellis Fielding sold little votives and Jamie held Bronwyn in his arms as she slept.

Jeeves went to the Biltmore in Coral Gables for a three week Christmas holiday. Bronwyn couldn't quite picture him on South Beach, but he seemed taken with the '100 wines by the glass' when she showed him the brochure. She'd expected him to choose the lights of Vienna at Christmas or a trip home to England, but he wanted to drive south.

Jamie asked Bronwyn to stay at Jeeves' flat with him, but she was reluctant. He had been firm about their platonic status and she couldn't fault him. After all, she was the one who declared they could be as close as they liked, without the complications of being lovers. But, she'd said it before Jack had married.

She decided to give Jamie a ring, but discovering his ring size was the problem.

She enlisted Grace and Jen to discretely get the size. Could it be a clipboard and form that everyone on the estate had to fill out? Slip him a Mickey and measure it? That idea had them rolling on the floor. Finally, Bronwyn said he'd only trust the innocent, and as none of them qualified, they agreed Jen's four-year-old daughter could get Jamie to do anything.

Jen had cleverly painted each ring a different color, from a plastic ring-sizer. Even Jen's husband got in on it, as Tricky Abigail was in training. She played a teapot game Jen and Bronwyn devised, and every time Abigail brought a ring out, she'd put it on Ken's fingers. The little sprite was carefully trained to check for a good fit, at her daddy's expense. They almost had to cut one off his thumb. It was Jen's job to observe, and see what color ring fit Jamie's right ring finger. Bronwyn decided measuring his left ring finger was presumptuous. She didn't want to think he'd ever marry, but she expected him to wear *her* ring through five marriages, if that's what the future held.

The day had come. Seated on the floor, opposite Abigail, Jamie began to play the game. He poured 'tea' into her tea cup until she heard a ring, grabbed it and placed it on Jamie's finger. End result – purple was the perfect fit.

Jen broke into flop sweat from the pressure of covert observation.

The day before Christmas, Bronwyn and Jamie were having their usual breakfast with Edgar and Clara, and they were coaxing her to stay with Jamie.

"I promise you, Bronnie, I'll fix you both a good Christmas breakfast. Here with us or over at the flat. You say. What about tonight? What can I fix you kids tonight?" Edgar implored.

Bronwyn was amused. Edgar didn't call her 'Bronnie' so it must be important to him. She looked at Jamie and realized he was hoping for a nice Christmas in Jeeves' gorgeous flat, and decided he shouldn't spend it alone. She'd had enough quiet Christmases.

"Tell you what. If you don't mind, maybe Jamie and I will have your five mushroom soup with hazelnuts at the flat. It'll be a soup party. Then I'll sleep over in the alcove bed, we'll get up in the morning and do presents, have breakfast back over here and," Bronwyn's eyes lifted to the ceiling "maybe we'll eat Christmas dinner at Pine Manor. What do you think, Jamie? Would that be too depressing?"

Jamie's face was in his wrinkled elfin smile mode. "Sounds brilliant, Bronwyn. Simply brilliant."

"Well, don't get excited, because I bought fancy new sheets and blankets for the residents, and I plan to change their beds while everyone's eating Christmas dinner. Are you up for changing a hundred beds on Christmas?"

"Bronwyn, you've no idea of my training, have you? No one wraps a tighter corner than I do. Have your sixpence ready for bouncing, my love."

They laughed and Edgar's wheels started turning, figuring he'd go over to Pine Manor and make a nice dish or two for the cafeteria.

Jamie wondered what Jack had sent to Bronwyn. He told himself he didn't want to upstage McClean, but in reality, that's just what he hoped to do.

Hardly a day went by when Jamie didn't wish he could talk to Clive. He hated being on this 'spark McClean's romance' path. At least they could have commiserated with each other. Clive had been under Bronwyn's spell. Of all people, he would understand why there was no future for Jamie as Bronwyn's husband. Clive knew the places they'd been, the things they'd done. It was a blessing and a curse to be on this seemingly benign side of the stone wall. Jamie could taste life with Bronwyn as keenly as he could savor the buttery morsels of lobster at the dinner table.

Bronwyn packed an overnight bag and headed to Jeeves' flat. She didn't mind leaving her home, one bit. It was large and empty and, other than the Dickens houses in her library, rather un-Christmas-like.

Jamie's squatter life had yielded a breathtaking Christmas scene. Bronwyn wondered how he'd managed it, and was stunned to see the overwhelmingly gorgeous Christmas decorations. The flat sparkled, shimmered, dipped and swooped all down the hallway and into Jeeves' library and living room, swinging from balcony to balcony. She was reminded of the Horne's store holiday decorators who told her 'too much is never too much'. The living room had an enormous Christmas tree, but one couldn't see much greenery because the tree was decked to a fare-thee-well in red, burgundy, dark green, lime green, gold and copper ornaments of all shapes and sizes. Bronwyn had never seen anything like it. If Christmas had ended at that moment, Bronwyn would be utterly happy.

She heard Edgar and Clara traipsing down the hall, clucking. Bronwyn saw a large package the size of a dishwasher, and went to the kitchen to retrieve the gifts she'd brought over.

Edgar served the Christmas Eve soup with jumbo gulf shrimp, cheeses, and seeded crackers; and returned with fudge brownies and cranberry ice cream for dessert.

After dinner, Bronwyn and Jamie bundled up for a quick dash back to Edgar and Clara's and wished them a Happy Christmas, leaving a wrapped package they'd chosen together.

Back at the flat, Jamie made a roaring fire and Bronwyn changed into flannel pajamas.

They didn't have happy tales of Christmas Eves to share, so Bronwyn didn't delay the viewing of *It's a Wonderful Life*, asking Jamie over and over, had he really never seen it before? They alternated bites of chocolate cherry fudge, courtesy of Clara, with popcorn, washing it down with Edgar's wassail. Next was *Miracle on 34th Street* and Jamie wasn't a bit surprised that a department store movie would be special to her.

As it drew near midnight, they donned heavy coats and boots and walked down to the edge of the lawn. Neither spoke, aware of the significant hush all around them. Bronwyn turned to see the shimmer of white miniature lights sparkling from the Factory balconies.

Jamie kissed her. It wasn't a long kiss and it wasn't a short kiss. It was a 'just right' kiss. The perfect Christmas kiss, sweet enough to stay with them as they both drifted off to sleep, he in his Jeeves bed and she in her alcove bed.

The next morning, Bronwyn had that Christmas morning fizzy feeling of anticipation. Jamie was already up, turning the Christmas tree lights on. As her alcove bed overlooked the living room, she leaned over the balcony in rapturous amazement. It was fabulous; she dashed down the stairs, tying her robe, certain she would never have such a wonderful Christmas again. She didn't think of Jack McClean for even one moment, until Jamie handed her a box from Jack.

Inside, was a diamond necklace. Bronwyn wasn't as delighted as she would have expected to be. She felt far removed from Jack. It had been almost two years since she'd seen or spoken to him. The necklace seemed to be an extravagant gesture that said, 'forgive me for shocking you with my wedding'.

Jamie wasn't prepared for Bronwyn's muted reaction, although he didn't mind it. He'd prepared himself to see extreme joy. Perhaps she was just sparing his feelings. He raved over the diamond necklace as much as a man could do. It really was outstanding. Perhaps his gifts wouldn't hold up.

Bronwyn had four gifts for Jamie and he opened them all together. He unwrapped a Prada garment bag, a cashmere herringbone tuxedo vest, a Polo Blackwatch hoodie that he immediately donned, and a navy corduroy Polo blazer. They laughed about her subterfuge during their recent NY trip.

Despite the Moss meeting, she'd managed to hit the Ralph Lauren store – hard.

They exchanged Harbor Candy, books, socks, and nuts.

She still had one more gift for him, but she'd wait, she said. He dragged over the enormous box, with its huge pale pink satin ribbon. She pulled the bow, sliding the ribbon down, when Jamie stopped her.

He caught his breath, then urged, "Go on."

She lifted the lid, and plowed gently through layers of tissue until she found pale copper satin. Jimey must have gotten her a dress. She realized there was a net petticoat; actually numerous net petticoats. Jimey must have gotten her a ball gown. "It's breathtaking," she told him, reverently. "Absolutely breathtaking."

"Go on, Bronwyn. Lift it out. Do you need my help?"

"No, I'll get it." And as Bronwyn saw the bodice, and then the sleeves, she couldn't believe her eyes. She felt decidedly faint, holding Deborah Kerr's gown from the 'Shall We Dance' scene with Yul Brynner. She laid the dress gently across the box, walked to the sofa and put her head in her hands.

"You fancy it? Bronwyn, you like it?" Bronwyn nodded, head still in her hands. "It's not just me. Graeme Woods helped. He was part of it."

Bronwyn lifted her face and smiled through tears. How delightful that Graeme and Jamie had conspired together.

"It's for me? It's mine?"

Jamie nodded.

"I'll get a museum case and put it upstairs in my theatre lobby."

"We thought you might. So, you really like it?"

Her head bobbed.

"Are you ready for your next gift?"

"Do you mind waiting a bit? After breakfast? This is so unbelievable. You could *never* top this," and Bronwyn threw her arms around him and hugged him hard.

They called Edgar to see if Christmas breakfast was nearly ready, and changed for the day. Jamie wore the Blackwatch hoodie under his new blazer, and well-worn jeans. Bronwyn thought he looked like a million bucks. She'd given her Christmas day look a great deal of thought, and buttoned a Lauren oatmeal shirtdress with suede elbow patches, over brown riding pants, leaving the bottom of the dress flapping open. Adding a narrow leather belt, she pulled on brown leather riding boots. She dashed back into the living room, gazed at the *King and I* dress again, and skipped down the hall to an appreciative Jamie.

Edgar had a spectacular buffet arranged on his sideboard…mimosas; Pain Perdu with candied pecans and maple syrup; Crab Louie with tomato wedges, sliced eggs and asparagus; lobster and asparagus quiche; crispy home fries; rashers of crisp bacon; almond croissants; blackberry scones; cranberry walnut toast; lemon-brown sugar meringue tarts and glorious Torrone parfaits, studded with flecks of nougat, pecans, cherries and raisins.

While they were still saying their good mornings, Grace and Hughie came down from the fourth floor. Grace's eyes were sparkling and Bronwyn asked why she had such a huge smile. Grace looked at Jamie, who shrugged, and turned to Bronwyn.

"You've got to see the Christian Louboutin heels Hughie bought me. Unbelievable. And a Von Furstenberg dress and Stella McCartney ballet flats and Ann Demeulemeester black leather boots, killer, and these."

Bronwyn stepped close to see her leverbacks. They were spectacular. "Cathy Waterman Love Earrings, they're called." Grace whispered, "Platinum and diamonds." Grace lifted her exquisitely groomed black eyebrows, for effect.

"Wow," Bronwyn said to Hughie, and she meant it. She'd made a shopping list for Hughie, from the Barney's web-site, and he'd done a spectacular job with the shoes and boots. But she had to hand it to the little devil – the dress was a brave add-on, but the earrings were an impressive statement of his love for Grace. The diamonds even spelled LOVE suspended in the circles. Bronwyn gave Hughie a hug that nearly squeezed the life from him.

"Good job," she pronounced, kissing his cheek with a loud smack.

Jamie was pirouetting in his new garb, for Grace's inspection. Bronwyn caught her looking down at his hand and Bronwyn mouthed, "Not yet."

As they moved through the buffet, Grace whispered to Hughie, "They're not done with their gifts yet," and he nodded.

When Bronwyn told them about the Deborah Kerr gown, they were shocked; even Edgar remembered the dress once Clara started singing 'Shall We Dance' while waltzing him around the kitchen. Everyone was impressed, but no one more than Hughie. He'd always enjoyed Jamie's company, but now he regarded him with profound respect.

After breakfast, Bronwyn and Jamie returned to Jeeves' flat, laden with iced cutout cookies from Clara.

She gave him his ring, a platinum band with a narrow bar of onyx and two diamonds on the left side of the bar, and explained that no matter what, she hoped he'd know how much she loved him.

"Any time you want to change the nature of things, let me know. I'm in! But I'll not bring it up, again. I'm happy, Jimey, and I'm happy because of you. If things stay exactly as they are, I am happy and content." He put the ring on his left hand, kissed her deeply, and beamed. Bronwyn hoped Abigail's measurement would hold true for Jamie's left hand, so she took his hand and gave a little tug.

Then, he handed her a flat, rectangular package, extravagantly wrapped in shiny emerald green, topped by a huge green bow dwarfing the box. "I hope you like it."

Opening it, she parted the tissue and found a beautiful pair of leather gloves. Bronwyn smiled because she remembered Grace insisting she try her gloves on, as a guise to judge her glove size. Jamie and Grace, working together. It surely was Christmas time.

"Try them, Bronwyn."

She slipped them on, first the right and then the left, but as she put her fingers in the left one, something was inside. She found a ring. An exquisite ring. Jamie handed her the robins-egg blue box and her fingers touched the embossed 'Tiffany'. She took a closer look at the ring. It was the most exceptional thing she'd ever seen…two open hearts, woven into an intricate design, with diamonds sprinkled about.

"It's Paloma Picasso, Bronwyn, called a Double Loving Heart Ring. White gold and diamonds and exactly what I wanted to give you this Christmas. I want you to know how much I love you, and I was deadly stunned when you gave me a ring, as well." He kissed her lightly. "I'm a lucky bloke to have someone who loves me and understands how we can still love each other no matter the reality. I hope you'll keep it and never forget that I bloody well love you."

He was prepared for waterworks, but she just smiled.

"It's two hearts, Jimey, for a reason. Just like your ring has two little diamonds on the side. If you look inside your ring, it says 'Never Alone'. That's us."

She put hers on her left hand, and Jamie looked like Santa's most enthusiastic elf, his face a roadmap of happy lines and wrinkles in a gravity-defying smile, curving almost up to his twinkling eyes. Bronwyn knew she'd never manage such a smile; who could? But she enjoyed looking at his. She hugged him with happy emotion, and knew at that moment, no matter what happened with Jack or anyone else in the future, she would never stop wearing Jamie's ring.

As January ended, Jamie girded himself to sit through the Golden Globe Awards with Bronwyn. She waffled between enthusiasm as the day approached, and quiet contemplation.

When she explained about the red carpet shows, he understood the cause of her anxiety. He was interested to see how well Jack McClean could pull it off, with Lara Blue there. As a courtesy, he called Dick Domitrovich to offer fair warning: Bronwyn would be watching.

Hughie was filming and Grace had gone on location. It would have been easier to have Grace at her side whenever Lara Blue popped up on the screen, but it was sweet of Jamie to join her. Bronwyn vowed to remain cool and indifferent to whatever happened on the television.

She chose the warming room for their viewing. Not realizing they were going to start their 'fun' several hours early at 5:00 PM, Jamie was relieved to see Edgar providing nibbles. Edgar promised to be in the kitchen all evening long, prepared to serve whatever the mood dictated. In Jamie's opinion, that man was a prince.

This was all new to Jamie, and it was odd seeing the actors and actresses sauntering down the line, with focus on fashion of all things. When Jack McClean came up to the mike, he was with his co-star and not Lara Blue. Bronwyn was so pleased, she dashed into the kitchen afterward. Jamie watched her scooping into a mini banana split and took the opportunity to visit Edgar and grab a plate of tapas.

Bronwyn wanted to comment on Jack's classic tuxedo. Too bad she wasn't watching with The Boys. They were always appreciative of a crisp shirt collar and well-tied bow tie. Their derisive comments could be brutal as the stars walked the red carpet. She knew they were having a field day, wherever they were, and each of them would be agonizing over Jack's wavy and rather long hair. It looked gorgeous.

Bronwyn finished her banana split just in time. Lara Blue was on-screen.

"Howya. It's been ages since I've been here. Yes, my Jack wanted to give Kate a hand. He's such a grand fella, isn't he? He's specky four eyes tonight, has a bit of a headache."

"You look beautiful, Lara. Turn around. Oh, those feathers are fabulous. Who are you wearing?"

Jamie stole a quick look at Bronwyn, who seemed calm.

"Hopefully, when you see me next, I'll be stretchin' it out. We're ready to start with the babbies."

"Really? Thanks for the scoop, Lara. We'll be here at Oscar time...think you can manage it by then?"

"Well, aren't you a wee bit cheeky...but yeah, could be."

Jamie hardly dared to look at Bronwyn, but she was smiling. "Let's see what Edgar has for us now, Jimey."

While they leaned over the kitchen island, nibbling on salted Marcona almonds, olives, stuffed new potatoes, and prime rib silver dollars, Bronwyn told them that Lara was a fraud. Jack couldn't have children so she was just putting on a good front.

Jamie offered, "She's quite common, Bronwyn, did you give a listen? And seems more than a bit thick."

She gave him a grateful hug. She was prepared for Lara Blue to look lovely, and she looked luminous.

Clara had warned Edgar what hurdles they'd have to clear. In fact, she was watching at home and calling Edgar from time to time, commenting on the red carpet and asking how Bronwyn was doing. Clara predicted Lara Blue would make a top 10 best dressed list; she was tiny and pretty with perfect features, shining hair, but in a horrid updo in the fashion, and a non-stop smile. When she began describing the pink feathers, Edgar tuned out until his wife asked how Jamie was holding up. Edgar thought how odd it was for them to worry about the feelings of an MI6 as he watched television.

The night he'd gone over to Bronwyn's and made cocoa, Edgar figured out Jamie held Jeeves responsible for her heartbreak. Edgar couldn't imagine someone turning his back on Bronwyn, so he wasn't inclined to cheer for McClean, tonight or in Bronwyn's life. Watching how Jamie sat with Bronwyn with simple class and elegance, knowing how he loved her, Edgar found himself hoping Bronwyn would give up on McClean.

Once the show began, Clara called and warned her husband that the screenplay award would be presented by Jack McClean, so Bronwyn would see him then, but the tougher time would be if Jack won for his role in *Hemingway*. He either would or would not kiss his brand-new wife, Lara Blue, sitting beside him at the *Hemingway* table.

Jack won. It didn't seem awkward at all, when Jack rose and turned to his left, hugging his directors and co-stars, walking the long way around his table. In his brief acceptance, he did the usual bit and then said, "I'd like to thank those who have always believed in me."

Jamie was relieved. McClean had done everything he could to make Bronwyn's viewing as painless as possible. He might just be worthy of her love.

Satisfied, Jamie got to his feet and asked Edgar to break out the bubbly so they could ostensibly toast Jack McClean's victory as 'Best Performance by an Actor in a Motion Picture – Drama'. In actuality, they were toasting their survival of a very tricky evening.

CHAPTER THIRTY FIVE

KEI TE PAI
2008

*G*raeme pulled the script from his worn leather messenger bag, and stroked the bag fondly, concentrating on the nicks and scratches that seemed to multiply each day, reminding him of the wrinkles on his well-worn face. Vanity, he sighed. An actor's best friend. Looking from the gilt ceilings to the marble floor, he appreciated why this hotel was a favorite of Bronwyn's. No matter that Jack McClean was staying dozens of blocks away, at the 60 Thompson. Graeme suspected Jack agreed to meet, because he hoped it was Bronwyn's idea. Surely Jack held no hope that the script was anything worthwhile and indeed, it wasn't. When Bronwyn had called Graeme, he protested that it would be impossible to find a script to pass off as a plausible project. For him, it was a dry-spell. Better they sort through the pile that Jack stacked up, he thought wryly.

Although he had taken his place in the elegant lobby fifteen minutes early, he expected Jack would be stuck in Manhattan traffic and settled back into the plush settee, closing his eyes. Moments later, when a waiter arrived with

Graeme's espresso, Jack slid into the settee beside him, with a nervous giggle.

"Hullo, mate," Jack breathed as he held his paw out for a handshake. Graeme was always surprised what a large presence Jack McClean was, just as Jack noted the incredibly shrinking man that Graeme was becoming. Jack gentled his handshake and leaned in to kiss his cheek. Graeme thought how easy it was to write Jack off as brash, and was reminded what a courtly gentleman he was. Open and affable, the crews always loved him. Graeme felt the current that vibrated beside him and understood why Bronwyn would be taken with Jack. And so he began the folly of the script.

After twenty minutes of false enthusiasm, the scripts were set upon the coffee table. They regarded each other, Graeme with hesitation and Jack with bemusement. Jack guessed his acting compatriot was about to fly without a net.

The twinkle in Jack's eye and his half curving smile unnerved the older actor. This wasn't something Graeme was used to doing, but he reminded himself that if he had a daughter, and Bronwyn was all that and more to him, he'd do it for her, so he gathered himself.

"How's married life?"

Jack inhaled deeply, all the way to the core of his belly. Graeme must have read the script of Jack's own desire; the script he'd been mentally writing ever since Graeme had called. This script that Jack had gotten on his knees and prayed to hear this very morning, opening with an inquiry as to the state of his wedded bliss.

However, the shock of being blessedly on the right track took the twinkle from Jack's eye and Graeme feared he'd gone too far. Jack realized he hadn't chosen the message he wanted to convey to Bronwyn, who startled so easily.

He weighed his words, tested his thoughts, and worried what to do with his golden opportunity. This lobby of the Waldorf-Astoria was as close as he'd gotten to Bronwyn in two years, and although he still had no idea where she was, he could feel her breath upon his face and was desperate not to make a false move. Seated as they were, both men were circling each other.

"Lousy, actually. Most bloody ridiculous thing I've ever done. Proving a point, I suppose. Both of us, proving a point."

Graeme's bushy white eyebrows shot up. "Sorry to hear that lad, truly I am. Tough spot."

He saw real regret in Jack's eyes. He often found it difficult to be around actors as they could be incomplete left on their own, or could take fantasy beyond the soundstage. But Jack was easy and genuine.

"I'm ashamed to say, after a week or so, we found we're copacetic as long as I'm on location and she's not there. She's busy spending my money – quite adept, actually. She seems to have her money tucked away for a rainy day. Torrential." He grimaced and said, "If I want to see her, I can watch 'E' and she'll be on the red carpets or doing interviews. I've moved her up the food chain."

Graeme studied him thoughtfully. "So, you're settled in then?"

"Would you be asking because Bronwyn wants to know?" That caused a nearly imperceptible flinch on Graeme's part.

"Certainly not. A moment of curiosity is all," Graeme hesitated. He felt uncomfortable with his struggle to appear unflappable. Drat. Why was this so hard? He could act, for Queen and country; what was so damned hard about this?

Jack's twinkle returned. "So, Bronwyn doesn't want to know?"

"I assure you, no, cross my heart."

Jack's green eyes narrowed. "So, is that how they cross hearts these days?" His wide smile and gusty laugh broke through the lobby's din, and Graeme smiled abashedly as they settled in as amiable friends.

It was noon and they moved to the bar at Sir Harry's, just off the lobby. Graeme ordered a well-earned Jameson Whiskey and Jack had a Bloody Mary. The men sat reflectively.

Jack spoke without looking at Graeme. "I suppose you heard about the *Maxim* interview? Lara said Bar Harbor was a boring death, while I was gadding about in Key West. We weren't even together then. My assistant showed me the Maine papers...*Blue Who*...and *Lara Blue Us Off.*" Jack grimaced. "Making light of whale watching and popovers on a wooden bench really set their teeth on edge."

"Well, my boy; I believe Lara's always spouted, hasn't she? She's a reputation for it. People don't think that's your attitude," Graeme said, without naming names. "She said last week you're trying for children. Start a family or whatnot."

Jack's lips were drawn to a thin line.

"Well, that would be a bloody miracle. There'll be no babies. Not with me, anyway." He remembered this was ground he and Bronwyn had covered the first time they were together. "Lara will do anything for some face time on the telly. I've never known anyone like her."

Realizing what folly a few missteps could produce, if marriage could ever be called a misstep, Jack felt thoroughly miserable. He left the prison of his dark thoughts for a moment and remembered he was sitting beside Graeme Woods, sent as emissary by his Bronwyn. He regained his footing and righted his path.

"I'm thinking of ending it soon. Lara was so bloody

aggressive with the pre-nup, she won't be surprised. Her ex has been making noises about getting back together, and I said if he's making noises maybe she should listen." He spoke even more quietly. "I don't like to admit it, but it's damn hard to have my mistakes bandied about. I know it seems I don't give a flying leap, but I've had quite enough. And it's about to get worse."

"Bloody hell. Jack, my boy, dear friend. Don't do this for the wrong reason." Graeme looked into Jack's eyes. "I only brought you a script. Nothing more."

Jack returned his look with soft eyes shining in the reflected light of the crystal barware.

"Would you like some chocolate cake, dear? With caramel icing," Clara gestured toward the table by the Orangerie's kitchen.

Bronwyn smiled at her. "No thanks. I'll take some when I go home, for sure."

It was one of those days when she found it difficult to eat. She looked at the cake with a faraway look, a cake like her mother had baked for her birthday, as long as Bronwyn could remember. Although it seemed a lifetime of cakes, she realized there'd probably been only six or seven of them. This day was becoming sodden with regret.

"Just tea now, if you're having some." She settled into a comfortable chair in the Orangerie and was glad to have Clara's maternal company. Waiting to hear from Graeme was unsettling.

The phone rang and after a moment, Clara emerged from behind crisp chintz drapes. She handed Bronwyn the phone and retreated to make the tea.

"Hello Graeme, what's up?" She glanced back where Clara had gone and answered, "No, just Clara. So, how did it go? Did you learn anything?"

"Oh, really?" Clara peeked out as she noticed Bronwyn's voice rise in pitch and saw some much-needed color come to her cheeks. "You're certain? That's sad news." But Clara saw no sadness in Bronwyn's demeanor as she put her other hand up to the phone and cradled it gently. She seemed to prize the phone and everything it said.

"That's nice. You think so? Really? How did he look? Well, what was he wearing? Try to remember, Graeme."

After a few soundless moments in the glass house, Bronwyn's face gradually fell into a stony hardness as she listened.

"No, you're right. That didn't happen. I didn't. That does explain a lot." She sat, listening. "I don't know if that would have changed anything – it might have. I don't know. You know how stubborn I can be," she said with a hollow laugh.

Her voice became stronger. "I'll not hold that against him, I'm just disappointed. That's what he does, maybe more often than I've known. I'll have to read my Wodehouse books again. Maybe it's part of Jeeves' charm."

Bronwyn was leaning forward with her elbows on the table. After a bit, she sighed, "When I think of Jack here, I picture my whole life being blasted open. I've always needed quiet and invisibility." She listened. "Well, perhaps someday. I'll think about it. I do know how much it would mean. It's probably a moot point, no matter what Jack said today."

She listened a bit longer and said gently, "Definitely. You're my true friend. My hero."

Clara could picture Graeme demurring as the aristo-cratic gentleman he was.

"I thank you, very much. I will. I'll think of a grand gesture." Bronwyn listened a bit more, laughed and promised, "Yes, Graeme, a truly grand one."

Hughie took a seat in Bronwyn's formal dining room. "Why can't we just have tea in your little tea room and pretend you haven't called a meeting and scared the pants off me?"

He'd feared there'd be a price to pay for enjoying her largesse these many months; had it been years already? He guessed the day to pay the piper had arrived. His heart pounded in his feeble chest and sweat beads started to appear on his forehead. "Perhaps some water would be nice."

"Nothing's wrong, Hughie. I just want your advice."

"Say what?"

As Bronwyn poured his water, she inquired, "I want to know if it bothers Grace when you kiss actresses on-screen and when she knows you're doing love scenes, days on end."

"Why don't you ask Grace? I'll fetch her," and he started to stand, on his way to bolting. She pulled him back into his seat.

"No, Hughie. I wouldn't want to put the thought in her head. I'm guessing it hasn't come up."

"Well, it is me, you know. I rather think she hasn't given it a thought."

A smile flickered briefly across Bronwyn's face. Then, she turned serious. "I don't want to get involved with an actor. Really. I hate Los Angeles, the phoniness, the paparazzi."

"Paparazzi? My God, who are you getting involved with?"

Ignoring his question, Bronwyn remarked, "I like a quiet life. I don't want to hurt your feelings, Hughie, really I don't. But we don't seem to draw attention here. Together.

I'm sure it's because you're from," she hesitated, "you know, across the pond."

"So, what you're saying is that I'm second rate. I suppose the bloke you have in mind has a Golden Globe? BAFTA?" His eyes grew bigger. "A damned Oscar?"

Bronwyn placed three fingers over her left, closed fist.

"Three? Oscars? Good God, who can that be?"

Hughie struggled with his awards trivia knowledge. "Someone living?" When her eyebrows rose, he said, "Sorry, of course. I can't think of anyone with three."

While he was deep in thought, she went to the kitchen and returned with a plate of shortbread. She waited, knowing how sensitive he was when his thought process, memory, or intelligence was challenged. Bronwyn was beginning to second-guess meeting with him.

She almost saw the light bulb, above his head. "You don't mean to say, Jack McClean?" Bronwyn slowly nodded. "He doesn't have three."

She smiled and said, "One supporting."

"Well, good lord girl, that's just two and a half."

Bronwyn waited for Jack's identity to settle into Sebastian Hughes' psyche. He'd be envisioning life with another star, top billing dissolving to a co-starring role. What delicate creatures actors are, she thought.

Finally, Hughie drew himself up in his chair, placed his hands together in a pious and gentle manner and asked, "What's the problem? Are you saying the paparazzi are the reason you haven't invited him here?"

"No, I'm saying that I can't imagine living life with that much attention. My life isn't about acting and movies and fame and publicity. I couldn't stand it."

He looked stunned. "Bronnie lass, your life is all about

acting. You made a movie with Graeme that won him the show-boatin' Oscar of which we're so suddenly fond. Everyone who knows and admires Graeme, himself included, knows his role would have been nothing without you. Why you insisted on the cutting room floor, except for an elbow here, a hand shot there, is beyond me luv, but we all know his reactions to you made the film. There was no *Find Me* without you. None of us would have decent careers if you weren't reading the scripts and spicing them up for us with a bit of business here and there. You're a natural with film and lighting. We're in awe of you and worried you'll drop us like hot potaties and we'll none of us reach a decent height again. If we haven't told you often enough, shame on the lot of us."

He nibbled shortbread and bits of crumbs from the plate. Reinvigorated, Hughie steadily gathered himself and began again.

"You rebuilt a grand movie house in town, you have a theatre in your home and popcorn is your major food group. Briar roses, Bronwyn, you're all about acting and film." She looked unmoved. "This estate is just one grand location and these homes you've built are movie sets. Don't you see that? Don't you recognize that? Look around. Think about it. We all of us marvel at your creativity and brilliance. You've given every one of us our parts, and we love them." He patted her hand. "But, dear Bronwyn, you never cast the leading man for yourself."

Proud of his eloquent delivery and prepped for applause, the silence was starting to unhinge him a bit. He watched quiet thoughtfulness settling over her as she seemed less and less present. "Don't give me the damnable silent treatment, Bronwyn. I don't deserve it." He sulked a bit, and then came around the table and put his hand upon her shoulder.

"I can't in good conscience say that I'm thrilled to be relegated to the top floor parapet, while fancy pants Oscar boy is sword-slashing and romping all over our grounds. But, it's nothing personal against McClean. I've fancied him myself for a half second…especially that Western. Oh, lord, and that Minuteman movie," he grinned. "This town loves you. They won't stand for paparazzi about. Our lobstermen will toss them into the bay. And everywhere I look, we have our own James Bonds, three abreast. It's a flippin' fortress here. I say, we'll all be safe and sound if you bring that Jack McClean around, I promise you."

He lifted her chin and looked quizzically from eye to eye. "You deserve to have a life."

Bronwyn researched horses for sale around the world and e-mailed young Paul, as he became her horse expert. What Bram's son didn't know, he found out, and she was impressed with his knowledge.

She had phoned Jack's parents with her idea of surprising Jack with a horse, and they'd been very encouraging. But, she was wary of getting too close to them. Experience had shown her it was difficult to lose families, along with a man.

It was for that reason Bronwyn vowed not to meet the McCleans face-to-face, when Paul delivered the horse. Bronwyn would be there to choose the horse, but Paul would be the emissary, delivering the horse and settling it in.

Involving the McCleans made the project more enjoyable. On the phone, Jack's dad explained sheep shearing to her. The 'New Zealand' method was the most popular method in the world, he claimed, sheering in one piece and constantly moving the sheep so it was relaxed and didn't struggle. She also learned of Jack's boyhood fondness for an alarming number of vigorous activities like rock climbing, caving, and surfing.

She found excuses to call the McCleans, watching the clock with the significant time difference in mind. Bronwyn appreciated their Irish accents mixed with whatever New Zealand accent or slang she was hearing. Both Mr. and Mrs. McClean greeted her with 'Tena Koe' (hello) and said 'Kei Te Pehea Koe' (How are you). They always giggled and tried to get her to say 'Kei Te Pai' (very well, thank you) but Bronwyn surprised them once and said, 'what if I'm *not* very well?', provoking their laughter.

Bronwyn considered using an international horse transport, but she decided shipping a horse from the states might be too stressful for the horse. One from Australia or New Zealand would be less traumatized in its new home. She and Paul settled on seeing one horse in Australia and three in New Zealand. Sounding as if he'd crammed for a final, the young man solemnly promised to judge its suitability, conformation, soundness, health, history, and temperament.

Jamie spent two weeks with Paul, visiting several Kentucky horse farms to better understand the selection process. Paul was excited and a little nervous at the responsibility, but gained confidence with Jamie at his side.

Bronwyn joined them in Kentucky to choose a saddle, selecting an Aussie trail saddle with a sterling silver star. The salesman touted the rear rigging options, changing from single tie to balanced double tie or western. What Bronwyn liked was the Gel-Cush seating for comfort. She figured that would really impress Jack. Jamie had suppressed rolling his eyes.

They would be staying in Sydney and then Wellington.

The McCleans insisted on putting Paul up at their sheep farm when he arrived with the horse and they hoped Bronwyn might come, even though she'd declined.

Back in October, Mr. McClean had warned Jack not to broach something as important as marriage, in a letter. However, Jack had said the letters he and Bronwyn exchanged over the past two years brought them closer than any time together could have done. They'd invested those letters with time and thought, exploring and sharing their days, getting to know each others' sensibilities and values, and amusing each other. It had been a fine courtship, with their letters as mortar. The miles, and sometimes, continents, meant nothing when they held each other's words in their hands.

As a father, Mr. McClean was sad when Bronwyn broke Jack's heart. The Bronwyn Jack had described didn't seem the kind of girl who would end things at the first whisper of marriage. On the other hand, they couldn't expect to understand how her orphan mind worked. His son was terribly hurt when Bronwyn stopped writing and decided to end things, sending her man Jeeves to heartlessly break things off, in no uncertain terms.

Still, they'd been shocked when Jack impulsively decided to marry Lara Blue. Good parents support their son, but their reservations had been right about the Blue girl, almost from the beginning.

Surprisingly, every good thing Jack had said about Bronwyn, seemed confirmed when she called about her horse idea. She had spark and her feelings for Jack were obvious. They hoped it was more than Bronwyn second-guessing herself and wanting what she'd thrown away. It was an effort not asking Bronwyn if this meant she wanted Jack back. It wasn't like the McCleans to leave anything left unsaid.

Plans were finalized and the trip was launched. Jamie and Bronwyn flew to Los Angeles with Paul and the prime minister's bodyguard, and then continued to Sydney, settling in at The Observatory Hotel near Sydney Harbor.

Bronwyn enjoyed hotel tea with Paul and Jamie; then rested before their dinner reservation at The Boathouse.

Jamie sat smiling to himself in his room. When they'd gotten off the plane, a loudly dressed, older couple had been standing beside their driver, who was holding up "McCALL". Bronwyn hadn't noticed, but when they collected their luggage at the baggage claim, the man, wearing a porkpie hat, snapped a picture of the woman in a sillier hat, near Bronwyn. They'd so awkwardly staged the situation; Jamie enjoyed watching the McCleans immensely. Bronwyn being Bronwyn, noticed the flash and volunteered to take their photo together. This was so much more than the McCleans had expected. Although they maintained silence, lest Bronwyn recognize their voices, they were noticeably thrilled to interact with her. Instead of just snapping a quick photo of them, Bronwyn looked up at the shafts of light and moved them in front of the windows. She asked them to look over her left shoulder, down a little, and Jamie suspected it would turn out to be one of the best photographs they'd ever taken. Minus the silly hats, of course.

Bronwyn never gave them a second thought.

While Paul finalized arrangements to see the first horse, Jamie went through the adjoining door and sat with Bronwyn, drawing a second chair to the window. After companionable silence, Jamie asked, "Bronwyn, is there anything you've always wished for?"

Bronwyn stared out the window and Jamie wasn't

certain she'd heard him. Eventually, she turned to him with a sweet smile he'd not yet seen and said, "I do. Do you?"

Jamie grinned at her. "I see what you mean. No one's ever asked me, either. I'll have to think of mine. What are yours?"

"I've always wanted a big front porch with a view, I've always wanted a child," her voice was a little breathless. "I've always wanted a dog of my own." Jamie looked at her, with warm, crinkling eyes. "A wiener dog. And most of all, I've always wanted to open my eyes Christmas morning with someone I loved, beside me."

She was earnest, but this quickly devolved to a look of embarrassment. She'd rattled off the list as if she kept it on the tip of her tongue.

"Those are fine things, Bronwyn. They suit you." Jamie turned back to the window, looking out at Sydney Harbor. "The front porch I don't understand, though. You built the house..."

"People shouldn't get everything they want. I made sure everyone else had a big porch or balcony with a view. That way, it would be special if they invited me over to sit with them."

Jamie took her hand, unable to bear the wistfulness in her voice. "Well, let me think. I've always seen myself on a boat. I've always wished I could build something, a chest of drawers or a table." Jamie glanced at Bronwyn from the corner of his eye.

"Go on, Jimey. I want to hear."

"I've always wished I could have just a day with my Gran and Pap. One more day. They're gone, you know."

"What do you think you'd do with that day, Jimey?"

And, together, they offered all the favorite places they'd been to in Ireland, Scotland and England – places to eat, golf, shop, sightsee and walk through gardens; pleasantly whiling away the hour.

Two days later, they flew to Wellington, New Zealand, and then helicoptered to Wharekauhau Country Estate, just ten minutes away. Bronwyn had chosen it because it was a 5,000 acre sheep station, and she wanted to feel closer to the McCleans who were just an hour away on their own sheep farm.

Once they settled into their expansive cottage, Bronwyn looked forward to reading the books she'd brought, but she'd chosen the place to please Jamie. He was a beaming ray of sunshine when she suggested he go on a four wheel drive safari, mountain biking, trap shooting, and horse trekking.

She phoned the McCleans and updated them. They were impressed when she correctly pronounced Wharekauhau (Forry Ko Ho). Both the McCleans and Bronwyn could feel the actual closeness, now that she was in New Zealand. They marveled when she told them Jamie and she had eaten at Shed 5 in Wellington. The McCleans hadn't been there, yet. She told them Good Son Jack *must* take them and that she'd ordered seafood chowder in a bread bowl with mussel and corn fritters and one of the best desserts she'd ever had…a parfait of caramel and sea salt with toasted marshmallows and chocolate sabayon. Mrs. McClean was sputtering at the thought of it. She asked what Jamie ordered and Bronwyn was obviously unimpressed with his choices…octopus salad and fig ice cream for dessert. When Bronwyn explained Shed 5 had been built as a woolstore, the McCleans said she was getting to be quite knowledgeable and they'd have to name the next lamb after her. Bronwyn sighed contentedly when she hung up the phone.

She couldn't imagine a lovelier place on earth than the

Wharekauhau Country Estate and tried to breathe it all in, each day. The germ-of-an-idea, getting Jack a horse, had become much more. The sheep were in such beautiful surroundings, that Bronwyn felt the urge to find a *Thorn Birds* dress, the color of 'ashes of roses'. She just hoped the horse would please Jack half as much as this grand and glorious place was pleasing her.

Bronwyn took charge of the souvenir buying and found carved jade Maori clubs, an assortment of Paua shell jewelry, wooden carved Maori figures, and lambswool muffs for the folks back home.

During the next two weeks, she chose a New Zealand horse – a black Morgan. The horse had a beautiful face and attractive head. Bronwyn learned Morgans were known for their stamina, bravery, and intelligence, and admired the distinctive way it stood with its front end thrust forward and its hind legs straight out behind. She hoped Jack would notice, and appreciate its sleek black coat and broad chest.

Bronwyn had a private talk with the horse, standing on a box to look him in the eye. She regretted leaving him, but kissed the horse as she held his muscular neck with both hands.

Over the next few days, Paul's efforts helped make a seamless transition and he was satisfied Jack's new horse would get great care from the stable boy and ranch manager.

Bronwyn was thrilled when Paul returned with a sweater from Mrs. McClean. When he explained Mrs. McClean had knitted it herself. Bronwyn stared. All this time in sheep country, staying at a sheep station and eating at a renovated woolstore on Lambton Harbour, Bronwyn hadn't made the connection with wool. The Bayside Blanket and Toboggan Company had been a woolen factory. And now fate linked her, continent to continent.

On the flight home, they were each deep in thought. Paul, anxious to expand his work with horses; Bronwyn picturing Jack's reaction to finding the horse; and Jamie, contemplating the selflessness he'd managed to find deeply rooted in one godforsaken corner of his soul.

CHAPTER THIRTY SIX

MAMA LOU'S

When Jamie and Bronwyn returned from New Zealand, they settled into a contented routine. Bronwyn continued to spend time with Jeeves, going to McDonald's for breakfast every Saturday and having lobster together at the Lobster Pound or the Wharf on Friday nights. Conversation was easy as long as they stuck to banalities, and neither felt the need to keep a conversation going.

It seemed Jeeves was testing Bronwyn, when he urged her to take Jamie to Pittsburgh and show him her favorite places. Knowing they were Jeeves' favorite places as well, she assured him she'd only be going to Pittsburgh and Sewickley with him.

Just as Jamie had done with Clive, he worked out early in the morning, then showered, dressed, and nursed a cup of coffee, waiting patiently for Bronwyn to awaken. They'd go to Edgar and Clara's for breakfast each morning, except for 'Jeeves Saturdays', and walked the estate – bird watching, walking dogs, visiting the miniature horses and investigating the greenhouse and gardens. It was a good life, but it seemed Clive should be with them, and there was a nagging uncertainty about Jeeves.

Jack McClean filed for divorce, but Bronwyn wondered if her feelings for him were more wounded pride than love. She hadn't forgotten his big wedding; it hadn't been a Vegas spur-or-the-moment thing. Jamie continued to encourage her about Jack, but one thing Bronwyn knew. She wasn't going to lose Jamie again.

Setting her Big Breakfast tray down, Bronwyn stabbed her sausage patty and placed it on Jeeves' tray. She buttered her English muffin, while Jeeves slathered two jellies on his biscuit and unwrapped his Egg McMuffin. Some of Bronwyn's scholarship kids worked at McDonalds and they were used to Ernest Rose ordering three Maccy D breakfasts at once…the Big Breakfast, an Egg McMuffin, and a Bacon Egg and Cheese Biscuit Meal. The kids vied to be on Saturday morning duty because Bronwyn left tips. It was amusing to see them elbowing each other to add ice to her cup, refill their coffee, and bring extra jellies.

"Really Miss. You must take Jamie around. How's he to come to grips with your life if you don't take him 'round the towns?"

"Nope."

"I'm at a loss, Miss. It's not as if I have special privilege. Just think of it, seeing him emerge from the Fort Pitt Tunnel for the first time, with the vista of Pittsburgh at night hitting him gobsmack in the face."

Bronwyn laughed. "You're convincing, Jeeves, but no."

"Then, take him somewhere else that's special to you. Save Pittsburgh and Sewickley for me, but find somewhere. You'd both enjoy a jaunt."

Even though they'd only been home a few weeks,

Bronwyn considered it. She hadn't missed it when Jeeves said 'save Pittsburgh' for him; he'd be crushed if she took Jamie there. She was angry with Jeeves about Jack, but she'd never hurt him that way. She and Jeeves were most happy together visiting Pittsburgh, and she wouldn't ruin those happy times.

"Take him to see someone who's special to you."

The early March weather was dicey, but her pilot landed Jamie and Bronwyn safely in Virginia. It would be a long drive with the rental car, but the real delay was waiting for a package from Jeeves. He'd decided Mama Lou should have lobsters after all, and they waited for his messenger. They killed time in the regional airport's lobby, watching the news and eating bags of potato chips. They'd polish off one bag of chips, have some bottled water, and then hit the machine for a bag of 'crisps', alternating the name but, unfortunately, not the food.

Bronwyn called Mama Lou and she said to stop at the restaurant and Ernie would bring them over to her house. Bronwyn called again as they approached the last major route change and Ernie answered.

"Hey, Bronwyn. Y'all just come by. Mama's gone home. We're fixin' to close up, but I'll have the side door open for y'all. Lights might be out, but jest come on in."

"We've just turned off. How long do you think it'll take us?"

"About half hour with the fog. Don't be speedin'. You tell that young man o' yours, don't be speedin'. I remember his drivin' Bron. You tell him to take it easy, easy."

"Okay, Ernie. Who's there? Is my little pal, Ernest Hemingway, there?"

"Couldn't keep him away, once he heard you was comin' over to the restaurant first. We'll save you a bite of sumpin'. Tell your Jimey we got some ribs for him that'll set his tongue to slurpin'."

"Do you want me to call when we get close?"

"Nah. Y'all just keep comin' and we'll see y'all when ya'll get here."

The road wasn't well-marked and Bronwyn kept her eye peeled. She ignored the honey-voiced girl spouting directions from the GPS, and Bronwyn honestly couldn't tell if Jamie listened to the girl or to her. Sometimes they talked over each other, with Bronwyn glaring at the box. She took Jamie's smile as happy anticipation for a late-night rib indulgence. He'd better not be smiling at me vs. the girl, she vowed.

It finally seemed familiar as they approached Mama Lou's Restaurant. The neon and parking lot lights were out, as were most of the lights in the restaurant, but Bronwyn could see movement and faint light from the kitchen area. She pointed to the side parking lot for Jamie, and by habit, he turned off his headlamps and coasted back to the employee cars. He smacked his lips at Bronwyn in the car and she laughed, knowing the smack was for baby back ribs and not for her. Jamie quietly closed his door, like always, and told her to wait. As he approached the side door of the restaurant, Bronwyn got out to retrieve the Styrofoam lobster box.

Jamie turned from the side door to scold her, when she heard a loud *crack*. He dropped at the door, half in and half out, his left arm outstretched, unmoving.

Stunned, Bronwyn ran to the darkness of the building's shadows and hid in the bushes. Someone was at the door with a gun pointed at Jamie. There were no other voices, except the sound of the man's cursing. She could only see Jamie from the chest up, and the man's leg prodded and kicked him. She leaned deep into the bushes and was glad she was wearing black and hadn't dropped the white box. Her heart had a life of its own, motoring with such velocity that it threatened to explode.

She couldn't hear Ernie, little Ernest Hemingway, or anyone else. Surely if there was more than one man, they'd be talking to the one at the door.

Jamie wasn't moving.

"Turn 'round! Now! Don't you look at me, boy. I'll shoot your head off, swear to God."

The shooter pointed the gun inside and reentered the restaurant, as the door swung back against Jamie's hip. The night was silent, except for chirping crickets. Bronwyn wished the restaurant was in a populated area. Was it possible that no one heard the gunshot?

The man was shouting, but whatever he was saying was unintelligible. Waiting a moment and holding her breath, she emerged from the bushes and, very slowly, moved toward Jamie.

His eyes were slightly open, perhaps in shock. She'd hoped he might gesture or whisper something to help her, but when he didn't, she gathered her courage. Analyzing the pattern of shadows cast over Jamie and through the doorway, she checked to see if interior light would catch her, and how much of the restaurant was dark. Satisfied that she could avoid light, Bronwyn peered inside.

The most obvious thing was the orange prison jumpsuit, and the back of the stocky black man's head and curly hair. She could see Ernie's worried dark face behind the counter and hoped he couldn't see her. Not yet. The convict was gripping Ernie's son, with the gun pointed at little Ernest's head.

Bronwyn charted a path through the darkness, imagining the GPS girl's voice in her head, robotically offering directions. She scanned the restaurant a third time and double-checked the faint light behind the counter. It was dark if she was low. If everyone stayed still, it wasn't far from the doorway to the convict. Bronwyn remembered the TV news reports back at the airport, saying a manhunt was underway.

She was surprised at her steadiness, most of all when she reached into Jamie's jacket holster and extracted his precious Walther P99. Jamie was a professional; the gun would be ready to fire. Just click off the safety. And, if she fired and nothing happened, she could leap up and smash Jamie's shooter in the head with a chair. She remembered the angle Jeeves had on Clive last year and was confidant she could re-create it.

Bronwyn took a moment to 'breathe' just as Jamie always reminded her. She took such a deep breath, that she feared she could be heard. Her exhale was directed at the bushes.

Mama Lou's son would be wondering where she was. Part of Ernie would hope she'd run away to safety, but being a dad, part of him would hope she'd rescue them. She'd seen enough movies to know that.

Time. Bronwyn wiped her hand on her trouser, shrugged out of her jacket, and pushed it against the dark wetness of Jamie's shirt. Removing her watch so it wouldn't tap against anything, she regretfully moved over Jamie, crawling across the dark path. The convict was edgy, talking non-stop smack. Bronwyn was directly behind him. Still in shadow, she rose in remarkable silence. Silence, until the gun fired and blood and brain matter were sprayed everywhere.

CHAPTER THIRTY SEVEN

BERGAMOT

*T*he men were playing poker in the Carnegie Suite, with Tiny watching and Jamie propped in bed. Satisfied they'd watch over Jamie, Bronwyn left the suite and walked slowly through the echoing lobby. Jeeves was seated on a couch by the enormous fireplace.

It was dark outside, and the lovely water view had disappeared, replaced by a night wall of navy blue. Sometimes it simply erased the outside world until sunrise, but tonight it seemed to press threateningly against the glass. Bronwyn sat across from Jeeves and surveyed the elegant furnishings. The balcony fronting her bedroom seemed to mock her. A cavernous lobby, an expanse of wrought iron holding back – no one. If Jeeves sniffed sadness in the air, he didn't let on.

They were adept at using silence and had run long streaks of it. Usually, Bronwyn broke the silence. This time, Jeeves gave in.

"He's settled, then?"

"Yes, with Snooks sleeping beside him."

Deciding she must be weary, Jeeves settled back and believed she'd do the same, content to watch the jumping flames. She leaned forward, about to speak, when Tiny lumbered down the hall.

"He pet her! He pet her! I saw him!" boomed Tiny and he told how he'd seen Jamie stroking Snooks. Bronwyn dashed off to see for herself. Despite finding Jamie's hand simply resting on Snooks' long back, she believed Tiny. Of course it would be Snookie who would get his first reaction. She was loving and warm and burrowing and Jamie adored her. Bronwyn told the guys, and they skeptically clucked over the news.

Tiny beamed with pride, basking in the dog's glory. Bronwyn gently kissed Jamie's forehead, and lifted Snooks. Snapping a leash on her and walking out the French doors, she praised the dachshund. Bronwyn returned just as Doc moved from Jamie's bed. She tucked Snooks alongside Jamie, instructed Tiny to keep watch, and walked back to the lobby.

Jeeves hadn't come to see. She hoped some of his repressed guilt would unrepress itself. It was time for a shot across his bow.

"Jeeves, I wanted to share something with you."

"Yes, Miss?"

"Jamie didn't kill that man. I did." To her satisfaction, Jeeves looked surprised.

"Jamie opened the door and was shot, but his legs blocked the door open. I saw the shooter had his gun pointed at little Ernest's head. I reached for Jamie's gun, crawled on my knees in the dark until I was close, and I shot the guy. In the head."

Jeeves betrayed no emotion, but was watching her carefully. This was a controlled Bronwyn, with bite to her words. What was she after?

"Ernie took the gun, wiped it off, and put it in Jamie's hand so his prints would be on it. But, he put it in his right hand and I said 'he's left-handed' so he wiped it again and put it in his left hand. I cleaned up and changed my clothes while the ambulance came, and Ernie said I was afraid and stayed in the car. The police accepted Jamie's attachment and credentials and that was that."

Bronwyn leaned forward. "I wanted you to know."

"You needn't protect Jamie Donald, Miss. I'm afraid you don't know how to fire a weapon."

"You'd think so, wouldn't you? But, remember when you were so angry with Clive for teaching me to fight and defend myself? He'd taken me to a shooting range. Three times. He didn't tell you because he knew you'd be angry."

"And, what was the result, Miss, with your three visits to the shooting range? Was your accuracy, spot-on?"

"Apparently," she responded, dryly.

"Why the revelation?"

"I think Jamie's in a state of shock, aware that I killed someone. It probably broke his heart. But he's going to get better, I know it. That's one reason."

She was keenly watching his reaction to her hope for Jamie's recovery. When she saw and heard none, she crossed the lobby to the ornate Brussels reservation desk. She glanced above at the magnificent clock, rescued from a London bank, then looked through the desk supplies beneath the marble counter.

Bending a paperclip, she returned to where Jeeves was sitting, knelt at his feet, and dragged the sharp end of the paperclip deeply across his beautifully polished leather shoe. Satisfied, she rose. If he had kicked her, she was ready. If he had slapped her, she'd have punched him. If he'd said one word, just one word, she knew all hell would break loose. But Jeeves, being Jeeves, said nothing.

Bronwyn threw the paperclip onto the fire, took her seat, and continued in a quiet voice. "The other reason is, I don't know how many coincidences there can be. I don't know how that man escaped prison. I don't know why he turned up at Mama Lou's. I don't know why you suggested we take a trip and I don't know why you helped make us late getting there. What I do know is that I killed a man." Bronwyn walked around the back of Jeeves' sofa and leaned into his right ear. "I'm huffing and puffing to blow your house down."

It was early morning, and Doc Larchmont came downstairs into the Carnegie Suite's bedroom. His sister Nan was with Jamie and Bronwyn. Nan Larchmont was happy to work nursing shifts at the estate, even though she missed her little home at the Bergamot Nine golf course. If it hadn't been for Bronwyn, she wouldn't live in the home of her dreams.

Over the years, when Graeme or Roddy O'Neal's visits turned to golf, Bronwyn enjoyed spending time with Nan. Of all the houses at the golf course, Bronwyn most loved hers. It was a picket fenced, white cottage with a small terrace. The tiny porch was screened, so they could watch the fifth hole action, in comfort. Nan's dining room windows provided a wide-open view of the sixth hole and Bronwyn loved the old trestle table with long benches around it. Sometimes they had lunch together and Bronwyn liked how clean and simple the white kitchen was with its blue slate floor. She had worked closely with Nan on the design and interiors, a fun project with a theme of old memories. The bedrooms had beautiful blue and cream quilts from Amish Lancaster, old wooden chairs they'd found in Sewickley, and blue enamel glossy floors. Shiny and bright, that was Nan's house.

It had been Nan who Bronwyn first overheard at the Sewickley Café, talking to Laura Larchmont about her marriage, and Peter Larchmont's depression over losing a patient. Of all the people Bronwyn 'found', she felt great satisfaction from finding the Larchmonts.

Doc's house at Bergamot was as grand as his sister's was quaint. Bronwyn wanted his home to reflect the Sewickley grandeur and civility she'd come to know. Doctors' houses were supposed to be impressive. Doctors and judges.

These days, Doc's new digs weren't grand at all, since Jamie had been flown back from Virginia. Doc temporarily moved into the quarters above the Carnegie Suite. Those secluded rooms were set back from a deep balcony, with thick greenery obscuring the upper tier rooms. When Laura stopped in to visit her husband, she often walked the estate with Bronwyn. Both women appreciated the fresh air. Jamie's near comatose state had unnerved them all.

Jeeves had known Jamie to have a beard from time to time, so his caregivers let it grow. By not shaving him, there was at least one intrusion they could spare him. Bronwyn began sleeping beside Jamie, with Doc's approval. She listened to the Golf Channel, HGTV, and ESPN, read books aloud, and brought over the most fragrant flowers Jen could find. She'd enlisted the ladies to manipulate Jamie's muscles and although they were slightly embarrassed, they owed it to him. They'd certainly taken every advantage to see his muscles before. Bronwyn worried that he was losing muscle tone, but was afraid to ask the ladies if they saw a difference. Since they didn't ooh and aah anymore, she suspected that impressive tone was already gone.

When Tiny had seen Jamie stroking Snooks Von Krinkles, Doc was skeptical. But Bronwyn knew Tiny. He wouldn't say something to make her happy. He was simply too honest for that. Snooks and Tiny gave Bronwyn a fresh determination, and she kept thinking of ways to help Jamie. She understood how important it was for someone to be silent, to let time heal. She was certain Jamie wasn't ready to restart his life. After her Oakley Forse beating, Bronwyn remembered her silence and how she didn't have the energy to let her thoughts escape from her soul and live on the outside. As anxious as she was that Jamie wake up to normalcy, she was patient.

In Jamie's world, he was hidden and making himself as tiny as he could. He had closed his eyes against the enemy's surprises, and remembered the yellow and orange glow of the poker as it danced before his eyelids. He thought he'd dodged the rod, but his eyes were sealed shut. Forever shut. But he was safe here, hiding behind his eyes. Safe from everything.

March was ending on a cold note, but Bronwyn had Jamie bundled into his wheelchair for some estate meanderings. With Doc Larchmont's help, they took him to visit the miniature horses.

From there, they wheeled over to Charlie's house. It was a sunny day, and the boy was shooting hoops, with the sound of the ball smacking loudly off the pavement. Charlie rattled off a running commentary; Bronwyn had no idea he could broadcast and showboat at the same time.

Jamie seemed tired and Van Tsang brought the Cushman.

They zipped back home for a kip, Jamie's term for nap. They kipped a lot.

The next day, Bronwyn went to Clara's and asked if she thought Jamie could float on a raft, in the pool he loved so much. When the Larchmonts volunteered as lifeguards and raft assistants, Clara took it as her singular duty to oversee Jamie's aquatic treatments.

Bronwyn appreciated how diligent Clara and the Larchmonts were, but she hated seeing floaties on Jamie's arms and legs, even as he appeared to be safely on the raft. Clara would go like gangbusters, and Bronwyn was impressed. The old woman was certain Jamie needed speed to remind him of his prowess, so she flutter kicked to beat the band, motoring him along. Laura and Doc would yelp at her to slow down, concerned it might tip over, but Clara figured they were the professionals and it was their problem.

Before, Bronwyn had been too shy to join the ladies watching half-naked Jamie at the pool, but she knew how much he loved going up there. She recalled how the rooftop pool house lit up late at night, shimmering with greens and blues. The first time she saw it, she'd checked with Clara the next morning, concerned something had driven her to leave Edgar's bed and have a swim. Ever the mermaid, Clara had done the requisite snooping and found it was sleepless Jamie. Now, Bronwyn prayed each day that the pool would work its magic, releasing the elixir Jamie so often sought in his 'able' days.

Bronwyn reflected on the shooting's aftermath. Jamie was suffering a post-traumatic condition, silent and unresponsive. But his vital signs were good, and he was recovering from the gunshot wound.

Doc Larchmont explained Jamie's traumatized state.

"I think we're on the right path with him. He needs rest and we have to be there and monitor things. But, you should know something." Doc's brow was furrowed. "I've been speaking to Jeeves and Van Tsang. Apparently Jamie endured a series of tortures, right before he was released from service. It wasn't the first time."

He watched Bronwyn to see how she was taking it. "Are you all right?"

Bronwyn was pale, but insisted she was okay.

"Go on."

"I've spoken to the medical people at MI6, and the people at Langley, as well. We feel the reason he hasn't fully recovered is a result of the psychotropic drugs he was subjected to. And, perhaps from a delayed reaction to the particular tortures he endured." He looked carefully at Bronwyn. "I think we can understand why this has been a slow process, don't you think?"

She answered him with a grimace, and while he waited for their lunch to be served, she walked back to the Carnegie Suite.

Glad of the doorway's solidity, she swayed slightly and leaned against it. One of Clara's well-worn quilts was tucked around their prized patient. It was Bronwyn who said not to trim Jamie's beard and it had become fuller each day and a bit wild and tangled; a furry mask. She noticed it had a red cast and his thick and substantial moustache was curling over his top lip. It had been a foggy night as they pulled into Mama Lou's parking lot, and a mist of fog still clouded her memories of that awful night. But Doc had succeeded in lifting her foggy notion of Jamie's MI6 days. Torture was something she hadn't considered. Restrained. Strapped.

Unimaginable pain. She closed her eyes and let her fingertips lightly cup her eye sockets, willing the tears away. For now.

She moved to Jamie's bed and spoke so quietly, the words barely floated through the air. "The last time we were together, it was under the cold moon and the stars. But there's sun now. We'll walk together soon. In the sunshine."

With a kiss on his brow, she paused and backed out of the room.

Bronwyn sipped coffee and waited till Doc ate his lobster roll and half of hers before she told him she'd killed the escapee, not Jamie. It started to make sense to Doc, because Mama Lou's son Ernie had a zipper on his lips at the hospital. Bronwyn's supposition was that Jamie had seen her shoot the man and was traumatized. Doc told her Jamie would have been in shock, and unaware, but Bronwyn was certain he knew. The two were close, Doc couldn't deny that. She might well be right.

Bronwyn and Jack McClean continued to write. She explained she couldn't deal with anything except Jamie's recovery, and Jack replied that he understood. His letters still brightened her day, at least twice a week, and it was good to lose herself. She read them to Jamie, omitting any mushy parts.

Jeeves stayed to himself after her veiled accusation. How could she ever think he'd put her in such danger? Or Mama Lou's family, who had been nothing but kind to him? And Clive's Jamie was like another son to him. If this was her way of hurting him, just because he'd done a bit or two to thwart her romances with Dominguez and McClean, she'd succeeded. He hurt in places he never knew existed.

His toes hurt, his heart broke, his head ached. The diagnosis would have been Prickle of Conscience.

Bronwyn stopped by from time to time and even shared McDonald's takeout breakfasts with Jeeves. She had a better appetite for those Egg McMuffins with him, than anything else. She wished he could be a part of Jamie's recovery, and yet she wouldn't have trusted Jeeves within fifty yards of Jamie.

Nevertheless, he offered his version of encouragement.

"Dr. Larchmont says that Jamie has no memory of the night, Miss. So there's no reason for you to ever reveal your role. The authorities were most grateful that our Jamie did the deed." She merely stared back, with a slight tilt to her head. "You were quite right, you know. Saving the boy and without question, everyone there. I imagine you felt anger over Jamie's being shot. Quite natural. But don't forget for a second, the people he murdered along the way, taking the car. Why he didn't change from his prison garb only proves his stupidity."

Jeeves' disgust was obvious.

"I was keen to speak with Mama Lou's family." With this, he sparked her interest. "Young Ernest is off to Math camp and they're ready to launch a much-needed refurbishing. They'll not breathe a word, Miss. They're grateful and quite glad to turn the page."

One morning, Bronwyn was arranging the throws at the end of Jamie's bed when Linda walked in.

"I don't understand you, Bronwyn." Bronwyn was alarmed at her tone. "How long are you going to do this? I mean, put the guy in a home. Until he gets better. *If* he gets better. You can't do this to yourself."

Bronwyn was turning rapidly pink.

"You're dressing him up like a doll. Don't look at me that way. You play with him."

Doc Larchmont was hauling his long body down the stairs at a rapid clip.

"You've gotta stop. Right, Doc? She's killing herself for a guy that can't even see or hear her."

"You should leave," he warned.

"Don't look at me that way. You've all been thinking it. I've just got the nerve to tell her."

Linda stood her ground, but he pointed to the door.

"I'll be back to finish up. Think about what I said," Linda said, sagely.

Doc noticed Bronwyn's cheeks were hot pink and the tips of her ears were scarlet. "I'm sorry Bronwyn. You're doing everything right. I don't know what got into her."

Bronwyn sat beside Jamie and tenderly kissed his forehead. She motioned for Doc to join her in the hallway.

Whispering, she asked, "Do you think he heard? I mean sometimes he has to really sleep, doesn't he, and if he was really sleeping, he wouldn't hear her, right?"

"He was sleeping, Bronwyn. I'm sure of it. I know the rhythms of his chest and he was definitely asleep. Don't give it a second thought. Sleeping."

She walked around the lobby's perimeter, calming down. Doc guided her outside for a quick breath of air. "Let's go up to the pool today. Jamie always enjoys that. I'll check with Clara and see if it suits her, all right?"

Bronwyn watched him go, picked up the phone and called Jeeves.

"This is right down your alley, Jeeves. I want you to find Linda and tell her she's not to return to my house. Period.

Tell her to have someone else do the cleaning." Bronwyn wasn't surprised when Jeeves didn't ask why. She could almost see him doing a happy dance with the joy of delivering the reprimand. She would have banned Linda for less.

Linda found her husband and self-righteously complained about her ill treatment.

When she came up for air, Matthew implored her, "You did not tell her that. Tell me you didn't."

"Are you even listening to me? That oaf Jeeves just banned me. I mean, I can clean her house and avoid her completely. This makes no sense. He sounded like he'd shoot me on sight."

Her husband tried a quieter tone. "Linda, do you remember what Bronwyn did for you, when you were going to have surgery?"

"What's that got to do with anything?" When he looked blankly at her, she retorted, "she was supportive, so what?"

"Supportive? Is that what you call it? Do you remember how she cut her hair off, so you wouldn't feel badly when yours fell out? Do you remember how she cancelled her trip with Oré to Bora Bora?"

"So, she cancelled a trip."

"If she hadn't cancelled her trip, he would have gone with *her* and they'd probably be married now. Married. Look what she gave up for you."

"That's what you say. You don't honestly think that's what she's thinking, do you?"

"Duh."

"Really. She didn't need to do that. I was with my sisters back home after the surgery. Didn't even involve her."

"Linda. She didn't know that. You didn't tell her you had a plan. You just told her how scared you were. She cut her hair off and cancelled her trip so she could be here for you, and then you left for three months. She thought you needed her and you didn't because you had *family*." He watched Linda to see if it was sinking in. "Jamie needs her. And she's there for him. He'd do the same for her. If you don't know that, then you don't know the two of them at all."

Matthew wanted to tell his wife he knew she'd happily ship him off to a home somewhere if he was ever in that state – that much he'd learned.

He left to see Bronwyn; Linda certain he'd gone to plead her case. Bronwyn assured him she wanted them both to stay. Forever. Nothing had changed. She just didn't want Linda at her house, and that was her prerogative. Matthew hadn't seen this side of Bronwyn, stern and no-nonsense.

"Just remember, Matthew, you're the one that brought Linda here. I wanted you and Coolidge." Matthew nodded. "You're not living in a huge Island House in the Factory, with a little western stable down by the water. I gave you the house that mattered. That was my choice. She's just along for the ride."

Nan and Doc were getting Jamie ready for the day, while Bronwyn waited around the corner. They were commenting on the photos she'd brought down from her bedroom, hoping to cheer Jamie when he awakened from his netherworld.

"Look at all of these pictures, Peter. I hadn't realized Jamie'd been to Hershey. Look how happy you look, Jamie. Gotta get back there, my friend. Eat some chocolate!"

Bronwyn heard the sound of Doc snapping his medical bag shut.

"Isn't she pretty?"

"That's Clive's mother. You remember Clive. He came

over to Bergamot to golf with Jamie last year. Remember, it was December and we thought they'd freeze."

"No, Peter, this is Ernest Rose's wife. Bronwyn told me."

"Yes."

"What do you mean, yes?"

"She is Clive's mum, and Ernest's wife. Van Tsang told me the other day."

"Oh, I never realized Clive is Jeeves' son."

Bronwyn almost fell out of her chair.

That day, she tried to put the pieces together. She wondered how she had never figured it out. She wasn't even certain they'd kept it from her, especially when Van Tsang apparently gave the information to Doc without hesitation.

It made sense now, why Jeeves and Clive had parted with such warm affection all those years ago. And she also surmised why Jamie and Clive high-tailed it out of the boxing ring last December. They hadn't wanted to tangle with Dad. It was sweet, really. Not the Jeeves part, though; not the crush Clive with a chair part. Of course Clive knew right away that all those photos Jeeves had given her were phonies. They weren't Clive's family. But that made her realize he deliberately kept the secret. When he gave her his mum's photo, he could have told her. She decided it was all part of being spies. Agents. Men of Espionage. There was a really good part to it, though. Jeeves must be in touch with Clive and that made her happy. She wasn't going to ask Van or Jeeves or even Jamie about the father and son bit. She'd act like she'd always known.

Bronwyn was waiting for another sign, like Tiny seeing Jamie petting Snooks. She watched Jamie carefully and was well aware of the nuances of his day. She anticipated what he might need, like putting his sunglasses on one morning when they sat on the patio. Bronwyn couldn't see Jamie's eyes. But if she'd seen through the dark lenses, she would have seen a tiny reaction; something that would have signaled an emergence. Then, just as quickly, it was gone.

Doc and Bronwyn were thinking of stimulating scenarios for Jamie. Their little excursions on the estate seemed to tire Jamie, but Bronwyn thought going to the Bergamot Nine would be a nice change. Jamie used to enjoy golfing, and with the course closed on Tuesdays, Doc and Bronwyn could hit golf balls. That's something she enjoyed, so Doc said 'yes' – as much for Bronwyn as for Jamie. They called it their Big Adventure.

Nan left early and made chicken salad, while Doc's wife frosted her strawberry pretzel salad. Nan was glad to be home and it had been a long time since Bronwyn sat on her porch. Her sister-in-law appreciated the heads-up and they agreed to have lunch over at the Big House. It was wheelchair friendly and Laura planned to play her piano, hoping Jamie would enjoy the music. She was enjoying herself, sorting through sheet music.

Van Tsang helped unload the wheelchair and lifted Jamie into it. When they had him settled with a St. Andrews throw tucked around him, Jerry, the Bergamot golf pro, came out with four buckets of balls.

For the first time in a long time, Bronwyn was engaged in an activity and although she glanced at Jamie after almost every ball she hit, she was enjoying herself. Doc gave her pointers and she returned the advice. They laughed and she thought the sound of the balls would be the 'call of the wild' for Jamie. She gave him a play-by-play of Doc's attempts to correct his slice. Bronwyn put Jamie's sunglasses on, since the clouds were parting to reveal the sun. Wap. Wap. Wap. She advised Doc to have a 'sword swishing sound' on the downswing, like José Maria Olazábal and stood beside Jamie with her eyes closed, judging the swish.

Jerry emerged from the Pro Shop, giving Doc a wrist check. Then he brought over a driver. "Here you go, Bronwyn. Remember you ordered this for Jamie at Christmas? It just came in."

Bronwyn pushed her lips out in a pained expression. She placed Jamie's hands around the driver, and then stopped, feeling guilty. The last time she'd put something in his hands, it had been the gun. Technically, Ernie put the gun in his hand, but Bronwyn hadn't put so much as a book in Jamie's hand and it didn't seem right.

She kissed Jamie's cheek and then wrapped his hands in the proper manner around the club. If it fell, she'd just pick it up and do it again. "Jimey, this is one of the new drivers I told you about. You're gonna be wicked good with this. Look, Doc hasn't hit a sweet spot, yet. But, you will. I love you," she said softly. And she turned back to her balls, glancing to see that Jamie's club hadn't fallen yet.

Bronwyn hit a sweet spot and as it sailed 150 yards on the fly, she was whooping and hollering. Doc congratulated her royally, and when she turned to see if Jamie had reacted to the sweet sound of a ball perfectly hit, by her nonetheless, she saw him standing shakily with feet apart, leaning on his new golf club in the fashion of Ben Hogan, smiling weakly and nodding at her.

Laura Larchmont moved in with Doc above the Suite, and they spent every day assisting Jamie with his recovery.

Bronwyn decided to sleep in the warming room, to be near the action, and Edgar spent much of his time making meals and snacks for the recovery troops. He needed to put some meat on Jamie's bones.

Two days after Jamie's awakening, Bronwyn walked over to the Island House and told Linda she was welcome back. Bronwyn noticed Linda's red hands and realized she'd been doing some wicked cleaning somewhere. They never spoke of what happened, but Bronwyn noticed Linda was extra cheerful at the house, probably hoping Jamie hadn't heard her suggestion to put him away somewhere. Things weren't quite the same between the women, but they were both relieved to move on.

Doc took great care to limit Jamie's enthusiastic return to physical training, but he felt a warm sense of accomplishment, seeing his improvement. He didn't let on to Bronwyn, but he was just as anxious to see Jamie's toned muscles. The exercise, weight training, and swimming fell under Doc and Laura's guidance, but the walking regimen was Bronwyn's. Clean-shaven Jamie and Bronwyn spent as much time sitting and chatting, as walking, and she was happy to know Jamie remembered petting Snooks, Bronwyn reading to him, and the laughter of the card games in his room. As each day passed, he continued to nudge Bronwyn toward Jack.

"Gentle and constant, that's us, Bronwyn. The world is jammers with unloved people. It's time to get him over here so Jack and I can be mates. It's been ages since you've seen him and more's the pity."

Bronwyn listened, but bringing Jamie all the way back was her priority. There were times when she could still feel her knee pushing into Jamie's legs as she crawled over him into the restaurant, and she wasn't able to shake it. She expected to remember firing the gun most of all, but it was the moment she crawled across him that most haunted her. She hadn't thought of it while he was comatose, but now she replayed that night, trying to think how she could have avoided pushing into him as if he were an inanimate object.

It was a welcome invitation, when Mollie and Wells Moore invited Bronwyn and Jamie for a sneak peek at the nearby Garden of the Five Senses – a sensory garden Mollie had envisioned. Mollie was a remarkable woman from Bristol, England, who had gone suddenly blind after an illness. Her husband Wells was a great guy; a friend to both Bronwyn and Jeeves. So, as soon as they could manage it, off they went.

The gardens were a wondrous achievement and they dashed here and there, labeling their discoveries as 'taste' or 'hearing' or 'seeing' or 'feeling' or 'smelling'. Jamie grinned when she whispered how Jeeves would be seeking 'umami' if he were there. A tall granite sculpture had a hole that reverberated in strange, whispering ways. Flower towers held edibles and Bronwyn planned to bring Edgar over so he could experiment with his own herbs in vertical plantings. Garden explorers could taste savory, minty, and sweet plants. Despite a nip in the air, they removed their shoes to walk in their socks upon smooth, egg-sized stones and Bronwyn appreciated the low striker stone curb to help people poking with canes on their fragrant and colorful journey. Planting tables were the right height for wheelchairs, while vertical planters over six feet tall were gloriously on display for people unable to crouch to look at plants. The interactive nature of the garden dazzled Bronwyn; such a realized vision in every way. Jamie reminisced with Mollie about England, while Wells told Bronwyn tales of their mischievous Welsh corgi, Morgan – a notorious yet adorable pickpocket. As they ended their tour, Mollie handed Bronwyn a basket of her homemade scones, for Jeeves.

Jeeves usually stopped over to the warming room near Bronwyn's bedtime, to watch television and have a cup of tea together. He envied the closeness the others shared, although he'd never admit it.

Jamie's recovery wasn't the only miracle. After fourteen years of marriage, Laura Larchmont became pregnant. When she took her home pregnancy test, she was convinced Jamie was a lucky charm. When they had the pregnancy quickly confirmed, Doc couldn't dispute her notion about lucky Jamie. They'd been an affectionate and tireless team because of Jamie, and they thoroughly enjoyed their happy little life, above the Carnegie Suite. This was a supreme reward for their diligence. They were certain if it hadn't been for Jamie Donald, there'd be no baby-to-be. And Bronwyn had brought them all together; Little Sewickley transported to the North.

CHAPTER THIRTY EIGHT

LARA BLUE

*B*ronwyn put the phone back in its cradle and sat for a moment as the earth spun around her. Walking zombie-like down the hall, with the intention of splashing water on her face, Bronwyn peered at a reflection she barely recognized. Nothing was real. Only the sick feeling deep inside had any solidity. Jeeves took her elbow and steered Bronwyn to the bench.

"He'll be fine, Miss. I spoke with his parents and they're at hospital. You're not to worry. You're not to worry a bit. Have a lie down." Jeeves gently steered her down the hall, past the dressing room and toward the bed. Bronwyn stopped.

"I'm okay." Bronwyn sank into the chocolate velvet couch. "I should make a list."

She jotted a few things, lifted her head, thought, and added a few more lines.

"Jeeves, I need you to tell his parents I'm coming. See if we can use the jet, or if Grace can charter one for us. I can't remember if it's out, do you? Have her get us rooms near the hospital. Would you call Doc? I'll pack – I don't need to take much. And, remember your passport. Even though it's Canada, we'll need our passports now."

"Pardon, Miss. Did you say 'we'?"

She nodded.

"You wish me to go? To see Jack McClean in surgery? I'm afraid you're not thinking clearly. I'll send Van Tsang. He'll be of great assistance to you, as always."

She shook her head. "No."

"Why ever not, Miss?"

Bronwyn turned and peered into his eyes. "When Jeeves sets you upon his shoulder, no harm can come to you."

"Forgive me, but you believe that, Miss? Even now?"

"I've always believed it, Jeeves."

Doc walked with Jeeves and Bronwyn through the Vancouver hospital and left them near the waiting room, promising an update when he knew something. He'd called the hospital from the airport, confirming Jack's status from his motorcycle accident. The fractured tibia, femur and three broken ribs had been addressed, but his most pressing problem was surgery to remove a newly formed blood clot.

Doc looked meaningfully at Jeeves, who nodded his assurance that he'd watch over Bronwyn. As Jeeves walked with her toward the waiting area, they heard an argument around the corner.

"I'm tellin' you, I'm not signin' anythin' till I find out what I'd fetch."

"Don't you think it would give him peace of mind, knowing this was tied up? You both agreed. Give him some peace now, when it matters. Sign it."

Bronwyn's eyes grew big and she stopped to listen. Jeeves stood at her side.

The girl's voice was a harsh whisper. "I'm tellin' you, I want to know what I get if he dies. I'm not a bloody fool. I'm not signin' if I'm about to get more, so sod off."

"Jack was right. You really are a bitch and a half."

Bronwyn turned the corner and walked without glancing back. Scanning for empty chairs in the waiting room, she took a seat. As Jeeves was sitting, an older couple approached them.

"Oh, Bronwyn. My dear," the woman said.

Bronwyn looked up to find the man earnestly saying, "Oh, dear girl."

She found herself staring at them. Although she expected Jack's parents to be there, these were two people she'd seen before, and then she remembered.

"The airport."

"Yes, luv, we couldn't stop ourselves."

Bronwyn smiled at them, remembering the scene. And, the hats. She rose and embraced them, asking, "Have you heard anything?"

They shook their heads.

"Maybe I shouldn't sit near you. I think Jack's wife is here."

Mrs. McClean clucked and her husband rolled his eyes.

"Don't you go anywhere, you sit right here. You know it was all supposed to be over by now. They came to an agreement," Mr. McClean said, with exasperation.

Bronwyn remembered Jeeves at her side, and introduced him. She was too worried to notice, but the McCleans were cool and barely acknowledged him. They had succeeded in doing what no one else had ever done – making Jeeves embarrassed and uncomfortable.

Asking Bronwyn if she needed anything, Jeeves excused himself. The McCleans spoke quietly, but Mr. McClean kept one eye out for 'the wife'. He didn't want a scene.

Twenty five minutes later, Jeeves brought Starbucks coffee for the four of them. He leaned into Bronwyn and said quietly, "They're signed. The lawyer chap has them."

She clasped his hand with a sigh, "Thank you, Jeeves."

After she shared the divorce signature news, they all got a second wind and talked optimistically about Jack's recovery. After what seemed an eternity, Doc came into the waiting room with the surgeon. Their good report brought exhausted relief and even Jeeves smiled.

Out of recovery, a sleeping Jack was wheeled to his room. The McCleans stood on one side of his bed while Bronwyn was on the other; Jeeves posted himself in the hallway.

Nurses frequently came to check Jack's vitals and Doc stopped in. It was reassuring for Jack's parents, having Bronwyn's own doctor there.

"I think he'll be coming around, Bronwyn," Doc said, encouragingly.

She looked up at the McCleans. Connecting the people she'd spoken with on the phone with these unusually dressed and down-to-earth people took a moment. Jack had said they were 'characters', and Bronwyn had suggested 'characters' were the perfect parents for an actor. She was comforted seeing them and when they looked back at her, there was a satisfaction from having lived through the trauma together.

Jack's eyes were opening and closing as he drifted in and out of consciousness. His father waved her over. "Look who's here, boy. Look who's here."

Jack's eyes were closed.

"Jack...it's Bronwyn." She hadn't seen him in two long years.

Mr. and Mrs. McClean smiled happily at each other, and Mr. McClean planted a kiss on his wife's cheek.

"When you get better," Bronwyn turned around and looked at the McCleans, then turned back, "when you're allowed to, I want you to come to my house and see everything." Jack's eyes flickered. "I have a theatre." She spoke softly, near his ear. "Actually, I have a real movie theatre in town and then I have a little theatre in my attic."

She tried to will his eyes open, observing the wrinkles that fanned out from his lashes. The bruised hollows beneath his closed eyes had sheen, as if someone had smeared them with an oily substance and she noticed a tear puddling at the corner of one eye. She hadn't realized how anxious she felt, having just gone through Jamie's worrisome and silent recovery.

Mr. McClean patted her shoulder and gave her a wink.

"I have little horses, Jack, little horses for you to see." Jack's eyes fluttered. "Miniature horses, you know the size of a dog."

Jack's eyes didn't open, but he seemed to register what she was saying. His mouth started moving and swept very slowly into a smile. The smile transformed his face and pushed his cheeks into small merriment. Jack's eyes were still closed, but he murmured, "Little horses. Of course. That's why I can't ride them."

CHAPTER THIRTY NINE

SNOWBALL

*D*ick 'Cleveland' Domitrovich was giddy with lobster. He'd just made himself a lobster omelette and dashed out the door and over the stone patio to give a full report to Mr. and Mrs. McClean. They'd walked out the French doors with cups of tea, and settled in to watch the water and discuss how many ways they'd eaten lobster.

Bronwyn was writing a letter at one of the sun-drenched tables in the lobby. Before signing her name, she reread it.

Dear Jeeves,

I miss you! I'm glad you're happy in your new house. I don't think Dubai would have suited you, and somehow I don't think we're 'Florida' people.

I wish I could have been with you, hearing Marvin Hamlisch and the Symphony. Glad to hear you had a date. I'm sure she must have enjoyed Hyeholde. Yes, you remembered correctly – I've been to the Duquesne Club. Just

*once. And you'll not be surprised that I only
saw the kitchen – just peeked at the rest. I can't
wait to hear what you think. I am so impressed
that you've discovered the Strip District and
Primanti Bros. That's one big sandwich, isn't it?*

*Everyone here is settling in. Dick loves
Joseph's house. I probably shouldn't call it
'Joseph's' house, but you know me, since
Jamie's staying in Jeeves' flat. Mr. and Mrs.
McClean seem to really like the Suite. They've
been through so much but they seem to be less
exhausted now.*

*You should see Dick at the Lobster Pound.
He's like a child! I can't imagine how he'd
behave on a lobster boat, but we'll find out.
Teddy and Charlie are taking him this weekend.*

*I hope this note doesn't make you homesick,
but if it does, I understand! Hope you'll be
planning a trip back in the near future. I'm
coming to visit you next month. I thought
the Penguin Bookshop was just a gorgeous
remodel. Thanks for filling me in on the LEED
designation. We'll check it out together and
have tomato dill soup across the street, okay?*

Kiss the fox for me, and pet his head!

With Love,

She signed it *Bronwyn* and addressed
and stamped it, glancing at the address –
Sewickley, PA 15143

It seemed as if Jeeves had royally called her bluff. He was gone, Jack and his family were there, she was still sleeping in the warming room, and her heart belonged to Jamie. She knew it. Jeeves probably knew it. And Jamie pretended not to know. The past several weeks had revealed Jack to be a good friend, but nothing more. Jeeves may have fancied himself her Henry Higgins and been more Fagin, but now that he was gone, she missed him. No longer riding Jeeves' shoulder, she had some sorting to do.

"And the role of Jeeves has been recast," Doc Larchmont said, in a theatrical voice. Bronwyn looked over at Doc and Jamie, seated by the enormous fireplace. Doc was pointing to Dick, who was gesturing animatedly, outside the window. Bronwyn joined them.

"You're writing to Ernest, then?" asked Jamie, with Snooks Von Krinkles tucked in beside him, sound asleep.

Bronwyn nodded.

"Doc was just giving me the Sewickley report from his Mumsey."

She shrugged. "Sounds like a perfect match. Elise Fairchild has everything Jeeves is drawn to and she'd get a nice financial infusion. Pesky stock market."

"Mother clued Elise into his money, so she'll be like a dog with a bone."

"And, you think they'll live happily ever after," Bronwyn said, doubtfully.

She rose to leave, lifted Jamie's chin and kissed him firmly on his cheek. As she passed the kitchen, she saw Edgar through the leaded glass door, working on breakfast. Snowball the cat wove through his legs. Bronwyn watched for a moment, then put the envelope on the hall table and listened carefully to the thumping of Jack's cane, upstairs.

Walking across the reclaimed floor, she wondered how many people had walked upon it over the past hundred years. She rolled back the metal sheath from the Dickens Village and threw the switch. It was always a revelation. The sound of distant trains echoed along city blocks with tiny streetlights, fountains, skating rinks, and cobblestone pathways winding along the streets. Buildings had charming scenes behind their tiny windows and were set amidst snow. Waterfalls and snow laden trees dotted the hillsides. Children were sledding in front of country churches, and horses crossed stone bridges, climbing the tiers of hillside. It was a life in perfect miniature, with a heart-wrenching vibrancy that always affected her. How often had she unveiled it to the complete and utter delight of children, over the years? And yet, no one loved it more than she did.

The moments of happiness, she reflected. That's what people have. Moments of happiness throughout a lifetime. She moved her gaze from corner to corner, street to street, mountain top to valley, absorbing the glory of the little lights as if they were a thousand candles.

The blissful moment lodged itself in Bronwyn's heart. Gazing at the leather sofas, she remembered Gus and Jeeves happily settled in, watching a horse race or hockey game from one sofa, or facing the fire in the other, with its tawny lion-like flames illuminating their faces. A prickly ball lodged in the back of her throat, its rough edges making her eyes tear. She missed Gus with a deep ache and she missed her enigmatic, elegant, exiled Jeeves.

A white ball of cat fur streaked into the library, pausing to ease into an Egyptian sphinx stance. When Snooks Von Krinkles plodded into the room, Snowball darted toward the other doorway. Scooping the dachshund up as Snowball made her teasing escape, Bronwyn lifted the red wiener dog so she could see the Dickens Village. The dog dutifully dipped her white flecked muzzle within an inch of Hollydale's Department Store and Lafayette's Bakery. They circled the display, with Snooks rhythmically thumping her tail.

"Look at all the pretty lights, Snookie. Aren't they nice? I know it's September, but it looks like Christmas, doesn't it?"

Bronwyn pulled a lightweight throw onto the leather sofa and suggested, "Let's get cozy, Snooks."

Lying with her back along the outer edge of the sofa, Bronwyn brought her knees up to limit the space as the dog made circles and settled upon the throw. "That's my snuggle bunny," Bronwyn cooed as Snooks sighed and closed her eyes. Bronwyn gently tucked the throw around her.

After a few minutes, Snowball made one of her mystical leaps onto the sofa. Bronwyn appreciated her airless agility. It seemed as if the mere thought of leaping was all that Snowball needed to be magically transported. There was no false start, no misstep, no run-up, no crouching and springing, no grasping and throwing a leg up. Snowball hypnotically blinked twice at Bronwyn before turning and flinging onto her back, with a languid stretch. The swish of her black tipped tail broached the distance to Snooks, who was too sound asleep to notice.

Shafts of morning light poured across the room, catching dancing dust particles. If Linda saw them, she'd yank the drapes down and beat them into cleaning submission, but Bronwyn contentedly watched the floating specks. It seemed to be a parade of pixie dust.

Gazing at the cat and dog, she murmured sweet words to them, and Snowball lazily swept her tail, unable to resist responding to the sound of Bronwyn's voice. When the tip of her tail swished across the sleeping dog, it provoked Snooks' long ear to twitch.

It gladdened her heart to see Snooks and Snowball. Only a moment ago, she'd been sadly missing Gus and Jeeves. Something emotionally yanked her, and she realized how much of her life had been spent in yearning. She yearned for the past, yearned for lost future, yearned for those who'd gone, and yearned for those who had left her as if enough fervent yearning might rise up and fill the gaping maw within her. In fact, the yearning emptied her, more than filled her. It tamped down her joy. She was expert at the yearning, but not so good at the having.

She peered with tender appreciation at the two small animals beside her, aching to preserve the look of them in her memory.

Glancing at the electrified village display, Bronwyn whispered, "God bless us every one." In the back of her mind, she could hear the detached, constant voice of Jeeves answering, 'Yes, Miss. Indeed, Miss.'

As carefully as she could manage, Bronwyn edged off the couch and stood above the snoozing animals, her hands relaxed in her pockets. Snooks was obscured by the drape of the throw, but the cat peered at her through slitty green eyes. Snowball's white underside was flat as a pancake with her right leg pointed to the west, her left leg bowed to the east, in an utterly vulnerable pose. The large black spot on her head looked like a jaunty beret. The sight of the cat basking in sunlight while fairy dust danced to tease and engage her, made tentative resolution play through Bronwyn's mind.

Time seemed to stand still. It was as if a silent battle of emotion was playing out in the room of Samuel and Paul's forefathers. A battleground where Bronwyn controlled all the troops – holding the past as if it defined her; feeling annoyance that the chasm between her bad luck and good fortune still seemed to matter; missing Jeeves, despite knowing he had to go. He couldn't stay at the estate with Jack there. Not after Jeeves had interfered. It would be easier if she didn't miss Jeeves.

Bronwyn observed the old black and white photograph of Menke's grandfather above the fireplace. Even though the portrait had had pride of place for many years, she examined it to see if there was some part of Mr. Menke that reminded her of Bram, or of Samuel or Paul. She peered at the factory owner's eyes, the set of his jaw, his classically stoic demeanor. She'd have to study the boys' faces, the next time they came to visit.

"Bronwyn," Edgar called from the doorway, "I'm sending Jack's breakfast up. Would you like anything? A croissant?"

"That would be great, Edgar. I could get his breakfast from the dumbwaiter."

"No, Bronwyn. I've got it."

"Okay, I'll be up in a few minutes."

"Oh, I forgot to tell you. I found some cherry cider up the road. How's that sound, with lunch?"

"I'm sure that'll be a big hit with everyone."

Edgar smiled, knowing that 'everyone' mostly meant Jack's father, who viewed food and drink with an explorer's rapture.

Her inner-battle continued. If she was finally coming full-circle, why was the circle not quite closing? It seemed as if something was missing, yet tantalizingly close to her grasp. The sun refracted through an Irish crystal vase, sending rainbow prisms of light flying around the room.

Lit like a spotlighted circus performer, the reclining Snowball continued to regard Bronwyn through hooded eyes, with a conspirator's aplomb. Bronwyn stared at her for several minutes, before nodding purposefully and quietly backing out of the room, so as not to awaken Snooks.

Dashing down the hall, through the lobby, past Jamie and Doc, and onto the stone patio, she asked a favor of Jack's shutterbug father.

Stealthily reentering the library, she was relieved to see Snowball and Snooks hadn't moved from their charming positions. She knelt at the edge of the sofa and sighted through the borrowed camera's lens. With a quick click and a flash, Bronwyn finally began to silence her anthem of longing, as Snowball's tail lazily twitched in the glimmering layers of sunlight.

READING GROUP

QUESTIONS AND TOPICS FOR DISCUSSION

1. Loneliness is one of the themes in the story. Do you think Bronwyn will choose happiness and leave loneliness behind?

2. "Home" is significant for Bronwyn, and returning to Pittsburgh, Sewickley, and Beaver is a pleasure for both Bronwyn and Jeeves. Do you have places you enjoy visiting because they hold memories for you?

3. Bronwyn is usually safe 'riding on Jeeves' shoulder'. Would you want to have someone like Jeeves looking out for you?

4. Did you guess that Clive was Jeeves' son? If so, when?

5. Why do you think Jeeves never told Bronwyn that Clive had died, or that he was his son?

6. Would you be able to forgive Jeeves for the things he did? And specifically, what do you think he was guilty of doing?

7. Why do you think Bronwyn stopped taking photographs?

8. What would you do with sudden, enormous wealth?

9. Would Jeeves have stayed with Bronwyn if she hadn't received such an enormous fortune?

10. In what ways do you think Bronwyn was emotionally stunted by being orphaned at eight?

11. Why do you think Bronwyn created so many homes on her estate and repurposed the Factory?

12. Which estate house would you most enjoy having?

13. What would Bronwyn's life have been like if she hadn't noticed Samuel and Paul being kidnapped, or hadn't responded?

14. What significance did Christmas hold for Bronwyn?

15. There are several mentions of after-life and other-worldly happenings (seeing Bram during the surgery, Pal the dog and David in 'Heaven', the Forever House, Snooks in the elevator, the Fox). Have you ever noticed unexplained things in your life?

16. What do you think happened during the Beverly Hills beating, between Oakley Forse and Bronwyn?

17. How did movies influence Bronwyn?

18. What man do you think would have been the best partner or husband for Bronwyn?

19. Who was your favorite character in the book?

20. There is a theme of second chances throughout the book. In fact, Bronwyn gives almost everyone (and several things) a second chance – Oré, Alex Ozwald King, Edgar, Vicki, Jack, Linda, the Factory, the reclaimed furnishings, even Jeeves. Have you given someone a second chance?

EXPLORE THE WORLD OF
NORTH
OF SUPPOSED TO BE

ON

Pinterest

www.pinterest.com/mfergusonnorth

Photographs illustrate the memorable places, beloved
objects, luscious food, and dear animals of the story
– just click on each Pinterest board

Visit the author at
www.twitter.com/Marcia_Ferguson

9 780985 781002